OLD FIRE EYES

Kathleen Valle

INTRODUCTION

I N THE YEAR 1806, TWO thirteen-year-old boys overcome their differences and strike up a friendship, as they work together to conquer wilderness dangers. Slavery was legal in those days, but many people disagreed with the idea that you could buy, trade, mistreat, and sell other human beings! Benjamin appears to be a runaway slave, but he carries secrets and responsibilities which burden him terribly. John has never encountered a black person before, and he struggles to understand this touchy young man, who seems a likely candidate to replace the friends he left behind in backwoods Virginia.

Because there were no meat markets beyond the cities, people hunted and trapped wild animals to feed themselves and their families, and they used their hides, pelts, and bones to create clothing and accessories. What they did not use, they traded, because coins were in short supply.

Native Americans were mistakenly called Indians in those days because the European sailors who first saw them assumed that they had fulfilled their mission of establishing an easier route to India. The name stuck, however, as did the derogatory terms *redskins* and *savages*. By the time our boys embark on their adventure, most settlers and frontiersmen deeply feared all Native Americans who inhabited the wilderness, because they had been forced to defend the land their ancestors had occupied since before written history.

Grizzly bears, which had once ranged across our continent as far as the Atlantic Ocean, struck such fear in the hearts of our early settlers that they were hunted down and killed in most areas east of the Mississippi River. In 1806, the huge predators still roamed freely in the areas west of the great river, however, and their intelligence and fierce attacks were legendary. To make matters worse, the bear in our story seems to possess magical powers.

I hope you will enjoy this work of fiction, as you follow John and Benjamin through one rip-roaring wilderness adventure after another. At trail's end, you will see that love and respect win out over hatred and mistrust every time they are given the chance.

DEDICATION

This book is lovingly dedicated to John, Tony, and Carey, my three sons, whose hungry minds and requests for stories never failed to inspire me. Together, we spun yarns to carry us through long road trips, bedtimes, fevers, waiting room fidgets, gray rainy days, and bouts of cabin fever. I also dedicate this book to my seven grandchildren, Madeline, Rachel, Shannon, Jack, Brady, Louis, and Addie, who carry on in my sons' story-hungry footsteps, and to all my future grandchildren waiting in Heaven's wings to make their appearance. Finally, I dedicate this, and all my flights of fancy, to my gentle, loving husband, Bob, whose patience and praise nourished my soul.

OLD FIRE EYES

by Kathleen Valle

RUN!

I T WAS EARLY SPRING IN the year 1806 and still unusually cold for Virginia plantation country. After sitting at his master's bedside for most of four days, thirteen-year-old Benjamin had fallen asleep in the warmth of the sun streaming through the rippled glass window. Laid up far too early in life, even for an old man, Master Jeffries rested stone-cold still in his large, hand-carved, four poster bed. Jeffries' good friend, Doc Graves, had come and gone many times, rubbing his scratchy whiskers, and tut-tutting helplessly. The two old men had shared whispers and secret looks when they thought Ben wouldn't notice. But the young slave boy caught and understood their secret glances, and he knew this beloved old man lying quietly in his bed wouldn't last many days before an illness like pneumonia would finish the job that Jeffries' startled horse had started. There was no cure for a broken back.

Unable to move his arms and legs and struggling for enough breath to whisper last secrets to the young black boy seated at his bedside, Jeffries had rushed to tell Ben of amazing plans he had made for him and for all the other slaves living on the plantation. Between fits of secret-telling, the old man drifted off to an exhausted sleep, eventually regaining enough strength from each nap to continue. Ben had used that precious time to digest and comprehend the wave upon wave of shocking facts that his old master hastily announced. Lack of sleep had finally caught up with Ben, however, and his efforts to stay awake and make sense of all Jeffries' secrets had failed during his master's last, lengthy nap.

A bright light awoke Ben. Something shiny outside had glinted in the sun, causing a dazzling reflection to bounce off a glass-covered picture hanging on Master Jeffries' bedroom wall. He arose quickly and looked outside, catching a hint of movement in the piney woods which stood between the river and the big plantation house. When he returned his gaze to Jeffries, the old man was awake and following Ben with his eyes. Ben sat back down quickly, hoping that his master hadn't known he was sleeping a moment before, but the faint, loving smile on Jeffries' face told him he was caught. The twinkle in the old man's eyes would have normally introduced a stream of soft chuckles, if Jeffries had been healthy and whole. As it was, that gentle smile would have to do.

The look turned serious and hinted at urgency. "Ben," Jeffries gasped. "There's more to tell and not much time. Important papers under my desk. Three loose floorboards. Pull them up. A strongbox set in stone down below. Key around my neck. Take it now. You are my son, Ben. Benjamin Jeffries. I adopted you. You are free, and so is everyone else. Promise me. College. The Law. Use your education. We studied hard, didn't we all? You are enrolled at Harvard. Cambridge, Massachusetts. All arranged and paid for."

Ben's heart leapt into his throat. "Your son? But I thought . . ."

"The key, Ben. Is it still there?" the old man interrupted.

Ben studied the old, iron key strung from a worn leather thong. It had hung around Master Jeffries' neck for as long as he could remember. Now it lay in a nest of grizzled gray hairs on the old man's sunken chest. Somehow, it seemed wrong to even touch it.

"Yes," Ben answered, "it's still there."

"Now, Ben," Master Jeffries gasped. "Put it around your neck. Don't lose it."

Ben did as he was told. When the leather thong was safely around his thin neck, and Jeffries had refilled his lungs, the old man continued. "Your mama will explain. Not your blood father. Just adopted, but you are my son in my heart and on paper. Remember those trips up to Pennsylvania?"

Ben remembered them well. At one time or another, every last man, woman and child on the plantation had traveled up north to the other Jeffries place, a small farm named *Haven*, which sat a half-day's carriage ride from Philadelphia. The young man smiled briefly, recalling the first time he had passed under the beautiful wrought-iron entrance, which seemed to drip with plump clusters of iron grapes and life-like grape leaves. Already an artist in his five-year-old heart, he had fallen in love with the iron work and asked Master Jeffries to stop long enough to study it. Mistakenly reading the word wrought within the curved arch, he had asked Jeffries if they truly were about to enter Heaven.

"Had to get you all to Pennsylvania. Needed to be sure," Jeffries panted, abruptly interrupting Ben's memories of that day eight summers ago. "There's talk here about changes in the law." He closed his eyes once again as he licked his dried lips and gathered his breath. Ben offered him sips of spring water, lifting the old man's head so he wouldn't choke. "Bad changes for black folk," Jeffries added, after wetting his parched lips with his tongue."

"Ledgers in the strong box," Jeffries continued. "Manumission papers and wages for everyone from the day they were freed. Accounts. The bank is in Boston. Calhoun will help. He knows. Trust him. Move everyone up to Haven and sell this place. 'Bound to be bad feelings around here when word gets out. My brother. Look out for him. Big trouble. Plenty of money in accounts. Not for him. Keep going forward, Ben. Promise me."

Ben was in shock. There was too much to take in, and he wasn't sure he could remember everything Jeffries told him. "I promise," he said, hoping he could keep his word. Then he realized the old man had mentioned something about a brother. "Brother?" he asked. "You have a brother? Wouldn't the law …?"

Jeffries seemed to read his mind. "No good slaver," he interrupted, dismissing his own brother as if he didn't matter. "Say it all back to me, so I know you understand," he gasped, "but first get me another quilt. I'm cold as death."

Ben shuddered at the horrible word Jeffries chose, but he shook it off and hurried to the new wing of the big house. He slipped into the small room called the press, where all the coverlets were stored. As Ben dug through the linens for the old man's favorite winter quilt, he tried to recall in order all the shocking secrets Jeffries had told him, but the sound of soft footsteps on the back staircase interrupted his thoughts. The servants were the only ones to use the back stairs, and someone had picked a horrible time to bother the old man, who was lockstep in a race against time. Except for Ben, Doc Graves, and Tom Beadles the overseer, the only other people allowed to visit Master Jeffries were Osha, the big cook who ruled the kitchens, and Obadiah, the house man who saw to cleaning and changing the master, now that he couldn't care for himself. The third step from the bottom always complained noisily about Osha's weight when she climbed the stairs, but Ben noticed the step remained quiet. It had to be Obadiah, he guessed, but Ben reckoned the bent and twisted old man had visited less than two hours ago to take care of the master's needs. The young man found the quilt he was looking for and hurried around the corner and into Master Jeffries' wing to try to stop Obadiah before he could enter.

But he was too late. As he moved into the doorway, he gasped. A tall stranger dressed in a fancy military suit of some kind was holding a pillow over Master Jeffries' face, trying to smother him! Ben ran into the room, nearly tripping over the dropped quilt as he rushed to stop the big man, but he was thrown against a bedroom wall by a swipe of the man's powerful arm. The wall knocked the wind out of Ben, silencing his calls for help before they could even begin. He tried to jump to his feet, but his legs had turned to willow whips. He had left his carving knife on the table next to Master Jeffries' bed. Now, it was hidden under the man's fancy hat. If he could get to it in time, maybe . . . But he was too late! The man returned the hat to his head and grabbed the knife like he had known all along that it was there. Now, it was Ben's turn to run for his life as the man rushed toward him and sliced through the back of Ben's left hand. Feeling like he was swimming through vat of molasses, Ben waded across the quilt and stumbled through the door with the man close on his heels. Desperate, the brave young man turned. He stooped to grab the edge of the quilt, yanking it as hard as his fear would permit. Sliding across the polished wooden floor, the quilt slithered out from under the stranger's feet, and he came crashing down. Without daring to look back, Ben ran down the back stairs like the devil, himself, was after him.

As he entered the downstairs hallway, he heard the man's footfall on the top step. There was no time to look for Osha or anyone else. He had to hide, and his hand was bleeding badly! He darted into the kitchen and grabbed Osha's spare apron, before leaving an intentional trail of blood to the back door. Then he squeezed the apron against his hand and hurried across the kitchen. He thanked the Lord above for making him small as he squeezed into the kettle bin, curling up in the biggest iron kettle he could find. Then he remembered the cabinet door. The man was down the stairs and headed for the kitchen. He twisted as quietly as he could and grabbed the back of the door with his fingernails, easing it toward him until he heard the quiet click of the latch. Did the man hear it? Ben held his breath until he was seeing stars, and he tried to squelch the fear that the sound of his pounding heart would echo around in the big iron pot like a muster-day drum, announcing his whereabouts.

The man was slinking about in the kitchen, coming closer and closer to the kettle bin. He might not have fallen for the trail of blood, after all. Suddenly his steps stopped dead-still, and he seemed to be standing right on the other side of the kettle bin door. After a long silence, Ben thought he heard the kitchen door squeak, but he wasn't about to test his ears. Just as he heard steps running toward the summer kitchen outside, Osha came muttering down the hallway from the front side of the big plantation house. She had a way of giving herself orders, as she marched through her days, and Ben was thankful for her habit, because her voice had scared away the stranger. His heart sank with disappointment as he heard the third step squeak. Would the man come back to search the kitchen once more if he knew Osha had gone up the back stairway?

The cook's wails echoed through the big house. Frozen with fear and wilted by guilt for failing to save Jeffries, Ben stayed put in the kettle, listening as Osha sent Obadiah to fetch the Reverend Stiles and Doc Graves. Within minutes, the sound of hoof-beats rattled the kettle bin as the old man galloped past the outside wall which separated the lane from Ben's hiding place. The frightened young man correctly guessed that Obadiah hadn't bothered to saddle the horse, but had chosen, instead, to ride him bareback right into town.

In his misery and fear, Ben lost track of time. It seemed to him he might have been hiding in that kettle for hours, when Osha returned to the kitchen to punch down a batch of risen bread dough. Sniffling and snuffling away her sadness, she kneaded and slammed the huge wad of dough onto the sturdy oak table made by the master's own father. Figuring it was safe for the moment, Ben climbed out of the kettle bin, nearly giving Osha a heart attack in the process.

When she had regained her wits, she reached out her huge arms to hug Ben. "Oh, Benjamin, I've got some terrible, terrible news," she said.

Ben melted into the warmth and temporary safety of her embrace, but he knew he had to act quickly. He told her about the military man smothering Master Jeffries, and he showed her the cut in his hand, cringing at the way he had ruined Osha's apron with his own blood. At first, she seemed to doubt him, but then he realized she had believed every word, because she ignored the bloody apron and wordlessly returned to punching her bread dough. From the squint of her eyes, Ben knew she was considering his news and its consequences. He stilled his tongue and waited impatiently, aware that she would best know what he should do, if he allowed her time to think.

"You need to talk with Doc Graves and Reverend Stiles when they get here," she finally reasoned. "They'll know what to do about this murderer, if . . ."

But Osha's speech was ended by a gasp, and she shot Ben a wide-eyed stare. Someone was pounding on the big front door of the Jeffries mansion. It was far too soon for Obadiah to return with the two men he had been sent to fetch, and besides, no one ever used the front door. It had to be a stranger to these parts, and the timing couldn't be worse. Ben had intended to tell her about their freedom and the hidden papers, but there was no time!

"Quick," she ordered, "climb into the apple barrel." With more speed than Ben would have thought possible for the big woman, she scurried to the trap-door set into the kitchen floor and lifted it. She motioned Ben down the wooden steps descending into the big root cellar and ordered him to keep quiet and stay put, adding a fierce glare to make her point. It wasn't a minute too soon. Before she had time to lower the door, the murderer marched into the kitchen like he owned the place. Ben had immediately rejected Osha's order to hide in the apple barrel, because it was too close to the ladder. If their visitor was the murderer, he had probably come back to find Ben. The man could look right down on him from the opening in the kitchen floor. Instead, he tiptoed into the darkest corner of the root cellar and wiggled into a large bin of potatoes, working quietly to bury himself among them.

Ben's hunch was right. The murderer was back, and he was obviously on a mission to find the only person on earth who could identify Master Jeffries' cold-blooded killer. As he had suspected the man might do, the stranger marched right up to the rim of the opening, looking downward into the gloom as he asked angrily, "Why was the front door unmanned, Cook? I have traveled a long way and expected to be received properly. Where is the house boy?"

Osha played her role well. "I'm so sorry, Massah, but we . . ."

"Then announce me to your master yourself," the man interrupted. "Tell him his brother has come calling."

Ben could hear Osha's reply clearly. Whether from real sadness or fear, her sudden sobs sounded genuine. "Oh, Massah Jeffries, Suh, my massah's dead! He jus' die. We got the doctor and the Reveren' comin' by'm'by. He been laid up wid a broke back, and he jus' die."

Ben could hardly believe his ears. Why was Osha talking this way? Master Jefferies would die all over again if he could hear her going on like a mistreated, uneducated slave. Osha had spent many hours up on the third floor reading hungrily through books and ciphering with such accuracy that Master Jefferies had turned over the household bookkeeping to her. She was anything but uneducated, and she might not know it yet, but she was no longer a slave, either. She was a free black, and so was he! So was Obadiah and so were all the rest of the blacks once owned by Master Jeffries. Then, as he listened to Osha's sniveling and the stranger's pompous raving, something else struck him for the very first time. He shouldn't be saying *Master* Jeffries anymore. The old man, who had been a combination guardian angel and grandfather for as long as he could remember, was actually his legal father! Imagine that! Now, he knew why Jeffries had insisted every black on the place should only use the term, "Master," when there were strangers around. He *wasn't* their master; he was more like a secret friend helping them along on their way to freedom!

When he realized the room had become silent, he mentally scolded himself for letting his mind wander at such a dangerous time. Was he right in thinking Osha had led the man up to see his brother? If Ben was going to fulfill his promises to his father, he needed to keep his wits about him and escape this murderer, who had strutted across the huge kitchen floor like an arrogant peacock. It seemed to Ben that his best chance to escape this man's evil intentions would come from staying put, so he used the opportunity to truly bury himself in the potato bin.

As he lay still considering his best course of action, Osha returned to the kitchen. She slowly made her way down the root cellar ladder, grunting with the effort. "Ben," she whispered hoarsely, "Where are you?" She began to systematically peer into each of the big barrels which stored dried fruits and vegetables. She was inspecting the last of the barrels with her back to the nearby potato bin, when Ben finally felt she was close enough to hear him.

"S-s-s-s," he hissed as quietly as possible.

Osha jumped so hard that one foot actually left the floor. After catching her breath and muttering up some courage, she whispered hoarsely, "Ben? Is that you, or am I talking to a snake?"

"It's me, Osha," he whispered from the middle of the pile of potatoes. "Behind you."

"Heaven's sake, child, you sure have found yourself a good hidey hole! You best stay right there until I come down to get you. It might be quite a while, but you stay still, you hear? When I say it's clear, you've got to run like the wind and get as far from here as you can."

"Osha?"

Yes, child?"

"Do you believe me?"

Osha sighed sadly. "Yes, Benjamin, I *do* believe you, but you've got to look at facts. That murderer up there says he's Master Jeffries' brother, and he sure seems to know his way around the older half of the house, so he probably is. Problem is, he's white and you're a black slave boy. The Master was on his way to dying. Now, even if you could get past this man without being murdered, yourself, who do you think will be believed, if you go try telling your story to the authorities?" She sighed again. "No, child, you've got to run far and fast. That scoundrel will be looking for you to head north, so if I were you, I'd head south first, and then I'd make for the western wilderness like your tail's on fire."

But the big cook didn't know Master Jeffries' secrets. "Osha," Ben began, before he thought better of breaking the shocking news. He had to have some quiet time to figure out on his own just what he should do. If he were caught, that evil man would see to it that his story would never be told! Changing course, he whispered fiercely, "I'm not going without my knife. Master gave it to me and told me to carve out a place for myself, and I'm not leaving without it."

She glanced at the empty sheath hanging from his leather belt. "I'll get it, just you wait and see. Now, you be still!" Osha gathered a spare apron from one of many pegs pounded into the root cellar wall, and she filled it full of last autumn's apples before struggling back up the ladder. Deciding that the events of the last few hours were too overwhelming to consider just now, she intentionally turned her thoughts to more familiar problems. She would focus on doing her job and bake a big pan of dowdy for that murdering scoundrel and his rag-tag bunch of men, she told herself. As she wiped away streamlets of tears from her plump cheeks, she considered what she should fix for all the visitors who would undoubtedly show up within the next few weeks. Master Jeffries was truly loved by whites and slaves, alike, and rightfully so. He was an honest and kind man. Any slave could count himself fortunate to live on the Jeffries plantation. Though the whites would come a-calling at the ornately carved front door of the big house, Osha predicted that many blacks from the surrounding area would quietly appear at the kitchen door to offer sympathy to their brethren and to demonstrate their high regard for Master Jeffries.

Osha sighed, pulled a large pan from a sturdy iron nail on the wall, grabbed a paring knife, and eased herself into the big hickory rocking chair she jokingly called her throne. Carefully removing each apple from her apron, she peeled and sliced it into the pan, absent-mindedly removing the peel in one long, curling spiral, as she always did. "*I wonder,*" she thought to herself with a shudder, "*what it will be like to have a murderer for a master.*"

During the next few hours, there was a great deal of coming and going through the kitchen, and as Ben had suspected he would, the man who called himself Captain Jeffries found an excuse to carefully search the root cellar, claiming he needed to conduct an inventory, since the house would soon be filled with friends and neighbors coming to pay their last respects. The man strolled right past the potatoes, studying the pile as carefully as he had examined every other possible hiding place. "*If he decides to stick that big sword hanging at his side into this pile of potatoes, I'm a gone sucker,*" Ben thought. Luckily, there was little room in the root cellar to draw such a lengthy weapon from its fancy metal sheath. Eventually, the man seemed to relax a bit, perhaps deciding that Ben had long-since left the plantation. As Ben listened, the man's heavy boots shuffled up the steps and the trap door squeaked shut, enveloping the root cellar in inky darkness.

By the time Osha opened the trap door and quietly ordered Ben to come up, he climbed the root cellar steps like a gouty old man. The only movement that seemed to come naturally to him was shivering, and he was doing that so well that it worried Osha. It was late evening, and he had fallen asleep listening to the murderer hob-nob with Doc Graves and Reverend Styles at the big kitchen table, like he was already the new owner of the plantation. Well, Ben guessed, he *was* the new owner, until Ben could prove otherwise. He had to get at those papers and hurry to Mr. Calhoun's office to tell him what had happened. Calhoun was a good lawyer and a best friend to Jeffries, and he would see to it that justice was served.

Clucking away about how what Ben really needed was a stout bowl of the stew that bubbled away in the kitchen fireplace but how there wasn't any time for such a luxury, Osha handed him a large kerchief filled with enough food to get him started. She also gave him three coins to use when he was desperate but not before. Finally, with a flourish, she handed him his beloved carving knife, which he quickly returned to the beautiful, hand-tooled leather sheath that always hung from his belt.

"I took it right out from under his nose," she whispered with a proud grin. "Grabbed it and said I'd been looking all over for my favorite knife. Now you've got to run like the wind. Don't even stop to say good-bye to your mama. It isn't safe. Captain Jeffries has men posted around this place, and I think they're watching for you, so keep to the shadows."

"First I've got to go to Master's office," Ben insisted.

Osha grabbed him by his belt. "No! He's in there, and he's already going through Master's books, the scoundrel!" she hissed. "Run, Ben! If he catches you, our hearts will break all over again!"

Ben had no choice. According to Master Jeffries, not even Mr. Calhoun knew where the will and manumission papers were hidden. With luck, Captain Jeffries wouldn't know about that secret hiding place, either, because it was under the new half of the house. For now, it made sense to get to Mr. Calhoun's office and tell him everything.

"Osha," Ben whispered, "Do you know how to get down into the old tunnel that leads to the river?"

"Of course I do, child, but so does the captain, I'd venture to say. It's in the old part of the house, and he grew up here, you know. I've been outside a few times, and it looks like the captain has men watching the doors, just in case you're still hiding inside. He's too smart and sneaky not to have posted someone at the tunnel opening. You just forget about that and do as I say."

She steered him away from the back door and led him to the first-floor linen press, where there was a window hidden from view by their master's pride and joy, three big lilac bushes, brought straight from Middlesex, England, many years before. Ben crawled through the opened window, and Osha closed it quietly behind him. As he crouched there, breathing in the wonderful fragrance of the blue blossoms, Ben waited for his eyes to adjust to the darkness. Osha was wise to lead him to the window. He could see strange men watching both the front and the back doors, acting disinterested as they waited for him to come out of the house. He stared longingly at the deeply shadowed piney woods that lay just beyond an open stretch of carefully manicured lawn. Ben thought to himself that he might be looking toward the very spot where the sun had glinted on something this morning. Now, he knew it was likely that the shiny thing had been a piece of polished brass on the captain's uniform, as he sneaked toward the house to murder his own brother! *Was that only this morning?* It seemed days ago. From the moment the bright light had awakened him, his life had changed course forever. He could waste time wishing it had all been a bad dream, but there was no need for that. This tragedy was real, all right.

The guards all turned suddenly toward the back door, and Osha stepped out to throw a large pan of water onto the ground, barely missing the boots of one of the guards.

"Oh! I'ze so sorry, Massah!" she exclaimed loudly. "I be seein' po'ly in de dawk de las' few years." She stepped boldly toward the man, continuing to hold the attention of all the guards nearest Ben's hiding place. "Lemme dry dem boots, suh," she whined.

Offering a silent prayer of thanksgiving for his big, brave guardian angel, Ben slipped unseen across the lawn and melted into the shadows of the piney woods. Osha kept up her act loudly enough to cover any sound he might have made while hurrying away. When he judged they could no longer hear his movements, he set out quickly to notify Mr. Calhoun of the day's events. The young black boy avoided the roads and stuck to the river, noticing that the mosquitoes had chosen the same vicinity. When he was sure no one was around to hear, he allowed himself to slap at the blood-thirsty creatures, but enough of them had enjoyed his momentary ceasefires that he was dancing with The Itch by the time he emerged from the woods behind Mr. Calhoun's simple frame home on Main Street. He stopped dead in his tracks, however, because two more strangers were posted by the aging lawyer's house. One more second out in the moonlight, and they'd have seen him! He ducked back into the deep woods, where he was greeted by a fresh horde of biters. Frantic, he melted backward into the deep shadows and silently waded into the cold river, feeling more relief with each step he took into the deepening water. Willing his teeth to stop their chattering, he allowed himself a few minutes to float silently, until he found himself under the old stone bridge that spanned Main Street.

The nearly full moon was high in the sky, but its light was slanted just enough to cast shadows onto the water over the spot where Ben lay partially submerged. He took a few precious minutes to calm himself and consider his next course of action, but the moment he invited in the calm, his grief came along for the ride, and he struggled not to sob. Today he had both gained and lost a father. He had loved gentle old Charles Jeffries with all the love he supposed a real son would have for his real father, and now, before they had even begun to openly enjoy that love, the old man was gone. He had also gained and probably lost a great deal of property and a chance to tell all his people at the Jeffries plantation of their freedom. He owed so much good news to so many people who weren't even aware of their wonderful circumstances, but he could see no way to get around Captain Jeffries.

As if thinking of the man had conjured him up, he heard a now-familiar voice. The bluster from the man's kitchen table speeches had left, but Ben was certain the voice floating quietly from above him belonged to the captain. When four men neared the far side of the bridge and he saw their silhouettes on the water, his artist's eye carefully studied the shadow of the villain standing above him, from the jut of his ears to the strange bump on his nose. Ben suspected that nose had been broken more than once, from the look of it. As he lay in the water, he vowed to carve the man's head and face, from the top of his military hat to his braid-trimmed, stand-up collar. He had been frightened and had only caught quick glimpses, as he fought the man in Jeffries' bedroom, but he was enough of an artist that he had memorized every little feature on the man's face. As soon as he was safely away from the area, he would carve an exact likeness of the captain. Then let people try to tell him they didn't believe him! If he was gone by the time the captain arrived at the front door, how could he have known what the man looked like? He smiled at his decision, but his smile quickly slid into a look of worry as he listened to the captain's words.

"I don't care how you do it; the boy has to die. They say he likes to carve animals and people and he's good at it. That should be a clue you can use. Head north and spread the word you're looking for a runaway slave boy who's thirteen and small for his age. Don't kill him 'til you get him alone with no one to watch, and then bring me his left hand. It should have a fresh cut across the top of it where I caught him good with a knife, and I'll know if you try to trick me by bringing some other boy's hand. Bury the body where no one will find it. There's a nice pile of gold waiting for the man who brings me that hand." The three men nodded silently. "And one more thing," the captain said. "There are three of you and one of him. If you *don't* get him, heads will roll. Understand?"

Ben stayed in the cold water under the bridge well into the night. He was so numb and exhausted when he climbed onto an isolated island well downriver, that he didn't even feel the few mosquitoes still out on the prowl. Just before plunging into an exhausted sleep, he decided his course was set. Osha was right. Whether he wanted to or not, he was about to become a wilderness man.

SMOKE DREAMS

AS HE HAD DONE FOR as long as he could remember, thirteen-year-old John Cooper lay as still as death on his corn-husk palate, feigning sleep. He knew from experience that he would learn the most private business of the village as long as he managed to lie quietly and listen carefully to the men assembled below his little attic room. At least once a week for a string of years, the men of Stowe's Fork, Virginia, had gathered in his parents' cabin at the edge of town. While John's ma fussed around with pewter mugs of cider warmed by her white-hot poker, or gingerbread baked to perfection, the men's conversation was jovial and light-hearted. They would never worry a woman with their manly cares. But after they had offered her their wishes for a restful sleep and smiled reassuringly as she entered the little lean-to bedroom beside their cabin, the real business of the night would begin.

There were no schools in Stowe's Fork, but John's secret listening post above those late-night gatherings had become a kind of classroom. Straining to hear the men's whispered conversations until he gave in to the sleep so inescapable to a young man full of growing muscle and fresh air, he learned a great deal about the bloody history of the seemingly peaceful place he had always called home.

The Stowe's Fork settlers had lived through many years of struggles with starvation, storms, blizzards, and Indians. Most of all, Indians. Johnny's neck tingled each time he thought of those late-night tales carried on the pipe smoke that drifted up to his news-hungry ears through the cracks between the boards, right along with the flickering firelight. One crack was big enough that, if he lay just right and squinted, he could look down upon the men as they stared into the firelight and quietly discussed their dreams and fears.

In his younger years, Johnny had imagined the menfolk were holding a special ceremony, because their ways were always the same. They would scrape chairs across the stone floor to get closer to the warm embers. When talk would quiet down and Miller Brown, the oldest man at Stowe's Fork, would clear his throat and spit into the fire, Johnny knew another Indian tale was on its way. Everyone respected Brown, because he had kept track of everything that happened from the day he arrived to build his mill so many years ago. It was a chancy thing to set up so far into the wilderness of Virginia in those days. If you found a big enough clearing to stand in, and if the sun and the sky were just right, you could see the mountains off to the west.

Brown told of the Indians' attempts to stop him as he struggled to build his mill. He won out, though, and got it built. Other friends who had traveled here with him had run into Indian troubles, too. Just when the settlers believed the old chief had finally given up his campaign to drive the settlers out, and they could breathe easy, a bushel of young braves would sweep down and scatter their milk cows or carry off their sheep or hogs. And they never disappeared back into their wilderness haunts without setting a fire to a barn or a cabin or two.

Johnny had heard the tales of how Grandpa and Miller Brown had fought together during the freedom war. As they battled the English redcoats, Brown poured out his brags about the mill and the bountiful settlement he had left behind when he mustered to fight for independence. By the time freedom was won, Grandpa Cooper knew there just wasn't any other place for him but that settlement Brown kept jawing about. Still a young man, himself, he took a bride and, with other eager friends, they followed Brown back to his spot a hawk's flight away from the mountains.

What they found when they returned would turn a skunk's stomach. The Indians had overrun the settlement and had carried off women and children, burning down all the buildings as they left. The men who had stayed behind to run the settlement had been cut down wherever they stood. John Stowe's body was still hitched to his plow when they found him. Like the other men, buzzards and night critters had picked away at so much of Stowe's body, they couldn't have identified him without his father's pocket watch. Stowe had been right proud of that watch. It had come all the way from France. They hurried to bury and pray over all the poor souls they had found at the settlement, and then they mounted a search party to find the women and children, but it was no use. They were never found.

"They was growed men a-crying, walking around like they was dreaming, when they come upon the settlement," Brown whispered hoarsely one night. "One woman in the group commenced to screaming and never did get her senses back. She died a few months later from pure scare."

Winter was approaching, and all the crops had been destroyed. Whole families had been wiped out. The only things left from Brown's mill were the two huge grinding stones he had struggled so hard to bring to the settlement. Those two stones were the very heart of his mill, because it was with them that he ground everyone's grain into flour or meal. Without flour or meal, the people might starve to death!

Angry and grieving, the new crop of settlers had squeezed their strong hands into fists and shouted that the marauding natives would never, ever use this land again. They built a small fort on the spot where John Stowe's body was found, and then they set about making shelters and rebuilding the mill. They won. The Indians finally gave up and let them live in peace. In honor of the Stowe family that would never exist again, they agreed to name their settlement, which rested at the fork of a big river, "Stowe's Fork."

It had not been an easy life, working from daylight to dark through rain, wind, snow, and floods, but things improved. Crops appeared and then became bounteous, as they cleared their lands. More settlers came. Johnny's own father, Matthew Cooper, was born in the cornfield a few minutes' walk from Grandpa Cooper's cabin. Although all the rest had the good manners to wait until their mothers were conveniently inside their homes, many more babies arrived over time, increasing the population of the settlement one lusty bawler at a time. Stowe's Fork was growing into a respectable little community.

Early one spring morning a one-eyed, strangely clad man named Cyrus Beade led a heavily loaded mule to the edge of the settlement. By the time the sun set, he had built himself a small lean-to up against the south side of Ring Rock. He stowed all his belongings in the new little shelter, watered, fed, and hobbled his mule, and crawled inside to sleep atop his merchandise. The settlers quickly found their way to Beade's lean-to, where he traded during daylight and slept at night. Before the first flakes of snow blew in on late autumn winds, he had built a fine log trading post with a bedroom for himself and an attached shed for his mule.

Trails branched away here and there, allowing settlers to venture farther and farther out to build their cabins and tend their lands. Most of all, the Indians changed their ways. Some even took to wearing white man's clothes and poked their noses into Beade's trading post. By the time Johnny was born, they could be seen strolling through the settlement, visiting, and doing business with their white neighbors.

Well, you can bury old hurts, but somehow, they always sprout up later to pester you worse than thorny thistle. The older settlers who remembered their lost friends and families could not tolerate the men and women they considered "savages," especially since they could look right out the church window any Sunday morning and see the graves of friends and family the Indians had killed. Bad feelings festered up among the older Indians and settlers, even though their children and grandchildren tried their best to get along and help each other. Miller Brown, himself, shakily announced late one night that the ghosts of his long-dead wife and children had come to him in his sleep and had told him not to let the Indians stand on the ground stained with their own blood.

One meeting night several weeks ago, Johnny's own father, Matthew Cooper, had dared to take the Indians' side. The only natives he had ever known were fine people who honored their promises. He even went so far as to ask how the settlers would have felt if they were there first. Like many of the second generation of Stowe's Fork citizens, Matthew Cooper had developed friendships with the Indians. He had learned about their belief that people could not own land, because the land owned itself. They believed that the land was kind to allow them to use it to feed their families, and like any kindly being, it should be respected and thanked, but never owned. *Never* owned!

From that night on, it was plain from the way Matthew Cooper's entire family was treated that the people of Stowe's Fork no longer considered them entirely welcomed. To make matters worse, to Johnny's way of thinking, his father wouldn't leave the subject alone. He kept going back to his opinion, like a moth drawn to a flame, and added to his list of beliefs. The women who had always been happy to visit Johnny's mother, eager to share a recipe or bring the latest news, avoided the Cooper cabin, and so did their children. Except for his friend, Rebecca Mobley, John Cooper lost every friend he had.

Set on convincing Matthew that he was wrong in his thinking, the men continued to gather for their late-night meetings below Johnny's sleeping pallet, and the young man grew angrier with every word his father spoke. If nothing else, why couldn't his father just keep his opinions to himself?

And tonight, his father had taken that final, irreversible step. He announced that he and Ma were going to move west into the wilderness, where white man had not yet battled Indians over land. He and his family would prove his beliefs by starting right out living in peace with the Indians. As Johnny lay worrying that the men gathered below would hear his heart slamming against his chest, he clamped his hand over his mouth for fear he would cry out in anger and shock.

No one had told *him* they were moving, and as for himself, and probably Ma and baby Hallie when he thought about it, he didn't want any part of it. He panicked. His mind raced. Maybe he could take over the farming duties and become the man of the place. The more he thought about it, the more reasonable a solution it appeared to be. With Grandpa and Grandma nearby to help him, Ma, and Hallie, they'd get along just fine. Pa could go off on his own if he was so all-fired keen to prove his beliefs. Maybe after Pa had been gone for a time, the people would take up their old friendships where they'd left off before his Pa started spouting off. He'd miss his Pa, for certain, but not so much that he was willing to risk his scalp to prove it. And what about Ma and Hallie? Their scalps were a whole lot prettier than his!

Johnny stopped listening to the men below and began to plan how he would announce his intentions to stay and take care of his family. After all, it was mostly his pa that was doing all the wild talking. No, he would go talk to Grandpa first thing in the morning. He was certain the loveable old man didn't know a thing about Pa's plan, and he guessed Ma didn't, either. He fell asleep assured that he had found the perfect solution.

MISS POLLY

FTER AN EXHAUSTED BUT DREAM-FILLED sleep, Benjamin awakened before sunup the following morning. Hoping his hunters were snoring happily away, he swam from the island to the far shore of the river and made his way south through the thick growth of weeds and young trees that always seem to border streams. He had been on several carriage rides with old Jeffries, and so he had a good idea of where the villages and nearby plantations were. Except for watchful hounds baying along the way, he passed without notice. The hounds, whose instinctive love of running off after a stray rabbit or raccoon caused them to be penned up when they weren't called upon to hunt, could do nothing more than bark.

Jeffries had taken Ben on many business and pleasure excursions through the years, hoping to expose him to the ways of white people. This could be good and could be bad. Ben knew the roads, fields, and villages like the back of his hand, but the people hereabouts knew *him* on sight. Jeffries had insisted Ben accompany him as he moved about, conducting business. If word had spread about the search for him, there were many white folks, and even some blacks, that would jump at an opportunity to turn in the young "upstart," who didn't know his place.

Before the sun cast enough light to see more than dim shadows, a wide tower of dark clouds thought better of it and rolled across the sky, rumbling deeply as they moved. Soon Ben was slogging through a downpour, hoping the driving rain would discourage his hunters. He headed into deep woods and ran until he could run no more. In his science studies, he had learned that lightening most often strikes trees, and here he was in a whole forest of them. The leaves had only begun to turn from little green buds to anything that would provide cover from the rain, anyway, so he avoided the temptation to seek shelter and dropped to his knees near the edge of a small clearing. Exhausted and hungry, he opened Osha's large kerchief and dug through its contents, uttering a prayer of thanksgiving through an unexpected smile. The river had turned his bread to sodden mush in the bottom of the bundle, but Osha had thought of other necessities that had escaped the damaging river waters. There was Jeffries' compass, which she had dared to take from its place of honor in the front hallway and store in its waterproof case. Except for the time Jeffries, himself, removed it from its display case in order to teach Ben about the great Chinese invention that changed the world, no one had been allowed to touch it. There was a precious needle from old Mistress Jeffries sewing kit, as well as a spindle of cotton thread. The thread was wet, but it would dry out with time. A square cake of homemade soap nested in the soggy remnants of bread. For the first time in a whole day, Ben was smiling. Old Osha was truly an angel in disguise. He promised himself he would avoid the two apples and the smoked fish she had carefully wrapped. Hunger would keep him company every step of the way, and he might as well get used to it and make that food stretch for as long as he could.

His stomach complained bitterly as he gathered fists full of soggy crumbs and tried his best to squeeze out water before stuffing a small, sticky wad in his mouth. What had once been a delicious-smelling, crusty loaf of manna, had turned into a soapy-tasting paste with little satisfaction to it. Nonetheless, he carefully squeezed every last crumb, chewing and then swallowing it, until it disappeared far too soon. Fingering the three coins in his pocket, he knew he couldn't purchase food until he had gotten himself far away from Jeffries' usual circle of travels. He would just go hungry until he absolutely had to eat, he thought, shivering with fear and unaccustomed exposure. The smoked fish and apples would keep him from starving. In the meantime, maybe he would come across something edible in his travels.

Soaked and muddy, his shoes and stockings had already rubbed his heels raw. Before Master Jeffries' startling announcements, Ben had not understood why he, and all of the blacks living on the plantation, had enjoyed yet another distinction among slaves. Twice a year, Jeffries had hired a shoemaker to see to the needs of many growing black feet under his care. Ben had heard the old man defend his practice to disapproving friends and neighbors, saying that he was simply protecting his investments. An injured foot is a non-working foot, he would say. Now, Ben knew the real reason behind Jeffries' shoemaker: simple kindness. With regret, Ben removed his shoes and stockings and scraped as much mud from them as he could. He tucked them into Osha's roomy kerchief, promising himself he would be able to wear them safely one day soon. For now, however, they stood out on his black feet like a sinner on Judgment Day. It would take several days to toughen up his feet, but he was not about to call attention to himself by wearing his shoes.

Hungry, cold, and soaked through to his weary bones, Ben sobbed bitterly. Would he ever be able to return to the Jeffries plantation? Was it possible to bring Master Jeffries' brother to justice? What was his mother thinking? If only he could have stolen just a precious moment to say good-bye to her and give her a last hug. Osha would take care of telling his mother what had truly happened, he knew. The biggest injustice of all was the fact that every single black who lived and worked on the Jeffries plantation was free! If they had those hidden papers, they could walk right away from that evil captain and make new lives for themselves as freed blacks. Why, Ben's own adoptive father had even been secretly paying wages into their own accounts for who-knows-how-long? They would have money to begin their free lives properly! Osha had kept Jeffries' books for several years, now, but somehow Ben was certain she had no knowledge of the ledgers that had kept track of each worker's earnings.

The more Ben thought about it, the surer he became that he needed to find a place to hide nearby. Eventually, the captain and his evil employees would believe he was long-gone, and they would stop searching. Then he would go to Mr. Calhoun, who would advise Ben and help to arrest Captain Jeffries and free everyone. That was his last thought before sleep caught him off guard.

Ben was awakened by the sound of hounds baying through the thrumming rain. They were nearby and barking like they had found his scent. He knew from the urgency of their howls that he had seconds before they would catch up to him. He grabbed his bundle and sprinted like his tail was on fire. Finally, fate handed him his only possible means to throw the dogs off his trail. A creek coursed right through the middle of the forest, and it was running fast and hard from all the rain. He bounded into the middle of the river and waded downstream, finally getting out on the opposite side. This would buy him no more than a minute or two, but it was the only chance he had!

It worked. At least it worked for a moment. The dogs stopped at the stream and milled around, searching for his scent. Their handlers finally dragged the poor animals across the river and set them to searching up and back. A high-pitched yelp announced that a hound had relocated the trail, and was off and running. Ben ran until the pain in his side nearly crippled him. He was a small for his age, and the men were long-legged and being propelled along by bloodthirsty hounds. They were gaining on him. Then the shots came. One shot rang out just as bark on a tree less than a foot from Ben's head splintered, and the men let out a series of war whoops. A second shot missed him widely. His luck changed with the third hunter. When the man pulled his trigger, the gunpowder must have flashed in the muzzle-loader's frizzen pan, because the man bellowed in pain. The side of his face would be badly burned, Ben reckoned, and he would need help getting to a doctor. As he ran, Ben even dared to hope the man's eye had been blinded. That would serve him right, he thought. With that happy thought, his pain went away, and he ran on. Sometimes fate has a way of evening things out.

As if the heavens, themselves, were crying over the tragic death of Charles Jeffries, the downpour continued, blown sideways by fierce winds. The temperature dropped suddenly, and Ben was pelted by stinging hail. He had to find shelter before he either froze to death or dropped to his knees from exhaustion and lack of food. He decided to risk being found and worked his way toward a back road he remembered, but when he arrived at the road, he recognized nothing. He struck out to the right, stepping into a rut filled with rushing water. The road led downhill, leading him to believe he was approaching another river. If he kept his feet in the rut, he thought, no one would see his footprints, and the hounds might become confused.

The hail left and the rain returned with a vengeance. As he worked his way downhill, he saw that the road ahead disappeared into a flooded bottomland. As he watched, a hog house spilled squealing young piglets into the rushing waters as it tumbled end-over-end. Benjamin knew he could not help the poor pigs. If he tried, he would undoubtedly drown or be caught. Up a long lane to his right, a small farmhouse perched atop a hill. It was surrounded by a broken-down barn and a few other buildings but seemed to be placed high enough that the flood would not affect it.

Struggling against a fit of shivers, he worked his way to the little farm and fumbled with the slippery latch on a gate leading into a chicken yard. Within minutes, he was inside a cozy chicken house, feeling with his numb fingers under the warm, plump bodies of two irate hens. Enduring their angry pecks, he snatched one egg from under each bird and retreated to a warm corner, where he sat in dry straw. Benjamin shuddered, thinking about the prospect of swallowing raw eggs, but he knew he needed their nourishment. Gritting his teeth, he cracked the first egg on his knee and threw back his head, dropping the egg into his mouth. He swallowed it quickly. He gagged on second egg, but he got it down. Too exhausted to move, he curled up into a ball, soothed by the constant murmurs of the chickens and warmed by their body heat. His shivers finally ceased, and he fell into an exhausted sleep, too tired to consider his next move.

"Stand up, young man!"

Benjamin opened his eyes to find the barrel of a rifle mere inches from his nose. His eyes followed the length of the rifle to a gnarled, age-spotted hand peeking out from a cuff of tattered lace ruffles. A tall, elderly woman was holding the rifle like she knew how to use it. Benjamin tried to jump to his feet, but his body wouldn't cooperate. He fell against the side wall of the chicken house, finally using a wooden ledge to pull himself up.

"I'm sorry, Ma'am," he said, "but I was lost and I needed a place to get in out of the storm."

The old woman's eyes shifted to the emptied eggshells. "You steal my eggs?" she asked, squinting at Ben accusingly.

"Yes, Ma'am, I did," he answered. "I was very hungry and cold. I'd be happy to pay you for them." He thought of the three coins Osha had given him, thankful to be able to keep his word."

She waved the gun toward the hen house door. "Get to the house," she ordered.

Ben wanted to follow her orders, but somehow, his legs did not. The woman sized up the situation and shifted her rifle to her left hand, grabbing it by the barrel as she put an arm around Ben's waist. "Appears to me you are in need of some help," she said. "Come on, now; we might as well get inside before these hens take a liking to you. Fetch your bundle."

Ben didn't know what to make of the strange woman who seemed old but stood ramrod straight, like she was either very proud or very stubborn. Maybe both. They slogged together across the muddy chicken lot and passed through a squeaky gate. When she opened the door and helped him into her kitchen, he nearly cried when he felt the pure comfort inside. There was a perfect fire in the stone fireplace. Three big loaves of freshly baked bread sat atop the kitchen table, and he smelled tea! Hot, wet tea! His mouth would have watered, but he was far too dry, in spite of all the rain.

The woman pointed to a chair beside the table. "Sit yourself down there and don't move," she ordered. Feeling dizzy, Ben gratefully sat before his legs buckled under him. His eyes closed all on their own, perhaps so his mind could pretend for just a minute that he was back home in Osha's kitchen and his bad dream had ended.

She carried a wooden pail to the fireplace and half-filled it with hot water. "First thing we're gonna do is get you cleaned up," she announced. "And then we're gonna get some food and drink down you." She stole a glance at his surprised face. "Don't suppose you'll mind that much, will you?"

"No, Ma'am, I'd be very happy for both."

When she tried to apply soap and water, he gently removed the wash rag from her hands and thoroughly cleaned himself. Standing to take away the pan of dirty water was impossible, he found, so he tucked it under his chair. The woman perched her fists on her bony hips and stood back to study Benjamin, causing his heart to beat nearly out of his chest. Was she going to turn him in?

"You look like a cherry jam man to me," she announced through squinting eyes, "but we're going to bring out the honey, cause that will help you faster. And am I wrong in thinking that you prefer your eggs cooked?"

"No, Ma'am, cooked is my favorite way, but . . ."

"Good." It was settled. She scurried around her kitchen, dishing up some bubbling oatmeal and smothering it with honey before setting it before the hungry young man along with a silver spoon. Silver! Next, she sliced off enough fat back bacon for both of them and fried up several eggs in the fat, cooking over the fireplace embers in her long-legged "spider" frying pan. As if by magic, she produced a pot of tea hot enough to scald his tongue and poured a generous helping into a pewter mug. "More honey," she explained, stirring the golden nectar into the steaming tea. "Good for what ails you." When she followed that with a slab of warm bread, Ben could have sworn for an instant he saw wings sprouting from her shoulders. He had never before been fed by a white woman, and it felt very strange. He wasn't sure he had ever seen a white woman cook, now that he considered the subject.

Benjamin ate like a field hand. The tea warmed the inside of his body while the fire warmed his hide. His eye lids felt like they had fishing weights attached to them, and he fought hard to stay awake.

"Can you walk yet?" she asked. When he teetered on his feet, she grabbed him around the waist once again and walked him right up the stairs, into a bedroom and to the edge of a feather bed. After motioning for him to sit down, she swiveled his cold, blistered feet onto the bed. "Lay down there, and I'll get you a coverlet," she ordered. He was asleep before she returned to cover him gently and tiptoe out of the cozy bedroom, closing the door behind her.

After sleeping through an entire day, Ben awoke. It was dark outside. He took a tentative step away from the bed and found that his strength had returned. Beside him on the end of the bed were a dress and a bonnet. Judging from their size, they must belong to a young woman about his age, he guessed. He felt a pang of guilt about forcing the girl out of her own room, but he was grateful to the old woman who had seen to his needs. He shuffled to the door and stood there momentarily, listening for the woman. He heard nothing but the crickets outside.

Ben hurried to the top of the stairs. "Ma'am?" he called. "Ma'am?"

Silence.

He panicked. What if the old woman had gone to bring back the authorities! He rushed downstairs on legs made strong by the fear in his pounding heart, and he grabbed his bundle, barely noticing the two places set at the worn kitchen table. He had lost his bearings yesterday, he thought as he paused long enough to search his bundle for the compass. Starting out in the right direction would save valuable time, and it just might fool his would-be captors, since they would be expecting him to head north.

"Name's Miss Polly," the old woman's voice croaked from the direction of the barn, "and it seems to me you must be Charles Jeffries' boy, Benjamin. The one they're all after."

Ben's heart sank to his toes and his legs refused to work. He swallowed hard, certain he was a goner, as he watched Miss Polly emerge from the darkness.

"You've gone all day without eating," she said, "and you'll need help getting past those scoundrels. Come on inside. I've cooked up too much to eat alone, and we have some planning to do."

At Miss Polly's insistence, Benjamin spent the night back in the comfort of the feather bed. During their hearty evening meal, she had told him a great deal about herself, including her life-long admiration for Charles Jeffries. She had been saddened by his death, and she offered her sincere sympathy to Ben, which surprised him. He was tempted to pour out his story about Captain Jeffries and the secret freedom papers, but he chose instead to be grateful for Miss Polly's help with just getting away. He did not want any harm to come to this strange old woman, and he realized, when she told him of her escape plan for him, that she was risking all kinds of harm, as it was. He wouldn't heap any more danger on her boney old shoulders.

Once again, she fed him a large breakfast, and she insisted upon packing additional food. She had washed his clothing after sending him to bed, and it was warm and dry as she tucked it into his bundle on top of his supply of food. Benjamin sheepishly donned the bonnet and climbed into the dress that Miss Polly had set out on his bed. It came complete with an underskirt, he found to his distress, but dressing like Miss Polly's slave girl was about the only chance he had to get through the ring of men waiting to screen everyone passing along the roads.

While Ben dressed, Miss Polly harnessed her horse to her dilapidated carriage. She was waiting for him when he emerged from her home. "You need to do something that will be very distasteful to you, Benjamin," she advised. "I think Charles must have taught you to look a person straight in the eye, whether white or black, but Charles is gone, now, and he can't protect you. With white folk, you must learn to keep your eyes down. It's a way of saying you know whites are the boss." She noticed Ben's jaw muscles working as he gritted his teeth to curb his anger. "Benjamin, I'm only telling you this to help you get past these scoundrels. The time and the place will come when you can lock eyes with anyone. You just wait and see. For now, though, try to get acquainted with every set of white feet you encounter. You'll know in your heart when you can stop that horrible practice." She lifted his quivering chin and gazed into his eyes. "That's one last look for good luck. Now let's get moving, Martha," she said with a wink. And move they did.

Miss Polly's warnings had been correct. The roads were swarming with thugs obviously promised a reward by Captain Jeffries. Ben wondered to himself just how many evil men the captain had recruited. Enough that he could not stay in the area, as he had hoped. Osha was right. He needed to keep heading west into the wilderness. Each time they were stopped, Miss Polly explained that she was loaning her girl, Martha, to her ailing sister, and they needed to get moving, because they had a long ride ahead of them. Martha couldn't talk, she explained, but she could hear and understand just fine. Everything went very well until they met up with a man who had known Miss Polly for years.

"Why, Miss Polly," he said, "I'm surprised you bought yourself a slave. I thought you were against such things."

"I was until I got old," she said with a scowl. "When you can't do for yourself, you change your mind about a lot of things. Besides, Martha can't talk, so she doesn't bother me with incessant babbling, and I got her cheap."

"I remember your sister," he continued slyly, perhaps trying to catch Miss Polly in a lie. "Susanna, isn't it?"

"Oh, Edward, you can't remember anything," she replied. "Susanna died years ago. The fever. Remember? No, it's Augusta."

"Augusta?"

"I don't have time to sit here giving you memory lessons, Edward. Augusta's son-in-law will be waiting to meet me half-way, and that weather already slowed me up. Now get out of my way before I forget about our friendship and take my whip to you."

Edward laughed and stepped back to let her pass. "Nothing I like better than to get your dander up, Miss Polly. You're beautiful when you're mad." Benjamin dared a backward glance and saw the man waving, but Miss Polly did not acknowledge his farewell. With her nose in the air, she flicked her whip above the ears of her old horse which reluctantly picked up his pace. Only then did Ben notice her hands were shaking.

"Thank you, Miss Polly, for being so brave," he said softly when he was sure that no one but she would hear.

Benjamin could not believe how far Miss Polly took him. She explained away her decision to keep going by saying that the road-watchers would not expect her back anytime soon, anyway. By the time he climbed down from her carriage and said his good-byes, darkness was beginning to fall. She explained she had a cousin who lived just down the road. She would travel on to his home alone, and she would be welcomed to spend the night, so Benjamin was not to worry about her. She suggested that Ben duck into the woods to change his clothes, warning him that he should keep the dress and bonnet with him, just in case he needed a quick disguise again.

As Ben settled down on a mossy spot far from the road, he marveled at his good fortune. He was well fed and well rested. He had food to last several days, and he was safely past the people searching for him. Thinking about his geography lessons up on the third floor of the Jeffries mansion, he decided he would seek out a large river and follow it south. It should eventually turn westward. Daniel Boone had already blazed a trail and led many settlers into the wilderness, so he should have decent luck staying within ear shot of settlers. He would undoubtedly run across them as he traveled. If his luck held up, maybe he could convince a good family to allow him to travel with them. Even the mosquitoes seemed to leave him alone tonight. It must be a good omen, he decided, as he drifted off to sleep.

FAREWELL

F ROM THE MOMENT JOHNNY AWOKE, it became clear that his plan for staying in Stowe's Fork would be a disaster. Smiling like the milk barn cat, Ma turned to greet him as he stepped down the ladder from his attic room.

"Well, it's about time you woke up, sleepyhead," she teased. "We have some wonderful news, and I was just about to climb up to shake you awake, I got so impatient to tell you." Perhaps from his groggy state, his spirits momentarily lifted. If this was *good* news, they were going to stay, after all. But his mother soon put an end to his dreaming.

"John, we're moving west! Isn't it wonderful? I wanted to tell you sooner, but your pa thought we ought to wait until now." Her smile turned to shock, when Johnny's legs buckled under him and he sat down hard on the stone floor. "Johnny! Are you hurt?" she gasped.

Of course, Pa chose that very moment to enter the cabin. He looked first at his wife and then at his son. "What happened?" he asked innocently. "Johnny, did you fall down the ladder?"

The young man's anger swelled his muscles, and he jumped to his feet quickly. "I'm fine," he answered through gritted teeth. "Ma just told me we're moving west." He wanted to curse and stamp his feet. He wanted to scream at the top of his lungs that he wasn't going. He'd stay right here, thank you very much, and live with his grandma and grandpa. But Johnny was raised to be respectful. He swallowed his anger and tried to think of a reason he should be staying.

"Are you sure you want to leave Grandpa?" he asked, hating himself for lying to cover up his fear. "He's getting pretty old, you know. Who will help him with his chores? Maybe I . . ."

Matthew Cooper interrupted his son. "He understands," he said, "and he and Grandma want us to do what's in our hearts. They know we won't ever be really happy until we test ourselves, just like they did when they moved out here. Maybe we'll even send for them when we get settled."

Johnny saw his opening. "That's great, Pa. I'll stay with them and help with the chores, and when you get . . ."

His father interrupted once again, this time with a hearty laugh. "Oh, no you won't!" he said. "We need you with us. Our work will be much harder than any chores Grandpa might have, and besides, there are plenty of willing hands right here in Stowe's Fork. No, you'll come with us. We're a family, Johnny, and we're going to stay together."

When Matthew Cooper made up his mind, there was no stopping him. John might be thirteen years old and tall and strong for his age, but he knew the fight was over, even if it hadn't begun. He swallowed hard and tried to calm his racing heart. Awash in fear, he wiped his sweaty palms on his pants and ran a hand through his curly black hair. Indians! He wished he was dead, and then he worried that he might get his wish.

"Getting ready will take a while," young Cooper reasoned aloud. "And there's so much to take care of right here. When will we go? Next year some time?" With enough of a delay, maybe he could talk them out of their insane plan.

Now it was Ma's turn to laugh. "No, Johnny; we'll be gone from here and on our way in less than two weeks. Isn't it grand? There's a new-fangled wagon almost done, and I've been sorting through our goods."

"Miller Brown's buying our place for his son," Pa added. "It'll be a surprise present for his wedding."

Johnny thought about their livestock. The sow was about to give birth to a passel of little piglets, and their milk cow had freshened. Who would milk her with Ma gone away? There was that mean old gander. Johnny had hated that old bird for as long as he could remember, and why not? That tough old honker had rushed out of nowhere and nipped him on the leg or the rear, or even on the arm at least a thousand times, and now that Johnny was big enough to fight back, they were going to move away? It didn't seem fair. There were the chickens. Who would feed them and gather their eggs? No, there was way too much to get done right here; too many responsibilities to just pick up and walk away into the wilderness.

It often had seemed to Johnny that Ma could read his thoughts, and this was one of those times. "Don't worry about our animals, Johnny," she said. "Grandpa is taking care of them until Josiah's wedding, and then he and his bride will just step right in with their own livestock. Isn't that a *wonderful* wedding present? And Miller Brown paid us a fair price for every single animal, young and old." She was practically dancing around the cabin in her excitement. Johnny wished he could catch some of her happiness. He surely could use it right about now.

True to his ma's prediction, they worked through the next fourteen days to prepare for their trek into the great, unknown West that Lewis and Clark had just recently dipped a tentative toe into, themselves. The only difference, Johnny thought to himself as he considered what the broadsheets had told of President Jefferson's exploration party, is that there are plenty of them. They're all strong, well-armed and well-provisioned men. And us? We're a small family of back-woods farmers with a baby and a single rifle among us. Sure, we have some knives and some tools, but what good will they be against bloodthirsty scalpers? As he labored beside his parents to empty their little cabin, sell or give away a lifetime collection of comforts, and stock up on simple provisions, he became more and more fearful. And then the time for leaving came before he felt he was ready.

The people of Stowe's Fork had come together the night before to wish them well, inclining Johnny to hold out one last hope that they just might unload the wagon and call the whole adventure off, due to patched-up hard feelings. Of course, his wish was not about to come true, he thought to himself, because his pa would be too proud to admit his mistake. And now he found himself hiding inside the covered wagon, peeking through a knot hole to watch his Ma and Pa say their good-byes to Grandpa and Grandma. He was afraid for anyone to see him. His heart was breaking with the need to give what might be the last hugs he ever shared with his grandparents, but he was a weepy-eyed, runny-nosed mess. He guessed he was a little too proud, himself, but he was doggoned if he was going to leave Stowe's Fork with his old friends running along-side the wagon yelling something like, *Baby Johnny's leaving town, because his tears are falling down!*

He peeled his thoughts off of leaving and tried to imagine what might happen during their long journey, but that didn't help, either. When his mind conjured up a picture of the unknown trail that lay ahead for him and his family, his belly fluttered like there was a full-grown chicken hawk inside, flapping around and trying to find its way out. One thing for sure, it would be exciting! They were bound to run across Indians out there somewhere. Would they be kindly people, or would they take his scalp and bones, like Miller Brown had predicted?

"There you are, John," his pa's deep voice boomed from the back of the wagon. He poked his curly head through the canvass flap long enough to flash his son an understanding look and a quick wink.

"John's in here, nursing his cold. Blow your nose, Son, and come on out to say good-bye to your grandma and grandpa." His blue eyes sent a message to John, saying he understood his sorrow, but the young man would be sorry for the rest of his life if he didn't say his goodbyes properly.

Wondering if anyone would really believe he had a cold but grateful for a made-up excuse for his appearance, he picked his way around the stores in the wagon and climbed down. Old Grandpa Cooper threw his work-strong arms around John's shoulders and locked him in a bear hug. From the corner of his eye, John caught sight of Grandma's apron flying up to cover her face. She always was one to cover her face while playing peek-a-boo with Hallie or laughing herself to tears over some little thing. This time John knew that Grandma was hiding pure sadness tears, and he almost began to blubber again, himself. Then, quick as anything, Grandma was smiling through her snuffles, laughing at her strange snorts that so often followed on the heels of her crying. As Johnny left his grandpa leaning against a wagon wheel and headed toward his grandma, she lifted the corner of her apron to wipe her wet cheeks, and then she fished up a small bundle from a roomy pocket of her long black skirt.

Offering it to John, she said, "This kerchief is for you, John." She reached out with her other arm to snag him in one last hug. "The ribbon tying it is for Hallie's pretty hair when she gets older, and what's inside is for everyone."

John's always-hungry belly forgot about the chicken hawk and sent up a grateful grin. Ginger cookies! John would do almost anything for just one of Grandma's cookies, and here he was, standing with a whole heap of her spicy treats tied up in a pretty, red kerchief.

All the Coopers joined together in a final, big family embrace, with kisses to go around. Ma and Grandma cried and laughed at the same time, and John's heart tugged away at his gizzard when he realized how much he'd miss those silly snorts of Grandma's. Pa and Grandpa locked in a final hug as each man looked forward and backward. Matthew Cooper looked over his own father's shoulder and saw all the days of love and work, from the first day he could remember, trailing his pa around as he journied through life to this day. Grandpa looked across Matthew's strong, broad shoulder and saw the trail that began here and then quickly disappeared into the deepest part of the forest. Would he ever see his son and his family again? Grandpa Cooper knew how Matthew felt, because he had found the need to search out a new place once, many years ago, himself. But they would be alone out there in the unknown wilds. Who would protect them?

His head popped up suddenly. "How could I forget? I have a going-away gift for you, too, Johnny."

He limped off to the barn while John's heart nearly pounded out of his chest. What could it be? Then, quick as a church-lady's sneeze, the old man reappeared with a grain sack, its bottom bulging. Grain. Grandpa meant for John to clear and plant his own patch of grain. He had been secretly hoping his grandfather might return carrying the shiny new rifle Johnny had admired every time he stepped into Beade's Trading Post, or maybe even a hunting knife with a fancy, carved handle. The gangly thirteen-year-old swallowed his disappointment that the gift wasn't more exciting, but he puffed a bit with pride when he realized this meant Grandpa thought he was grown enough to plant a field of his own. Maybe he would take his crop to market someplace out in the wilderness and come home with his own money jingling in his pockets!

"Thank you, Grandpa. I'll try to keep my patch as good as Pa's," he said.

Grandpa shot a wink at Pa. Matthew Cooper scooped up the sack and hustled John into the back of the big wagon, while Ma, with Hallie perched carefully on her hip, climbed up the wooden spokes of a big front wheel.

"Here, John," she said as she turned and looked through the front opening of the big canvas shelter. She lifted the gurgling baby toward her son. "If you tend Hallie until she naps, I'll start out our adventure watching your pa goad Jack and Molly."

John made his way across a jumble of sacks and barrels and crawled onto Ma and Pa's bed to reach up for his little sister. He didn't mind tending Hallie one bit. She was always bubbling away in her strange baby language, all the while smiling up rainbows. John loved to make her laugh. Threading his way to the back of the big wagon, he sat on a flour keg and settled his little sister to his lap. "Come on, Hallie, wave bye to your grandma and grandpa."

Hallie's chubby little fingers shot up to explore first his mouth, then his nose. "Aw, come on, Hallie," John giggled with a voice that sounded sometimes like a boy's and sometimes like a man's, "wave bye."

He took her dimpled little arm and waved toward Grandma and Grandpa. The wagon began to lurch and rumble as Pa commanded Jack and Molly to "step up" onto the trail which led out of their little Virginia settlement and disappeared around a bend into the forest. What noise! Kegs creaking and knocking, wheels and wood squeaking, canvas flapping, and final good-byes drifting away on the breath of the piney woods. Johnny watched his grandma and grandpa until they disappeared, when the wagon rounded a bend in the dirt trail. Now there was nothing but trees. Just as he had begun a game of peek-a-boo with Hallie, the big wagon lurched over a rut in the trail. The baby slipped from his lap, sliding down his legs to plop squarely on John's grain sack.

Mixed in with Hallie's gleeful giggles, John heard squeals of a different kind. The bag had come alive and was wiggling to who-tied-it. John snatched up his baby sister and propped her on his left hip as he carefully poked his curious nose into the sack.

"A puppy!" he yelled with delight. The young dog stumbled out of the open sack, squinted up at John, and then sent up a cloud of grain dust as she flapped her ears and shook from her nose to her tail. "Ma! Pa! Grandpa gave me a pup!" He lifted it to check its belly, and the puppy sneezed in his face. "It's a girl!" he shouted over the din.

"We were a-wondering when you'd get around to finding her," Pa bellowed from his post in front of the oxen.

Ma left her spot on the seat and carefully worked her way back through the stacks of furniture, barrels of supplies, and trunks of clothing.

"Here," she said. "I'll tend Hallie while you get acquainted with your new friend. What are you going to name her?"

Johnny ran his hands across the pup's silky fur. As the grain dust disappeared, he could see she had the look of a shadow-dappled pile of fallen leaves in the woods.

"She could lie down next to a rotten log, and not even an Indian could spot her," he marveled to himself. "I don't know, Ma," he answered. "A name is a serious thing. I'll have to get to know her better."

Ma and John settled in the back of the wagon. As Hallie drifted off to sleep on her mother's shoulder, John played with his new pup. The soft, warm ball of brindled fur had begun to lick John's neck, and it tickled. Suddenly, John's sadness and fear of the unknown trail ahead melted into pure delight.

"Come on, Girl," he giggled, as he lay back on the floor of the wagon. "We have a long trip ahead of us, and my eyes are tired of trees. Let's take a nap." He lay on his back, plopped the playful pup into the hollow of his belly, and stared down his nose at his new traveling companion as they rocked, bumped, and jostled along, until he drifted off to sleep.

TRAVELER

E ACH DAY OF THEIR JOURNEY, Johnny was amazed by the sights and experiences that popped up along the way. Rounding a bend in the trail was like turning a page in a bible that was nothing but pictures. The mountains marched closer and closer until one day, John noticed they had come up out of the thick growth of trees. They started to move upward through the first hills that formed the base of the mountains, themselves. Pa called these the "foothills."

John's pup enjoyed the journey and padded back and forth in the wagon on her big, clumsy-looking paws, yapping at everything from chipmunks to hawks' shadows. When Ma commented one day on what a good traveler the puppy had become, John was certain he had found just the name he had been searching for. He would call her *Traveler*!

Times got rough. Each day the wagon moved more slowly as the oxen struggled against their harnesses to pull the heavy wagon upward. At times, the Coopers unloaded several of their precious belongings to lighten the load for Jack and Molly. Then Pa would coax the oxen forward over a rise in the trail and leave them there to rest while Ma, Pa, and John carried, rolled, pushed, and pulled the kegs, barrels, and bags up the rough trail to the awaiting wagon.

Because the hard-working oxen tired more quickly, Pa decided they should begin setting up their overnight camp earlier than they did down below. While Pa unhitched Jack and Molly each night, it was Johnny's job to locate a clearing where the oxen could graze on what little grass was available. Then he and Pa would lead them to the spot, clamp a long rope on one back leg of each ox, and pound a long iron stake into the ground to hold the ends of the ropes. This way, the grateful giants could graze contentedly and bed down for the night without wandering so far away that they couldn't be found the following morning. Pa called this job "hobbling" the oxen. This was just about Johnny's favorite time of day. After he had helped Pa with Jack and Molly and gathered brush and dead wood for the campfire, he could find an open spot on a wind-blown rock and look down on the land they had covered since leaving Stowe's Fork.

John's favorite activity was gobbling down Ma's mouth-watering campfire cooking. He was *always* hungry! After they had eaten and cleaned up their dinner mess, they sat around their fire and stared like they were hypnotized, dreaming their own private dreams, while the wood burned down to white-hot embers.

There were times when they encountered other travelers along the trail. Sometimes they invited those people to join them, and even to stay the night near the fire. Whether they were camping out in the open with nothing but boulders and scraggly grass, or in the woods, surrounded by a thick, black curtain of trees and brush, there were all kinds of dangers lurking out there. The inky space away from the campfire's light came alive with strange sounds in the dead of night, and it seemed to the Coopers they were always better off with as many people as possible to grab their rifles. And of course, the women felt just about as safe when they reached for a big iron spoon or poker. Johnny and his family were fascinated by the collection of people they encountered on this first section of their journey. If they happened to be alone for the night and they had extra time after chores and dinner, their conversations somehow always turned to the people they had met and the advice they had been given about how best to get to Lewis and Clark's big river. The Indians called the river "Mississippi," which means *Father of Waters*.

Among the follow adventurers they met along the trail were the Hooples. Ma Hoople must have towered a full head above her husband and had to be as strong as the back half of an ox, but she was fresh-egg neat and as womanly as any two-legged being could possibly be. She herded her gaggle of five young Hooples around with no more than a smile here and a pat there, and never once in the three days the Coopers and Hooples had spent together on the trail, had a Hoople child been seen to step out of line. Mr. Hoople and his children seemed to worship Ma Hoople like she was a queen right out of the Bible. Yet, when a strong shoulder was needed to help roll a wagon up and over some obstacle, it was Ma Hoople who would wedge herself under the back corner, lifting and shoving, while Pa Hoople took the reins, yelling "gee" to make their big mules turn right, or "haw" to turn left. What a group those Hooples had been! More than one tear had fallen when the news friends so quickly parted as the Hooples took the south branch of the trail.

Pa Hoople had sighed and looked up longingly at the rocky towers that jutted toward the sky like giant church steeples, but he turned his family down a trail that led southward, saying they "weren't ready yet to conquer no mountains."

There were the McGraths. Johnny was the first to spot them that day, when two weather-worn fur caps popped above the rise in the trail behind the wagon. From his perch on the tail of the wagon, he thought they looked like two scruffy hunters out to do no good. There was something strange about them. The season was warm enough for green sprouts of corn to have shoved through the dirt back at Stowe's Fork, yet here they came, sporting the mangiest looking raccoon fur head covers that John believed he had ever seen. One man was the size of a brown bear and appeared about as gentle, with a bushy beard springing out from his iron cheeks. The other adventurer was smaller and looked as if a gentle wind blowing around some pass could have knocked him right off the mountain. They must have seemed a curious sight to Traveler, too, because she braced her front paws up on the back of the wagon and stared and sniffed so hard that she altogether forgot to yap her puppy-sized warning.

On they came, with friendly smiles and gestures of peace. That evening as they sat Indian style, staring into the campfire, John learned their secret. The small one, who never opened his mouth, turned out to be a woman! A woman with long, bright-red hair that just might interest some Indian who would like to add a little variety to his lodge pole! That was why they dressed so strangely and wore those terrible hats. She was hiding her beautiful hair. The McGraths stayed for only that night, just long enough to share with the Coopers their plans to walk all the way through the mountains and settle in Daniel Boone's land of promise down on the other side. Ma and Pa wished them farewell and waved them on their way, but their smiles soon sagged into something that looked more like worry. Johnny caught the look in their eyes that said they doubted the red-haired woman would make it to Kentucky alive.

Why are they acting scared for that woman? Johnny thought to himself. *If the McGraths are headed out to where us white folk haven't tried to take hold of Indian land, and if they are peaceable, then they should be safe. . . if Pa truly believes what he's been preaching.* He was so thoughtful, as he shook out his quilt and spread it in its usual place under the wagon, that Traveler, who could already read her master's moods, tried to cheer him up by chasing her tail.

The boy and his dog grew together, with Traveler becoming less of a puppy and Johnny becoming more of a man. Ma busied herself at night with sewing up rips and tears and moving out seams as Johnny grew lean, hard, and tall from life on the wilderness trail. Pa stood by with a speck of pride in his eyes as he watched John and his dog become a part of each other. Traveler grew to know her master so well that she could read his mind, fetching this or that without a word passing Johnny's lips. She was a possessive dog, who seemed to know when to protect her family of humans from harmful people or animals and when to keep still. From morning, when Johnny and Traveler headed out to get Jack and Molly, until night, when the boy and his dog would hunker together under the wagon, Traveler stuck to John like a trail burr.

Did Traveler know what Grandpa had known so many weeks before when he looked down on her for the first time there in the back of Miller Browns barn? Did she know that she was put there for a special time when she would save Johnny's life? Grandpa had felt it deep in his old bones the instant he laid eyes on that pup. She was there for a purpose ... to get Johnny through some special danger that lay ahead, hanging like a ghost over some hidden place in the wilderness. Was it Indians or some wildcat? Maybe it was a robber. Grandpa hadn't known what the special danger was, but he knew it was there waiting for Johnny, just as he knew Traveler was put here on earth to save his grandson from whatever it was. He bought the dog.

Traveling on the wilderness trail had become a part of everyday life. It was hard to see the progress they had made, because so many of their days were spent surrounded by high, rocky peaks. When he thought about it and began counting up the weeks they had spent working their way toward the wide Mississippi River, he realized the cold winds which blew through the high mountain passes day after day had tricked him. It was early spring when they said goodbye to Grandma and Grandpa Cooper. Not a seed had been planted, because there was still danger of a late frost creeping down from the mountains to kill the young plants after they sprouted. If they had stayed back at Stowe's Fork, the corn would have baked in the summer sun long enough to stand as high as his waist, at least, and he was a mighty tall boy for his age.

Like his pa, John sported that same curly black hair that seemed to be natural to all the Cooper men. The work and strain of life in the wilderness had built up sturdy muscles in his legs, arms and shoulders. There was a new look in his eyes as he learned to harness his love of adventure with the wisdom to expect emergencies. The sun and chilly winds working their way down through the high, stony passes cured his skin to a tough, brown hide that fought off anything Mother Nature sent his way. John learned to see hidden hazards ahead as he scanned the rocky ledges and cracks with eyes as blue as a high-country lake. At the same time, his dog grew before his eyes, but Johnny was so busy keeping track of everything else, he didn't notice.

Instead of walking beside or behind their wagon, as they had seen other families doing, Ma, John, and Hallie rode in the wagon with the many necessities and treasures that Ma and Pa had so carefully packed away. One windy morning they learned the danger of their ways.

As they bounced along the winding trail through rocks and across ledges, their first warning came from Traveler, when she began to pace and whine nervously through the wagon. Suddenly, she lunged up onto the seat and begam barking fiercely at Pa and the oxen. The fur from her neck to her tail stood up, as she curled back her pink and brown speckled lips to reveal threatening fangs. A fierce growl surged upward from deep in her throat.

Everyone in the wagon grew silent as Molly and Jack understood her warning and hurried their upward struggle, digging their hooves into the solid path. Their ears stood forward as they stared ahead to search out the danger that Traveler was clearly trying to point out. From his seat atop Ma and Pa's bed in the front of the wagon, John felt a wave of fear grip his body. Looking up, he locked eyes with his ma. Instantly John and Ma bound together their resolve to get the family through whatever danger was awaiting them. They had come to learn that Traveler was never wrong about danger, and this was the most upset they had ever seen the young dog.

Suddenly, a loud rumbling sound filled the air behind them, and the big wooden craft began to slide backward. Without looking, Pa knew the ledge under the back of the wagon was giving way. The rear wheels dropped, giving life to Pa's big barrel of seed grain. It tipped over and, in an instant, had rolled back, pinning Ma and Hallie against the tailgate. The barrel was followed by kegs and sacks. In seconds, Ma and Hallie were trapped as the wagon continued to slide backward toward the huge, yawning gorge cut hundreds of feet below.

Pa struggled, urging Jack and Molly to pull the wagon up and out of danger, but it was no use. The wagon scraped backward, as hunks of stone loosened and hurtled hundreds of feet downward into the gorge, crashing and breaking as they went. Soon the whole wagon and its precious contents would fall backward over the edge, and Ma and Hallie had no way of getting out.

In a flash, Johnny and Traveler each knew what they had to do. Traveler jumped down from the wagon and frantically joined Pa's efforts to move Jack and Molly forward by attacking their heels. Johnny knew that Pa could not turn away from the oxen. It was up to him to free Ma and Hallie and somehow right the wagon. He eased cautiously toward the back. The wagon shifted more as he moved. He had to get rid of that weight in the back. Pa dared to glance over his shoulder, as he shouted encouragement to the oxen. Now the wagon was hanging so low in the back that John looked out over the tailgate into open space. He knew what he had to do, but was he strong enough? He quickly picked up the sack directly in front of him. Oats. Gritting his teeth, he threw it for all he was worth. The bag cleared the wagon's tailgate and began its long fall to a spot hundreds of feet below. Next to go was Ma's cornmeal, then her flour. John grabbed the handle of Pa's tool chest and dragged forward, quickly lifting it to the seat beside Pa. He hurried to the back of the wagon. Out went Ma's beautiful three-drawer chest and a box of quilts. Finally he was down to the big grain barrel.

Ma sat still as a statue, staring up at her John with eyes filled with terror. Hallie screamed in pain, for somehow her little leg had gotten wedged under Ma's and the barrel lay over the top of both of them.

John grabbed the pry-bar. Too short. Looking around him desperately, he spotted the spare oxen yoke lashed to the supports over Ma and Pa's bed. He quickly untied it and carefully edged his way back to the barrel. Try as he might, he couldn't get the right angle on the barrel. The only way he was going to budge that barrel was to move himself to the outside of the tailgate. If he stepped out that far, would his weight tip the wagon over the edge? He had to risk it. Carefully, he swung one leg over the tailgate. Edging his toes across the ledge at the back, he located an iron strap. Slipping his left foot through the strap as if it were a stirrup, John braced his knee against the outside of the tailgate and slowly brought his other leg over the gate to the ledge. Now he was on the back of the wagon, trying to ignore the deep emptiness that lurked below him.

Poking one end of the long, sturdy yoke out the open flap of canvas, John began to search for the right spot to set the other end. He wedged his massive pry into a spot near the fattest part of the barrel and began to push upward, then pull downward. Ma's eyes lit with a spark of hope, and she held her breath as she tried to help John roll the barrel off her legs.

"It's moving," she whispered.

But so was the wagon. As it lurched backward, John's right foot slipped off the ledge of the wagon, but his left foot was still held firmly in the metal strap. He pulled himself up and resumed his battle with the barrel. Finally it moved, as John and Ma gave a desperate shove.

Just pretend you're Mrs. Hoople, he told himself.

His strength was about to give way when Ma shouted, "We're free!" Afraid to stand up, she dragged herself and Hallie across the floor to the front of the wagon.

"Get out!" Pa bellowed.

As John swung his legs back over the gate to the interior of the wagon and edged his way forward, Ma scrambled down the left front wheel and reached up to receive her crying daughter into her arms. John climbed down after her and ran past his snarling, snapping dog to the head of the oxen team. He ducked under the yoke and wedged himself between Jack and Molly's straining shoulders. Feeling every muscle in his body bulge with the effort, he braced his back against the center of their yoke and pushed as they pulled. Traveler lunged afresh at the heels of Molly and Jack, while Pa continued to wield his long goad. Finally, the wagon edged forward, and its back wheels rolled up onto solid ground.

"Keep them moving," Pa shouted.

Inch-by-inch, the Coopers coaxed the oxen forward to an open, level area well away from the broken ledge. Ma kept Hallie cocked on her right hip and, with one hand, slapped Molly's rump to urge her to keep moving forward. John was proud of his Ma. She always stayed calm in an emergency and never failed to surprise her family with talents even she hadn't known she had. He remembered her big, blue eyes looking up at him from under the barrel. For the very first time in his life, he had seen fear in his mother's eyes, and he hoped he would never, ever see it again.

The grateful oxen were freed from their heavy yoke and stood panting, too exhausted to move away just yet. John noticed that their big, muscular haunches and shoulders were quivering, and he felt sorry for them. Every muscle in his body seemed to be twitching, too, like dried birch leaves on a windy fall day. He knew just how they felt! Like magnets, Pa, John, and Ma, with little Hallie still perched on her hip, were drawn together into a quiet family hug, holding on to each other tightly. Their danger had been so terrible that they couldn't talk about it yet. Each knew in his heart that this day would never be forgotten. Not wanting to be left out, Traveler squeezed between Pa and John's legs and licked his master's bare feet. As John stooped to stroke his dog, he suddenly realized that she had grown up. She had some filling out to do yet, but she wasn't a pup any longer. No, she was his best friend and the greatest traveling companion the Cooper family could have. Like a four-legged guardian angel, she knew many things which even Pa overlooked. They all loved their wise, brindled dog more than they could ever say.

"Oh, thank you, Grandpa," John whispered as he rubbed Traveler's silky ear. "Thank you!"

SMELLY JACK

THE VERY NEXT DAY, THE Coopers threaded their way through a mountain pass and whooped with joy when they read a hand-lettered sign wedged into a crack in the stone. The sign told them they had found the opening which would let them cross over to the other side. Stopping to gaze at the beauty of the mountains which marched down to a distant point at the edge of an ocean of green forest, they could hardly believe their eyes. The wilderness seemed to stretch on forever.

The wind whipping through the pass brought all sorts of dust and stone with it, and a speck found John's right eye. He was happy to have an excuse for stopping to take care of his watery eye, because it gave him time to study the far-off wilderness. He wondered if they would ever get to where they were going before the snows came.

Thirty-three years before, in the year 1769, a pack-horse man by the name of John Findley had guided Daniel Boone through that same pass, which is now known as the Cumberland Gap. Daniel Boone saw to it that people learned about the pass, which gave them a way to get from the east side of the mountains to the west side.

Jack and Molly must have begun to smile somewhere deep inside, because their path turned easier as they ambled downward. The trail wound its way around boulders and across rushing streams day after day, until the mountain-weary family found themselves on rolling land guarded by close-standing pine trees. How nice it was to smell the piney woods once again! John guessed that, as in Virginia, this ocean of pine trees would soon give way to giant maples, then oaks. How strange it seemed that there was a wilderness area so many weeks away from Virginia which was actually a state called *Kentucky*. That man, Daniel Boone, must be some kind of trail-blazer to direct people to the eye of the needle through those mammoth mountains, and then drum up settlers to struggle through the stone giants to find likely spots to sink family roots.

Matthew Cooper wasn't called to settle in Kentucky, in spite of all the stories which had drifted back through the mountains to Virginia. There had been tales about corn as tall as a mill wheel, month-old pigs that were full grown, even melons that grew so fast they got dragged around by their vines until their skin wore off and they were ready to be eaten. No, Kentucky was too settled for Pa's wants. He was drawn to the Louisiana Territory that Lewis and Clark had explored. The territory had been sold, lock, stock and barrel, to the United States. First the French trappers, then Lewis and Clark, had spun yarns of Indian tribes up and down the mighty Mississippi River. The stories had reminded Pa of the natives who fought Miller Brown when he first tried to settle Stowe's Fork. This would be their chance to live side-by-side with Indians, showing them how peaceful and co-operative white folks could be. Both white people and Indians could learn a lot from each other. Pa believed that, if the Cooper family could get to the Indians first, hundreds of people, both white and Indian, could be spared from ugly deaths and torture.

Pure excitement traveled with the Cooper family the summer day that Pa pointed Old Jack and Molly toward the trail that led away to the Oyo River, the smooth-riding waterway to the Mississippi. *Oyo* was the name the Indians used for this wide waterway, but some white people, when talking about Lewis and Clark's adventure, had taken to calling it the *Ohio River*. John's keen eyes immediately caught the signs in the trail. No longer were the Coopers moving in the mainstream of traffic. Their last trail had been littered here and there with evidence of other recent travelers. This trail looked as if all beings but God had forgotten it. Ivy had begun to creep across to explore the other side. A rotten tree rendered itself back to the earth smack in the path of the oxen. Animal tracks tattooed dried mud patches, and last year's empty nut shells and husks lay where hungry squirrels had dropped them from ancient limbs that formed umbrellas over the old deer trail.

Their fourth day on the trail to the Oyo, Ma spotted a patch of black berries begging to be picked. Because Pa was searching for a spot to lay over for the night, they took note of the location of the berry patch and coaxed Jack and Molly to a clearing beside a beautiful, clear lake just a short distance away. As Pa climbed down wearily from the wagon to free the oxen from their burden, Ma snatched a wooden pail and handed it to her son.

"Here, Johnny; you head back and fetch those berries while Hallie and I get dinner started."

John set down his little sister, who immediately pulled herself up on her feet, begging for a finger to hold, so that she could practice walking.

"Not now, Hallie," John chuckled. "I'll bring you some big, juicy berries. Then we'll practice our steps" Hallie plopped down on her chubby bottom and rolled over to her knees. She fixed her eyes on a fallen limb and crawled full-speed toward it while John and Traveler retraced their steps to the berry patch.

John loved the quiet times he and Traveler shared away from the wagon. They were on their own and relied upon each other like a bee and a blossom. It was at these times that John's senses were their keenest. Would danger lie around the bend? Did an Indian lurk in the deep shadows? His ears and eyes strained to pick up any strange noises, as he watched Traveler closely for signs that she sensed danger. Today, the gangly dog located a soft, cool patch of moss and dropped to rest her boney body. Cradling her chin on the soothing, green blanket, she rolled her eyes upward as if to say, "Don't worry, Friend. All is well. And now if you'll excuse me, I'm going to take a nap."

Confident in his dog's judgment, John turned his attention to the tempting berries and began dropping handfuls into Ma's pail. After giving in to the temptation to eat a few, he respectfully moved aside a vine and stepped carefully to a spot deeper in the patch. Suddenly, an odor worse than the world's most frightened skunk attacked his nose. Traveler undoubtedly smelled the foul thing, too, because John heard her sneezing like a preacher in a dust storm, and then whining a complaint.

"Boy, if you don't pay attention to yore signs no better than this, you'll never make it to wherever it is that yore a-going."

John dropped the pail and spun around to see a wild old man with a flowing white beard, who stood less than ten feet away from him.

"Traveler!" John threw a panicked look at his dog. She sat peacefully and, except for a fit of sneezing, casually watched the woodsman as he were an old friend come back for a visit.

What a sight that man made! Dressed in years-old clothing and a mangy fur cap, he bristled with firearms, knives and hanging pouches of assorted sizes. Johnny reckoned the old man must have been on the older side of seventy hard winters. He stood there, eyeballing Johnny and his dog through cornflower blue eyes that twinkled with laughter.

"Well, Boy, do you aim to let those berries set there to rot, or air ye taking them to yer poor ma?" The old man picked at his ear, and then stepped a moccasin-clad foot forward and began to scoop the spilled berries back into the pail. John's eyes watered as the man neared, and the boy's poor nose identified him as the cause of the terrible odor.

"Name's Smelly Jack," the old man proudly proclaimed, "and I'm the orneriest-smelling creature in this here country. Why, I'm so smelly, there's nary a varmint hereabouts that will so much as think about botherin' me, from a mosquito to a grizzly bear, and that includes women. They all leave old Smelly alone. Why, it was only last month when a deerfly flew a might too close afore he realized it was me he was a-considerin', and the pore creature fell flat down dead from six feet in the air."

It was plain to Johnny that he and Traveler needed to get away from this man fast, before their noses dropped off from pure disgust. Seeing John begin to edge away,

Smelly Jack plucked at the boy's sleeve and made it clear he expected his audience to stay put until he'd bragged his say. John rolled his watering eyes longingly at his dog as she backed away, belly to the ground, snorting her opinion of the smelly old hunter all the while.

The ancient man continued his sermonizing. "I'm a Long Hunter. 'Been ever'where from the Mohawk to the western mountains. Yes, Sir, I knows my way 'round these here parts. They've changed. Too many peoples 'round here these days. One thing fer sure, though, you've got a lot to learn if yer a-going to wander 'round in this here territory, and we mought as well start now."

While his mouth rattled on, Smelly Jack herded John out of the berry patch and prodded him back along the trail toward the Coopers' wagon. The boy grew painfully aware that old Jack wasn't going to stop talking any more than he was going to stop smelling. Edging around the man and his captive far enough to keep out of nose-range, Traveler circled back to camp and bellied her way under the wagon to await further developments.

And they weren't long in coming. Hearing the old man's voice, Ma and Pa looked up to see the scruffy-looking Long Hunter amble into camp with one arm wrapped around their son's shoulder while the other cradled two long rifles. The pained look on Johnny's face clearly asked for help, and as the boy's parents advanced to meet the pair, their noses told them why.

"Smelly Jack's my name," the old character began anew. "Why, I'm so smelly there's nary a varmint . . ."

John snatched the opportunity to slip away from the hunter's bony arm and eased quietly out of nose range, eventually working his way to a spot next to Traveler under the wagon. From his refuge, John watched his Ma square her shoulders and grit her teeth as she nodded at the man's lengthy speech. She had a firm hold on poor Pa, so there was no escaping for him. If she had to be polite to that stinky old man, then by golly, so did her husband!

On and on the old man jawed. He casually walked over to lift the lid on Ma's stew kettle to sniff its bubbling contents. John's mouth popped open as she saw his Ma smack old Smelly's hand with her big wooden spoon. The old visitor dropped the lid back on the kettle with stunned surprise written all over his face, and he finally stopped talking long enough for Ma to speak her say.

"Mr. Smelly Jack," Ma began, crossing her arms and stepping between the old man and her stew, "if you're hungry and would like to share a meal with us, you're welcome to, but not until after you have washed away that terrible smell."

John caught a look of surprise, then pride cross Pa's face, as Matthew Cooper stepped up beside his wife and nodded his agreement.

"We appreciate your offer to help us," Pa added, "but we will not abide your terrible smell."

Smelly Jack's shoulders drooped with shock and disappointment. "Why, how can you say such a thing? Here I offer to help you peoples out of the kindness of my heart, and you ask me to go wash off a smell I worked years to git just right. This weren't easy, you know. Why, I had to search high and low fer just the right combination of stinks to get me this here one. There's full-growed men that'ud give their sharpest hatchet to know my secret!"

On Smelly Jack begged, but John could see from the set of Ma's shoulders that she would not back down. As he and Traveler watched, she walked to the wagon and fetched Pa's change of clothing and a chunk of soap. Just as Smelly finished a story about a fish that jumped into his frying pan just so the old hunter would move his stink away from the river, Ma set her bundle at his feet and backed away, arms folded.

"Mr. Smelly," she quietly interrupted, "We will be ready to eat in about an hour. That should give you enough time. I'm off to grub some roots, and I promise I'll stay away from the lake so you can bathe in privacy. I'll have a nice blackberry cobbler ready for dessert, and after dinner I'll wash out your clothes for you."

Without waiting for his response, Ma turned on her heel and reached for the pry-bar she used to dig up tender plant roots to add to her stews. Picking up her skirts, she stepped around her napping daughter and headed to the woods' edge.

The old man stared at Pa with a question in his eyes, and Pa answered with a firm-set jaw and a nod toward the water. After a few seconds of shocked disbelief, Smelly Jack reached down to gather up Ma's bundle and turned slowly toward the lake. Shaking his head all the while, Jack muttered his way to a wash-hole behind a stand of fox tails which guarded the water's edge. John and Traveler stayed put in their spot under the wagon and hoped for a wind to carry off the smell that hung around the camp like an uninvited uncle at dinner time.

For the next few weeks, Smelly Jack traveled with the Coopers. John learned that a Long Hunter was a man sent out in the early days of the colonies to explore. Hired by wealthy men interested in owning new lands that were right for settlers, a Long Hunter would journey through the wilderness for years at a time, living off the land. When he returned, he would give details of the likely spots he had found in his travels. Smelly Jack had gone out as a Long Hunter before the freedom war. On one of those trips, he had somehow lost track of why he traveled in the first place, and he had gone to seed. Now old Smelly preferred the feeling of loneliness over the nervous jitters he got whenever human beings were within a mile of him.

But there was something about this particular family that drew him nearby to protect them. He had watched the Coopers for days and saw that they were headed for disaster if they didn't learn the laws of survival in the wilderness. Something about that black-headed, blue-eyed young sprout and his brindled dog tugged at Smelly's heart, and he knew he would have to overcome his fear of humans long enough to help this family.

Smelly's knowledge of the woods and the Indians seemed endless. He taught the Coopers to listen as carefully for silence as they listened for noises, because silence meant that *man* was moving into the area.

"When the forest around you grows quiet," he warned, "someone's sneaking up on you, and you'd best be ready."

Smelly had his opinions about Johnny's readiness to take on a man's job in the wilderness, too. He steadily won Pa over to seeing the value in teaching John how to hitch and unhitch Jack and Molly, how to lead the team, and how to cross streams and rivers. Finally, the day came when Smelly tackled the biggest convincing job of all: giving John shooting lessons.

"Johnny is only a boy," Pa had argued, "and he shouldn't yet be forced into killing. I'll take care of our hunting. I can always provide meat for our kettle. We have but one rifle, and I will use it."

"But what if yore laid up with the fever or a broke arm or the like, and Indians or some bear attacks? How air you going to use yore rifle then?" Smelly questioned.

John had already used those same arguments with his pa, but they had never worked. He was amazed when his Matthew Cooper turned a thoughtful eye toward his son and, after taking a long time to ponder Smelly's advice, he agreed that it was time for John to try his luck with a long rifle.

Johnny waited patiently while Pa carefully loaded his flintlock rifle. Setting the butt of the long weapon on his left foot, he pried the cap off of his powder horn with his teeth, then tipped the horn over the barrel head, forcing black gunpowder to run down inside the length of the barrel. Next, he reached into his shot pouch for a small patch of linen. Pulling the ramrod out of its slot under the barrel of his rifle, Pa gently tamped the linen patch into the barrel, nesting it on the gunpowder. Finally came the lead ball, the bullet. After ramming the ball carefully into place with the powder and patch, he slid the ramrod back into its place on the underside of the gun barrel and declared the rifle loaded.

"Here, Son. Let's find a good tree fork to rest this old soldier in so you can shoot it."

Smelly found a likely tree with a limb coming away from the trunk at just the right height for John. Turning the gun on its side, he tapped ever so lightly so that a tiny bit of gunpowder trickled out the touch hole into the frizzen pan over the trigger. Pulling back the flint lock, he cocked the rifle. Now, except for aiming it correctly, it was ready to shoot.

"Here, John," Pa said quietly. "See that white birch tree over there? Well, set your weapon in the crook of this tree and pull the trigger when you think you can hit the birch. Get a tight hold, 'cause this old gun will kick worse'n Beade's mule ever did."

Breathlessly, Johnny laid the gun barrel on the fork formed by a low branch jutting out from the trunk. Dropping to his left knee, he shouldered the stock of the rifle and eye-balled the white birch. He squeezed the trigger.

John's ears rang from the sound of the blast as he picked himself up off the ground. The gun had bucked just like the horse Miller Brown was always trying to saddle and ride. His ears reddened with embarrassment as Pa and Smelly slapped their knees with laughter. He couldn't ruin his chance to show he was ready for the rifle. John dusted himself off, quietly took the powder horn and shot bag, and reloaded the rifle. Serioused-up by the boy's determination, Pa and Smelly watched quietly as Johnny propped the gun in the crook of the tree once again.

This time he was ready. Bracing himself, Johnny pulled the trigger and withstood the full force of the flintlock rifle, as it loudly belched out its lead ball. Pure pride surrounded John. He stood up and walked quietly over to inspect the birch tree. He hadn't hit it, but he hadn't fallen down this time. He was getting better. Pa smiled and nodded his approval. Yes, it was time John learned to shoot. "Always collect your shot, Son," he advised. "Lead is precious, especially out here where it can't be replaced. Come with me, and we'll dig those balls out of the trees they hit."

During the next several days, John practiced using the rifle every chance he got. Traveler sat proudly at attention during each training session. She knew her friend was becoming a man, and this was as it should be. They were growing together.

Each evening, Smelly Jack told of the path that awaited the Cooper family. While John melted down fresh lead and spent rifle balls to mold new ammunition for Pa's rifle, Smelly would find a whittle stick, spit into the red coals of the campfire, and begin his advice.

"Well, I reckon if you head straight for the North Star from this point, you'll come to a fair-sized settlement. You can outfit yerself a flat boat there. Now, whatever you do, don't settle fer no keel boat. They set too low in the water for the Oyo. That dang river's got hunerds-a logs and such hiding just out of sight, a-waiting to ram a hole below yer waterline. Even if you got to stand in line fer one, you git you a flatboat."

Smelly talked about the natives that awaited the Cooper family. "Now, steer away from the land to the north of the Oyo. That there's sacred ground to the Indians. Don't even matter what tribe they're from. Ever' last one of'em holds to that purticklur belief. They've got this old tale they've handed down fer maybe four er five lifetimes. Some tribal holy man saw a pack of white ghosts a-hunting in the forest on that side of the river, and he claimed the land was to be used only by them spirits. Ever since that time, it's been a terrible sin for them Indians to even set foot on that holy ground unless it's to defend the area from settlers."

Smelly squinted at a glowing coal that had popped itself a step away from the fire and spat it out of its misery. "To put it short, if you set foot on the land north of the Oyo, them scallywags will have yore hide strung for window coverings on their hogans afore you shake the sand from yer toes."

Johnny's heart thudded in alarm. Was this the kind of Indian that Pa aimed to get friendly with? The whole Cooper family would be nothing but ghosts by the time they got to where they were going! John's eyes rested on the curly, blond head of his little sister. Hallie lay asleep on Ma's piecework coverlet. With her arms tucked to her chest and her knees folded up under her tummy, her little rump made a mound under the blanket that begged to be patted. As he did many times each day, he reached automatically to pat that little mound as he stared into the fire. Was the worst part of their trip about to begin? As if she sensed John's worry and sought to reassure him, Traveler padded quietly to her master's side and wedged herself under his arm. Sure enough, John felt better.

Smelly plucked a long wood chip from his deerskin leggings and set it near the fire. All eyes watched the shaving slowly begin to curl and smoke as the ancient Long Hunter painted new pictures with his words.

"There's people can help you along yer way. They have ears up and down the river to tell them which way the Indians are a-blowin'. Used to be you didn't need to worry much about the Indians. That was before the French and the English commenced a-stirrin' the waters and muddied things up. They taught the Indians not to trust white men, and them peoples learned their lesson so good, it's gonna take three hunert years to unlearn 'em."

Smelly scratched his neck just under his beard and shifted on his achy, old haunches. "There's other folk along the river that'll do you in if they take a notion. They look for peoples like you, what would make easy pickin's. Now, I know you ain't wealthy folk, but you'd best take what money you do have and hide it well, just in case."

Ma glanced uneasily at Pa, and John recalled the hours she had spent the night before they left, sewing coins into unlikely spots on dresses and pants. The very coverlet Hallie slept on contained hidden coins. Who would suspect such a rag could contain such hard-earned wealth? Johnny's spirits lifted a bit. Maybe they were better prepared than old Smelly thought.

"A day or so this side of the Mississippi," Smelly continued, "you'll pass by the dangdest sight yer eyes ever met, and you'll know in your gizzard that you want to hurry on to get away from the haints what hangs 'round it."

"What sight is that?" asked Pa.

"Well," answered old Smelly Jack, "I cain't ezackly say *what* to call it, but the Indians or *somebody* went and put this giant monster on the side of a cliff. I don't know how they did it, 'cause that cliff goes straight up more'n a hunnert feet from river at the bottom to nothin' at the top, and there that huge monster stands, carved and painted smack-dab in the middle. They wuz a Indian a-travelin' the Oyo with me once, when we passed that demon. When I saw the way he eyed that thing, I decided that the Indians hadn't put it there at all." Smelly tossed his whittle stick into the fire and turned to look John square in the eyes. "It was the *Devil* did it!"

Johnny caught his breath as Smelly cleared his throat and continued. "Down river from the monster, you'll run into Crazy Sir Edward. He and his Missus live in a grand cave on the north side of the river. If yer bent on goin' up the Mississippi, Crazy Sir Edward will keep yer stores fer you 'til you find you a spot to settle."

The grizzly old hunter turned a kindly eye to Ma and added, "If I was you, Rachel, I'd keep little Hallie and stay with Crazy while Matthew and John go on ahead to seek one out."

Ma looked a bit upset by Smelly's suggestion. "Just why does the man have a name like Crazy Sir Edward?" she asked.

"Well, his name is Edward," the old man answered, "and he's plumb crazy."

Gently cradling Hallie in her arms, Ma arose and announced that she was going to sleep. She climbed into the wagon, muttering to herself about the strange characters who wander around in the wilderness.

Smelly watched quietly while Ma stepped into the wagon, and then he stood to brush wood shavings from his deerskin leggings and moved to a spot closer to Pa. "There's just one more warning, Matthew," he whispered hoarsely, "and it's the most important one of all. Watch out for the grizzlies."

John leaned closer to hear the men's whispered conversation.

"I don't know that I've ever seen a grizzly bear, but I've heard tell of them," Pa said. "What sets them apart from any other old bear that we should be so all-fired afraid of them?"

"A grizzly's different all right. You just take my word fer it. First of all, he's bigger. Why, I've seen grizzlies what stood eight feet tall, easy. They got a big hump 'tween their shoulders, and their colors is different. Their fur is silver tipped. Their muzzle is broader than other bears' an' it's covered with long, gray guard-hairs." Smelly wiped his sweaty hands on his leggings and forced his excited voice to quieten back to a whisper. "If yer out huntin' and you run across bear tracks, take a good squint at the hind feet. If they're longer than the front ones, it's a grizzly and yer in fer trouble. The best thing to do is to say yer prayers and turn around right quick. You never can tell what a grizzly will do. He mought just knock you off the face of this here earth for the pure fun of it, or he could decide to have you fer supper. Grizzlies 'r' meat eaters, you know."

Pa was quiet for a long time while he studied the fire. John was struck with the feeling that Smelly had come close to revealing a terrible secret he held close to his heart.

"Used to be," Smelly continued calmly, "you could run across grizzly just about anywhur on this here land. Nowadays, it's a pretty rare thing to see one this side of the Big Muddy."

John shook out his quilts to rid them of varmints, and he built a nest for himself and Traveler. His dog gratefully snuggled next to him. From their bed beneath the big wagon, the boy and his dog watched the men bank the fire for the night. Pa and Smelly Jack sat down to continue their talk. They had become close friends in the short time they had known each other. Each knew that the other would be terribly missed when they parted ways. As Johnny drifted to sleep watching Pa and Smelly hunker near the fire, he knew their trails would soon part, and he felt sadness creep into his heart.

The boy thought about Smelly's future. He was getting old. Who was going to take care of the old stinker? There had been times when John knew Smelly's knees ached so badly that he could hardly stand. Why did this man, who meant so much to the Coopers, insist on living alone out in the wilderness? What if a bear or an Indian attacked him? What if he was sick with the fever? Who would care for him? Johnny could stand it no longer. Late one night he carried his troubled thoughts to his parents. In the privacy of the wagon, they whispered their thoughts.

"John, you've heard us ask him to stay with us for keeps," Pa answered.

Johnny recalled the number of times the old man had managed to steer conversation away from invitations, sometimes before they were even spoken. "What makes Smelly such a loner?" he asked.

Ma answered thoughtfully, "I think that man has gone to seed. He's been tramping out here alone for so many years that he's gone wild. He gets to feeling cooped-up if he's around too many people."

"I'll bet it's been years since he's set foot in a settlement or town," Pa added.

Finally, John began to see what made Smelly tick. He was people-shy, like a hunting dog gone wild. Maybe that's why he wore that awful smell; it kept people away. "But why did Smelly decide to join up with us?" he asked.

"Son, I just can't figure it," answered Pa, "but we should be thankful for the time we have with Smelly, 'cause we've learned so much from our old friend. We might not have made it this far without him."

Feeling lucky to have run across his stinky old friend, John climbed down to his spot under the wagon. As the boy shook out his quilt, Traveler loped into camp. She gave up her night time hunt and rolled her warm back against John. After cocking her ears to pick up any strange noises, she laid down her bony head and closed her eyes heaving a big sigh that announced her plans to sleep. Maybe old Smelly's trail would take him away from the Coopers, Johnny thought, but

Traveler would stay. Nothing could his dog away from her important, family duties. The boy fell asleep with his arm around his furry friend.

Three days down the trail, Smelly circled back to the wagon after a quick scouting trip through the woods ahead. "Well," he announced, "I reckon you pilgrims will get along just as good without me now. There's a settlement dead square ahead about a half-day's walk from here. Why, I can smell them peoples already!" His face wore a disgusted look as he continued, "I don't know why them humans think they have to bunch up every whip-stitch. Why, you'd think they wasn't strong enough to cuss without some fool friend a-holding them up! Probbly have to spit downwind! It's flat unhealthy for so many bodies a-sharing the same air. First thing you know, there'll come a fever that'll lay every blamed one of 'em low."

Smelly kicked at a fallen limb. As he turned to talk to John, his weathered old face softened. "I taught you about a thimble-full of what I know, but there's no more time. You keep aholt of yer wits and you'll make it. Now there's just one more thing."

From the crook of his arm, the old Long Hunter lifted a flintlock rifle. John's eyes widened as Smelly continued. "You got yerself a fine family and the best dog I've knowed, but there's one more thing you need to be a man." He handed the rifle to John. "Years ago, I come across this here weapon wedged into a Sycamore tree with the body of my best friend. From the looks of old Harper, a bear surprised him afore he could think. Prilla, here, was loaded and ready to shoot, but she wasn't of no use behind Harper's back. I buried my old friend and promised I'd look after Prilla for him. She's a fine long rifle, and I want you to have 'er."

John's mouth hung open like the hayloft door. "Smelly, I reckon you love your rifle and need her. I can't take her," he said, wishing he'd kept his mouth shut but knowing he shouldn't.

Smelly grinned inside, because he knew John had fallen in love with Prilla the first time he shot her. He had felt the boy's longing for the rifle as plainly as if he'd asked for it.

"Son, I got no more time to hang around and protect you Coopers," Smelly said as he thrust the gun into John's hands. "Why, there's things a-waitin' to be done what needed me a turtle's lifetime ago." Smelly turned to Pa and grabbed his big hand and pumped hard as he spoke.

"Matthew, you fare thee well. For a addle-headed farmer, you managed pretty good to keep yer family alive out here. You keep on a-doin' it."

Smelly held back his tears until Ma stepped up to give the old character a hug. She handed over Hallie for a quick good-bye kiss, and Smelly's eyes filled. John's throat swelled up with a sob stuck inside, and he looked at Pa. His ox-strong father locked Smelly in a bear hug and cried openly. The old man turned, waved, and disappeared into the woods beside the trail as silently as he had arrived at the berry patch so many memorable days before.

"Well," Ma sighed through her tears, "we've got half a day's journey ahead of us."

The Coopers turned their eyes to the trail ahead and quietly moved on. Not a word was said for several minutes as each one enjoyed special thoughts about their dear old friend.

THE RUNAWAY

T RAVELER PICKED UP SIGNS OF the settlement first. John knew
from the way she tilted her nose that strangers were upwind and close by.
Before the sun had begun to set, Jack and Molly kicked up dust along a
road that led into the heart of the settlement, which had sprung up at the edge
of the Oyo River. What noise! John heard sounds he had long forgotten. Mostly,
the sounds were made by people. When he began to feel nervous, he understood
what had happened to Smelly Jack.

Pa led Jack and Molly into a large pen by the biggest barn John had ever
seen. He propped his goad against the wagon and spoke with a round little man
who led the lumbering team closer to the building. The man would unhitch the
oxen and turn them into cool stalls where hay, grain, and water waited for them.

Leaving Traveler in the wagon to guard their precious belongings, the
Coopers walked across the road to a large, two-story inn. Johnny's trail-sharp-
ened nose picked up a happy memory floating along on the air: ginger cookies!
They all entered the tavern side of the inn. John saw a small number of men
enjoying ale and quiet talk as Ma hustled herself and Halle into a separate room
for the women and children. Not sure whether he belonged with the women and
children or with the grown-up men, John shot a look at his Pa. It was clear from
Matthew's actions that he meant for his son to stay with the men. He was pleased

but tried not to show it. Otherwise, the men gathered here would know this was his first time spent in such distinguished company.

While Pa and John each enjoyed a spring-cooled mug of buttermilk, the boy sized up the tavern's customers. All but one of the men seemed to know each other. They probably lived around the settlement. The lone stranger gave John the shivers. Unlike the other men in the room, he wore his hat, which was considered rude, even in the wilderness. The hat reminded him of the one that Miller Brown wore every Muster Day. It was a big, black hat with the brim turned up in the front and back, and out straight over each ear. John knew Miller Brown was the head man on the Muster Day maneuvers, so he guessed the man was some kind of military officer. He wore a dark Blue jacket with two neat rows of shiny, brass buttons marching from his upturned collar to nearly the bottom. There were gold stripes on each of his sleeves. The way he was dressed reminded him a lot of a navy officer he'd seen on a big hand bill back at Stowe's Fork. Maybe he had a ship somewhere, but what was he doing out here in the wilderness? Could a full-size ship come down the Oyo River? From what Smelly had told them, it would be too dangerous.

The man sat in the shadows. A flickering candle stood at the center of his table, and in the candle light John caught flashes of evil in the man's yellow-green eyes! Surely a man so dangerous looking wouldn't be chosen to lead a group of men! The boy was relieved when the plump mistress of the inn opened a door and stepped in to call the men to dinner. Like a pack of hungry wolves, they all scrambled to a long table in the next room. The evil-looking stranger hung back in the shadows until the tavern had cleared, and then he slowly moved to the dining table and seated himself across from John. This time, Pa sat beside John where his observant eyes could study the stranger.

Feeling safe at his pa's side, John's nose turned his thoughts to food, causing his mouth to water uncontrollably. Mistress Lanier walked quickly around the table, carrying hot stew, biscuits, and greens, to the hungry men. Again and again, she pulled her big apron up to wipe her sweaty face. It was plain she had cooked at the hot fireplace for hours. The women and children waited in a third room for the men folk to finish and leave. Soon they would enter and seat themselves for a fine meal of leftovers.

While John waited inside the inn for a round of ginger cookies, Traveler sat patiently in the wagon. Her tail wagged as she felt the quiet approach of a stranger. She jumped up and, with a friendly lick, she greeted Ben as he slipped quietly over the tailgate. Traveler and Benjamin sized each other up and they each liked what they saw.

"Hello, Girl," Ben crooned quietly, extending his hand for Traveler to sniff. She stepped forward to offer the top of her head, snuggling it up against his opened palm. "I need a place to hide," he explained in a whisper. "I hope you won't mind, but I won't stay any longer than I have to." Ben searched for a likely spot, starting with the grain barrel, but it was filled to the brim. He spotted the dark shadows beneath Ma and Pa Cooper's bed. There was a coverlet hanging over the edge that would help to block anyone's view. Offering Traveler's silky ear a last scratch, he darted under the bed and wedged himself into the darkest corner, tugging the coverlet down as much as he dared.

Within minutes, Traveler felt another stranger nearing the wagon. This time, her special sense warned her that this was no friend. With her fur raised from head to tail, she silent padded to the back end of the wagon. Baring her sharp fangs, she waited in silence. The evil-looking face of a man appeared over the tailgate. Traveler lunged fiercely at the man and attacked him, forcing him to jerk his head back so far that he almost fell. As quickly as he had come, the man was gone. The mean-hearted captain would have to search for Benjamin somewhere else. He reasoned that the vicious dog inside the wagon would never have permitted a runaway slave boy to enter, anyway. In fact, he concluded, if there was anyplace Benjamin *wasn't*, it was inside that wagon.

As Captain Jeffries rubbed a mole on his cheek, he plotted his evil plans. The black boy was near here. He could feel it. Besides, he had proof. He smiled as his hand squeezed the walnut wood shavings in his pocket. That young slave's habit of carving things from prime hardwood would trap him. An ordinary whittler would never waste such good wood. The captain would soon find and kill Benjamin, and then he could return to the plantation with no fear of ever being found out. He practically drooled when he thought of the money to be made on all those acres. If he wanted, he would never have to set sail on another foul slave ship, living off sea rations and sleeping in a cramped bunk. He had always known he was much too good for that kind of life. Now, he was about to clear away the very last obstacle to what he *truly* deserved: the Jeffries Plantation.

As the captain moved his search to the inside of the huge barn, Traveler got acquainted with her new friend. She dragged her belly across the wagon's floor, shimmied under the bed and stretched her neck to lick Benjamin's smiling face. He dared to move from the deep shadows, but he appreciated the dog's friendship. The boy shifted enough to return her attention by stroking her strong back. It felt wonderful to have such an accepting friend, even if it was a dog. Benjamin had spent so many days and nights alone and on the run that he was tempted to stay put and enjoy this dog's affections. He knew, though, that he needed to move away and find himself a better, more permanent hiding place. Captain Jeffries had an uncanny way of tracking him down. More than once, he had barely escaped being captured. He had to keep moving until he was so far into the wilderness that the captain would give up and go home. If only he could find a family that would allow him to travel with them! It would be ideal to float downriver in a boat of some kind, he reasoned, because his poor feet and legs could use a break from the running. If he couldn't find a friendly, accepting family, maybe he could hide away on one of the boats until it got far downstream, and then jump off in the dark of night.

When Pa and John returned to the wagon, Traveler greeted them with joyful wags of her brindled tail. Pa smiled with pride. The big dog had protected the wagon as he knew she would. Not a single thing was out of place. There was no visible sign that Traveler's visitor had come and gone. Until they unloaded the wagon, no one would see the tell-tale curl of walnut wood hiding in the deep shadows under the bed, and by then it wouldn't matter.

During the next few days, the Cooper family made their travel arrangements. Pa bargained for a flatboat that would hold their belongings, oxen, wagon, and all. Ma arranged for new meal and flour from a local mill, and she haggled with a store owner for necessary supplies to replace the equipment now resting in pieces at the bottom of a mountain gorge. Johnny was amazed at her good humor, when she laughed about how many unnecessary items she had insisted upon hauling. Although he had never mentioned that nearly fatal day, he had noticed that Jack and Molly had made much better time and seemed to be in better shape at the end of each day that followed. He guessed Pa must have noticed the same thing, but no one in the family had uttered a single word about that horrible day since it happened. It was if they might lay a curse on themselves, if they even thought about it.

While Pa and Ma hurried through the little river town arranging for a flatboat and supplies, John explored the settlement with Hallie in his arms or tugging at his finger as she practiced her steps. It was during such an adventure down near the mill race that John met a black boy for the very first time in his life. He had heard of black people slaving away on the land of rich men and women, but he came from such a poor part of Virginia that everyone worked for himself. There were no black people at Stowe's Fork. Even Hallie, as young as she was, noticed the difference in this boy's looks, and she stared openly at his dark skin. Johnny felt both embarrassed and curious. In fact, the only member of the Cooper family that behaved sociably was Traveler. She hurried to Benjamin and greeted him by tucking her head under his palm, begging without shame for attention. Johnny had never seen Traveler greet anyone but her family with such obvious joy.

The black boy focused on Traveler's silken ears, and she responded by wedging her head against the front of his legs. "Hello," the boy said with an open smile. He nodded toward his four-legged friend. "Are you her owner?"

Hit by a sudden attack of shyness, John could do no more than nod. He picked up Hallie, just for a way to look busy. He was never shy with people, and he wanted to talk to this black boy, who was smaller than him, but the sharp look in his eyes said he was at least as old, if not older. A million questions popped into his mind, but he couldn't seem to get started talking, and he didn't want to ask some nosy thing that would upset this friendly-acting stranger. His tongue refused to work, and he found himself turning his eyes to the huge mill wheel. The miller had opened the gate to the millrace, forcing river water to rush past the mill down a narrow chute. It churned through the millrace with such force it turned the big mill wheel around and around as it pushed against the wheel's giant wooden paddles. Johnny even felt a cool breeze created by the rushing water.

"My name's Benjamin," the boy announced. "What's yours?"

John felt his shyness melt away, and he sat down to dangle his feet over the mill race wall. He beckoned Benjamin to take a seat beside him and carefully eased Hallie to a spot beside him, circling an arm tightly around her so she couldn't fall into the mill race. "My name's John," he answered, "and this is my little sister, Hallie."

Traveler firmly planted herself between John and Benjamin the moment he sat down. This was probably her idea of Heaven, because now she had the opportunity to be petted from both sides. She sat lean and tall, waiting impatiently for an introduction. Johnny obliged. "This is my dog, Traveler," he announced proudly. "My grandpa gave her to me when she was just a pup."

As Benjamin ran an admiring hand down Traveler's strong back, John wondered about the pinkness of the palm side of his hand. Had the black color rubbed off of that side? John figured he had a lot to learn about dark-skinned people, and he might as well start now. "You a slave?" he asked innocently.

Ben curbed his first reaction, which was to slap the stone wall in anger. Instead, he answered, "No, my master freed me. I'm a free black now, on my way west."

"So are we," said John. "Are your ma and pa a-looking for a flatboat?"

"I have no mother or father."

Johnny blushed with embarrassment. He just naturally figured . . .

"I'm looking for a family to travel with," Benjamin went on. "Do you think your father could find room for me? I'm a hard worker."

John's jaw dropped with surprise. The thought of having a slave had never entered his mind. Somehow it just didn't seem natural. "I don't think Ma and Pa would take to having a slave," he began.

"I won't **be** a slave!" Benjamin interrupted, almost in anger. "I told you, I'm a free black. I'm hoping to work for my passage west."

"I'm sorry." John blushed once again, puzzling over this strange new boy. "I don't know much about slaving. I feel like a fish out of water. Let's go talk to my pa."

When Matthew saw the boys approaching, he smelled trouble. He hadn't seen many black folks, but he figured they weren't much different from white people, However, there was a sparkle in this particular young man's eyes that looked like fear. Pa reckoned the boy was a runaway slave. After hearing the boys out, Pa shook his head sadly. He didn't want to accuse the boy of lying, but . . . "Benjamin," he began, "we can't take you along. I am against slavery. Now, I know you want to hire on. You wouldn't be a slave. But to other folks, it'd look like you're our slave, and I'll not have it."

Benjamin's shoulders drooped with disappointment. He had been secretly watching the Coopers since they had rolled into the settlement, and he liked what he saw. Matthew Cooper stacked up to be a fair and honest man, and Mrs. Cooper seemed as gentle as his old master's dead wife. His heart ached to be part of a family again.

"I wouldn't mind if people thought I was your slave," he said, hoping he could persuade Mr. Cooper to change his mind.

But Matthew Cooper was one of those men who made up his mind and very seldom changed it. He stood silently, then finally answered. "I'm sorry, but it would make me feel like I owned you. I just won't have it."

"Well, thank you for hearing me out," Benjamin said. Secretly, he vowed not to give up on these Coopers. Giving Traveler a farewell pat, Benjamin turned toward the mill. When he was out of view, he edged through the woods and angled toward the waterfront docks. He had a plan.

At the same time, two wicked men were secretly meeting in a small clearing in the woods on the other side of the settlement. Their words must not be heard by a soul, or they both would be in deep trouble with the law. One of the men was the sinister captain that John and Pa had both seen. Traveler had even met him. The other man was an Indian who had been sent away by his tribe. He had done things that were unfair and against both white and tribal men's laws, and his people had made him pack up what little he owned and leave forever. The two men were talking quietly, just in case someone might happen into the clearing where they were holding their secret meeting.

"You'll know him when you see him carving things out of wood. When you're sure it's him, I want him killed quickly and quietly. No one is to know of this but me. Understand?" the captain whispered.

The Indian's black eyes glittered with greed as he gave the captain a nod.

"I'm a rich man," the captain continued, "and when you take care of the boy, you will be rich, too. I'll set you up with land, a trading post, whatever you want." He opened a leather pouch heavy with coins. "Here are five gold pieces," he said, counting out a small portion. "You bring me a hand of the dead boy and one of his carvings, and there'll be many more of these coins waiting for you."

As the men plotted, the Coopers made their final arrangements and planned to begin their trip downriver at dawn the next day. They said good-bye to their new friends in the settlement as they enjoyed Mistress Lanier's wonderful cooking one final time at the inn. Not a single Cooper knew that their journey would carry them into the web being spun by the evil captain. Not even Traveler!

THE RIVER'S SECRETS

JOHNNY MARVELED AT THE BIG, smooth-riding flatboat. With the wagon lashed to its deck and Jack and Molly on board, there was still room for the Coopers to move around the edges. From the oxen and dog to the people, each one had earned a slow, smooth trip down the Oyo. Jack and Molly had become sleek, fat, and well-rested during their pampering in the big barn, and it seemed to suit them well, as they often lay in the straw of their pen and chewed their cud peacefully, content to flap an occasional ear or tail to discourage flies, while they dozed in the warm sun. While Pa walked the big tiller pole back and forth across the rear of the boat, Ma and John used fishing as an excuse to gaze over the side and watch the underwater world swimming beneath them. When the river curved, causing the boat to cast its big shadow on the water, they clearly saw the bottom of the river.

River life was new to the Coopers, and they constantly spied strange sights, totally different from those they had enjoyed along the trail. Muskrats, otters, and beavers popped wet heads above the water to study the large boat as it passed. With water dripping from their chins, deer raised their heads and paused to watch, and an occasional black bear could be seen fishing or swimming in the giant green waterway. A lone Indian approached the northern bank and inspected them through glittering, black eyes.

Ma set out a fine meal to celebrate their first day on the Oyo. At Midday on the trail, they would have been chewing on dried meat or stale biscuits as they walked. Today, however, they had a stew, biscuits, even river-cooled buttermilk. Ma surprised them with a berry cobbler that Mistress Lanier had tucked into her basket at the last minute. John and Pa took turns at the tiller pole so that each could eat his fill at this feast, so unusual for the middle of the day. Johnny could not recall a time he'd eaten while floating along on water. In fact, he wasn't sure he had even been in *any* kind of boat in his whole life!

Ma announced that, for the first time since she was a child, she was taking a nap. Lifting Hallie to her hip, she climbed into the wagon and soon the two were gently rocked to sleep. Pa and John spent the remainder of the day discussing plans for the rest of their trip, and their talk often drifted back to Smelly Jack's advice.

As the sun began to settle behind the trees, they spotted the ferry station that Smelly had described. There was no sign of life at the ferryman's cabin. It seemed to be deserted. Squinting through the long shadows cast across the water by the sun setting behind the forest, Pa spotted a lone man huddled near a campfire across the river from the cabin.

He shouted to the man, "Hey there! Could you use some company for the night?"

The man called back hoarsely, "Suit yerself."

Pa and Ma traded questioning looks. Was this man safe company? Would they be better off to go farther downstream, risking running into a floating tree in the darkness?

"The man sounds sick, Matthew," Ma whispered. "Maybe he needs our help. Besides, he already has a fire going, and it would save John and me a heap of work."

Pa guided the big boat toward the southern bank, and soon they were face-to-face with the strange man. His long gray hair and beard needed cutting, and his clothes were nothing more than rags. He stared blankly at them through bloodshot eyes that seemed to be two hundred years old, and he looked so thin a good wind could have knocked him right into the river. After Pa introduced his family, the man took his turn.

"I'm Zeb White," he announced weakly. "I'm the ferryman here 'bouts."

John's warning system needed no help from Traveler this time, and he saw Ma and Pa sending messages to each other with their eyes. If this man was the ferryboat pilot, what was he doing on this side of the river, and where was the ferryboat? He should have been across the water in his comfortable cabin.

"Is that your cabin over there?" Pa asked Zeb with a nod toward the dark, empty-looking log house across the river. When the man gave a slight nod that Johnny took to mean yes, Pa added, "Why are you on this side? Is there something wrong with your ferry boat?"

John saw fear cross the man's face like the shadow of a buzzard, and he felt the hairs on his neck rise. Something told him he was about to hear a story worse than Miller Brown could have told in a thousand years of tales, and he wasn't at all sure he wanted to hear it.

"This side suits me," the man answered flatly.

Handing Hallie over to Pa, Ma guided John toward their flatboat. "Come on, John, you can wade out to get our dinner," she said. "I put the leftover biscuits and cobbler away in the bench back by the tiller pole. Since we had such a big meal earlier, let's just make do with them tonight.

It was almost dark enough to need a lantern as John crawled on-board the flatboat. Lifting the bow bench lid, he poked through the stores for the leftovers. There were none. The biscuit and cobbler pans were there, but they were empty. John grinned as he pictured his hungry pa sneaking the last of the midday meal.

"It's all gone, Ma," John whispered. "Pa must have finished it off when you and I were fishing a while back." He could feel his mother's disappointment as they returned to the campfire. Now she would have to cook the fish they had caught.

There were only two medium-sized fish hanging on the stringer, which dangled into the river. The two fish would not begin to fill all their stomachs.

"John, where is that fishing line?" Ma asked.

"Right here in my pocket." He pulled out the two lines he and Ma had used. Reading her thoughts, he hurried back to the boat, where he would put bits of fatback on the hooks and throw them over the back of the flatboat, and then tie them to the tiller pole. They'd soon have several fish browning on sticks propped around the fire.

When he returned with five good-sized catfish, he saw a strange sight. There, on a green willow whip strung over the fire, was pair after pair of frog legs, cooking tender. Zeb White had shown Pa the secret of frogging. Armed with a fiery pine torch, they had easily speared several frogs.

Tasting the delicious meat for the first time, John was puzzled about the man who felt well enough to spear frogs, but too poorly to eat them. Ma added the catfish to the fire, and soon the family was stuffed and happy. Just as Pa reached for the last, sizzling catfish, Zeb grabbed his sleeve.

"Hear that?" Zeb whispered hoarsely, his ear cocked toward the river.

"Hear what?" Pa asked, looking automatically at Traveler. Unconcerned, the dog sat happily licking catfish from her muzzle.

"There they are again!" Zeb whimpered. His face was drawn with fear. "I knowed they was a-comin' back."

Ma and Pa looked at each other. Was this man sick in the head? "Who *are* they?" Pa asked quietly.

"Them redskins," Zeb answered, as he jumped up and began to pace.

Fear grabbed John right in the belly. Smelly had spoken of murderous Indians, but they were supposed to be on the other side of the river. Were they coming over to the south bank? He squinted into the thin layer of fog settling onto the river and saw nothing but blackness.

"Here, Son," Pa said quickly, "you take my rifle while I go for Prilla." He hurried to the boat while John clutched Pa's flintlock. Loaded and ready to shoot, it felt comforting in his hands ... until he considered the idea of shooting another human being.

Zeb continued to talk. "They won't let me rest. I was only doing what I had to do. It was either them or me!"

Squeezing Hallie close, Ma edged toward John's side. She didn't know whether she was more afraid of the Indians or Zeb White. There was something wild about the way he talked. As John looked around for suitable shelter from an Indian attack, Zeb rattled on.

"That first one made me sick. He came on so fast I didn't have time to grab my gun. I hit him with my shovel. I had to hide his body from the others, so I just buried him where I was digging my root cellar."

Ma's eyebrows shot up in surprise. "In your cabin?" she gasped, immediately covering her mouth to keep herself from saying anything else that might get Zeb White riled up. She had no reason to fear Zeb. As the strange man hugged his knees to his chest, Ma squeezed John's arm. Were there really Indians out there?

Rocking back and forth, Zeb moaned, continuing his tale. "The next two come together. They jumped me. I got my knife into one of 'em, but he didn't die yet. He just laid there staring, while I fought the other one. I chopped that second one in the chest with his own hatchet. There was too much blood for me to drag 'em to the river, so I buried them, too. I had to finish that one devil off while he stared at me."

John was regretting having eaten those frog legs, because Zeb White's story sickened him right down to his toes. He shot a look at his ma and reckoned she felt the same.

The strange man shuddered, and then continued. "That's when the curse started."

"What curse?" John asked, immediately wishing he hadn't.

Zeb ignored John's question and began to moan, "Oh, them eyes! Them eyes! They stared at me even when I worked to get him buried. Listen!" He jumped to his feet suddenly, startling Ma and John.

Pa returned with John's rifle as Zeb began to pace around the fire. Pa watched the ferrymen mutter and pause to listen to sounds only he could hear. Traveler wasn't worried about a thing across the river, but Pa noticed she was beginning to move back and forth, posting herself between Mr. White and her family, like she thought she might need to defend them from the wild-eyed man.

"Why won't they leave me alone?" Zeb pleaded with Pa. "I didn't want to kill them. I was only protecting myself!"

Pa saw immediately what was happening. "How many were there, altogether?" he asked quietly.

"Seventeen of 'em," Zeb answered. He shuddered. "Except for number two and number three, they come at me one at a time."

"Where are they now?" Pa continued his questioning.

"They're in my cabin," Zeb answered, pointing toward the deserted log building across the river. "Buried 'em. Had to so's the others wouldn't find out and come after me."

Pa gave a quick, nearly invisible nod, and Johnny relaxed his tight grip on the rifle. He dropped his sweaty hand to Traveler's strong, sleek back. As the Coopers quietly gathered their things to wash them in the river, Traveler walked slowly to the edge of the black water. She stood stone still and cocked her ears toward the cabin across the river. Raising her nose, she howled mournfully. A shiver ran through John. Maybe those Indian spirits *were* making noises that only Zeb and Traveler could hear. After all, who would blame them? They nodded their goodbyes to Mr. White and climbed silently onto their flatboat, leaving the man alone to suffer the attacks of his guilty conscience. Pa nodded at John, indicating he would stay awake and watch for both Zeb White *and* Indians.

With the rising sun, John and Traveler walked a short distance to a clearing where Jack and Molly had been hobbled for the night. The boy led them back onto the boat and they went willingly into the pen, where they would ride for another day. The Coopers left Zeb White at the mercy of his ghosts and resumed their trip down river. In the daylight, the ferryman had become a much different person. Strong and cocky, he had eaten an enormous breakfast. Then he had launched his ferry and hurried to the northern bank. He was scurrying up the hill to his cabin when the Coopers shoved off, and he seemed in such a hurry that he didn't even turn to wave. John doubted that Zeb remembered what had happened the night before.

Pa gritted his teeth with pain when he took the tiller pole. As strong as the big man was, he had used new muscles as a river man. Ma laughed and said that she would have to make him new shirts by the time they got to the Mississippi, because all that fresh muscle wouldn't fit into what he was wearing. Pa puffed out his chest, spit into the palms of his hands, rubbed them together, and grabbed the end of the tiller pole. He leaned into the pole like he had been born on a flatboat.

There were two tiller poles on the flatboat. One was in front and was usually tied down with a thick rope. There were times when John and Ma needed to untie the front tiller and work to keep the boat headed in the right direction. Those times were exciting and risky, but Ma and John always managed well, and the boat moved smartly down the river. Pa relied on the current to do most of the work, while he swept his rear tiller here and there to skip the boat past sand bars or around half-sunken tree trunks. Smelly had been right again. The flatboat eased over hidden logs and snags that a keelboat would never have passed.

As John sat up on the lashed tiller pole to watch for snags, Ma busied herself with woman's work. Singing to Hallie, she gathered her stores to fix a midday meal. Ma lifted the bow bench lid and removed the empty biscuit and cobbler pans.

"Matthew, I've never known you to sneak food," she said, smiling broadly as she teased her husband. "If you weren't busy a-building new muscle, I'd be wrathy at you."

Pa's eyebrows lifted with surprise. "Woman, sometimes you don't make sense! What are you talking about?"

"I planned for us to eat left-over biscuits last night so I wouldn't need to cook," she explained, "but you ate them, and the cobbler, too!"

"I didn't eat your leftovers," Pa said with mock seriousness. "I'm not the only one a-building new muscle, you know."

Despite his innocence, John's face stung when Ma and Pa turned to him.

"John! How could you accuse your father?" Ma scolded. "I've never known you to lie before. I allow if you need food, you should eat, but not without asking. The worst of it is the lying!"

John couldn't believe what he was hearing. "I didn't eat anything after midday until those frog legs!" he insisted, wide-eyed.

Ma and Pa squinted at each other. It was plain to John that they didn't believe him and that they were hurt. "It's over," Pa ordered. "There will be no more talk of this."

Knowing the seriousness of Pa's command, John swallowed his defense. His cheeks stung with embarrassment. Had Pa eaten the food and lied? That didn't make sense. They had been gone from the boat for only a few minutes. Maybe that strange Indian they had seen at the river's edge had been following them. Maybe he had stolen the food. John's mind wouldn't rest until he found an answer. He automatically reached for his dog. Stroking her muscular chest, he buried his face in her brindled fur.

"I wish you could talk," he whispered to his dog. "I'll bet you know who did it." The big dog stayed close to her master, seeming to understand his sadness and need for comfort. "*I wish Grandma and Grandpa were here,*" John thought with a lump in his throat. "*They would trust me.*"

"There!" Ma's shout startled John. "There, Matthew; see those berries? They're just what we need. Let's tie up here for a few minutes. We'll stretch our legs and pick berries."

Pa nodded. He hadn't said a word since the scolding. Johnny wondered if things were gnawing at him, too. As the boat neared the bank, John jumped out with Traveler at his side. He tugged the rope and eased the boat in close, tying it to a tree. Pa threw John a line from the rear of the boat. Soon the big craft was held near the bank, and Pa was easing Ma down into the water. She whooped like a twelve-year-old when her bare feet hit the water, and she reached up to receive Hallie into her arms. Hiking up her skirts, she danced through the cool ripples with the baby on her hip. Pa and John laughed at Ma's delight.

"Why, you didn't want berries at all. You just wanted to take a swim," Pa teased Ma.

Rachel Cooper had soon finished with her dancing, and she turned to the business of picking berries. "John, why don't you take Prilla and hunt us up some meat for our kettle?" she suggested.

John knew that Ma wanted to send him into the woods so she could talk to Pa privately. Well, that set well with him, because he'd just as well get away on his own for a spell, anyway. Traveler pranced with excitement when John reached for Prilla and his shot pouch. The two companions set out with Prilla loaded and primed for game. Would it be squirrel or rabbit? Looking at the oaks towering above them, John guessed it would be squirrel, and he was right. Before an hour had passed, John had brought down two large red squirrels. He carried them back to the river to skin and gut. As he washed his knife and arms in the cool water, John sensed that the problem about the leftovers had passed. Pa and Ma seemed themselves again. The young man laughed at his full-grown parents. Their faces and hands were smeared with purple berry juice.

"You must have been taking eating lessons from Hallie," he laughed.

Showing purple-toothed grins, Pa and Ma carried Hallie into the water. With hoots and splashes, they cleaned up, and soon they were loading the boat. John had to wait for Traveler to return from the woods before he could climb on board. The rest of the family was settled and ready to go when he hefted his dog onto the boat and untied the lines. In no time at all, they were down river.

After digging into the stores for her dried beef, Ma looked up with a frown. "John, come here," she whispered.

John climbed down from his perch on the tiller pole. "What's wrong, Ma?" he asked.

"We're missing some dried beef," she whispered.

His face reddened with sudden anger. It *wasn't* over. What was going on?

Continuing to whisper, Ma said, "Johnny I want you to go take your pa's tiller pole and send him here."

His anger was replaced with something like fear. Why was Ma whispering? He hurried back to relieve Pa and sent him hustling quietly to Ma. John leaned into the tiller, steadying the big boat as he puzzled over the latest development. He watched his parents pow-wowing at the front of the boat. They didn't seem to be talking about him. That was good. His eyes strayed to Hallie as she reached for a light brown, curly object and popped it into her mouth.

"No, no, Hallie!" John warned as he released the tiller. "That's wood. It'll hurt you." He snatched a wood shaving from Hallie's hand and thrust his fingers into her mouth to force out another piece. Suddenly, the boat thudded against a half-sunk log and shuddered to a momentary stop. John heard Pa shout angrily as he and Ma were thrown against the bow bench. Hallie began to cry from surprise. Johnny gritted his teeth with dread as Pa hurried back to grab the tiller pole. The flatboat began to swing dangerously sideways.

"Go help your Ma with the front tiller," Pa growled, glaring at his son.

The boys' stomach knotted with frustration. Pa never mistrusted him. Suddenly, here was Pa with frowns and harsh words aplenty. He hurried forward to help his mother, and after five minutes of struggle, the boat was once again floating peacefully down river. The words that Johnny had dreaded hearing came from the back of the boat.

"John, come here," Pa said sternly.

The family gathered near Pa's tiller pole. Some fire burning inside the boy made him look his Pa straight in the eye. He refused to be wrongly accused of something he had not done. Pa looked at John long and hard, and the black-haired boy stared right back, his blue eyes filled with icy fire.

"Son, whatever made you let go of that tiller pole? Don't you know what happens when you let the river take over?"

John fought down his anger. "I was afraid Hallie would choke on those wood shavings. She had one in her mouth before I knew it," he answered.

As Ma reached down to pick up the wet curls of wood at the edge of Hallie's coverlet, Pa blurted, "Wait a minute!" He grabbed the shavings from her hand and examined them. "Where did these come from? John, have you been whittling?"

"No, Sir," came John's quick reply.

Matthew Cooper pulled off his sweaty hat and ran a big hand through his black, curly hair. As he mulled over the mysterious wood shavings, his eyes darted from one spot to another on the big flatboat. "Son, throw over the anchor," he ordered. "We're gonna search this here boat."

The anchor took hold quickly and Pa lashed down the tiller pole. Carefully, section by section, they searched the big craft.

"Pa, if someone was hiding out, Traveler would find him," Johnny reasoned.

"Yes, Johnny, I think she would let us know, but something is wrong here. I don't believe you took that food or left those wood shavings. We've got to get to the bottom of this."

Johnny felt relief knowing that his father trusted him. He would tear the boat apart board by board, if that's what his pa wanted.

And them Ma called from inside the wagon, "Matthew! I found him!"

In three huge steps, Pa was inside the wagon. As John watched, a black face popped through the canvas flap into the sunshine. It was Benjamin! Pa's face was red with anger as he hustled the young black boy down to the deck. "I told you that you could not come along," Pa said angrily. "What do you think you're doing eating our food and sneaking around on our boat? I ought to turn around and take you back to the authorities. You *are* a runaway slave, aren't you?"

"Mister Cooper, Sir, you *can't* turn me in. I'm a free black. My master turned me free when I did a good deed for him." Benjamin hated to lie, but he wasn't about to tell them what had *really* happened. If they weren't willing to believe that he was free, they *certainly* wouldn't believe he was running away from a murderer! "Please, just let me travel with you, and I'll do all your chores."

Like a mother naturally will, Ma moved to Ben to comfort him. "Benjamin," she said softly, "are you thirsty? Do you need food?"

Ben longed to let her mother him, but instead, he said, "No thank you, Ma'am. I've eaten and drunk only what I absolutely needed. It pains me to act like a thief, but I have no choice. I'm sorry if I've caused you trouble, but well, I …"

Ben's voice trailed off. There was silence as Pa considered. This Ben seemed like a boy in trouble. He probably had escaped from a master upriver somewhere. Pa could get the whole family in deep trouble if he kept a runaway slave. It went against Pa's ways to turn down anyone in need, but then he never broke the law, either. If only this boy would tell the truth! Somehow Pa knew the young man was lying.

"Benjamin, we'll not turn around, nor will we keep you," Pa finally announced. "We will give you food and necessaries and drop you off with the next settlers we see."

"Yes, Sir," Benjamin said quietly, as he felt that now-familiar old fear creep back up his spine.

As if conjured up by Pa's very words, a cabin appeared around the next bend in the river. Ma quickly gathered supplies for Benjamin, and Pa skillfully pulled the boat into the bank. While John and Traveler protected the boat and the womenfolk, Pa walked up to the cabin with the young black boy. There were signs of life at the log home, but the settler was away. From the looks of the stew pot hanging from an iron hook over the glowing embers of an outdoor fire, he would be back soon. Pa walked around the building, calling toward the hills for the man, but there was no answer. Finally, Pa returned to the flatboat, leaving Benjamin sitting near the bubbling stew pot. The young man would have to do his own explaining when the settler returned.

The Cooper family shoved off from the riverbank with confused and troubled hearts. There was something very likeable about Benjamin. He had spunk. But they would not break the law, and it seemed plain that Benjamin was hiding something.

From his spot near the pot of stew, Benjamin watched the Coopers leave. He smiled openly. There was something very likeable about those Coopers. They had spunk. He would win them over yet. Shouldering his small bundle of supplies, he walked to an animal trail that wound through the woods. His bare feet broke into a run. He would have to push hard to keep the boat in sight.

From a hill overlooking the cabin, a pair of snake-like eyes watched Benjamin. A greedy Indian fingered the gold coins in his pouch and smiled to himself. Very soon he would be presenting the black boy's hand and a carving to Captain Jeffries. He liked white man's ways. His tribe didn't understand him like this captain did. Soon he would be wearing white man's clothing and spending white man's gold. He sneaked quietly down the hill to follow the boy. The flatboat continued its journey toward the Mississippi. John went back to fishing, while Ma readied food. This would be a light meal, because no one felt hungry. Not a word was said of poor Benjamin, but John, Ma and Pa secretly worried about his safely out in the wilderness.

A pain stabbed Ben's side as he raced to catch the big flatboat. The pack that Mrs. Cooper had prepared for him slowed him down. He had to stay away from the water's edge so the Coopers wouldn't spot him, and the trail suddenly took a turn toward the river, where it ran so close to the water's edge that the young man could have taken one step sideways and been in the water. He searched frantically for a trail through the woods that more-or-less followed the river, but he found nothing but choke cherry, wild grape vines, and whips of willow mixed in under the big trees which made up the woods. Since there was no trail that he could follow and stay hidden, he decided to blaze his own way, jumping brambles and ducking branches as he ran. Despite his efforts to hurry, the flatboat was soon out of sight ahead of him. Ben resolved to eat a full meal, then empty his pack of things he didn't absolutely need. Then he would continue his chase at the water's edge. Travel there would be much faster. He found a shady spot below an overhanging stone ledge and settled down to enjoy Ma Cooper's dried beef and berries. From his pack, Benjamin pulled out a fist-sized head he had been carving. He was almost finished. He looked down at the face. There, staring back at him from beneath a strange military hat, were the piercing eyes of the captain. From the wispy eyebrows to the mole on his cheek, the carving looked exactly like the evil Captain Jeffries. Ben smiled. He could not do anything about the murderer until he grew older, but this carving would be his memory. He would never forget the promise he had made himself to come back to bring justice in honor of his dead father.

Peering down from the ledge above Benjamin, the Indian admired the carving, too, but for a different reason. It was the proof he needed. It was the final link in the chain that led him to endless bags of gold coins. Stepping to the edge of the ledge, he silently drew his knife and prepared to jump.

Ben heard a rock fall from above and looked up. There, screaming past him and falling into the river below, was a strange looking Indian. In the instant the Indian plummeted past his face, they looked into each other's eyes, and Ben could see the man was filled with surprise and fear. Like a glittering icicle, the native's drawn knife had flashed in the sun and chilled the young boy to the bone. Benjamin knew it was pure luck that the copper-skinned man had slipped, and he immediately wondered if the Indian would have drawn his knife on just anyone, or if there was some reason the man was particularly after *him*. Deep in his belly, he sensed the Indian was stalking him, and him alone. Ben grabbed the wooden head and jumped to his feet. Now it was doubly important that he reach the Coopers. Maybe he could catch up with them when they camped for the night.

The Coopers quietly went through the motions of preparing to eat dinner on the flatboat as it eased downriver. John couldn't get the black boy off his mind. What kind of man was this settler they had left Ben with? He had heard talk back in the river settlement about rewards being made to people who caught runaway slaves and turned them in to the law. Would this man decide to claim an easy reward? Or would he make Benjamin his slave and put the small boy to work doing man-sized chores? The more he thought, the more he worried.

His thoughts were interrupted by Traveler as she brushed past him, growling her way to the front bow bench. She braced her front feet on the back of the bench and stared toward a high, rocky ledge just down the river. She growled more fiercely and barked a ferocious warning.

In the late afternoon sun, it was difficult to see. Shading her eyes with her hand, Ma squinted and pointed toward a patch of white in the shadows high above them. As they came closer, the patch became a woman who was holding a young girl in her arms.

"Help!" the woman shouted desperately. "Up here!"

Shocked, the Coopers stared upward as Traveler continued to growl and snarl fiercely. She was obviously warning her family about whatever was up there.

"What's wrong?" Pa bellowed.

"It's my man," the woman wailed. "He's been mauled by a bear, an' he's hurt bad. I'm, afeared he's a-dying!"

As the young girl screamed and trembled, the Coopers hurried to help. While Ma rushed to the wagon to grab her homemade medicines, Pa steered the big flatboat to the bank. John jumped out to pull the boat in as close as possible and tied it, front and back, to trees. Without wasting time setting the big wooden ramp across to the shore, Pa ordered Johnny to tend Hallie, and he carried Ma across the shallow water to the bank. They rushed up through the trees and soon disappeared.

As he climbed back into the big boat, John watched his dog carefully. He didn't like the way she was acting. Pacing nervously with her hair raised from head to tail, she growled and snarled like a cornered wild dog. John reached for Prilla, his shot pouch, and powder horn. With shaking hands, he quickly loaded his long rifle and sat on the bow bench. From his spot at the front of the boat, he could keep an eye on the trail that Ma and Pa had taken. Within minutes, he saw his parents stagger back down the steep trail. He gulped when he realized their hands were raised and wild-looking men holding guns were strutting along behind them. John dropped to the deck and propped Prilla's long barrel across the flatboat's side, keeping the closest of the strange men in his sights as the group approached.

Seeing John's plan, Pa shouted to him frantically, "Don't shoot, John. Hold your fire! It's no use!"

From inside the wagon came the babbles and coos which announced that Hallie had awakened and was ready to eat. John's stomach twisted with fear for his little sister. Echoing in his ears came the sound of Smelly's voice, saying, *"There's other folks along the river that'll do you in if they take a notion."* And now the old stinker's words were about to come true.

How John wished Smelly was here with them now! He would have known just what to do. John's pa yelled again, to put the rifle down. The boy propped his treasured weapon against the tiller pole and moved away from it with his hands raised. Traveler continued her snarling and John could hear Hallie's whimpers from inside the wagon. Those whimpers would soon become full-blown complaints that the strangers could easily hear. He knew he shouldn't enter the wagon to comfort her. He would be shot before he reached the step-up. His feet froze to the deck of the boat and a cold sweat began to trickle down the middle of his back.

One of the men pulled a wide plank from the bushes and laid it across from the bank to the boat. He was a mean-looking follow, about as big around as a willow whip, and his black eyes seemed to throw out sparks of hatred, as he bared his rotten teeth in a false smile. His hair was probably brown, although John judged it to be so filthy it actually might have been just about any color, short of black. With all that dirt and grime matting it together, it was hard to tell. There were two other men brimming with firearms, and John realized they probably had so many guns so they wouldn't have to stop shooting to reload. His eyes ticked off a total of seven guns of one sort or another between them. Add the pistol tucked into the smiler's belt, and that made a total of eight shots the three men could fire off without wasting a second. John didn't like the sound of that, since there were only four Coopers to begin with. That made two chances for getting hit by a lead ball for each of them, including Hallie!

"Now git up there and be quick about it," a snaggle-toothed snake of a man said, as he prodded Ma and Pa up the plank to the boat. Noticing the man's fiery red hair, Johnny recalled tales he'd heard about the bad tempers that red-headed folks carried around with them. He never knew if those tales were true, but just then, it seemed a likely possibility. This man, who didn't think Ma and Pa were moving fast enough to suit him, looked like he might have the worst temper this side of a cornered wildcat.

John looked at his Ma and was reminded of the time the wagon almost slid backward down the mountain. Her eyes were filled with terror once again, and Johnny knew she was scared breathless. However, Pa secretly shot him a wink, as if to say, *"Don't worry, Son."*

The big red-headed man was the first to step onto the boat behind Ma and Pa, and before his foot even touched the rough wooden deck, Traveler lunged savagely for his throat. The skinny man with rotten teeth must have expected her attack, because had had pulled his big pistol out of his belt. With lightning speed, he swung his gun up and brought the handle crashing down on her head. Traveler dropped to the deck with a thud and lay, unmoving, on her side. Pa locked John in place with his eyes. Biting back screams, John watched in horror as Traveler's bright red blood began to spread across the deck from under her head. John prayed she wasn't dead and hoped for a way to help her.

The men moved quickly, snatching John's howling little sister from the wagon and dropping her roughly into Ma's arms. The third man tied Pa's and John's hands together behind their backs and ordered them to march with Ma across the plank and up the steep hill leading to the bluff where the woman had been. The climb was rough. With their hands tied behind their backs, they were unable to catch themselves when they lost their footing, and they fell on sharp rocks and thorny plants. When they finally reached the top of the bluff, they stood, bruised and bleeding from fall after fall, and they found themselves at the mouth of a cave set in a huge expanse of rock. The men prodded them roughly, ordering them to enter the yawning black hole. As they marched into the cave, John looked over his shoulder. From this high perch, there was a clear view up and down the river. Those robbers could sit in their cave like a flock of buzzards, waiting for unknowing travelers. John noticed that there was not another boat in sight, and he knew it would soon be dark. There was no chance for help from the river. What was to become of them? Smelly's words echoed through John's head again. "... *that'll do you in if they take a notion.*"

After rejecting the idea of staking out Jack and Molly for the night, the lazy men busied themselves with tying up their captive's hands and feet and propping them against a hard, damp wall of the cave. Only Hallie was left free to wander around freely. She seemed to be under the supervision of the young girl that John had seen in the arms of the screaming woman. Johnny studied the girl, estimating that she might be six or seven years old. How filthy she was! Her matted brown hair sprouted burrs and bits of dead plants, like she had slept in a patch of weeds.

Her mouth hung open and gave her the look of a child whose wits were in short supply. Her hands were dirty, with mud caked beneath her long fingernails. John looked at Ma and could see that she felt the same sickness he felt at the thought of Hallie being touched by the girl. Fortunately for Hallie, the girl was more interested in following her mother around than in tending the baby.

The woman busied herself with bringing firewood to the entrance of the cave, where a large kettle of smelly stew bubbled. John spied dirt-caked roots that the woman must have grubbed, waiting beside the iron kettle. She snarled something at the skinny man who had clubbed Traveler, apparently asking for a rabbit or squirrel for her pot. It was clear from the way the man marched back down the hill that he was headed for the boat. He was more interested in stealing than in hunting.

The Coopers had no choice. They were forced to sit against the cold, stone wall of the cave and divide their time between worrying about Hallie getting too close to the fire and fretting about what would happen next. The three men returned, carrying Prilla, Pa's rifle, and their shot and powder. They also brought Ma's salted pork and little else of consequence. The woman pounced on the pork and took it to the back of the cave, where she hung it from a jagged piece of rock that looked very much like a hook. John could feel Ma's anger at the loss of the pork that she had preserved so carefully. Hallie finally gave up her hungry howling and crawled over to John. She fell asleep with her head cushioned by his belly, and he was relieved that she was out of danger for the time being.

As darkness settled in, the robbers gathered at the big kettle, where the woman dished out a watery, meatless stew. Smacking and slurping, the outlaws ate the mess noisily and wiped their beards with greasy shirt sleeves. The Coopers were so sickened by the sight that they lost what little appetite they'd had a few short hours before. As the crickets outside announced nightfall, the men stretched out on furry bear skins near the entrance of the cave. Yawning, burping, and scratching, the filthy scoundrels soon fell asleep. With the sound of snores echoing back through the cave, the woman banked the fire under the kettle. She settled the young girl onto a bear skin pallet back near Rachel's salted pork and left the cave. After a time, she returned with a wild turkey. She must have surprised it roosting low in a tree and caught it before it could awaken enough to flap away. The woman picked up a long, thin log from the fire. Holding it like a torch, she burned the feathers off the turkey, and then tossed the charred bird into the pot. The Coopers looked at each other wide-eyed. She had not removed the head or feet or gutted the bird. What a lazy woman! Johnny's stomach knotted, and he couldn't tell if the knots came from the horrible smell of burning feathers, or if they came from the thought that he might be forced to eat that horrible stew. Maybe they wouldn't be fed at all. He nearly decided that he'd rather starve to death than eat that witch's bubbling garbage, and then he hoped he'd get a chance to make that choice.

With a long, dirty fingernail, the woman scratched her head and picked at her matted hair until she caught a bug. She threw it into the fire, where it quickly sizzled away its life juices. Finally, the woman sank to the bear skin on which the girl had fallen asleep. She roughly pushed the child aside to make room for herself, and then quickly drifted off to sleep as if she didn't have a worry in the world. One-by-one the Coopers, too, fell into troubled sleep filled with nightmares of the day's terrible events.

Benjamin made good time. The moon was up, and he could clearly see his path near the water's edge. His mouth was dry from breathing hard as he ran. His side ached from the effort of gulping, air, but he pushed himself onward. Surely the big boat would be showing up soon. He *had* to find the family and persuade them to accept him! Ben had no idea how he would win the Cooper's trust, but he knew how to use his wits. Somehow, he vowed as his feet flew along the dimly lit path, he would find a way when the time came. His sharpened senses told him his very life depended upon convincing them.

The night sounds comforted Ben. Crickets urged him on, while bullfrogs and peepers along the river set his pace with their rhythmic croaking. But now and then he surprised a raccoon or opossum at the water's edge, and its startled cries would bring on a bad case of dread. Would Traveler give him away too soon? He hoped that he could count on her friendship as he had done twice before.

Suddenly, the silhouette of the big flatboat loomed ahead. Ben was puzzled by the quiet. Traveler must be out on a nighttime hunt. Surely, Pa had fallen asleep at his watch. Ben waded through the shallow water to the boat.

"Mr. Cooper," he whispered as loudly as he dared. "Mr. Cooper, it's me, Benjamin."

The boat rocked silently in the river and he thought he heard a snuffling noise coming from the pen where Jack and Molly spent their days. Why weren't they hobbled in a nice clearing filled with juicy grass? Ben's head buzzed with other questions. His senses told him that something was wrong. Quietly, he pulled himself up onto the boat. Something wet and sticky oozed between his toes. Looking down, Benjamin saw poor Traveler lying at his feet. In the moon's light, the large pool of blood surrounding her looked as black as tar. Ben dropped to his knees beside the dog and felt her silky side. She was warm and still breathing. Afraid of what else he might find, the boy stood and turned to search the rest of the boat. The Coopers were gone. Benjamin shook his head. Those people had gotten themselves into some kind of trouble. He had learned to smell trouble, and this situation was getting mighty stinky!

As Ben looked for a cloth to use on the dog, his keen eyes picked up more clues that confirmed his conclusion. The wooden plates which Ma so carefully cleaned after each meal were dirtied by half-eaten food. Very sloppy eaters had used these trenchers. Bits of food lay on the deck of the boat. No, the Coopers had not eaten this meal. Someone else had. Was it the Indian?

Ben located a cloth and dangled it in the water. Wringing it out, he hurried to Traveler and gently cleaned her cut and swollen head. Ben wondered if the big dog would live. She had lost so much blood! How long had she been there, lying on the deck? Carefully, he lifted Traveler and struggled with her weight as he moved her to John's quilts under the wagon. If he didn't make it back to the boat before the sun came up, at least she wouldn't bake to death. Stroking Traveler's silky side for good luck, Ben tiptoed to the side of the boat, where he spotted the plank. No, it had not been the Indian. There were other people around here. He stepped across to land. As he scanned the bank, his eyes rested on what might be a path. It seemed to angle up the hill through the brush. He checked the river's muddy bank for footprints, but the trees overhead cast a deep shadow near the water's edge, and it was too dark to see clearly.

"Well," Benjamin thought, "*if the Coopers are alive, I guess I'm the only one around who can help them.*"

After taking a deep breath and crossing his fingers to the count of seven, Ben began inching his way up the path. As the brush grew thicker, he found it hard to see, and he stumbled and fell rather loudly. The boy lay quietly, straining to hear over the pounding of his heart. Either no one had heard him, or there wasn't a soul around.

Finally, after restocking his heart with courage, he picked himself up and continued his climb, using his bare feet to feel out the path. Pausing to listen, he heard something growling ahead of him. Or was it hogs? Hogs wouldn't make sound like that at night, he reasoned. From the dense forest at the top of the bluff, he stepped suddenly into a clearing. In the light of the moon, he clearly saw the entrance to a large cave. Lying helter-skelter on the ground outside the mouth of the cave was the source of the sound. Three men were sprawled across bear skins, snoring like champions. Benjamin waited for a warning bark from a dog, but there was none. He moved into the center of the clearing, ready to dash toward the river if he was discovered. Nothing but snores. Knowing he needed to get his bearings, Ben took a moment to look back toward the river. The beauty of the silver ribbon of water winding its way around a bend nearly took his breath away. He had to admit that anyone interested in robbing travelers would find this particular knob of land an ideal spot from which to spy on river traffic. The yawning cavern would even give them shelter from the weather. It was a perfect hideout.

"If those Coopers are anywhere around here, they're in that cave," he reasoned to himself, *"and I've got to help them."*

He slowly paced off the remaining distance and picked his way through the snoring guards, grinning as he reached the cave's entrance. So far, anyway, this was easy! Like a silent ghost, Ben glided into the deep shadows and stood quietly, studying the sight. A kettle of foul-smelling stew bubbled near him. From the rear of the cave came more snoring. From the sound of it, a hard-sleeping woman was back there. Ben's eyes shifted to the right. There, tied up and laid out like firewood, were the Coopers. Were they alive?

Benjamin edged his way to Hallie. She was asleep. He could see that the other Coopers were asleep, as well. The young man quietly slipped his knife from its leather sheath and got to work. Beginning with Matthew Cooper, he stealthily awoke the man and cut the ropes tying his wrists. Then he handed his knife to Matthew and searched the cave for another knife. Returning to Ma with the robber woman's butcher knife, he soon freed her, as Pa cut through John's ropes. Ma stood up stiffly and reached to pull Ben into a grateful hug. He felt her body shake with silent sobs.

After wiping her dress sleeves across her wet cheeks, Ma scooped up her sleeping baby and motioned for Ben to grab the sack of belongings the men had taken from the flatboat. Pa snagged Prilla and his own rifle, and he motioned for John to take the powder and shot. Finally, with a gleam of revenge in her eyes, Ma tiptoed to the back of the cave and rescued her salted pork. Standing proud and tall, she lifted her chin and hurried from the cave with her precious pork slung over one shoulder and her baby over the other.

Pa handed Prilla to John and motioned for him to guard the rear. Then, checking his own gun to make sure it was loaded, he led the family down the hill to the flatboat. As silently as they had moved along the path, they walked across the wide board the robbers had put down. Johnny stayed on the river bank long enough to untie both ropes from the two Sycamore trees to which the boat had been lashed, and then he sprinted across the board and landed on the deck of the boat with a muffled thud. He grabbed the board and pulled it into the boat.

"There," he thought, "*they'll have to find themselves another board. In the meantime, they're gonna get mighty wet if they try to capture and rob anyone else.*"

As quietly as the ghost of Mr. Stowe, the big boat eased away from the bank and moved down river. John stood with Prilla loaded and ready to fire, but there were no threats from the shore. He was grateful that his doubts about ever being able to shoot at a person were not tested. The boat quickly carried them out of danger, and Pa motioned for John to relax. With his guard duty over, John turned to the spot where Traveler had fallen. She was gone!

Benjamin touched John's shoulder and whispered, "She's alive. Come with me."

John followed Ben to the wagon. There, sleeping peacefully on John's quilts, lay the big brindled dog, with Ma's wet apron resting on her swollen head. John picked up Ma's bloody apron to inspect the dog's wound. "Ma will tan your hide good for using her best apron," he said, but then he smiled. "No she won't. She'll probably want to hug you and give you a big, wet kiss or something."

The boys were grinning at each other when Pa whispered hoarsely for Benjamin to join him at the tiller pole. "Young man, I can't approve of your following us when I ordered you back to where you came from," Pa began. He spat on his hands and rubbed them together. "But I have to say I'm right glad you disobeyed me. We Coopers owe you our very lives, I'm thinking. Now, I still stand tight on my first say about you joining us."

John and Ben automatically traded looks as Pa settled into thought. Finally, it was decided. "We'll keep you with us as far as Crazy Sir Edward's cave," Pa announced. "After that, you're on your own. And Son, thanks again."

Johnny smiled at Benjamin. Somehow, the brave, determined black boy had found and saved them all. Even Traveler seemed to be healing, thanks to Ben's quick doctoring. As Benjamin smiled back, John secretly crossed his fingers. He wished there was a way this mysterious boy could join their family and stay with them for good. "Let's go tend to Traveler," he said quietly to his new friend.

RIVER HAUNTS

T HE BIG FLATBOAT PICKED UP speed and, by the time the sun was
up, the Coopers had left the Cave-In-Rock robbers far behind. Ma busied
herself cleaning up the mess the thieves had made, and John and Pa taught
Benjamin the many tricks of wrestling a tiller pole. Traveler was awake from time
to time, but she wisely stayed on John's quilts under the wagon. She seemed to
know she would heal faster if she stayed put.

When Pa called for John to lash the front tiller, he was freed to stake out
a friendship with Benjamin. As the huge flatboat eased down river, the boys
pampered Traveler. Ma offered bits of meat, which they took turns feeding to
her. Johnny noticed how Benjamin's hands seemed to work on their own to seek
out ticks behind Traveler's ears, and he wondered if the black boy had owned a
dog before. Could slaves own things? John puzzled over the many questions he
was storing away for the right time. Remembering Benjamin's anger back in the
river settlement, John vowed to guard against using the word *slave*.

The time came when Traveler thrust her strong legs in front of her and
stretched from her toenails to the tip of her tail. She opened up with a yawn so
big, it curled her tongue. Benjamin and John nodded knowingly at each other. This
was a good sign. Only healthy animals stretch. As the dog scooted over to John
and laid her head across his legs, Benjamin reached automatically for his wood
carving project. From deep in his possible bag came a lump of walnut. Soon he was

frowning over his work. John gently edged Traveler's head from his lap and moved to Benjamin's side. He could see a face staring back at him from the wood. Who was this man? John's skin crawled as he felt the evil coming from those eyes. He couldn't help but feel that he had seen this man before. "Who is that?" he asked.

Startled by John's questions, Benjamin stuttered, "Well, it's just supposed to be a man. Just some man."

"What kind of hair will he have?" John asked, trying to get a clearer picture of the finished carving.

John noticed the speed of Benjamin's answer. He was pretty sure the boy was carving a real person, and he felt from the chill in his bones that he had seen this person somewhere, himself. If only he could remember!

As the day unraveled toward sunset, Benjamin and John worked together as closely as a tick and a hound. When John carried grain and hay to the stock penned up in front of the wagon, Benjamin carried them water. John was struck with how much Benjamin knew about things that he hadn't even thought about. He knew the value of snakeroot, for instance, and carried a piece with him to ward off evil. One of the most powerful ways to defend yourself against an enemy was to chew snakeroot, then spit on his shoes, according to Benjamin. John was amazed that he hadn't been told this important spell before.

The boys wove their friendship tight through the day, and John learned that his new friend preferred to be called Ben.

"What's your last name?" he asked, suddenly wishing he hadn't opened his mouth. Maybe Ben wouldn't have a last name. He wondered to himself if slaves had more than just a first name.

"Jeffries," Ben answered immediately.

Pa broke into their talk. Pointing toward the bow, he said, "Stand up there and look for a likely spot to tie up for the night."

Sounds of Ma singing to Hallie floated softly to John's ears. He noticed Ben's eyes shift to the northern bank. The side of the river was closely guarded by a sheer wall of stone that rose about one hundred feet straight up from the water's edge. Knowing they couldn't tie up on the bluff side, John turned Ben's attention to the southern bank.

"We need a place we can get ashore to hunt and build a good fire," John told Ben. "It helps if there's a solid tree or two a-standing out a ways in the water. It can't be too deep, so we can stretch our ramp across to the bank. Then we can unload our gear and lead Jack and Molly across for a night of grazing."

Together, Ben and John spied the perfect spot for the night and as they were pointing, Pa's hoarse voice pierced the air. "Well, I'll be squint-eyed, hump-backed..."

"Matthew!" Ma interrupted from the wagon, as she poked her head out to scold her husband. She turned to see what he was staring at. "Lord a'mighty!" she gasped, covering her mouth with a shaking hand.

The boys looked up the stone wall on the north side of the river and saw the reason for Ma and Pa's surprised comments. Guarding the Oyo from forty or fifty feet above the water was a gruesome, winged monster, painted and carved into the limestone wall. The size of a half-grown oxen calf, it glared down at them through angry, red eyes set into a bearded face like a man's. It's antler-like horns threatened to pierce their very souls! From below its beard began the writhing, snake-like tail of a dragon that passed around its body, over its head, and between its legs.

Ben quickly pulled a length of snakeroot out of his pocket, broke it in two, handed one piece to John, and jammed the other piece in his own mouth, chewing for all he was worth. John watched Ben closely, to be sure he chewed the snake-root correctly. This was no time to ward off an evil spirit not knowing what you were doing. He would have sworn his heart had turned to ice, but he could feel it beating so hard it just might hammer itself right out of his chest.

Clearing his throat, Pa was the first person to free himself from the monster's spell. He could see that darkness was rushing in, and this time the clouds covered the moon. If they continued down the river without light from the moon, they were sure to get snagged by a floating piece of trouble. Squinting as hard as he could through the darkness and fog, he searched farther downriver for a good place to tie up for the night. He couldn't find a single tree or even a big rock formation they could tie the boat onto. They had no choice. They either camped straight across the river from the monster, or they risked ramming their floating home into something which would sink them all.

"Boys, get ready to grab that tree," Pa shouted, pointing toward a dead Sycamore standing in the water.

"But Matthew!" Ma gasped, nodding her head toward the monster, "we can't tie up here!"

"Look downriver, Rachel," he answered quietly. "We've got no choice."

Pa steered the flatboat beside the first, big Sycamore, and John quickly hugged the trunk as it passed, passing the rope back around to Pa. In no time at all, the rear of the boat was tied securely, leaving the front pointed in the direction they were traveling. John jumped into the water and slogged toward the river's bank as Pa threw him a coil of rope from the bow. With muscles bulging, John strained to pull the boat away from the current and in toward the bank. Suddenly, Ben was in the water beside him.

"I can do this myself," John barked at his surprised young friend. "I always do this, and I don't need any help from anyone."

Ben apologized and scrambled up onto the bank to watch, thinking he had a lot to learn about this big white boy. John coaxed the boat toward him, and soon he had it tied only a few feet from the bank.

"Let down the ramp, Pa," John shouted.

Pa motioned for quiet. "Not yet, John," he whispered. "Not until we've scouted this place for Indians or varmints like the ones back there in that cave."

Motioning for Ma to stay put with Hallie, Pa grabbed Prilla and his own rifle, strung himself with shot, powder and possibles, and eased down into the water. Traveler surprised everyone by leaving her spot beneath the wagon and padding over to the side of the flatboat. Wisely, she did not try to go with John and Ben, but instead stood on the deck, guarding Ma and Hallie.

The trio of explorers smiled at each other over Traveler's improvement, and then set out to search the area. Quietly they stood, listening as Smelly had taught them, for tell-tale silence from the woods. Crows in a giant oak complained of the day's end, while three male woodpeckers called *flickers* argued from tree to tree over the love of a nearby female. From the riverbank on both sides of the boat, the bullfrogs forgot about the humans and their traveling home and returned to their evening songs.

Their listening completed, Pa motioned them into the sparse woods. Ben walked behind John as they searched carefully for signs of Indians or dangerous animals. Suddenly a dead limb cracked loudly and a deer exploded away from them and up the slight hill to their right. John and Ben caught their breaths, grinning at each other as the deer's white tail disappeared into the brush.

"I wish we could have shot it," John whispered to Ben. "We could use some good meat."

Quietly the boys began to circle toward the riverbank. Their arc would bring them back upriver from the boat. Their silent feet climbed the small rise which the frightened deer had covered a few seconds earlier. *Whoosh!* John spun around to see Ben step into a thicket and retrieve his knife. He had brought down a large rabbit. While lifting the rabbit by its ears, Ben wiped his knife on a handful of Sycamore leaves. "Good meat," he whispered, smiling proudly.

By the time the boys reached the bank, the sharp-eyed marksman had killed another rabbit with his swift, silent knife. He presented Ma with the fresh rabbit meat and two pelts ready for scraping and stretching, suggesting they use the furry pelts as foot-warmers for Hallie when winter set in.

Pa returned with good news. There was no sign of Indians, and he had found a perfect stand of cool, juicy grass and wild clover for Jack and Molly. John and Pa stretched the wide, strong ramp across to solid ground at the water's edge. They coaxed the lumbering oxen across the plank, then down the bank into water up to their bellies. Their legs and feet were soothed by the cool current as they drank away a day's thirst. Knowing what usually came next, the oxen happily followed the Cooper men to the clearing. Pa pounded two iron stakes into the ground near the center of the clearing. To each stake he attached one end of a long rope. The other end of each rope was tied to a clamp that encircled each of the oxen's' left hind legs. Now they were watered and hobbled for the night in a field of delicious grass. They could eat to their hearts' content, roll around in the sweet smell of wild clover and grass, and sleep. Molly began to gather in bunches of clover with her long, rough tongue. Tearing off the grass easily, she raised her head and settled down to some serious chewing. Jack spied a patch of grassless, dried ground. Loosening the hard earth with his giant hooves, he eased himself into the brown powder and rolled happily, creating a cloud of dust all around him. Satisfied that he was well-powdered, he sought out a good stand of grass and began to eat. Flies wouldn't bother him now. They hated to go near that brown, powdery earth now embedded in Jack's hide. John knew that, before night fell, Molly would also take advantage of the "dust bowl."

Pa cut new bedding for the stock, using a long, sharp, quarter-moon-shaped knife attached to a long, curvy handle. Stepping and swinging, stepping and swinging, he had soon cut enough straw-like weeds to cover the stock pen. He set aside his sickle and helped John gather the fresh bedding.

By the time Pa and John returned to the big flatboat, Ma's kettle was bubbling up mouth-watering aromas. Ben had mucked out the stock pen and was tending Hallie, while Ma washed out diapers and clothing at the river's edge. Rachel Cooper had found a perfect bowl hollowed out in the smooth, stone riverbed. Into this bowl she stuffed clothing, one piece at a time. She rubbed each piece with rendering soap, and then returned it to the bowl. Handling her washing stick like a war club, she beat the linsey-woolsey garments until no self-respecting stain or smell would be caught dead hanging around. As she squeezed, poked and beat the clothing, cloudy white water churned up bubbles from the bowl's depths.

Pa watched Ma proudly. "Boys, don't you ever cross this here woman if you know what's good for you," he said through a made-up frown. "She's liable to take after you with her wash stick and beat you into white foam." Ben laughed at the thought of this gentle woman doing such a thing, and Pa winked at him. "You laugh, Benjamin, but I wager she could even turn *your* skin into white foam!" he chuckled.

John felt himself blush deeply and he watched Ben to see if Pa had offended him with his joke. He was surprised to see Ben laughing heartily. Either jokes about the color of his skin didn't bother him, or he was a good actor, he thought to himself. Still and all, he felt fluttery inside with worry that Ben's feelings might have been hurt.

Pa pulled a chunk of Ma's soap from the supply box. Taking Hallie from Ben's arms and stripping himself to the skin, he waded into the river and began to bellow a hymn, as he scrubbed himself and Hallie. John looked at Ben and wrinkled his nose, knowing what would come next. "Ma insists we bathe at least every two weeks," he muttered. "Most people think the change of seasons is often enough, or even once a month, if they're real picky, but not my ma. If she had her way, we'd be baptizing ourselves every whip-stitch."

"Your ma's like my master's wife was before she died," Ben said. "I can remember how she used to send me to the creek with enough soap to choke a whale. I always wondered if she was trying to find out if my black would wash off." He rolled his eyes and laughed at his own joke.

John laughed along with his new friend to cover his own embarrassment. A short time ago, he had noticed the palms of Ben's hands and had wondered the same thing. Maybe the black wore off a person's skin, instead. Or, maybe that's just the way black people's hands were. John sneaked a peek at his own hands, which were turning a golden brown from being in the sun, now that they were traveling by river. Except for developing a few tough calluses from the tiller pole, his palms had remained the same color. He shrugged his shoulders and reached for a chunk of soap, hoping that they might become such good friends that they could talk about their differences without either one of them being hurt or embarrassed.

When Ben and John hit the water, Traveler could stand being an invalid no longer. The boys squinted through soap-stung eyes to find her swimming beside them. Happy for an excuse to stop scrubbing themselves, they gently washed the dog's bloody wounds. When they returned, their just-washed clothing was drying on bushes, and neatly folded stacks of fresh, clean duds awaited them. Without a pause, Ma had turned from laundress to cook. She was busy dishing up rabbit stew. The Coopers and their guest drew close to the campfire and said their thanksgivings, along with a few well-worded requests for an uneventful night, while the inky sky crept in close.

"It's as dark as the inside of an ox," Pa commented as he chewed. Dark clouds had rolled in, completely covering the moon and stars.

"It's just as well," Ma said, "because I allow as how I don't care to see that monster across the water." She poked at the campfire, trying to stir up brighter flames to stand guard against the velvety, black curtain surrounding them.

"Just the same, don't you feel like it's still there, a-staring at us?" asked John. He noticed he was whispering, but he couldn't seem to make his voice louder. "I've felt all evening like we're being watched."

Ben remembered the strange Indian who had fallen past him into the river. "Maybe we *are* being watched," he said quietly.

Ma removed a bit of meat she had been chewing for Hallie and placed it in the baby's mouth. "Matthew, do you reckon that monster is the demon that Smelly mentioned?"

Smelly's voice echoed in John's mind, "*It was the devil did it!*"

"Smelly?" Ben interrupted. "Who is Smelly?"

The fire had died to a flicker by the time the Coopers had finished sharing their memories of old Smelly Jack. Without meaning to, each person had settled into quiet memories. The Coopers thought of their favorite old long hunter, while

Ben pined for another old gentleman. His old master had been like a grandfather and the Archangel Michael, all wrapped up inside one skin. Master Jeffries had pulled him in from his mother's side one day, where he had played while she picked squash.

"Joshua is getting old," Master Jeffries had said, "and I need to train someone to take his place."

Being only five years old at the time, Ben hadn't understood he was too young to train. Before that day, he had seen his master often. When the old man rode his fine horse through the fields or stopping at the slave quarters to pay his respects to Old Mary, the master usually had a wink and a nod for Benjamin. He always had a kind word for Ben's mother when she passed his office on her way to her lessons up on the third floor. Like everyone who worked on the Jeffries plantation, Ben's mother could read, write, and work with numbers. Master and Mistress Jeffries had seen to their education, just as they had seen to teaching them about the world that lay outside the boundaries of the Jeffries land. Now, as he thought about it, Benjamin understood why. They all needed to be as prepared as possible for the day when they would take their secret earnings and live in the world as freed blacks.

He hadn't understood this any more than he had understood why the kindly old couple had taken an interest in his ability to grasp his own mother's lessons so quickly. By the time Ben left his mother's two-room cabin to move into his own bedroom in the plantation house, it seemed a very natural step for him. After all, he already spent several hours each day in that third floor classroom. To live in the big house was much more convenient, and Mistress Jeffries made sure that Ben and his mother ate a hearty breakfast together in Osha's big kitchen before they began each day. Ben was always free to visit his mother, and he occasionally slept in his old bed back in her cabin. Raised in this place where his black friends and family were treated with respect, Benjamin took a great deal for granted. In their desire to set their little part of the world straight, the Jeffries had failed to teach Ben the most important lesson he needed to survive. He needed to know how other slaves were treated. If he knew how to behave, he could avoid calling attention to himself.

As Ben sat staring into the embers of the campfire, he realized that old Master Jeffries hadn't needed a houseboy that day so many years ago. With no living relative but a wife and a faraway brother, Master Jeffries was lonesome for family comfort. What he had needed was a son, and he had chosen Ben. But the old man that Ben had mistakenly called *Master* was dead now. Ben knew the secret of his terrible death and could do nothing about bringing justice. To save his own life, he must disappear into the wilderness, but he would return as soon as he could safely do so, and he would keep those promises he had made to Charles Jeffries. Ben fingered the beautiful knife that his old adoptive father had given him so many years ago. The master had told him that he must one day carve out a life for himself. Now, sooner than he expected, he needed to do just that.

The thoughts of the homesick travelers were interrupted by a loud screech, as a large owl appeared from out of the deepest darkness, passing just over their heads. Ben and John each clearly saw its huge, yellow eyes staring at them as it approached the fire.

"Listen!" Pa whispered hoarsely, as the owl disappeared into the darkness beyond the fire's light. "The crickets and frogs have gone quiet!" Had the owl's call caused their songs to still? After all, those small critters were usually at the top of most owls' list of druthers.

But Smelly Jack had warned that the sudden silence of woodland critters meant danger was lurking nearby. Pa and John reached for their rifles and checked them. They were ready. Maybe the owl had caused them to go silent, but Johnny didn't really think so. Owls might hunt up a frog or two, but they would not bother themselves with measly little crickets.

"Good old Prilla," John whispered to his flintlock rifle, as beads of sweat popped out on his face. From the fringe of the woods came a blood-freezing scream. John felt his whole body lock up with fear.

"It's a panther," whispered Ben, grabbing his knife.

"Rachel, throw those branches on the fire," ordered Pa, snatching up Hallie and turning her over to Ben.

The big cat's scream had awakened and startled Hallie, and she was crying. Ben stuffed his knife in its holder and rocked the baby gently, calming her with whispered promises. It seemed strange to him that Matthew Cooper had reversed Rachel's role with his own. Pa had given orders to Ma and had given the baby to him. Ben guessed Matthew truly was uncomfortable with the whole idea of slavery, and his admiration for the man multiplied.

"Matthew! Jack and Molly are out there with the wildcat," Ma gasped. "We've got to get them to safety!"

Pa had already thought of the oxen and was preparing a torch as he barked orders to his family. "Ben, help Ma and Hallie onto the boat. Do you know how to shoot a rifle?"

"No, Sir," came Ben's quick answer.

"Then John, you keep Prilla and guard the boat. Let nothing up the ramp but the oxen, Ben and me. Then get ready to pull that ramp *fast!*" He lifted the lighted torch and wind-milled it, whipping the flame to a frenzy of light. Then he set out for the clearing, saying, "Ben, you stick to me like a burr."

Leaving the kettle to boil away their leftovers, John, Ma, and Hallie made tracks for the boat. When John reached the top of the plank, he turned in time to see Pa's torch disappear into the woods.

Once again, the cougar screamed. Pa and Ben stumbled over roots, rocks, and fallen limbs as they ran toward the stranded oxen. It seemed to take them forever to reach the clearing, and their torch was dimming. Pa swung it in a circle to rekindle its dying flame.

"Ben, we've got to work fast," urged Pa. "This torch is a-dying."

They had just reached the edge of the clearing when the huge cat attacked. It must have stalked the pair from behind, for it hit Pa's back with such force that both the torch and rifle went flying.

"Ben! Ben!" Pa screamed, as the huge cat snarled, raking him with its claws. "The gun!"

Ben knew better than to fumble in near darkness for a gun he could not shoot. Automatically, he reached for his knife and without thinking he jumped onto the warm, silken mass of rippling muscle. The cat released Pa and turned to attack Ben. The frightened boy jerked his head away from the snarling cat's teeth as he felt its warm breath brush past his shoulder. The big cougar's claws laid open skin on Ben's left arm and the young man felt his own blood quickly soak his shirt as he struggled with the determined cat.

As Pa wriggled from beneath the cat and stumbled to his rifle, Ben shoved upward with his sharp knife. The cat jerked and howled in anger but returned quickly to his attack. Again, Ben plunged his knife into the animal. Again, the big cat moved and screeched in angry frenzy. But then Old Jack joined the fight! Ben fell to the ground and lay still. In the flickering light of Pa's torch, he saw the huge ox toss the wildcat into the air with a butt of his massive head. The cat landed with a thud, but Jack was not finished. He lowered his huge head and ground the carcass of the dead attacker into the dirt, finishing off the job with his massive hooves. Finally, the brave ox stood and bellowed his victory song to all who would hear. When Jack moved forward, Ben could see that Jack had ripped his iron stake right out of the ground to get to the wildcat.

"Mister Cooper?"

"Yes, Ben," Pa grunted. "You saved our lives." He struggled to where Ben sat. "Are you hurt bad?" he asked.

"No, Sir, I don't think so. At least I don't feel hurt too badly."

Not to be left out, Molly pulled up her stake and joined Jack. The two oxen snuffed and snorted, blowing dust into clouds as they examined the scene of the struggle. Finally, the torch flickered away the last of its light, and Ben felt a wet, leathery nose nuzzle him in the darkness.

Slowly, Matthew and Ben felt their way along the ropes to the useless hobbles and removed them from the oxen's hind legs. Gathering in rope, they worked their way back to the dangling iron stakes. After locating the knife and rifle, they led the lumbering animals back to the boat.

"Matthew?" Ma's worried voice called as they neared the light of the campfire. "Is that you? Are you hurt? Where's Ben? Where's Ben?"

Pa's calm voice answered from the darkness. "Now, quieten down, Rachel. Ben's here. We're a-coming with Jack and Molly. Be at peace, Woman!"

The light of a burning, sap-laden pine knot gave them all a chance to see their injuries. Pa's back was striped with bloody claw marks and his shoulder had a rip from one of the cougar's long teeth. Ben's left arm was badly torn by the animal's claws, and he had a crease on the side of his face and head where the creature had tried to bite him. Ma went to work with a wild alum salve to stop the bleeding. An oatmeal poultice soon took away the pain and swelling.

"Matthew, I need to sew that rip in your shoulder," she said firmly.

"I reckoned you would want to use your needle," Pa answered, "so go ahead and do it."

Ma and John stood watch through the rest of the night while the others slept. By sunrise, Pa and Ben were ready to take over some of the lighter chores, as they prepared to leave. John's new friend helped him clean the boiled-out kettle, while Pa went to fetch the big cat's body. He returned empty-handed, with word that the night animals had already gotten to it. The weary travelers broke their fast with dried beef and leftover biscuits, and then they set out down river.

In the shade of the wagon, John quickly dropped off to an exhausted sleep. Inside the wagon, Ma slept away cares and worries of the night's demons. Ben and Traveler tended Hallie while Pa guided the boat downstream. They were all happy to be away from the monster on the rock and its evil spirit.

After several hours of sleep, John roused himself and stepped to the side of the boat. Stretching and yawning, he stared through sleep-blurred eyes toward the far bank.

"Hullo!"

John looked down into a pair of blue eyes set in a round, hairless head which popped out of the water.

"Hullo, again!" the stranger said. "I say, may I board?" His round, bald head bobbed along in the green water like a float on a fishing line, and John wondered how this strange creature could keep up with their boat so well.

"Pa!" John called. "There's a man down in the water who talks strange. He's a-wanting to climb up onto our boat." He turned back to study the man's face. "What's your name and what's your business?" he asked in his deepest possible voice.

"I am Sir Edward Goodwin, and my business is caring for your cherished possessions," answered the man with a thick British accent. John remembered all too well the Cave-In-Rock gang and was not eager to be waylaid again. He scowled down at the man, hoping to intimidate him.

"That would be Crazy Sir Edward," laughed Pa. "Help him up, Johnny."

With a look that doubted the wisdom of his father's decision, the young man helped the stranger onto the boat. Ma popped her head out of the wagon. There, dripping onto the deck, stood the strangest person she had yet encountered. The man had managed to bring with him a soggy, beaver top-hat, which he swept through the air as he made a deep bow. Besides the hat, which he placed on his bald head, he wore nothing but a short, bearskin skirt. Grinning through a stubble of whiskers, the round little man stood about five feet tall. He didn't seem at all concerned about the water dribbling down his face from inside the waterlogged hat. Once again, he bowed low.

"Sir Edward Goodwin at your service, Madam," he announced.

Ma lifted her apron to fan her face. She looked at Pa, trying not to frown. Was this the man Smelly had mentioned? Was she supposed to stay in a cave with this man, while Pa marched off into the unknown? Ben and John traded looks. This man was crazy, all right. It was hard not to laugh when they looked at him, and yet Pa took the man seriously. After inviting the strange gentleman to the back tiller pole, Pa followed his directions carefully, and soon they were tied up at the base of a path. The trail cut straight up to the mouth of a cave. On the bird-spattered stone over the cave's entrance was painted, **Crazy Sir Edward's** in bold, black letters.

With a nod from Pa, Johnny hurried through his job of pulling the boat toward the bank and knotting the big ropes around two handy trees. Ben and John questioned the wisdom of Pa's orders to stretch the ramp across to the riverbank, but they obeyed him, keeping their doubts confined to the looks they gave each other when Pa wasn't looking.

"Pay no mind to what I do next," whispered Crazy from the side of his mouth, "and just walk into the cave."

Suddenly Crazy's arms shot out toward a Sycamore tree near the river's edge. He ran down the plank, grinning like a kitten in the milk house. "Friend!" Crazy shouted, hugging and kissing the tree. "Have you missed me? What's that?" Crazy snuggled his ear up tight against the trunk and rolled his eyes upward. "You did?" he questioned loudly. He began to laugh hysterically, slapping his leg and dancing a silly little step. Then he hugged the Sycamore once more, laughing through tears as he wished it goodbye. Crazy moved on to greet a birch tree, and his guests studied each other quietly.

"Walk into the cave now," said Pa. Ma's eyebrows shot up in surprise, and she worked so hard at keeping her thoughts to herself that her face turned nearly purple.

With Ben bringing up the rear, the Coopers entered the big, dark cavern. Ma squinted, adjusting her eyes to the darkness. There, about fifteen feet from her, stood an elegantly dressed woman, who held a whale-oil lamp near her face and smiled gently.

"Won't you please step inside and make yourselves comfortable?" she invited. Her speech had a beautiful, foreign-sounding lilt. "We are most happy to receive you into our home. I am Lady Eleanor Goodwin."

Ma tried not to stare at the lady's lovely gown. Surely it was made of silk or some such fine fabric. With bits of lace here and there, the deep green dress was the most beautiful garment she had ever seen. When Crazy's rants and bellows broke the silence, Lady Goodwin smiled and said comfortingly, "Please do not let my husband's wild actions disturb you. He discovered some time ago that the Indians treat addlepated people with deep respect. He hopes to convince them that he is quite mad. We live safely here, regardless of the moods of the natives. Edward will join us shortly."

The woman gently took Ma by the arm and led her into the second room of the cave, and the men followed quietly, hoping not to be noticed by the fine lady in green. As Lady Goodwin conducted a tour of the rooms naturally formed inside the ancient cave, her visitors gawked at the collection of finery. There in the large, cool cavern, stood furniture fit for a king and queen. Gleaming brass and crystal lanterns glowed here and there. Every man, woman and child in Stowe's Fork could have been seated in those chairs, with several to spare.

"Won't you make yourselves comfortable while I fetch some tea?" asked the regal woman. "Perhaps I can find a biscuit for your beautiful daughter."

As the stunned travelers seated themselves in ornate chairs, a beautiful tall case clock began to chime the hours.

"How pretty!" Ma said, listening to the musical tones made by the old clock. Within seconds, several clocks in a third room added their chimes to the first. Ben and John stared toward the room open-mouthed. What seemed like a hundred clocks were making enough noise to curl the bark off a gum log.

"Please forgive us," Lady Goodwin offered. "We are saving those clocks for travelers. Sir Edward insists that they must be kept running for their good. One gets accustomed to the noise after a day or two."

"I like the clocks," Ben blurted with a big smile. "They remind me a little of…well, excuse me. I should not have spoken out of turn." He jumped from his chair and moved quickly to a spot near the wall, reminding himself that he must act like the Coopers' slave. To do otherwise might bring on questions that would force him to reveal his identity. Hoping that Pa had forgotten his plans to leave him behind with Crazy Sir Edward, Ben slipped his left hand into his pocket and squeezed his snakeroot.

The clocks had their say, and the sudden silence was interrupted by insane-sounding laughter, as Crazy Sir Edward seemed to wander into the large entrance of the cave. John noticed Ma's back stiffen, and he knew that she was bracing herself to endure the man's frightening behavior.

"Please excuse me while I remove my costume," Sir Edward said with a bow.

Within a few minutes, a new man appeared from a side room of the huge cave. Dressed in a white shirt, velvet jacket and dress pants, he looked quite distinguished. He clicked together the heels of his shiny black boots and bowed deeply, offering Ma a dazzling smile. She had to admit to herself that, except for the horrible stubble decorating his face like dandelion fuzz, he was really quite a handsome and distinguished-looking fellow.

"Please allow me to properly introduce myself. I am Sir Edward Goodwin lately of England and loyal liege of good King George, and I am pleased to meet you all," he said politely. "Have you fared well on your journey? We are eager to hear about your travels."

As Pa and Sir Edward discussed business, Lady Goodwin led the others through the cave, showing them five large rooms. Each room contained treasures left behind by people moving on to find land. Sir and Lady Goodwin lived quite well, she explained, using the possessions of others as well as their own.

"When are the people coming back for their things?" John asked innocently.

The elegant lady sighed and studied her feet. "Many will never return, John," she said sadly. "It has been more than three years since some of our people have left. It seems they may have met with foul play." She straightened her shoulders and smiled. "We can always hope that one day they will return. For that reason, we keep every item entrusted to us."

For the next three days, Ma and Lady Eleanor sorted and stored most of the Coopers' possessions. John, Ben and Traveler scouted the countryside and supplied Lady Eleanor's kettles and spits with game of all sorts. Pa questioned Sir Edward about the land to the north and west. He learned that it would be faster to strike out through the wilderness and head northwest than it would be to follow the Oyo River any farther south. There were animal migration trails which cut northwest through the forest, easing the journey most of the way to the Mississippi River. Traveling along these paths, Sir Edward explained, they would encounter huge bluffs and deep ravines, as well as dense forest. Pa hated the thought of leaving behind the easy days on the river, but he needed to buy all the time he could. It was decided. He and John would cut northwest through the wilderness to the "Big Muddy." Pa eagerly asked about the land west of the mighty river, because he was convinced in his heart that it would be much easier to neighbor with Indians there, who had never known the land-grabbing nature of white folk.

"I must warn you of the danger there," Sir Edward said with a frown after listening intently to Pa's theories. "There are tribes of savages that blow with the wind. One can never predict when they will attack."

"What tribes are they?" Pa wondered aloud. John noticed his father's deep blush, a sure sign that he disagreed with his host's description of the natives.

"They are the Quapaw, the Sauk and the Fox," answered Goodwin. "Do not trust them. They cannot be tamed. There are many displaced Shawnee hereabouts, as well, since all the massacres among them and the militia trying to take away their lands."

John could tell by the set of Pa's jaw that he was gritting his teeth to keep from expressing his anger. When Pa ground those big, white teeth of his, there was no changing his mind, and John knew for a fact that his father had made up his mind that there was no such thing as a savage or a group of people *needing to be tamed*. And when he thought about it, he agreed with his pa. Who were white folks to decide if a group of people was less civilized than they? Maybe it was like Pa had said. Maybe Indians were just different, and it was a matter of learning about each other's lives. He took a deep breath and let it out slowly, hoping that those Indians knew what they were up against. Matthew Cooper was a keen-eyed, leather-belted giant so stubborn he could back a bull off a bridge, and come to think of it, John had to admit he was proud of his pa. Well, most of the time, anyway. Yes, Sir, those Indians had better be at least as friendly as the Coopers, or they'd better watch out, cause his pa would soon see to their friendship needs right quick!

Ben sat on a ledge above the cave entrance. His carving of Captain Jeffries was almost finished. All day Ben had felt like a June bug was crawling up his leg. He wasn't ever one to accept the superstitious beliefs of old Osha, but why take any chances? He could almost hear her scolding and warning everyone about the signs. Whether Ben was a believer or not, he could still clearly see that there were signs aplenty! First, there was the falling star he'd watched last night. Osha would have said a falling star meant death was coming. Then John whistled in the cave. Ben shook his head at the thought of such irresponsible behavior. Why did John have to go and whistle in there? A believer would say that whistling inside the house invites the devil in, and Ben allowed as how a cave wasn't much different from a house; especially a cave filled with such finery. Ben reckoned the Coopers had their hands full with Crazy Sir Edward. Why invite the devil, too? They might think old Goodwin was right in the head, but Ben knew differently.

Sometimes the strange little man would laugh and mumble for no reason *inside* the cave where the Indians couldn't possibly see him. No, the moon had gotten to Crazy, and Ben didn't trust the old coot. Matthew Cooper had said nothing of his plan to leave Ben with Goodwin. Was it possible that he had changed his mind? The young black boy wished the big man would just speak up about it and get the wondering over with. Well, John and his pa were leaving tomorrow. Ben had only one more day of waiting, but he suddenly wished it were a month.

With a few well-placed cuts, Ben finished his carving. He was thinking so deeply that he didn't notice his accomplishment any more than he noticed the Indian assassin spying on him. The evil man had caught up with Ben and had been watching him for more than a day. From his hiding place in the shadow of a huge Maple tree upriver, the greedy, would-be murderer curbed his impatience, as darkness sifted down. He knew Ben would be sleeping inside the cave. This was his chance. Tonight, he would kill the black boy.

After a meal of venison pie, the family enjoyed their last evening together in Crazy's cave. They heard tales of England and its finery that made John's head spin. He was glad to be a wilderness boy, because he would never know how to act in England. The oxen were moved to a new patch of grass for the night, and it was time for sleep. John thought about Ben's choice of sleeping quarters and scratched his head. From the very first night, his new friend chose to sleep in the room filled with those noisy clocks. John didn't understand that the sound of clocks was comforting to Ben, because they reminded him of the faithful tall-case clock back in his Virginia home that had announced the passage of time every fifteen minutes, whether day or night, for as long as he could remember. These clocks soothed him with memories of the nights he would lie in his own bed, in his own bedroom, and feel safe, secure, and loved. Mostly loved. When John questioned him about his choice, he had simply said the clocks gave him lucky dreams.

Ben rolled up inside a quilt and burrowed down in his sleeping pallet. Tomorrow he would hear Matthew Cooper's decision. What with all the bad signs recently, Osha would have had a fit by now, he thought with a tinge of fear in his heart. He certainly could use a lucky dream tonight. In the dim, flickering light of a whale oil lamp hanging on a far wall, he stared hard at his carving, studying its lines and wondering if any additional touches might render Captain Jeffries more recognizable. It had to be such a good carving that there would be no doubt in anyone's mind that it was the head of Captain Jeffries. After forming a plan for two final lines to be added around the captain's eyes, he carefully placed the carving beside his pallet on the cool, stone floor of the cave and closed his eyes.

Traveler paced nervously at the entrance to the cave. Pa watched her closely. "What is it, Girl?" he asked her quietly, rubbing her silky ear. "Are you nervous about the trip?" Traveler shook herself and sniffed the air. "Don't worry, Traveler. We won't leave you behind. John and I need you."

Pa reached down with his other huge hand and continued to rub both the dog's ears, and then he scratched her neck. In a way, he wished tomorrow wouldn't come. He hated to leave Ma and Hallie. He even wished he hadn't told Ben he'd be staying with Crazy. He liked that young man. Ben seemed honest and very smart, but why did he get the feeling that Ben was lying about his freedom? He supposed he really had no idea what a slave felt. How could he? What would it be like to be owned by another person; a person who controlled everything about your life? Pa had never liked the idea of slaving, even if it was the law of the land. Well, he thought as he turned toward the room where Rachel slept, maybe someday he would meet up with Benjamin when he was a full-grown man, and he could ask him. For now, though, maybe the young man had his own, good reasons for hiding the truth. Pa went to bed. Traveler left her sentry post at the entrance of the cave and trotted off to the back room where John and Hallie slept. She belly-crawled along John's quilt and wedged her head under his arm. Soon she, too, was asleep.

When the moon was high, the crickets outside the cave grew silent. In time, a dark figure edged around the rocky entrance into the shadows of the first room of the cave. His mouth dropped open as he stared at the strange surroundings. In what should have been darkened corners, large, golden-colored lamps burned low. The Indian's shadow danced on the rocky walls as the flames sputtered and flickered. He drew his knife and stood silently, listening to the sounds of sleep coming from other rooms. Moving quietly to investigate the first room to his right, he found a white-skinned man and his woman sleeping.

The slippery Indian glided silently to the next room. He was in luck. There in the back of the room, surrounded by ticking boxes, was the black boy. The Indian looked around him in the flickering light. He must first locate the carving. There might not be enough time to find it after he killed the boy.

As he moved closer to his target, he spied the wooden head beside the sleeping young man. The last requirement the captain had given him was met. Even in the poor light, the Indian could tell this boy was the one he was after. His carving looked exactly like the man who had promised him piles of gold and riches beyond his wildest dreams.

Quietly, the Indian clutched the wooden sculpture and raised his knife high. Suddenly the old, tall case clock in the main room of the cave chimed. Midnight. All the clocks surrounding Ben joined in, filling the small room of the cave with their noise.

"Aargh!" the Indian screamed in fear. "I-e-e-e!" These strange, ticking boxes were screaming at him, and the noise was bouncing off the stone walls, rattling every bone in his frightened body! Ben awoke to see the Indian crashing into clocks and furniture as he tried to find his way out. Pa heard the screams and bolted from his bed. He and the Indian collided as the frightened savage hurtled into the main room, wild-eyed with panic. Traveler leapt through the air and struck at the assassin's chest, knocking him over. Ben's carving dropped to the packed dirt floor of the main room of the cave and rolled several feet, skidding to a stop against the tall wooden leg of a fancy chair. At the same time, five shiny gold coins fell from the invader's pouch and rolled noisily to a stop in a dark corner. The Indian fumbled with his knife as both Pa and Traveler closed in for a final attack. Before the clocks finished their midnight announcements, the frightened, would-be killer had jumped up, knocked over several chairs, and had run out of the cave screaming in terror.

"Well, Ben, I think it's time you told us the whole of this here matter," demanded Pa when the cave was straightened up and everyone gathered in the main room. "It's plain to me that Indian was after you alone; you and that carving of yours." Ben stood silently, studying his toes.

Pa continued his questions. "Have you ever seen that Indian before?"

"Yes, Sir," answered Ben soberly. He told of his attacker's accident that day upriver.

The gold coins caught Ma's eye as they glittered in the flickering light of Sir Edward's lanterns. Curious, she wandered toward the corner and pointed, gasping, "Just look at those gold pieces!" Rachel hurried to scoop them up.

"No man out to murder someone would come across those coins honestly," insisted Pa. "Do you know anything about them, Ben? What did he want? What is important about that carving?" He pointed toward Ben's masterpiece, still wedged up against the chair leg. "Let me see that."

John picked up the carving, wiped smudges of dirt off the wooden man's fancy hat, and he handed it to Pa. Matthew Coopers eyes opened widely as he nearly shouted to the group, "It's that soldier fella from Lanier's Inn! I'd know those beady eyes anywhere. Remember, John? We sat across the table from him. What does that devil have to do with you, Benjamin?"

It was Ben's turn to open his eyes widely as pieces of the puzzle began to fall into place. Now he knew without a doubt that Captain Jeffries had sent the Indian to kill him! Ben shuddered like a spider had just crawled up the middle of his back.

"Tell us, Son," urged Lady Eleanor softly as she drew near to comfort him.

Ben could keep his secret no longer. He was beginning to like these Coopers a great deal, and he needed their help. They seemed to be his best chance to stay alive. "That Indian was sent by Captain Jeffries to kill me," he blurted. "Captain Jeffries murdered my ... my master. I saw him do it, but I couldn't stop him. Then the captain saw me, and I had to run. He came after me with my own knife!" Quick as that, Ben had decided to keep secret the fact that he had been adopted;

that he and every black living on the Jeffries plantation were legally free blacks. He reasoned that his story was nearly unbelievable as it was.

The group turned as quiet as an empty church and listened carefully, as Ben relived that horrible day. "Master Jeffries' horse, Old Buck, got spooked by a bunch of quails hiding in the tall grass near the river. Old Buck's as steady as a horse can get, and Master Jeffries can sit a horse better than anyone in Virginia, but those quails popped right up under Buck's nose, and he jumped and kicked like a nest of hornets was stuck to his belly. My master fell off and a big stone sticking up out of the ground hit him right between his shoulders. All of a sudden, he couldn't move. He was paralyzed."

Ben's eyes overflowed with tears, as he continued his story. His shocked listeners stared into the shadowy recesses of the cave, as his words painted dreadful, flickering images like ancient pictographs on the cave walls.

"We took him up to the big house and Osha sent for Doc Graves. Osha's the cook and pretty much runs our household since my master's wife died. It didn't take Doc long to figure out that the master's back was broken, because he couldn't use his arms, and he could hardly even breathe, but he could still whisper and smile. Doc told us to put him to bed and keep him warm and clean. We needed to feed him and be sure he got enough water to drink."

Ben dropped his head and stared at his toes, trying to swallow the lump in his throat so he could continue. Lady Eleanor's warm hand dropped automatically to his back and softly rubbed little circles on his boney shoulder blade, giving him a sharp reminder of how much he missed his mother.

"Doc Graves and Master Jeffries were good old friends. They grew up together," Ben explained. "When Doc sent us all out of the room and pulled up a chair to sit next to Master Jeffries, I sneaked a look back over my shoulder, and I saw Doc pick up my master's hand and hold it like he was protecting a baby bird. I knew then, when they looked at each other right in the eyes, that Master Jeffries would be dead before long, no matter *what* he and Doc Graves told us.

"Each day he had a little more trouble, but he could still whisper, and he had a lot of things he wanted me to hear, so I spent more time with him every day just keeping him company and promising him I'd do everything he asked of me. We both knew he was talking about things he wanted me to do after he died, but we kept acting like he'd be fine in a day or two. It finally got to the point that I was with him every hour of the day and night."

Ben rubbed his neck and took a deep breath. "One day he woke up and told me he felt cold as death. He said to go to the press and find a quilt to cover him up. While I was digging through a stack of coverlets, I heard someone coming up the back stairs. I figured it was Osha coming up from the kitchen to doctor Master Jeffries. She likes her own cooking too much, and she's heavier than anyone on the place. She's the only one the third step on the back stairs will squeak for. Well, that third step didn't squeak. There are only two other people besides Osha and me that use that back staircase, and I knew neither of the other two should be bothering the master. I found the quilt and hurried back to shoo away whoever it was.

"When I got to the bedroom door, there was a strange man holding my master's pillow over his face!" He pointed to the carving of Captain Jeffries in Pa's hand. "It was that man there, and he was smothering my master! I couldn't move for a second, and that was all it took. That stranger put the pillow back behind Master's head like he had all the time in the world, and then he picked up his hat. I dropped the quilt and ran to stop him, but he grabbed my knife off the table and cut my hand. I ran for the door and pulled the quilt out from under him when he came at me. When he fell down, it gave me just enough time to scoot down the stairs and hide in Osha's kettle bin."

Ben caught his breath and continued. "He sneaked away and then rode back in on his big, gray horse later to say he was the Master's brother, come back after many years to visit him. 'Said he'd been traveling long and hard since he had a dream that his brother needed help. He put on a big show about grieving, but even Osha knew the truth by that time."

"Were you in the kettle bin all that time?" Ma asked.

"No, Ma'am, Osha moved me to the root cellar. I was hiding in a potato bin. The captain made a show of taking an inventory so he could look for me down there, but I'd buried myself pretty well, and he couldn't find me. I think he finally decided I'd gotten clean away, but he had guards posted outside the house and even at the home of my master's attorney. He wasn't taking any chances." He rubbed at his face like he was trying to erase all the horrible sights, and then he finished his tale. "Old Osha had been telling me I should head south and then get myself into the western wilderness, but I didn't want to go. I wanted to get the law after Captain Jeffries. I finally had to give up when I saw what a powerful man the captain was. He had his look-outs posted everywhere, I heard him order two of them to kill me and bring him my cut hand, just so he would know I was truly dead." Ben's eyes filled with fresh, angry tears as he thought about his kindly adoptive father and the home he'd so quickly left; a home that now belonged to him!

Ma Cooper wrapped her arms around Ben and tried to hug away his grief. She whispered to him, trying to comfort him. "It's over now, Ben. You don't need to tell us more. It hurts too much to remember. How horrible to watch a man you loved being killed by his own brother!"

But Pa thought differently. He laid a big hand on young Ben's shoulder and said, "I'm sorry, Ben. I didn't reckon on the likes of this." He drew a deep breath and added hoarsely, "You must go on with your story, though it hurts. We have to figure things out."

So, Ben unraveled the rest of his tale. "Things happened so fast while I was at the house. Most of the time I was hiding, but by nightfall, Osha had pulled together a bundle of food and a compass and things she thought I'd need. She even sneaked my knife right out from under the captain's nose while he was bawling like a stage actor. She sent me out through a window and then went to the back door to draw everyone's attention away, while I ran into the piney woods. When I saw his guards everywhere and I heard him order me killed, I knew Osha was right. I had to get myself into the wilderness. That's when I made up my mind to carve the captain so I could remember exactly what he looked like. Then, when I can get back to bring him justice, I'll be able to prove I actually saw him murder his brother.

"I was hungry a lot of the time, but a woman named Miss Polly fed me and dressed me up like a girl, and then she drove me right past all the people waiting to catch me. I think I probably owe Miss Polly for my life. I spent my days hiding and my nights running. I kept to rivers and woods and finally got myself to the settlement where I met you." He decided not to mention having met Traveler first, since it was wrong of him to sneak into their wagon. "You know about my hiding on your flatboat, and I'm sorry I did that, but I had this feeling someone was about to catch me. I just didn't know who. It was after you put me off at that cabin that the Indian flashed his knife at me as he fell into the river. And, well, I guess you know the rest."

Ma and Pa locked eyes over the weary young man's head. John caught that look and his heart leapt, because he knew in a flash that Ben would not be left behind with Crazy Sir Edward.

Pa spoke quietly. "You will come with us, Son, and you will be a Cooper for as long as you want."

Ben slumped with relief, but John whooped like a moonstruck crazy and slapped Ben on the back affectionately. "Hallie slept through this whole mess," he said through a wide grin, "and she's gonna wake up with a new brother!"

Sir Edward cleared his throat and interrupted the celebration. "I quite agree that Ben should travel with you," he said, "but it should appear that he is your slave."

Pa's eyes fired up in anger but quickly calmed, as he saw the wisdom in Crazy's statement. No one would question the possession of a slave, but having a black family member would cause plenty of stir. Sir Edward led the group to a room filled with wooden boxes of all sizes and shapes. He stepped up to a large trunk.

"Hold this lantern, John," he directed. The gentleman opened the trunk and carefully sifted through a stack of important looking papers. "Here is what you need, Matthew," he said. He turned toward the young black boy. "Read this, Ben," he said, handing him the important paper.

Ben's eyes opened in surprise. How had Sir Edward known he could read? Master Jeffries had warned him often that many white people frowned upon blacks learning to read or work with numbers. In fact, he had predicted that the day would come that to do so would be against the law!

"You must learn to be a better actor, Ben," the Englishman warned with a twinkle in his eye. "Your speech is too proper for a slave. And when I found you looking through the books, I knew in a flash you could read, despite your act. I'll wager your master favored you like a son or a grandson. Am I not correct?"

"Yes, Sir," answered Ben. Never again would he think that the moon had gotten to Sir Edward. He was as smart as they came. Benjamin took the document and held it near the lantern, reading it aloud clearly as John squinted at it over his shoulder. The paper was a bill of sale which proved ownership of a slave called *Joshua*. The slave would be a little younger than Ben, but Ben was small for his age, so that would go unnoticed. Whoever owned the paper also owned the slave.

"Under any other circumstances," Sir Edward explained, "I would never allow a document like this out of my care, but this is a critical situation, and both Joshua and his owner have been gone so long without returning that I think I can safely say they will never be seen again upon the face of this earth."

"Most travelers in these parts cannot read," Sir Edward explained. "Matthew, I'll wager you would be safe in showing this document to almost anyone, but protect it carefully and do not produce it unless you are forced to." He folded the paper, returned it to its oilskin packet and presented it carefully to Pa. Then he turned to Ben. "Remember that you are a slave, Lad, and act like one. Never let your act go for a minute. Your name is Joshua for now and forever, but to Mister and Mistress Cooper and even to John, you will simply be *Boy*. Do you understand?"

Benjamin's face heated up just thinking about the way he would be treated, but he nodded, just the same.

Sir Edward turned to John. "Young man, it is clear that you admire Ben. This must never show. If you truly care for him, then you must treat him as a slave."

John's heart resisted, but his mind knew Crazy was speaking the truth. He looked at his good friend with sadness. "Ben, can you be a friend to a boy who treats you so?"

Ben smiled. "I learned from my master to do just that. He warned me that he would always treat me as a slave until the time was right. I knew he loved me. That's why I always called him *Master.*"

Ma was puzzled. "What time was your master talking about, Ben?"

"I don't know," he answered. "He just told me to have patience and trust him." Ben hated to lie, but he felt no one would believe the truth, and he wasn't at all sure he wanted this important secret told, anyway. His instincts told him to keep it to himself.

Pa took charge. "We have work to do," he warned, "and the moon is fading. If we want to get away from that Indian, we must hurry."

Quickly, Pa, John, and Ben gathered their necessaries. Slinging packs over their shoulders, they hugged Ma as they fought back against fear and sadness. They walked together to the back room where Hallie slept in a beautiful cradle left by long-ago travelers. Pa set down his pack and gently reached into the cradle to touch Hallie's blond curls. His eyes welled up with tears and he snatched his daughter up into his strong arms. He held her tightly, patting her diapered bottom and quieting her startled cries. She soon drifted back to sleep and her bear-sized father gently returned her to the crib. Pa, Ma, and John circled into a family hug as they straightened their backs, lifted their chins, and looked into each-other's eyes with sparks of determination. John was reminded of the day that they had pulled the wagon back from the jaws of the mountain, and he knew they would all be safely together again one day.

When he looked down into his Ma's blue eyes, he realized that he was nearly a head taller than she was. When had *that* happened? He wished he had something of hers to take with him. As if she had heard his wish, she stepped up and pressed a knotted kerchief into his hand. It was the kerchief that Grandma had given him so long ago. The ginger cookies were all gone, but there, woven into the know, was the ribbon for Hallie's hair.

"Take care of this, Johnny," she whispered, "and bring it back to Hallie and me."

THE TRADING TREE

LONG BEFORE THE SUN ROSE, two boys, one dog, and a man crept away from the mouth of the cave and made their way along the bank of the mighty Ohio river. Traveler gave no sign that the Indian was nearby, but they could take no chances. They hurried westward, hoping not to be tracked.

By high sun of the following day, Pa pointed to a cone-shaped boulder at the river's edge. "That's the sign Crazy told of," he said with relief. "Now we can lose ourselves in the woods." He led the weary boys to a deer path in the forest. They walked until John and Ben were sure their legs would fall off.

"Now," Pa said, panting from working his way up a steep hill, "we can rest."

The three explorers dropped their packs, and then Pa and John gently laid down their rifles and pulled off their powder horns. Using their packs like pillows, the three weary adventurers quickly drifted off to a deep sleep with their faithful dog standing guard.

John marveled at his pa's sense of direction. Ben had offered the use of his compass, but Pa preferred to follow his senses. There were times when the mammoth trees blocked out the sun. Still, John knew his father was not lost. Day after day, Matthew marched northwestward, encouraging the boys with a joke, a massive hand on a shoulder, or a strong back to ease their loads. Ben became so exhausted that he forgot to notice the beauty around him. Instead, he watched the path, wary of a stone or small limb which might snag his dragging feet. Even John, whose longer legs could cover more distance, lost track of the days and nights. His mind focused on putting one foot in front of the other until Pa's welcome announcement that they could camp for the night. Finally, just before dark exactly two weeks after they had left Crazy Sir Edward's cave, they came upon a broad river.

"This is Lewis and Clark's river," Pa declared through a big smile. "We're almost there. I can feel it!"

John and Ben gratefully dropped their packs. Soon they would be busy felling trees and building a home, but for now they could rest. They camped for the night and feasted on frog legs.

Pa's steps quickened. It was harder than ever for the boys to keep up with his long, strong strides. They traveled on excitement now, eager to plant themselves for good. Again, they camped, and again they filled their hungry bellies with frog legs. They fell asleep while leaning against their packs and watching a flickering campfire across the wide river and south of them. Was it the Indian? Probably not. He would be too sneaky to build a fire. Besides, how would he have crossed such a wide body of water?

Early the following morning, Traveler jumped to her feet and looked downriver, standing as still as a statue. She sniffed the air and moved her tail slightly, whining her questions. Following her gaze, the weary settlers spied a large keel boat. The craft was being moved upriver by a group of rough-looking men. Each man held a long pole. After sticking one end of the pole down into the mud at the bottom of the river, each man walked from the front to the back of the boat. When he reached the back, he carried his pole and walked behind the other men back to the front, where he began the process all over again. The big, floating trading post was making good speed, although it was loaded with barrels and crates of supplies.

"Bonjour," bellowed a large, round man standing in the bow of the boat. This man seemed to be the commander.

Pa and John were puzzled. They could not understand what the man was saying. Matthew raised his hands, palms up, and shrugged his shoulders. Was this one of those Frenchmen that Smelly Jack had mentioned?

Ben confirmed Pa's suspicions. "He's speaking French," he explained from the corner of his mouth. "He's saying good-day; hello."

The man's laughter skipped across the water. "Good day, Pilgrims," he shouted in a heavy accent. "I am Jean-Baptiste Le Claire, Captain of this ship. May I be of help to you?"

Pa stepped to the edge of the water. "Might you be crossing to the other side?" he yelled.

"But of course, if that is where you wish for going," the captain yelled with a deep bow.

"I have little money to pay you," shouted Pa.

John thought of the five gold coins sewn into Ben's pants and tightened his lips.

"I will not require payment," said the Frenchman with a smile, "for I am a wealthy son-of-a-gun. Ha!" He slapped his muscular thigh and began to laugh at his humorous remark.

The men poled the boat as close to the bank as they dared and stretched a sturdy gangplank across to a flat boulder. John was jolted by the memory of the horrid Cave-In-Rock gang. His heart skipped, but he realized that Traveler seemed happy to see this strange crew. That had not been the case when the woman at the top of the bluff along the Oyo River tricked them. Suddenly, his heart felt light enough to grow wings and *fly* across the river! He stepped onto the plank behind his pa, and Traveler hurried across to the boat on John's heels. When Pa waved his hand at Ben and signaled for him to move their gear, John felt his face redden in shame, but he knew they were only doing what they had agreed was safe.

"She is a fine *chien*," the captain said, pointing to Traveler. "You will sell her, yes?"

Pa smiled down at their big brindled dog. "No, but thank you, just the same."

As Ben moved to a corner near their gear, Pa purposefully ignored him and motioned for Johnny to step forward. "This is my son, John, and I'm Matthew Cooper," he said, offering his big hand. Le Claire grabbed Pa's hand and gave it one, hard shake. The men talked of Indians, settlements, and business. John strained to understand the sturdy Frenchman until his ears buzzed like a hive of honeybees. He longed to sit beside Ben but ignored him and climbed to the top of a bale of blankets, instead, feeling miserable without his friend at his side. John had understood enough to learn that a large settlement called Saint Louis was down river from them. This man was a merchant, and St. Louis was his home. His business was to load his large boat with blankets, hoes, hatchets, even rifles. He and his men would struggle against the current, stopping to trade their goods for pelts. Indians needed Le Claire's supplies, and white men would pay a great deal for the Indians' pelts, especially beaver. Le Claire seemed to be very rich and very jolly.

Soon the boat had crossed the wide, muddy river. The big Frenchman shook Pa's hand once more and turned to John. "For you," he bellowed with a smile, as he handed John a large axe. "*Bon chance!*"

Pa motioned for Ben to follow them with two heavy packs. "Don't be lazy, Boy," he said.

John's heart raced with anger and embarrassment. He knew that Pa was acting, but it hurt to see his friend treated so. "Thank you, Sir," he mumbled to the Frenchman. John thought seriously about returning the man's powerful-looking gift, because he felt like he didn't deserve it. "*If I was a dog, I'd have my tail between my legs,*" he thought to himself.

Le Claire began to curse in a mixture of English and French, giving sudden speed to John's bare feet as he grabbed the axe tightly and ran to the bank. It was obvious the Frenchman was against slavery. Pa fought down the urge to explain and walked down the gangplank to the western bank of the mighty Mississippi.

With Traveler leading the way and Ben struggling along in the rear, the Coopers moved upriver at the water's edge. Ben fell farther and farther behind. At the point where a fallen tree blocked their way, Pa turned into the woods. "We'll wait here," he said to John.

Within minutes, Ben came stumbling up the path with his load. "Master Cooper, I know for certain I want to be a free black," he said with a tired smile as he slumped against a large tree root. John and Pa rushed to take up Ben's burden.

"I'm so sorry. I'm so sorry," Pa muttered as he fussed over the young black boy. "And *please* don't call me Master unless your life depends on it!"

The three explorers rested in the woods, out of sight of the Frenchmen, until they felt it was safe to move back out to the river's edge. Both Smelly and Crazy had warned Pa of the dangerous woodland Indians who could cause a party of white men to disappear without a trace. Ever northward they marched, camping each night at the fringes of the water. Early each morning, Pa would kneel and raise his arms toward the heavens.

"Father, send us a sign," he would beg.

John and Ben read each other's thoughts. Would a sign ever come? Would it come and they wouldn't recognize it? John was worried. One evening just before they slept, he sat by the campfire. He missed his ma and Hallie. They hadn't jumped into the river to scrub themselves since the day before they left Crazy's cave, and it surprised him that he yearned for her orders to wash. He missed her cooking and her quiet, gentle ways around the camp. His arms ached for Hallie. How he wished he could be bouncing her on his shoulders right now! The miserable young man wondered if Hallie missed him. Would she remember him when they got back? His gizzard swelled with tears as he fished Ma's kerchief out of his pocket and held it close to his nose. After all these days, the faint odor of her soap conjured up a lump in this throat. Could he smell Grandma's ginger cookies, too, or was it his imagination?

John twisted the kerchief and curled Hallie's ribbon around and around his finger. Before he knew what he'd done, the ribbon had slipped out of the knot. John untied the kerchief to rejoin it with the ribbon. His eyes widened with surprise and then overflowed with tears. Resting safely inside the knot was a lock of his Ma's beautiful, light brown hair. Beside it was a little golden curl from Hallie's mop of ringlets. John sobbed in misery. Quietly, his pa knelt beside him and wrapped his strong arm around Johnny's shaking shoulders.

Ben watched from across the fire. He wished he could have said goodbye to his own ma. He liked these Coopers, but he longed for Master Jeffries, his very own father whom he would never again see. He wanted to eat Osha's cooking again, and he yearned to be fussed over. As his people had learned to do, he sat quietly, hiding his thoughts and feelings.

Just before sunrise the following morning, Traveler's insistent whining awakened the three weary campers. Their eyes followed her curious gaze. A jet-black owl perched above them on the limb of a Sycamore tree, and it was way past time for the owl to have disappeared into its nest somewhere deep in the forest. Owls only fly at night. Besides, they had never heard tell of a black owl! To rattle their bones a bit more, this yellow-eyed bird seemed to be staring directly into their eyes as if it were trying to send them a message.

"The sign!" Pa whispered hoarsely. "Collect your packs right quick!"

The owl sat like one of Ben's carvings, waiting silently. As Pa shouldered the last pouch, the bird silently spread its broad wings and drifted through the quiet, early-morning air into the mist of the woods. Pa and the boys hurried at a trot, following the owl. Traveler set the pace, darting ahead to keep the bird in view. Like a silent ghost, the creature drifted on its broad wings deeper and deeper into the forest, waiting at times for the breathless trio to rejoin it.

John followed Pa, wondering if Ben was as worried about his crazy chase as he was. Sometimes Ben was a hard puzzle. When he didn't seem to want to share his thoughts, he had a way of hiding his eyes behind some kind of invisible curtain. He could look right at you, but his thoughts would disappear somewhere between his eyes and yours. This was one of those times. It seemed to John there was a good chance the moon had gotten to his pa … or maybe the owl had! Who ever heard of chasing a fool owl through the forest? Owls aren't even supposed to fly during daylight. For all John knew, this owl was sick or something.

The lay of the land began to change, swelling into low hills and plunging into ravines. Suddenly, the exhausted runners found themselves at the edge of another, smaller river. The owl had crossed the river and disappeared into the dark woods on the other side. Traveler plunged into the water and began to swim across. John watched as the waters parted into a large V behind his dog's raised head. Could they trust her judgment? Traveler always seemed to know if danger was poking up its ugly head. Pa scouted out a likely spot to cross the stream, and they waded across, tripping over slippery stones hidden beneath the waist-high water that churned around them. Quickly, they angled through the woods toward their barking dog.

They broke through a tangle of wild grapevine into a wide, heavily shaded deer path. The earth beneath their feet was soft, cool, well-packed black clay that cushioned their feet as they stepped. Traveler stood at the base of a large tree in the center of the deer path. Her bark told them that the owl could be found in the tree.

Ben gasped with shock, and John followed his eyes to the tree, almost crashing headlong into his pa, who had stopped dead in his tracks.

"The tree," whispered Pa. "Look at the tree!"

After staring in silence at the huge Sycamore tree, they eyed each other with what looked suspiciously like they each wanted to hightail it away from that strange place right quick, but no one wanted to be the first to break rank. The trunk of the tree looked as if a giant had tried to walk through it, forcing out the impression of his head, broad shoulders, chest, and right leg, from the inside! The tree had held the giant prisoner, however, turning him into wood.

Ben reached for his snakeroot. As he felt John's eyes boring into the side of his head, he turned to share a frightened look.

"Do you remember how Old Smelly pulled Prilla out of the tree?" Pa croaked.

John's heart hammered in his ears, just about drowning out the memory of Smelly's voice as he told his tale about how he had found his partner inside the trunk of a tree where a bear had mauled him to death.

Ben interrupted his memories. "How? I don't think you told me about that."

"I'll tell you later, when we've got ourselves away from this here tree," Johnny answered, "but as soon as I'm done, you'll know why Pa and I are so spooked."

"I don't know his story, and I'm *already* spooked!" Ben observed with a shudder.

As Traveler circled the tree, Ben, John, and Pa moved in closer. They discovered that the huge tree was hollow, with an opening in the trunk nearly large enough for the three of them to walk in side-by-side. Had Smelly Jack been this far west? Was this the very tree in which the bear had cornered Smelly's partner? Had his partner made the impression on the back side of the tree? If old Smelly hadn't told them he had buried his partner, they might have concluded the wood had just grown around the dead man where he stood, finally revealing nothing but his shape inside the wood. It made John shiver just to think about it! He gripped Prilla as he peered into the fringes of the dark woods surrounding the deer path. Was the bear still out there after all these years? If so, he must be about twelve or thirteen feet tall when he stood up by now. When another shudder caught John off guard, he closed the gap between Pa and himself.

Traveler turned to sniff the air. After stretching her neck to give a mournful howl, she walked slowly into the woods. The explorers followed her, discovering that the ground steadily rose into an area where more daylight filtered through the dark green leaves. Johnny could feel his hopes rise and his fears melt away as he walked toward daylight. His nose picked up an almost-forgotten smell. Dry earth!

Whooping with joy, Pa danced out of the woods and into a large clearing. Waving prairie grass greeted them, brushing against the boys' chests as they walked. Pa closed his eyes and took a deep sniff. His nose sent a message to his lips, and his whole face broke into a satisfied smile. "We're home!" he announced.

John pulled a long stalk of prairie grass and crushed it in his hands. Its smell reminded him of Grandpa Cooper's wheat. Yes, this was home. Except for boulders shoved up through the earth here and there, the land was clear of trees and waiting for a plow. Pa looked at the bluffs surrounding the open area and smiled once more. This was just what he had hoped for. Water was a short walk away, there were plenty of trees nearby for a cabin and a barn, and the tall, rocky bluffs would protect them from those dangerous, twisting winds that Crazy and Smelly had described.

Pa thought they should explore the bluffs, just to make sure there weren't any huge boulders that might loosen some day and come crashing down the hill to smash the cabin they planned to build. While they were there, Ben discovered a cave, and Pa declared it a perfect residence for them until they got the cabin built. He mulled over the idea of putting their livestock and grain in the cave instead of spending time and effort building a barn. The animals would be safe from wind, rain, and fire. A barn could get blown over by one of Crazy's spinning winds, or it could catch fire. In the meantime, they had a comfortable place to sleep, cook, and keep their meager supplies.

From sun-up to sunset during the weeks that followed, the bluffs echoed with the ringing sound of axes striking wood. John and Ben exploded with new muscle. Their hands grew hard with calluses as they swung, swung, swung their axes. The three settlers raced with time. If winter caught them without a cabin, there would be terrible hardships.

The only breaks for John and Ben came when Pa would send them out to hunt meat and roots to roast near the fire. At those times, the two friends always arranged for a visit to the strange tree in the woods. They climbed into its leafy limbs far above the deer path. There was no sign of the giant black owl which had led them here. They searched for remnants of a grave, hoping to solve the mystery of Smelly Jack's old partner. One afternoon, as Ben and John sat propped against the tree and wondered aloud about its strange shape, Ben caught sight of something hidden in its root.

"Look, John," he said, pointing at a brownish-yellow object. "What do you make of this?" Trapped in the growing root was a knife handle carved from what may have been a deer's antler.

"Smelly's knife," gasped John. "That looks just like Smelly Jack's knife!"

"How long ago did you see Old Smelly and his knife?" Ben asked.

"It was late this spring, just before we came to the settlement where I met you," John answered, his voice trailing off somewhere into the haze of a memory.

"Well, this knife has been here for years," Ben pointed out. "See how the roots have grown around it?"

John crawled on his hands and knees to inspect the knife more closely. "That's right. It couldn't be Smelly's knife. As they each felt hairs on their necks and arms standing at attention, they stared eye-to-eye like a couple of magicians trying to read each other's minds. Finally, John took his first breath in several seconds.

"This has to be the tree, all right."

Ben fished a hunk of snakeroot out of his pocket and began to chew on it like he hadn't eaten in a month.

"Ben, tell me again why you are always chewing on that dang fool weed," John said. "It doesn't taste good. I've tried it." Ben was quiet for so long, John wondered if he had a secret he wouldn't share, which made him even more impatient for an answer.

Finally, Ben answered, "Snakeroot is powerful magic, John. It wards off evil."

John shook his head. "Pa always says such things are heathen superstition," he said. "A God-fearing man wouldn't depend on foolish superstitions to carry him through life."

Ben smiled, and John thought he caught a little twinkle in his dark brown eyes, like he was pulling a joke on his tall, white friend. "Don't be so quick to judge, John," he replied. "Why, if you wanted, I could tell you about a cure for that wart on your hand. I'm not superstitious; I'm just careful." He secretly watched from the corner of his eye as John shoved his hand under his thigh.

"It seems to me you're a-poking your nose into what's no concern to you," John muttered. "I suppose you'd have me howl at the moon or drown a squirrel or some such foolish thing."

Ben was silent.

"Well," John allowed, "I'm not saying I would ever *do* such a foolish thing, but just to give me a good laugh, why don't you tell me what *you'd* do for a wart?"

Ben slowly leaned back against the tree and spat snakeroot juice in the direction of the ancient knife handle. "I won't tell you," he said.

"And I'd like to know why *not*," said John angrily. He could feel himself blushing, a sure sign of upset, and he wished for just an instant he was as black as Ben, so it wouldn't show. At least he didn't *think* it would.

"Because I don't want you to get hundreds more warts on my account," Ben answered.

John sat up with a frown. "What's *that* supposed to mean?" he demanded. "Are you fixin' to put some kind of a spell on me?"

Ben looked his tall friend square in the eye. "Look," he said seriously, "it's well known that anyone who laughs at a cure will be twice afflicted. That's pure truth. I can swear to it. Why, Old Osha . . ."

"I don't want to hear about Old Osha," John interrupted impatiently, "I want to hear about the cure."

"Why?" asked Ben.

John pulled at a tuft of grass. "I just want to know how far your superstitions are leading you down the wrongful path," he said as he rubbed the wart. "I won't laugh; I promise."

Ben's mind smiled, but his face was stone-cold serious. "Well, it's hard to find just the right conditions," he began. "First, you have to be the first one through a brand-new door. Second, that door has to have leather hinges. They can't be some old store-bought hinges, or the cure won't work." Ben laced his fingers behind his head and leaned back to gaze up through the big Sycamore leaves, wondering why they had fuzz on them.

"Is that all there is to it?" John asked in amazement.

"No," Ben answered.

"Well, then, what's the rest of the secret?" John urged impatiently.

"You have to suck real hard on the wart and don't dare swallow," continued Ben, "then, as you walk through the door, you spit over your right shoulder. You spit on the middle hinge and then say . . ." He seemed to be trying to remember some important detail.

"What do you say?" asked John impatiently.

"I'm thinking," answered Ben with a frown. He leaned back once more and studied the leaves. "Let's see. You, say, 'Leave me, wart, and stick to the hinge,' I think. Yes, I'm sure of it."

John stood up and looked thoughtfully at the ugly bump on his trigger finger. "Going in or going out?" he asked.

Ben considered the rustling leaves above him until John wondered if his friend with a sudden twinkle in his eye had heard his question.

"Out," Ben answered. He rolled over to retrieve a pair of freshly killed rabbits. "We'd better get back to the cave or there'll be no meal tonight."

The boys returned to the sunny field and the ringing of Pa's axe. Soon the rabbits were cleaned and hanging from green sticks propped near the fire.

The cabin began to take shape. Pa carefully notched and saddled the logs and fit them together, notch to saddle and saddle to notch. Even with the block and tackle Pa had brought with him, the chore of raising the logs became impossible without Jack and Molly to help.

The day arrived when Pa announced it was time to return to Crazy's cave. Their struggles with logs were over for a time. Carefully, they hid in the cave all that could be left behind. By Pa's reckoning, it was August thirteenth when they began their trip back toward the rising sun. They stepped lightly, proud of their accomplishments and eager to see Ma, Hallie, and Sir and Lady Goodwin.

Ben and John led Pa back to the ancient tree to see the buried knife handle. It seemed to John that Pa's face whitened a bit when he caught sight of the familiar handle. When the boys stepped inside the hollow trunk for one last inspection, they were startled by a small doll sitting atop a large, smooth stone, smack-dab in the center of the clay floor.

"That's *you*, Ben!" John whispered shrilly. "Look! It's got your black skin and your brown pants. And look at your hair. They used dried blackberries to make your hair!"

Ben stared at the primitive doll. Was this a gift or a threat? Traveler poked her nose in the tree and quickly joined in the excitement. Her tail wagged as she brushed past the boys and hurried to the doll. Picking it up in her mouth, she trotted to Ben and raised up on her lanky hind legs. She rested her front paws on Ben's shoulders, and her tail beat back and forth merrily.

"She wants you to take it, Ben," John said.

Ben hesitated. If he took this doll, what would the Indians think? What did they *want* him to do?

"Take it, Ben," John urged. "Pa is calling us to move on."

Ben took the doll from Traveler.

"I don't think Pa should know about the doll," John whispered as they stepped out of the tree. "I don't think he'd understand."

"*I* don't think *I* understand!" complained Ben.

"S-h-h-h," Johnny whispered. "I don't either, but that doll gave me a good feeling when I saw it. Traveler doesn't see any danger to it. Maybe the Indians want to be your friend."

Ben gave a shrug, stuffed the doll into his shirt, and dipped his hand into his pocket to check for his snake root supply. "I'm ready," he announced. "Let's get out of here!"

SECRET GIFTS

IT WAS LATE AT NIGHT almost three weeks later, when the three adventurers and their dog trudged wearily up to the mouth of Crazy Sir Edward's cave.

"Hello in there," Pa shouted through cupped hands. "It's the Cooper men here. Can we enter?"

They waited impatiently while the brightening flicker of a lantern slowly approached the mouth of the cave from inside. Ben and John stared at the ghostly looking character who had come to greet them. It was Sir Edward, himself, dressed in a linsey-woolsey nightshirt with a sleeping cap over his head. His puffy eyes squinted through the darkness at his friends as he mumbled an invitation into the cave.

Soon Ma and Hallie were awake. Crying with happiness and relief, they all pounded and hugged each other. It seemed to John that Hallie had changed. Would she remember him?

"John and Ben, I do believe you turned into men somewhere out on that trail," Ma pronounced as she stood back to inspect them, squinting in the dim light of the lantern. First, she studied John and then, Ben. "There's a difference in your eyes."

"And in our hands," John said through a crooked grin. He raised his palms to show off his large calluses.

"And in your smell!" exclaimed Ma as she sniffed the air. "Whew! How long has it been since you washed?"

Pa's chest puffed up with pride. "We washed every day!"

"Your hands and face?" Rachel asked, perching her hands on her hips.

"Yes," Matthew answered proudly.

"Anything else?"

"No," said Pa with a sheepish grin. "No soap."

"Lady Eleanor gave me a large stock of soap to take with us when we leave," Ma announced proudly. She paced off three steps to a big trunk. "You might as well wash off that stink right now, because there's not enough wind in here to blow if off." Because Ben was closest, she handed him the soap.

Ben, John, and Pa smiled knowingly at each other, shaking their heads in mock disbelief. They were back, for sure. Soon, splashes and laughter arose from the great Ohio River, as the three weary woodsmen and their dog bathed happily in the moonlight. Surely the Indians would never bother a hair on their heads, because anyone bathing in the middle of the night and splashing around with such wild glee would be considered touched in the head. Plumb crazy!

After only two days of rest, story-telling and non-stop eating, the Coopers stood at the mouth of the cave saying their last farewells. Lady Eleanor and Ma hugged and said their goodbyes with huge tears and smiling mouths. John and Ben traded a look. How was it that women folk could smile and cry at the same time? Sir Edward appeared in his bearskin skirt and top hat to escort the Coopers to retrieve their oxen and wagon. Bouncing wildly from tree to tree, he began his act, while the Coopers prayed silently that the Indians were watching from their secret hiding places along the river.

Jack and Molly were well-rested and fat from days spent eating the lush grass on the plateau above Crazy's cave. The British aristocrat had visited them every day, taking them water and seeing to it that the Indians were aware the oxen were his and not to be eaten. Now, the sleek animals stepped out smartly in their yoke, full of new energy as they pulled the trail-worn wagon.

The flatboat was left to Sir Edward. It looked empty and lonesome floating in the shade of two Sycamores which shaded the water's edge. John had forgotten how truly large the flatboat was. Loaded with their wagon, the oxen, supplies and five people, it somehow had always seemed small to him. The people of Stowe's fork could hold a dance on that boat, he thought to himself, for it was surely big enough! John realized it had been a long time since he had thought of their old friends back home. He brushed a stray black curl away from his blue eyes and gazed back up the river. The Coopers had come a very long way since that early spring day when they headed into the mountains. Because so many people had woven their way into and out of his journey, it seemed to John that he was a different person, looking back on someone else's life. He thought of his grandma and grandpa and knew in his heart that they were fine, and that their lives were pretty much the same as they had been since before he was born.

He looked up the path they were about to take. "I'll carry Hallie for you, Ma," he said, lifting his little sister to his hip. Rachel Cooper moved closer behind her strong bear of a husband as he hacked away at stray willows blocking the path. Like a pair of faithful pet dogs, Jack and Molly followed along behind Matthew and Rachel Cooper, pulling the wagon. Ben and John, with Hallie perched on his hip, were content to plod along at the back end of their little parade.

It was easy to see that few white men had traveled by land through this new western country. In the place of the well-traveled roads or trails they had covered before their flatboat trip, they now struggled through deer trails, sometimes needing to cut away small trees and brambles so that their wagon could fit through. They stared at the hundreds of giant trees which met them along their journey. Such trees had long ago disappeared from the Virginia country to become cabins, barrels, tables, benches, beds, wagons, barns, and all the rest of the necessary wooden trappings that turned a wilderness into homes and towns.

Several days later, the weary pilgrims arrived at the eastern bank of the Mississippi River. Ma stopped quietly, looking first up, then down, then across the big, muddy giant which blocked their path westward. With a strong arm wrapped around her tiny waist, Pa stood beside her.

"It's beautiful, Matthew, but it is so big! How will we ever get ourselves across?" she asked. "Jack and Molly are good swimmers, but they would never make it through all this fast-running water. What will we do?"

Pa dropped to his knees and removed his large hat. John saw his father's black, sweat-curled hair glisten in the sun, and he decided he'd better drop to *his* knees, too. Soon, Ben and all the Coopers but Hallie were kneeling in the sun-warmed, damp earth of the riverside. "Lord," Pa prayed aloud, "you've been a-watching over us and carrying us in the palm of your hand all our lives. We need to get across this great river of yours." His prayer had ended, but Pa stayed in place, and so, of course, did they. After a silence so long that John pictured roots sprouting out of four pairs of knees and working their way into the ground, Pa added, "Amen!"

They all stood up together and began looking up and down the river, waiting for some sign that God had heard their prayers. Johnny wondered sarcastically to himself if everyone expected the waters to part like they did for the Israelites fleeing from Egypt. His Pa seemed certain that they would get across. They weren't being chased by the Pharaoh, but Captain Jeffries was just as bad an old coot, from the sound of him. Ma and Pa began lashing down all the loose items inside the wagon, acting as if they fully expected to cross the river any minute, and they smiled excitedly as they discussed the cabin.

John sneaked a look at Ben, who shot back the same questioning glance. What was about to happen? Would they swim the wagon across after all? The boys shrugged their shoulders and joined the preparations. Suddenly, as quickly as it had begun, the job was finished. Pa plucked a long weed from nearby and popped one end of it into his mouth. He sat Indian style at the water's edge, and he waited.

Too embarrassed to watch his pa make a fool of himself, John concentrated on an iridescent blue dragonfly flitting from reed to reed near the riverbank. Ma cooed and talked quietly to Hallie, as the toddler teetered over to investigate a brace of wildflowers. Quietly, Ben seated himself next to Pa and began work on a new carving. Now that the image of Jeffries was forever trapped in wood, Ben would carve a more pleasing piece. It would be Hallie. He began to carefully shave away pieces of wood and soon the shape of Hallie's head and neck magically appeared in his hands.

John blushed with anger. How could everyone just sit there? He heard a brazen horsefly pester Jack and Molly. The swish of a tail and the kick at the belly meant the fly had bitten Molly. Harness chain rattled, and then all was still, or *was* it?

John pricked up his ears and looked at his dog. She had heard it, too. A man was singing. From the sound of him, he was coming toward them on the river from up north somewhere. John remembered the big Frenchman and his crew. Was it Le Claire? His boat would certainly be big enough to get them across, if he had traded away all his supplies with the Indians. He didn't figure animal pelts would take up much room on that big river monster.

Traveler danced lightly with excitement and ran upriver at the water's edge, barking her welcome. The Coopers followed her eagerly. John smiled with anticipation, but then gasped in amazement. This was not Le Claire's boat. From the sound of the strange ditty the man bellowed, he was French, like Le Claire, but that ended any kinship. The man, dressed in skins and sprouting firearms like an adolescent cockerel growing pin feathers, was perched on his knees inside a large, round boat made of animal skins sewn together like a crazy quilt. The seams appeared to be sealed together with some kind of black, sticky-looking goo. With a short-handled paddle, the man guided his boat down the river, relying on the current to carry him forward. Occasionally, his boat spun totally around, but he simply stopped its spin when he reached the front again. Stacked around him were bales of animal pelts. The man waved and shouted, and then he began to maneuver his round craft toward them. He smiled and chattered away in his strange-sounding tongue, as he expertly guided his boat to the riverbank. Quietly, John reached for Prilla. She was primed and ready. This man might be just as bad as that gang of outlaws back in the cave. From the looks of him, he was certainly as dirty.

The stranger quickly pulled his boat up onto the bank and hurried to shake hands with all the Coopers. He even shook Ben's hand, which gave the young black boy a start. It's hard to act like a slave when a white man just walks right up and shakes your hand, he thought to himself. It didn't seem to matter to the man that he could not be understood. Ben wished he had taken his French language lessons more seriously. He could follow a bit of the man's tale but wouldn't dare offer to translate. Besides, doing so would bring on questions from both sides that he just as soon wouldn't want to answer. When Pa attempted to speak, it became clear that the man could not understand him. He did recognize that Pa spoke English, though, because he proudly nodded his head and said, "Yes!"

Soon, their visitor made it clear that he planned to stay with them for the night. He unloaded his round boat and stacked his bales of pelts and skins. Then he did a curious thing. He turned his boat upside down, and he used a short, forked stick to prop up one side of it. The boat became a domed lean-to which would shelter him and his pelts for the night. He could lie under the boat and look out across the mighty Mississippi. After slinging himself with firearms and possible bags, he strode toward the woods, continuing his chatter. Within five minutes' time, they heard three separate shots.

"Did you hear that?" Pa asked with surprise on his face. "That man must be some kind of wizard to be able to load and prime so quick!"

"Or maybe he just used one gun after another," John offered. "He had enough firearms if they were already loaded and primed."

"Matthew, did you ever smell such a gamey man?" Ma asked, wrinkling her nose dramatically. "He needs a month of baths with a chunk of Lady Eleanor's soap!"

"Rachel, I'm surprised at you," said Pa. "Have you already forgotten Smelly?"

"How could I ever forget that lovely man?" she answered. "Why, Smelly was like family, so he doesn't count. It's plain this man plans to stay with us if we're still here by nightfall. We have to do something, or none of us will be able to eat!"

It seemed to Ben that Rachel Cooper was forever thinking about how someone smelled and how clean they were. Then, he remembered how Mistress Jeffries used to set him up in a bathtub in the summer kitchen. She'd have Osha heat up some water until it was steaming, even in the middle of the summer. Then, she'd hand him a beautiful, soft towel and a piece of wonderful-smelling soap and warn him she'd be checking behind his ears and he'd better scrub up well, or he would be in for a pretty bad spell. He recalled how hard he had cried, right along with Master Jeffries, when she came down with a fever and died shortly afterward. It all seemed a lifetime ago, Ben thought to himself. Life has a way of changing for you, whether you want it to or not.

"Maybe if we bathed and offered him some soap, he'd get the idea," suggested Pa.

John rolled his eyes at Ben. Now *Pa* was finding reasons for them to wash! He dragged his bare feet as he headed toward the river, hanging his head like he was about to drop over from some rare disease that had taken all his strength. Soon Matthew, Ben, and John were scrubbing themselves as soap bubbles foamed around them in the river.

The Frenchman stepped out of the woods carrying a turkey and two crows. He continued to chatter away in French as he proudly stepped up to Ma and deposited the bloody birds at her feet.

"Yes!" he said.

She stuck her hands on her hips and stared at the Frenchman as he smiled at her proudly. She was to clean and cook the birds with no questions asked. Then Ma froze in her tracks. The Frenchman stripped off his deerskin pants and shirt, leaving himself totally bare, and deposited his clothing in a second pile beside the birds.

"Yes!" he said, and then he returned to his French language, talking and singing gaily. Walking into the water, he joined the bathers for a good scrub, leaving Ma to stew and sputter over the strange man who had paddled himself into her life. Well, even though her men always cleaned their own game, maybe it was worth it to clean the birds herself, if it meant her nose would get a rest. And yes, even wash his cloths. She hoped the man had a second set of clothing, but something told her he traveled light. Would he want to sit by the fire as naked as the day he was born?

"Well, Hallie," she said, "we've got some quick washing to do!" with her toddler perched on one hip and the strange Frenchman's deerskin clothing on the other, Ma hurried to the riverbank and soaped and beat the shirt and pants with frenzy until they foamed up into a million bubbles. Then just as quickly, she beat the soap away. This Mississippi water was muddy, but she'd take mud over stink any day of the week! She wrung out the clothing and stretched it over a bush to dry, promising herself she'd move it to a spot close to the fire when she got one started. She knew from experience that clothing made of deer hide dried very slowly.

Ma's hands flew as she gathered twigs and dried grass. From Pa's possibles bag, she quickly pulled the steel and flint and began striking sparks. Grateful that a spark had finally caught, she crouched low and gently blew a glowing trace into the tiniest of flames. Ma nursed the flare-up into a first-class blaze and added more twigs and dead grass. Small limbs and broken branches joined the burning pile, and finally larger pieces of driftwood topped it off.

Quickly returning the steel and flint to the possibles bag, she turned on her heel to clean the birds. "Crow!" she muttered to herself as she picked up the large black birds. "Next thing, some Egyptian is going to march up to me and throw an asp at my feet!" But the fire in Ma's blue eyes quickly turned to shock as the silhouette of the naked Frenchman walking out of the river appeared between her and the setting sun. She cleared her throat.

"Matthew," she called in a too-sweet voice, "hurry up here and do something about this heathen Frenchman. He's a-strutting around here like the general at muster day, and he's wearing naught but his curly hair!" Ma hurried off to clean the birds.

The Coopers were nicely surprised by the crow. It tasted sweeter than the turkey and was much easier to chew. Pa tried his best to follow their guest around and cover him with John's blanket each time it fell. Ma moved the visitor's clothing closer and closer to the fire to speed up the drying. When the shirt steamed and the pants scorched, Pa insisted she move them back a bit.

At last, the chores were completed. Ma hurried off to the wagon with Hallie, and Pa soon followed. John eyed his blanket. If he had it, he and Ben could crawl under the wagon and get some sleep. Ben looked just as longingly at the cover. As if reading their minds, the big, hairy fur trader walked over to them and gave John the blanket, but John returned it to their visitor. The Frenchman seemed to want to chat, and he stood in front of them, reciting his story. It seemed to be a funny tale, because every now and then the man would slap a bare, white knee and laugh until tears flowed into his curly black beard. The boys laughed with him. The more they sized up the situation, the harder they laughed. Their laughter encouraged the man, who would then launch into another hilarious tale.

"John, we have to do something," Ben wheezed. "I'm so tired I could fall of the ground lying down! What can we do?"

"I think my brain hates crow meat, Ben," said John out of the corner of his mouth. "I've been a-laughing away here, a-staring at this strange man, and my mind froze up."

Three belly laughs later, Ben had an idea. "Just act like I do this every night," he whispered as if the Frenchman would understand him.

Ben's hands stretched to the stars. "Silence!" he shouted.

John?" Ma called softly from inside the wagon.

"Ben is just a-trying to get Frenchy to bed, Ma," John answered. "Just go back to sleep."

"Silence!" Ben shouted again.

The Frenchman's tongue stopped dead in its tracks, as his eyes rolled a question John's way. John stood with his arms folded, smiling quietly at the fur trader, and then he turned to watch his friend. With his arms stretching toward the heavens, Ben walked stiffly toward the water's edge, pretending to be in a trance. Traveler belly-walked her way from under the wagon and sat alertly beside John, taking in the show.

Slowly, Ben stooped to pull hands full of grass which he threw in each direction, shouting, "North, south, east, and west." He walked toward the fire. Circling it again and again in a little dance, he chanted, "Leave me wart and stick to the hinge! Leave me wart and stick to the hinge!"

John worked so hard to hold back the laughter bubbling up through his chest that his eyes overflowed. The Frenchman turned his silent attention from Ben to John and his face became the perfect picture of sympathy. When John saw the man's reaction to his tears, he all but choked with the need to laugh.

"Silence!" shouted Ben seriously. The act was over. He walked solemnly to the wagon, dropped to his hands and knees, and crawled onto a patch of grass. He turned around three times, like a dog checking out its bed, then lay down. Rolling onto his left side, he immediately began to snore loudly.

From inside the wagon, John caught the muffled sounds of his parents laughing into their covers. To hide their laughter, John immediately began to wail loudly, acting like he was broken-hearted about his friend's mental ailment. He, too, dropped to all fours and hurried to Ben's side, where he lay, sobbing miserably.

Traveler sat watching the stunned Frenchman, Ben and John. When the show was over, she stood, shook herself, and trotted off into the woods. Alone in silence, the Frenchman crawled under the wagon, pulling the quilt with him. Gently, he covered both boys, then he shuffled off to his overturned boat, muttering in disbelief. He crawled under it and lay quietly for a long time, gazing out across the river, puzzling over these strange people who run around covering him with blankets, turn green at the sight of crow meat, and pray in such strange ways.

"Yes," he said, shaking his head sadly. He rolled over and fell almost immediately to sleep.

As the birds along the river sang to the rising sun the following morning, Traveler tugged gently on John's pants. No response. She licked his bare foot.

"Yeow!" John squealed. He sat up with a start and banged his head on the back axle of the wagon. Rubbing his throbbing head, he squinted toward his wet foot. "Traveler, you scamp," John scolded, but Traveler had jumped up into the wagon and was tugging on Pa. He awoke immediately, understanding that the dog's silent insistence meant something was wrong. Quickly, he pulled on his boots, grabbed his hat and rifle, and stepped lightly down onto the grass.

"John, Ben," he whispered, "fetch Prilla and come with me quietly."

Ben awoke immediately. He softly touched his knife for good luck and rolled out to the back side of the wagon. John bellied out right behind him, dragging old Prilla, his shot pouch, his powder horn and his possibles bag.

They eyed Traveler. She stood frozen like a statue, staring upriver. Her head shifted slightly as she spotted movement on the water through the low-hanging trees. As the brindle dog crouched, her fur raised from the back of her head to her tail. A quiet, warning growl rumbled up from her broad chest and curled her lips on its way out. The sight of her long, sharp fangs was a sure sign she was ready for a fight.

John and Pa quickly prepared their rifles, and none too soon, because the tips of dug-out canoes soon appeared. "Indians," Pa whispered hoarsely. "A whole *tribe* of 'em!"

The Indians had seen the wagon, but they didn't appear to be interested in nearing the bank until they cleared the trees well enough for the fur trader's boat to come into view. Suddenly, the canoes turned and glided swiftly and quietly to the bank, stopping on each side of the round boat. They were after the Frenchman and, judging from the deep snores coming from inside his animal-hide curiosity, they weren't going to have any trouble catching him by surprise.

Pa and John raised their rifles and Ben's trembling hand groped for his faithful knife, but the leader of the Indians raised both palms toward the Coopers, signaling for them to stop.

"Pa?"

"Lower your gun, Son, and look at Traveler," Pa ordered, barely moving his lips.

John dropped his eyes to the empty spot his ferocious dog had occupied seconds earlier. She licked John's hand, and he was surprised to see her sitting calmly between him and Ben, watching the Indians without a sign of fear.

"Stand your ground, Boys," sad Pa, but don't fight unless they come after us or the wagon. Their fight is not with us. They sure seem mighty wrathy at Frenchy, though."

When the Indians had surrounded the sleeping trapper, they pulled him out from under his shelter, heels first, quickly standing him up. He squinted through sleepy eyes, unable to understand for a breath of time just what was happening. Suddenly his eyes popped awake. Captured!

"Pa, we can't just let them take him," urged John.

"Look at all those men," whispered Ben. "Can you count them all before the sun sets?"

"Ben's right, Son," Pa said, "and besides, look at how they're talking to him. They seem to know who he is. That head man is madder than a wet hen about something."

Now it was Pa's turn to be right. The Indians poked and prodded the Frenchman around, laughing at his nakedness, and then they settled down to business. Their leader began an angry lecture which the visitor seemed to understand, because he stood quietly and hung his head like he was ashamed of himself. As the native leader spoke, a group of Indians removed the bales of pelts from under the man's boat and loaded them into their dugouts.

"Matthew, what …" Ma's head appeared through the back flap of the wagon. "Oh, my dear Lord in Heaven!" she muttered, ducking back inside.

The pelts were loaded. Now the Indians were obviously debating about what was to be done with the Frenchman. Quietly, the leader raised his hands and signaled for silence. After a quick order from the tall, bronze-skinned man, the trader was loaded into his boat. His paddle was thrown away, and his boat was taken to the middle of the river to float downstream, spinning wildly out of control. The Coopers and Ben watched quietly, pitying the naked man who floated away with nothing but his strange boat to show for his struggles.

The man's firearms and knife were handed over to the Indian leader, who turned to hail the Coopers and Ben before stepping into his dugout. The canoes were soon away from the bank and headed back upstream. Strong red-brown arms shoved paddles deeply into the churning waters and sped the long canoes northward. The men disappeared behind the same trees which had sheltered their arrival, as Ben and the Coopers stood like statues, afraid to move.

Ma was the first person to break their silence. "Well, there's no sense in wasting a perfectly good set of deerskins," she said as she climbed down from the wagon and headed for the bush holding their visitor's clothing. She removed the shirt and pants and held them to her nose, inhaling deeply. "Except for smelling a little burnt, they're fine," she declared, and she took them to the wagon.

It was dead noon. The sun baked bare heads and blistered lips. John prayed silently for a breeze as he hauled water to Jack and Molly. Ben had propped himself against the trunk of a shady Sycamore and resumed his work on the carving of Hallie. As if she was coming to model for the young artist, Hallie toddled to Ben's tree and sat squarely beside him. Soon her tiny fingers reached up to help with the carving. Ben sheathed his knife and pulled his little blond helper to his lap, where she waited patiently for him to tickle her toes. She could count on Ben to tickle those toes any time she wished, which was often, these days.

Traveler bounded into camp from the north, barking excitedly and wildly wagging her tail. She darted into the water, then back.

Pa grinned. "Well, folks, get ready for something good to happen," he announced confidently.

Within five minutes, Le Claire and his men appeared through the trees. Except for his men, the huge boat seemed empty, and the fur trader stood solemnly at the bow, studying his feet. He was changed from the jolly man they had met before.

"Le Claire," Pa shouted across the water. "Hello, Le Claire!"

The sturdy Frenchman glanced up and, for a moment, looked right through the Coopers. He was troubled. When he recognized his old passengers, he jumped into action shouting French commands to his crew. The men at the tiller swiftly turned the big craft toward the Coopers, and the men on the downstream side of the boat shoved their poles deep into the mud of the riverbed. The floating store abandoned its run downstream and turned cleanly. Within minutes, Le Claire had offered to haul the Coopers, Ben, and their wagon with Jack and Molly still hitched, across the river. Brawny, shirtless men covered with honest sweat lowered a large gangway to the bank, and Jack and Molly pulled the wagon onto the keel boat. Le Claire ordered his men to lash down the wagon, and Ben saw to Jack and Molly. John felt shamed as he watched his black friend step into his slave act.

Bowing deeply, the captain introduced himself to Ma. "Captain Jean-Baptiste Le Claire at your service, Madam," he announced. He gently placed a huge, work-roughened finger through one of Hallie's golden curls. "Madam Cooper, is it that I may hold your child for you?"

Ma's eyes widened with surprise. "Thank you for your kindness, Captain, but Hallie's no burden. I've carried her most of the way from the Virginia mountains."

"Madam, it would be for me a joy to hold your child," Le Claire explained. "I am a lonely and troubled son-of-a-gun. I am a father to eight childs. These childs I am not seeing for three years. I may, if you please?"

Ma's heart melted. "I am a might weary, Captain. It *would* be a help if you held Hallie for me."

The French bear lifted Hallie into his arms. "*Bonjour, ma petite chere,*" (Good day, my dear little one) he said. "You are a *belle femme.*" (beautiful woman). Le Claire played with Hallie's tiny toes, reciting a French rhyme, and then he turned to Pa.

"This wealthy son-of-a-gun is worth for nothing, Cooper," he said. "I am returning to St. Louis without nothing."

Pa frowned in disbelief. "What happened, Le Claire? Why is your boat empty?"

"There is big sickness in two village of the Indians. They stand two guards at the river and say I will not come or I will get sick and die. Their *shaman* burns the pelts for to stop the sickness, they say. I tell the guards that sick Indians need supplies for winter, and we unload my boat.

"No worry for me, I tell to myself. Last village I will buy pelts. Those are fine pelts, I know, for I see them on my way north when my boat, she has no room for to take them." Le Claire shifted Hallie to his left arm and pounded the wagon with his huge right fist. "But when we return to the village to load the fine pelts, the people, they run and they hide. 'I am not, sick,' I tell to them. 'What is the problem?' I ask."

"The old chief, he comes to me and tells to me that the pelts are gone. That rogue, Rodier, he steals them in the night. Rodier, he is for ruining me with his black, stealing heart."

The boys locked eyes. "Pa?" John said.

"I know, Johnny," said Pa. "Le Claire, what does this man Rodier look like?"

Le Claire carefully placed Hallie in Ma's arms. "He is a grizzly rogue with the heart of the devil," he began. He is using his rifle like magic. Rodier is for smelling so that a skunk would call him *mon oncle* (my uncle).

"Does he have black, curly hair and dress in deerskin?" Pa asked.

"Black hair with the curls, yes," said Le Claire, but this wild man will wear what he can steal. He is a thief!"

"Does he have a boat?" Pa asked.

"His squaw, she is making the boat each winter for him. Bull boat. She is making it of the hides of the bull buffaloes. Each year he is trying for cheating Le Claire out of pelts."

The captain's hands suddenly reached up and clamped themselves onto his head, as if he was planning to try to squeeze his brains out. "My mind remembers!" he said, wide-eyed. "The squaw of Rodier, she has two no-good brothers. I say to myself when I see those guards on the river, 'Le Claire, there is something you are knowing of these men.' They are strangers for me, but I know them."

He turned to Pa. *Mon Dieu* (my God), Cooper, is it that these men are the brothers of the squaw? They are looking like her!"

As the big boat reached the western bank of the broad river, Pa raised a hand to silence the excited captain. "There is something you must know," he began.

While Le Claire's men unloaded the Coopers' wagon and oxen, Pa and John told the Frenchman of their strange encounter with the fur trader. They left out no detail. The captain listened carefully, asking few questions.

Le Claire's usual broad smile returned to light up his face, and he clapped a large hand on Pa's shoulder, saying, "You are for saving me with your good news! We will return to the three village. My heart, she is telling to me there is no sickness and my pelts wait for me. That rogue, Rodier, is for cheating me, but I will win. You will see!"

The big man pumped Pa's hand excitedly and pounded John's shoulder, as he continued to bellow his thanks. Soon the ramp was stowed and Le Claire's men were busy poling their way back north, singing together in their excitement. After waving goodbye and shouting their thanks, the adventurers turned Jack and Molly northward, using the open space between the river and the forest as a road. Three days later, they reached the spot where they had been met by the strange black owl, and they turned their oxen into the bowels of the thick, dark wilderness. Both Pa and John took the lead, chopping away small trees and undergrowth with their big corn knives so the oxen and wagon could pass through.

The going was slow, and night had begun to sift down when they reached the strange tree. Ben touched the bulge under his shirt. All his luck had been good since they found the black doll left in the tree by unseen Indians. Maybe John was right. Jack and Molly caught wind of the prairie grass waving in near darkness at the edge of the forest, and they stepped out with sudden energy, pulling their load up the last hill with ease. In no time, the wagon rolled to a stop in a sea of grass, and the oxen dropped their massive heads, straining against their yoke. Racing with the darkness, the men scrambled to remove the yoke and hobble the oxen.

Ma caught sight of the partially built cabin and ran to inspect her new home. Her hand explored the rough logs, and she paced off the length of the front and side. "It's perfect, Matthew!" she exclaimed. "There's room for all of us, just like you said!"

As soon as the settlers had moved the necessary supplies into the cave, Ben and John yielded to the temptation to visit the hollow tree. John snatched up a pine knot and lit it in Ma's cook fire. Soon, the boys were picking their way through the dark woods to the soft earth of the deer path.

The tree loomed ahead, and the shadow of the wood-captured man seemed to perform a devilish dance in the flickering fire of the pine knot. John caught his breath with a stab of fear.

"Leave me wart and stick to the hinge," Ben chanted in a loud whisper. John exploded in giggles, seeing the silliness of his fear. Shoulder to shoulder, they edged around the trunk to its hollow opening.

"Ever hear of bears sleeping in trees?" John asked his friend. "I think we'd better throw something in there before we just step in bold-like. You never know what varmint might be holed up for the night."

"Good idea, John," said Ben as he searched the ground for a stray piece of wood or a rock. He found a likely chunk of dead wood and tossed it into the hollow darkness of the old Sycamore. The boys waited, but nothing happened.

"That's no good, Ben," John declared. "You've got to really fling it! Throw as hard as you can." He pried a fist-sized stone from the soft earth. "Like this," he said as he reared back and threw for all he was worth. The flames on the pine knot nearly blew out from his efforts, and the stone hit the interior of the tree with a loud thud. Silence.

"What are we a-waiting for?" John asked, nudging his friend forward. They each took a deep breath and stepped together into the shadowy darkness.

"Here's my rock," John said.

"And here's my stick," Ben observed. "Don't this tree's insides look different at night? Without your torch, it'd be as dark as the devil's soul."

John kicked at the soft sawdust and leaves carpeting the ground. "This would make a nice shelter for someone," he said. "It's so soft, you could lie down and sleep like a baby." He planted his pine knot in the soft earth, stretched out on his back, and laced his fingers behind his head, staring upward into the darkness.

"Sure, you could lie down in here if you want to spend the night with some lonesome bear who . . . What are you squinting at?" Ben asked, suddenly jerking his face upward. "Do you see something up there?"

Johnny jumped to his feet. "I'm not sure, Ben," he said, grabbing the little torch and holding it above his head.

The boys whistled softly. "Well, I'll be a ring-tailed roarer," John croaked. "A spear! Do you reckon we can reach it?"

Ben's eyes measured the distance from the ground to the spear and guessed they might just make it.

"Here, Ben," John said. "You climb up on my shoulders and see if you can get it." He squatted, bracing himself against the tree's wall, and Ben quickly scrambled onto his back.

"Now straighten up," Ben grunted.

With John stretched to his full height, Ben's fingertips were able to close on the lance. "It won't budge, John," he said. "Wait a minute."

Johnny felt Ben's feet leave his shoulders. He looked up to see his friend swing, hand-over-hand to the end of the long spear and begin to bounce.

"Look out!" Ben warned. He was still gripping the end of the lance, when he dropped with a thud onto the soft earth. His victorious smile told John he was unhurt. "Look at this thing!" Ben said with awe.

John carefully passed the pine knot over the long weapon, from one end to the other as they inspected the lance. Decorated with beautiful feathers, colorful beads and strips of rawhide, the weapon was obviously very special.

"What do you make of this, Ben?"

The young black stroked a long, bright-blue feather as it caught the brilliance of the fire. "I could take an oath that this wasn't here the day we found the doll," he said. "Why do you think it's here now? Did the same people who left the doll put it here?" He looked upward into the darkness above them. "And think about *this*. If they wanted us to take it down, why did they put it up so high? Maybe we should have left it there."

The boys studied each other's eyes, and this time it was John who fingered his snake root.

"Ben, what if this tree is sacred to the Indians and we're here a-trespassing?" John asked. "Or maybe they put it here for *us*? What should we do?" Their thoughts were interrupted by the distant sound of Pa's special call. It was time to return to the cave.

"Let's leave it here and decide tomorrow," Ben suggested. "If they want us to have it, it will still be here then." His hand dropped automatically to scratch Traveler's rump, and she swung her rear back and forth in that little dance dogs always do before they start scratching their belly with a hind paw. She loved Ben's attention. "Come on, Girl, it's time we left this place to the bears." They agreed to keep the lance a secret, along with the doll, at least until they decided what to do about it.

Early the next morning, Pa shook his young helpers gently. "Come on, Men," he whispered. "We can get another row of logs up before we break our fast. Jack and Molly are already harnessed and ready to go."

Happy to be back at work on the cabin, the boys eagerly jumped into action. The oxen leaned into their harness and pulled. Chains rattled, ropes squeaked, and a long log moved up into place with Pa guiding one end and John steadying the other. Ben coaxed and prodded Jack and Molly until the log hovered above the wall. Pa and John eased it into the saddles of the logs below, as Ben urged the oxen backward a few steps. Done!

With each log hoisted into place, the men and oxen improved their partnership, and soon the job was running smoothly. With Jack and Molly on their team, they were able to accomplish in hours what had taken days before. Each day the boys vowed secretly to get back to the tree, and each night they dropped to their pallets at the back of the cave, too exhausted to do more than sleep. Finally, the walls were finished, and it was time to begin the roof. Pa gave the boys the morning off while he began to split some of the logs into boards. Setting wedge after wedge into a log, Pa drove each deeply into the wood. With loud cracks, the rough boards splintered away in broad planks. Splitting logs was a long, hard job, but Pa was a patient man.

John and Ben were eager to take Traveler out for a good hunt. John's mouth watered as he pictured a plump turkey simmering in Ma's cook pot. There had been no time for hunting, and their bellies were angry about recent meals of roots and berries, but Ma had different ideas.

"We're out of water, boys," she began. "Will you fetch some from the river?" she held a wooden bucket in each hand. Her determined blue eyes had a look that said this would be the first of several chores.

Hallie toddled to her brother and hugged his leg. "Can we bring Hallie along, Ma?" he asked.

Rachel Cooper shot her son a grateful glance. "That is a fine idea, John. I've been too busy these days to play with her. This will be a treat for our little angel."

To get to the river, the boys had to cross the deer path. Their minds raced to the tree. Was the lance still there after all these days? When they reached the soft, damp earth of the deer path, John set Hallie down. Her little feet pit-patted here and there, as she walked from rock to stick to branch, investigating each thing she spied.

"Come on, Hallie," said John as he pointed a finger for her to grab. He led her into the tree, and she immediately chose a soft pile of saw dust in the center of the opening, plopping down to play.

The spear was still there. It had been moved from where they had left it and stood to the right of the entrance, just inside.

"No bear did this," declared John. "What do you reckon is the meaning of this?"

"John, have you ever had that feeling on your neck like someone was staring at the back of your head?" Ben whispered.

"Yes," John answered. He looked into his friend's large brown eyes.

In the dark undergrowth at the edge of the deer path, two other sets of large brown eyes followed each move the boys made. These same eyes had tracked them, along with their father, and now the two light-haired females, since the day they first arrived. It had been a simple matter to glide unnoticed through the tall prairie grass to the cabin and to the cave entrance without ever being detected. Only the large brindled dog had known they were there, and she silently tolerated their presence, as long as they made no threat to her family. Their eyes were especially drawn to this young black man who worked magic with his beautiful knife. The Indians had heard of black people, but they had never before seen actual proof that such people walked the earth. This young man appeared handsome and noble. He would bring pride to any tribe he joined. Traveler left the company of the boys and stood alertly outside the tree's entrance, sniffing in the direction of the Indian scouts. She stared at the underbrush, and it was plain to the natives that she saw them. They dared not move.

"John, I know what to do about this spear," Ben said suddenly. "We need to leave a gift in the tree and see if it gets taken."

John grinned widely. "That's a perfect idea, Ben. If it's gone when we get back, then maybe we should take the spear. What can we give that Ma and Pa won't miss, I wonder?"

The boys followed Hallie as she toddled out of the tree. John caught her hand and steered her toward the buckets. "I don't reckon there is one solitary thing that we don't need," he said. And then like a flash, it came to John. "Ben, you know that statue of Traveler you carved? Well, could you carve another one if you happened to *lose* this one?"

Ben's handsome face broke out in a dazzling smile as he turned toward the river with his bucket. "That's it, John. We can bring it back today. I'll carve another statue of Traveler. In the meantime, we have something to offer the, the, the . . .. who?"

Both boys looked deadly serious as they said the dreaded word together. "Indians."

For the next few days, Ben and John continued to take care of chores for Ma. Occasionally, Pa would put them to work splitting the long oak logs into planks, so that he could rest, but their efforts never lasted longer than two or three planks. Pa would find his strength and return to the job. Because the boys were free to hunt, the cook pot was once again filled with juicy meats. Pa claimed the meat brought back his strength, and soon the planks were ready to be laid across the roof. It was an exciting time, for their cabin would soon be ready to move into.

The boys had visited the tree each day, and each day they felt disappointment, as the wooden dog stood, untouched, on the smooth stone they had moved inside the tree. On the fourth day, they paid their final visit. Pa had warned them they would be working on the cabin once again. There would be no time for hunting. This time, their luck had turned. The dog had disappeared from its perch on the stone. In its place on the same stone, rested a small pair of deerskin moccasins. Laid carefully across the moccasins was the lance. The boys whooped with joy.

"These are definitely gifts!" shouted John, dancing with excitement. "We're a-trading with the Indians!"

Ben picked up the tiny moccasins. Decorated with beautiful red and blue beads and lined with rabbit fur, they spoke of hours of effort and care. "Remember that day we brought Hallie to our tree?" he asked. "Well, we *were* being watched. I'll wager the Indian knew just what size to make these from all Hallie's little footprints in the dirt."

The boys stared at each other. This was serious business.

"We have neighbors, Ben," John said quietly, "and they're a-telling us they want to be friends. Pa will be happy about this, I *think*. He *says* he wants to show them we want to live side-by-side in peace, but look at how we built the cabin. It's like a fort. No windows, an' built like a block house with those peep holes, so's we can look down on whoever's outside. I don't think Pa really trusts the Indians. What if he loads his rifle and takes out after them?"

Ben hooked his thumb through his belt and stared at the moccasins he held. "You might be right, John," he observed. "Sometimes a man can rush to judgment when he thinks his family might be in danger. This spear might cause him worry, but I don't think the moccasins would. And if it's all the same to you, I think we ought to keep this trading tree a secret."

John was busy nodding his head in agreement before Ben had even finished having his say. "I feel the same, Ben. Let's hide the spear and find a way to give Hallie the moccasins."

"Done," agreed Ben.

By the time the pals showed up at the mouth of the cave, the lance had been well hidden and the moccasins were concealed in John's pants.

Pa met his young fellow-builders, saying, "Men, I have good news!" John had noticed lately that any time Pa called them men, it meant there was hard work to be done, and this time promised to be no different.

"We can start the wattle now," Matthew announced proudly. He handed John a shovel and a wooden pail with a rope handle and gave Ben a hand sickle. "Let's see how much we can get done by nightfall," he challenged them.

John dutifully marched off toward the river, with Ben in hot pursuit. "I don't want to sound like some addle-headed fool," the young heir to a fortune asked, "but exactly what *is* wattle?"

John was surprised Ben didn't know, but he was pleased that, for once *he* could do the explaining. It sometimes seemed to him that Ben must have read every book ever written, because he knew about things that John hadn't even dreamed of.

"You chink the cracks between the logs with wattle, so that the wind and rain and cold can't come a-seeping through," John began.

"How?" Ben asked simply. "What do you use?"

"Well, I got this here pail and shovel, 'cause Pa elected me to be in charge of digging up clay. Now *you*, you get to be the sickle man. You go out and cut dead, dried-up grass.

"Then what?" asked Ben.

"We dig ourselves a good mud hole near the cabin. I dump in the clay and you dump in the grass. We'll mix in a little water and tromp around in the ugly mess like a couple of old hogs, until it's all mixed up. Then the fun begins. We tote the wattling to the cabin and begin to chink and smooth, chink and smooth, until there's not even space for a red ant to sneak in."

"Is it really fun, or are you just trying to joke with me?" Ben asked with the look of suspicion in his eyes.

John said nothing, but he wrinkled his nose in disgust.

"Oh," Ben said.

Ma supervised the mixing of the wattling, wanting first more water, then more clay, than more dead grass. The boys began to understand what she wanted, and soon she turned the job over to them. The day wore on. John had lost count of the number of times they had filled the hole. They had stared at everything in the general area as they slogged up and down, back and forth, through the wattle, mixing, mixing, and mixing.

Ben studied a black wasp working at the edge of their brown ooze. Its large abdomen pulsed up and down as it gathered mud. "I've been thinking, John," he said.

"You're lucky. My brain turned to wattle about two hours ago," John commented over his shoulder.

"This batch we're mixing up has to be the best wattle west of the Mississippi," Ben continued, "because every wasp within three days hard flying has dropped in to use it. I figure if we had all the ooze they've buzzed off with, we'd have finished about the time your brain turned to wattle."

John grabbed his bucket and filled it with the heavy clay mixture. "I'll take the inside this time, Slave-Boy," he said. "It's my turn to be cool."

Ben smiled at his friend. Being called *slave* didn't seem to anger him any longer. He knew John was joking, but all the same, he felt like a freed black. Suddenly, thoughts of Osha, his ma, and old Obadiah crept into his mind, and his stomach lurched. He knew for certain they all would find meaning in the word *slave*, and it would be a new, harsh meaning which would be totally different. Master Jeffries hadn't even used the word unless he was talking to a white person who he thought might accuse him of breaking the laws of slavery. The *new* Master Jeffries would probably be meaner than anyone in the whole area. After all, he was cruel enough to murder his own brother! As with every other time he had thought of the black folk of the Jeffries plantation, he felt deeply guilty. If he had just stayed to report Captain Jeffries . . .But then he knew he had done the only thing he could do. He gritted his teeth and stomped harder, marching through the wattle, as he promised himself for the hundredth time that he would find a way to return and free the already-freed blacks of the Jeffries plantation. He would see to it that they received their earnings, so that they could get the very best of starts in their new lives. *A promise is a promise*, he thought, fingering the iron key that hung on a leather thong looped around his neck.

The cabin passed Ma's critical inspection. Working with Pa, the boys had done a very good job. "Now for the stonework, Men," Pa announced, rubbing his hands together like a visiting preacher at Sunday dinner.

John knew what was coming. Ma had been in and out of the cabin for days, inspecting the huge opening where the fireplace and chimney were to stand. He could tell from the gleam in her blue eyes that she had her heart set on a just-so-fireplace, and he hoped they would understand what she wanted.

Jack and Molly were led back from their temporary retirement and hitched to the wagon. The boys were split up, with Ben in charge of wattle for the chimney and John heading up the stone operation. After showing Ben her recipe for a thicker wattle, Ma walked with John to the river. Jack and Molly followed, easily pulling the empty wagon. Ma led John to a large, jumbled mess of river-bed stone. Thousands of years of freezing and thawing had broken the stone into large flat pieces that John could barely lift into the wagon. Ma helped him with the first load of stone and kept him company on his return trip, and then he was on his own.

The settlers lost track of the days. Because Ma was working beside Matthew, meals were scarce. Traveler was sometimes left to entertain Hallie as she toddled between her parents and the boys. Hands were cut and bruised by the jagged rocks. Bodies ached and cried out for rest, but the fireplace, and then the chimney grew steadily taller. Finally, the day came when they had built the chimney high enough that there was little danger of it catching the roof on fire. From that point to the top, they used thick sticks which had been chopped to just the right length. This part of the chimney was mostly wattle, with the sticks used to keep its shape while the wattle dried. When it was completely dry, the wattle chimney would be as hard as stone.

The pain was forgotten by everyone the instant the last layer of wattling was smoothed over the stick frame, and the top of the chimney was squared off neatly. Ma stood back and clasped her clay-caked hands together. Then she cried. John couldn't understand what made a woman cry when she was happy. Maybe when he was full grown and had a wife of his own, he would understand. Pa climbed down from his tall, hand-made ladder and wrapped his big, muddy arms around Ma. He seemed to understand the mystery just fine.

That night, as John lay on his pallet in the back of the cave, he formed a plan. He knew the perfect time and place for the moccasins to appear. As he fell asleep, his thoughts drifted to the tree in the deer path.

The very next morning, Pa was ready to hang the door. He had saved the straightest planks and had planed away their rough spots. With its thick, smooth boards and hickory peg-work, it was a beauty. John and Ben helped Pa set the door into place, and then John and Pa held the heavy door while Ben pounded precious iron nails through the thick, tanned-leather straps that would act as the door's hinges. Soon the door hung on its own. When Pa released the door, it swung shut, closing off the last source of light. The three door-hangers found themselves in near-darkness. As Pa started for the door, John's quick thinking stopped him.

"Look, Pa," he blurted out, "when the door is closed you can look up and see just where the cracks are in the roof. Why don't you study those for a minute, so you can remind us where we need to chink."

Without waiting for a response, John reached the door in three quick strides, opened it, and stepped through. In the darkness he had sucked hard on his trigger finger. Now he spat over his right shoulder and grinned as he saw his spit land squarely on the middle hinge.

"Leave me, wart, and stick to the hinge," John muttered as quietly as possible.

Ben stood beside Pa in the cabin and fought down a belly-laugh as he watched the man stare in amazement.

"John?" Pa shouted.

John ducked back in the door. "Yes Sir!" he said loudly. "There's nothing like a little spit for a bad squeak in new leather." He grabbed the door and fanned it left and right, cocking his ear toward the hinges. Then he spat on the hinge once more. "There, that ought to do it," he said with a look of confidence. He shut the door on his way back outside.

In the near-darkness, Pa turned to Ben. "I must be losing my hearing," he said. "Did you hear anything?"

Pa heard a huge smile in Ben's answer. "Oh, yes; I heard it, all right."

Matthew Cooper put the boys to work splitting shingles. The roof would hold up well enough to move into the cabin, but a lasting roof needed shingles sealed well with pine pitch. He showed the boys how long to cut the logs from which they would split off shingles, and then he put them to work with a crossbuck saw while he went off in search of weeping evergreen trees. Pa would gather tree sap for making the pitch, while the boys added muscle to muscle as they sawed logs. John and Ben worked well together, stationed at opposite ends of the long saw. First, John would pull the saw toward him, and then Ben would reverse the process. The sawing went especially well, when they learned how to start the slice without bucking the saw out of the splintering bark.

About the time the boys felt they might never stand up straight again, Pa returned with his first of many collections of pine sap. He read the signs that said he might have a rebellion on his hands if he asked for one more log to be cut, and he took them aside to learn a new skill: splitting off shingles. He showed them how to set the one-handed splitter, and then drive it home through a log. John was strong enough to split off a shingle in two solid whacks with the heavy wooden maul, and Ben was happy to let him pound away with pride, knowing the maul alone might tax him beyond his limits.

Ma and Pa began to sniff the air early each morning, and then eye each other warily. "It's a-coming, Rachel," Pa said one evening at dinner. "I smelled sure signs of it this morning. I can't put off the trip much longer."

The boys knew Pa meant he would soon be leaving for St. Louis to buy winter supplies. They needed staples to carry them through the winter, because the day the wagon almost slid backwards down the mountain, John had thrown out bags and barrels of the very things Ma would need to keep them all fed until they could grow food for themselves. They had already used up a large part of the staples they bought at the river settlement, and they had arrived too late to plant any crops.

They would have to wait a long time to replace the furnishings John had thrown out. Some of the things he had hurled out of the wagon to save Ma and Hallie had been very precious to Ma, but she had long ago decided those things were not nearly as precious as having all the Coopers alive, instead of lying dead somewhere at the bottom of a deep ravine.

"Men," Pa began while Ben and John rolled their eyes at each other, "You've got to set aside the shingles for a time and lay in grass for Jack and Molly, while I set them up with a winter shelter."

Happy to be occupied with a change of jobs, they started near the cabin with the sickle. Taking turns to rest their weary backs and arms, they steadily cut in an ever-widening circle around the log building. They were clearing an open space and gathering in hay for the oxen at the same time. In the wilderness, it was a good idea to cut down anything surrounding a cabin or barn that could catch fire or hide a varmint, whether of the four-legged or two-legged type.

Their old cave-home was chosen as the best place for their animal shelter, and Pa set to work enclosing the opening with wooden planks. He quickly built a door, and the three weary workers hung it with ease, because it wasn't nearly as heavy as their cabin door.

Late that night, Pa gathered his family together. They sat proudly near their brand-new fireplace with a cozy fire crackling away and trying its best to shoot them with sparks as the burning wood popped from hidden droplets of sap and water.

"Tomorrow at sunrise, I will head for the river," he announced. "I'll be leaving the wagon and oxen here so I can make better time. If I can catch a ride downriver on a boat, I'll get there sooner. Then, after I've got our staples, I hope to find Le Claire. I'll figure out a way to get the supplies back, anyway. When I get back, I'll hide our staples at the river and come for Jack and Molly.

He looked proudly at his tall, strong son. "John, you know what this means. You will be responsible for the lives of yourself and three other people. You must provide them with food and safety."

As much as John felt pride in his father's trust, the thought of being without Pa scared him 'til his hands felt cold and clammy, and his teeth hurt.

Pa ran his fingers through his curly black hair and crossed the room, staring into the fire as he continued. "Make sure you always have two-or-three days' worth of water. Keep meat in the pot. You need strength. John, while I'm gone, I want you to sleep down here near the door. Keep the bar down and leave the latch string pulled inside, even when some of you are outside. Always call for a name if there's a knock at the door."

Pa's thoughts turned to the oxen. "Put Jack and Molly in the cave each evening and close the door on them. Keep plenty of water in there for them in case you have to hole up in the cabin for some reason. With all that hay and enough water, they should get along."

It was plain to John and everyone else that Pa dreaded leaving. Although John felt able to take on the responsibility, it frightened him to hear such talk about "calling for names," and "holing up."

Rachel read her son's thoughts and reached out a reassuring hand. Gently, she squeezed his shoulder. Her wink told him Pa sometimes had a way of worrying too much and all would be fine.

"When I get to St. Louis, I'll hunt up some ink and paper, and I'll write to Grandma and Grandpa," Pa continued. "I'll tell them all about our new home and about our times in the woods and on the river. He reached out and clamped a huge hand on Ben's shoulder and smiled. "Why, I'll even tell them they got themselves a new grandson, name of Benjamin. They'll be interested to hear about how he happened into our family."

Ben decided to let slide Pa's talk about his membership in the Cooper clan, but with mention of ink and paper, he immediately considered writing a letter to Mr. Calhoun, Master Jeffries good friend and lawyer. Surely he could find a spare sheet of paper or parchment somewhere in Rachel Cooper's supplies. But what would he use for an envelope? He could make one, he supposed. But then the door slammed shut on the idea when he thought about the consequences. Captain Jeffries was sure to be watching for mail addressed to Mr. Calhoun. As soon as he sent a letter, he would be announcing his location as boldly as printing up a hand bill for everyone and his brother to read. He thought of the Cooper family and all they had done for him, and he knew he couldn't expose them to the horrible danger that might find its way to their doorstep. No, it was far too soon to do anything. His hands were still tied. As he climbed the ladder to his pallet in the attic and lay down next to his best friend, he felt as if the troubles of the whole world were crawling under the coverlet with him. He was still awake when he heard Traveler answer the chilling howl of a faraway wolf.

"John?" Pa called from below.

"Yes Pa?"

"Starting tomorrow, you keep Traveler inside at night."

"Sure Pa," John answered, struggling with a fresh crop of goose-bumps that had nothing to do with the cold creeping in from outside.

Ben sighed, knowing as he drifted toward sleep that he wasn't the only person taking the world's troubles to bed. John would have a challenge on his hands until Pa arrived safely home.

DEADLY ATTACKS

D ESPITE HIS FEARS THE NIGHT before, John stepped easily into his new responsibilities, feeling the strength that daylight gave him. When you march them out into the fresh air and sunshine, a parade's worth of night-time worries usually break ranks and skitter off, never to be heard from again. John and Ben even found time to add to the growing stack of shingles. Within a few days of Pa's departure, John found he was even enjoying his new role in the family.

"You know, Ben, I think I'm probably working harder now than I did any time before Pa left," he said as they walked to a nearby piney woods. "This'll probably sound strange, but I think I like the work more. I'm doing it because I *want* to do it, not because someone tells me I have to, and it's the same work. Maybe that's because I'm working for myself."

Silent, Ben kept walking. Finally, he spoke up. "I understand, John. Believe me, I understand."

Within a few steps, however, John realized he wasn't totally working for himself. After all, they were headed out to the woods, because Ma had asked them to collect pine needles. Every day Ma kept them busy with projects. The pine needles were to be added to the home-made mattresses they slept on, called pallets. Ma wanted to freshen and fluff them up for the winter. She had even made a pallet for Hallie. From now on, John would carry his little sister up to the loft at night. He and Ben would take good care of her. It was time she had a pallet of her own.

Kicking his way through a skiff of colorful autumn leaves, John tried to cover his blunder. "When Ma wants me to do something, she never orders me to. She asks me like her heart would break if I said I had something else to do, and I'm not one to break my ma's heart."

Thy boys returned a few hours later with four large burlap sacks filled with wonderful-smelling pine needles. Ben propped one bag against his knee and banged on the thick, wooden door. "It's the pine tree brigade," he shouted.

They waited, but the door remained shut with the latch string stuffed inside where they couldn't reach it. They were locked out. Just as they were beginning to worry about Ma and Hallie, dirt, wood chips and sawdust drifted down onto their heads. Ma was cleaning up in the loft, and she had swept the dirt right out through one of Pa's famous peepholes.

"Well, at least those holes won't go to waste," Ben said with a smile. He sat himself down on a sack of pine needles. "We might as well wait right here until she decides to come outside, because she can't hear us. She's probably up there singing like she usually does."

Ben was right. Ma had been busy from the minute the boys left for the piney woods, and she had sung nearly every song she knew by the time they got back. In a burst of energy, she tidied up their new home. While she sang, Ma had tightened the ropes on the bed so it wouldn't sag and creak so. She unpacked one of the trunks which had made it through the trip without being thrown overboard, setting precious platters, pitchers, and bowls on the mantel. Carefully studying her new home, she planned for a table and benches and even some chairs. Ma set up her spinning wheel and wished for wool. Maybe next year at this time she would be spinning, she thought, smiling to herself.

Unseen by the Coopers, another mother had already begun *her* spinning. For her home, she chose a peephole at the back of the loft. After a brief courtship with her mate, she killed him. Now she wound his lifeless corpse with round after round of web. His body would provide the first meal for her young ones when they hatched. Ever so quietly, she had spun, until the peephole was filled with her silky web. Soon she would begin to lay her eggs. She was a black widow spider!

John and Ben took pride in the fine shingles they created each day. The blade on the splitter was dulling from the miles of wood it had splintered through, and John considered sharpening it, but he never seemed to find the time.

Pa had been right. Winter was coming. Frost glistened on the prairie grass each morning, and leaves fell into a noisy carpet that warned animals of John's whereabouts. Hunting was getting harder these days. Then his luck changed. He shot a deer that would give them a good supply of meat. Skinning it on the spot, he gutted the animal and threw its innards into the small river that eventually found its way to the Mississippi. Then he cut out the heart, ribs and hind quarters, dragging them home atop the deerskin. When he and Ben returned for the rest of the meat, it had already been carried off by hungry animals. Because the big buck was too heavy to carry, he had done the best thing he could. He took the meatiest parts and risked losing the rest.

Ma had wasted no time when she saw John's meat. When the boys returned from the piney woods, one hind quarter was already roasting on the spit, and the rest of the meat hung from a rafter in the cabin. After letting in the boys and their dog, she returned to scraping the inside of the deer skin.

"This skin is beautiful, John," she said. "We need so many things. You boys have grown so much that you each need new shirts. Maybe we could get pants for you out of this, too."

Ben offered a wise suggestion. "I've been thinking maybe John could get the new clothes, and I could use the ones he grows out of. I *am* a lot smaller, even though my brain holds more." He smiled, and then joined in Ma and John's laughter.

When the leg was well-roasted, Ma served up a meal that left the boys sleepy. Happy and satisfied, they stretched out on the bed. As he watched his Ma scrape, scrape, scrape, John drifted near the edge of sleep, and darkness closed in on the cabin.

Traveler had paced nervously for hours and refused to eat her share of fresh meat. Now openly upset, she whined and scratched at the door.

"Traveler!" Ma scolded loudly. "Not my new door!" Her shout awakened John with a jolt. He and Ben sat up in time to see the dog's fur raise as she growled ferociously.

Ma's frightened eyes darted toward John. "There's something out there!" she whispered.

The big brindle dog left her post at the door and went to the back corner of the cabin. Standing stone still, she cocked her ears toward the outside. All was quiet but the crackling of the cook fire. As if frozen in fear, John, Ben and Ma sat quietly, searching each-others' eyes for an answer. What was out there?

Suddenly, through the walls of the cabin came the piercing sound of splintering, cracking wood, followed quickly by the agonized bellows of Jack and Molly, and John jumped to action.

"Ben, fire the lantern." He shouted as he reached for Prilla and checked her prime. Do you have your knife?" Ben nodded, touching the polished handle of the knife hanging at his side. Angry at being caged inside when she was needed to be *outside*, Traveler jumped furiously at the door, barking insistently, raring to attack the unknown beast that had dared to invade her territory.

"Ma, bar the door behind us and keep the latch string in," John said quickly, "but stay near the door to let us in fast if you need to."

Ma nodded in stunned silence as the boys lifted the bar and the latch and stepped outside into the crisp, windy night. Traveler shot through the dried leaves up the hill to the cave barn. The boys hurried through the darkness holding their lantern high in the hopes of seeing ahead. Stumbling over stones hidden by the swirling leaves, they worked their way up to the cave.

Traveler had already inspected the oxen and was ranging across the open area outside the cave, whining and baying at the strong scent that her nose caught at every turn. It was plain the oxen's attacker was gone, but how *far* gone?

Ben raised the lantern once more and the light revealed that the planks had been splintered totally in two by a massive force. The door was broken and hanging open. What kind of animal had such strength?

"Listen," said Ben in a whisper. "It's gotten to the oxen."

John heard pain-filled moans coming from inside; moans he had never heard before. "Come on, Ben," he urged. "Traveler, you guard, Girl."

With their dog posted outside, they stepped timidly into the cave.

John's stomach knotted with fear and sickness when he saw old Jack. The ox stood with his front feet set wide apart and his bloody head hanging low, as his sides heaved with his efforts to breathe. Ben held the lantern closer. Huge flaps of hide and torn muscle hung from one side and shoulder. White patches of bone showed through the bloody flesh. Molly stood nervously behind Jack. She had not been touched.

"Jack, you old fighter, you kept it away from your girl, didn't you?" John said softly as tears clouded his eyes. "Oh, Ben," he sobbed. "I'm afraid he's a goner!"

Ben gently lifted a piece of bloody flesh and pushed it back into place. "John, once I saw Osha sew a slave back together. His back had been cut sort of like this by a whip. Everyone said he'd die, too, but Osha wouldn't let him. He lived, and my master bought him so he could stay with us where he'd be safe for the rest of his life." Ben's heart warmed with memories of old Obadiah.

John gripped his rifle. "My mind tells me I should shoot Jack. Look at him suffer! But my heart just won't let me do it. What do you think Pa would do?"

"I don't know what he'd do," answered Ben wisely. "The question is, what will *you* do?"

They hurried back to the cabin and pounded on the door, yelling their names as they did. Instantly, they heard the bar and latch lift. The door swung open, and the boys stumbled in with news of their discovery. John reached out and pulled his reluctant dog inside before resetting the latch and bar. In their excitement, Ben and John talked simultaneously, and within seconds, Ma had a clear picture of the destruction they had seen. She paced nervously in front of the fire, eager to take action. "What could it have been, Boys?" she asked.

Ben and John eyed each other as their minds agreed. "A bear," they answered together.

"This bear has to be huge, too, Ma," John added.

"And be part devil," Ben chimed in.

"Ma, we've got to try to sew up Jack," said John. "We can't let him stand up there and bleed to death. We've got to try to save him."

Ma's fingers shot to the precious needle she always kept stuck through her dress. "I've sewed up people before," she said. "I guess I don't know as how a cut ox would be much different. Just tougher hide, maybe." She reached for her scissors. "Ben, this time you stay with Hallie," she said, "and I'll go with Johnny to see what I can do. Remember the bar and the latch."

"Ma, where's your thread?" asked John.

"I ran out of thread about a month ago, but I already know what I'll do. I'll use hairs from Molly's tail. It sounds like she owes him that." She tucked her scissors into her apron pocket and snatched a rag, a chunk of soap and a bucket of water. The soap followed the scissors into her pocket, and she draped the rag over her shoulders. After throwing a thick blanket over her head, Ma grabbed the lantern. "Ready," she said, lifting her chin.

Traveler was eager to get out of the cabin. She bolted for the cave as soon as the door opened, and John could tell from her actions that the danger from the bear had passed, at least for now. Just the same, he gripped Prilla tightly, watching and listening for signs of the monster's return.

Rachel cried when she saw Jack. His eyes had begun to glaze over with shock, but he stubbornly stood his ground, too weak to object when Ma began to poke and push. She stepped over to Molly and snipped several long, brown hairs from her tail. Carefully, she washed them in soap and water and placed them in her apron. Piece by piece, she sewed Jack back together. Because John had to hold the lantern, he was unable to guard the cave entrance. He had to be satisfied with knowing that Traveler was there to keep watch.

Too weakened to stand any more, Jack dropped to his knees. He wanted to lie down, but Ma wasn't finished. John wedged his knee under the ox's chin so that he had to lie upright. Finally, the job was done.

"Don't let his head go yet, John," Ma cautioned. "We've got to get some water into him." She carried one of the water buckets over and placed it under Jack's nose. "Now, I'll hold one horn and you hold the other, and we'll try to lower his nose into the bucket." She grunted as she grabbed a huge horn.

John quickly grasped Jack's other horn with both hands. He lifted with all the strength he had, as he eased his knee out from under Jack's chin. Although Jack's eyes were still open, John was fairly certain he could no longer see.

"He can't die! He can't die! He can't die!" his mind screamed.

Mother and son strained with the effort of easing Jack's massive head into the bucket. Too weak to hold it up himself, he left the job to them. They softly spoke their reassurances to the big animal and watched, as Jack began to drink.

"He knows we won't let him lie down until he drains the bucket," explained John's stubborn ma with a proud smile.

The water was gone. They lifted his head, and John kicked away the pail. Gratefully, Jack rolled onto his uninjured side in the dried grass bedding.

After wondering momentarily if there was anything else they should be doing, John grabbed his ma's hand and held it tightly. "God, we need your help again," he prayed simply. The weary pair trudged through the leaves back to the cabin. Immediately after their knock and shout, Ben let them in.

Against her will, John dragged Traveler back inside the cabin. "Girl, I'd love to let you stay with Jack and Molly to guard them, but we need you to guard *us*," the exhausted boy apologized.

With Ben and John stretched out on the clay floor near the door and Ma in her bed beside her sleeping daughter, they quickly fell asleep. Traveler gave up her vigil and cozied up to John's side. Soon the cabin was peaceful.

Early the next day, John and Ben checked on Jack. He had not changed. They bullied him into lying upright and gave him more water, but once again, he rolled onto his least-damaged side. Molly seemed reluctant to leave Jack in order to graze, so they fluffed up the dried grass and brought lots of fresh water. They fetched axes and chopped down two large oak trees, cutting off the limbs to save them for braces. Then they set to work driving wedges into the trunks and splitting off extra thick planks. It was a struggle to split off planks so thick from green wood, but they stubbornly kept at it. Late in the afternoon, they had all the planks they needed. They coaxed Molly out and harnessed her. She dragged the limbs to the cave's entrance, and the boys wedged them solidly across the opening. To make sure they could not be moved, John drove hickory wedges into the space surrounding them.

"I'd like to see the bear get through this," dared John through clenched teeth.

Next, the planks were set in place. John and Ben used the last of Pa's precious iron spikes for the job, but they felt sure he would approve. The door came last, and Ben suggested they forget about leather hinges and use a door that would lock into place using thick wooden bars and L-shaped iron braces, which they removed from the back of the wagon. Finally, the job was finished, and none too soon, for the sky was beginning to dim. They had spent the entire day working on the cave opening, but they felt proud of their accomplishments. They watered Jack one, final time and set out for the cabin.

The night passed peacefully, and the settlers awoke with new energy the following day.

The cave-barn looked just as they had left it. When they entered, they found Jack lying up on his knees, chewing peacefully on a large pile of fresh, green clover.

"Clover!" exclaimed Ben. "Where on earth did you find this, John?"

"Ben, I didn't put that there. I've never even run across wild clover like that. Are you telling me *you* didn't, either?"

"I slept up in the loft all night," Ben replied. "How would I have gotten past you?"

The boys stared at the clover in disbelief. "The Indians," they whispered together. Before they returned to the cabin, Ben suggested that Ma had enough to worry about with the bear's attack, and they agreed to keep the clover a secret.

Ben and John worked quietly near the cabin that day. They couldn't overcome the feeling that they were being watched. "I almost wish they'd step up and introduce themselves," John thought aloud. "Maybe they could tell us what to do about that bear."

The following morning, the boys found another pile of fresh clover in front of Jack. The huge ox struggled to his feet when they entered the cave. Slowly, he made his way to the water bucket and drank deeply.

Ben smiled at John. "I don't think he could take another day of being lifted by his horns," he joked. "He's getting back his pride."

In St Louis, Pa packed together the last items on his supplies list. Because everyone seemed to know the jolly captain of the huge boat tied to its own pier on the river, he had found Le Claire easily. Matthew had been surprised by the number of French-speaking men and women in St. Louis. Many people spoke English, but it was usually broken and heavily accented, like Le Claire's. He felt like a foreigner, and until a few years ago, he would have been. Now, thanks to the

President Jefferson's Louisiana Purchase, this land was Yankee, and he felt proud to be a part of opening the wilderness.

After packing, he hurried to the Troussard Hotel, intent upon conducting one last bit of business. Across the street, a pair of yellow-green eyes caught sight of Matthew. The man pulled his sea captain's hat down to hide his face and quietly followed Pa. An evil smile curled his lip. Thanks to his Indian assassin's report, he knew he had found Ben's trail once again.

Pa stepped into the hotel and asked for paper, pen, and ink, as he reached into his pocket. The man behind the desk smiled kindly and raised a hand. "There is no charge for this service, Monsieur," he said. "It is for our pleasure that we are giving paper." He produced two sheets of ivory-colored paper, an envelope, and a newly trimmed quill pen. "You will be finding a pot of fresh ink over there," he said, pointing toward the front window.

Pa thanked the man and moved to a small table and chair next to the window. He was happy to sit in the bright sunlight and enjoy watching the people pass by outside, while he composed a letter to his parents.

"Dear Ma and Pa," he wrote.

Soon Matthew was so deeply involved in his news that he did not see the captain enter the hotel. Jeffries moved to a spot near the desk and sat in a large chair facing away from Pa and the manager. Removing his hat, he smoothed back his hair and raised a handbill, pretending to read the latest news.

Pa's letter was finished. He folded the papers and slipped them into the envelope. Stepping up to the desk, he offered the man his letter along with the last of his money.

"Thank you, Monsieur. We will deliver this to the docks right away. There is a packet which sails for the ports of the north tomorrow," said Troussard. He looked at the address. "And this is for a relative, yes?"

Pa smiled. "Yes Sir," he said proudly, "John Cooper is my own father. He is still alive and well and farming back in Stowe's Fork, Virginia. He and my ma are both still healthy in their old age."

"And now you will be making them happy with the news of you," the manager said.

"I'm sure they're a-wondering about us," said Pa, as he turned to leave. "Thank you, Sir."

Jeffries had heard all he needed. He slipped quietly out the side door and followed Pa to a small stone house near the river. Matthew knocked on the door and was admitted by an elderly servant-woman.

Seeing Pa enter the house, Jeffries turned quickly and retraced his steps. He stopped long enough to stand in front of a shiny store window and inspect his reflection. Smoothing his hair and straightening his hat, Jeffries stood tall. He brushed off his blue jacket and adjusted his shirt sleeves. Finally, he masked his devilish plan with a confident smile, and he walked calmly into the Hotel Troussard.

"I beg your pardon," he said to the manager, "but I understand my brother has already posted a letter back to our father, John Cooper. Would you be so kind as to give me the letter so that I might add my news to it?"

"But Monsieur," began the manager. He turned to see Jeffries' impressive suit and smiling face. Surely someone so distinguished looking could be trusted. He paused to consider.

"John Cooper from Stowe's Fork, Virginia," Jeffries continued through his smile. "Surely you remember. My brother just told me he gave you the letter to post a few minutes ago." He could see that he was winning the man over.

"I have some good news for him," Jeffries continued. He leaned across the desk and winked at the manager. "Even my own brother does not know yet, but, after all these years, my wife is with child! We had given up hope, and now, by some miracle . . ."

Troussard glowed with goodwill. "But of course, Monsieur, I remember now, John Cooper of Stowe's Fork." He retrieved the letter and handed it to Jeffries. "I am congratulating to you and to Madam Cooper," he added as he gave a paper and pen to Jeffries. "You will be finding a pot of fresh ink which is there," he said, pointing graciously and giving a slight bow.

The evil captain flashed his broadest, most innocent smile as he turned and sought a private spot. He opened the letter and quickly studied it. His heart raced as he read about the black boy, Ben. Matthew had even been kind enough to point out the location of their new home. It would be a simple matter to find this boy, Benjamin, and to kill him. Jeffries smiled at his good fortune. Very soon, now, nothing would endanger his inheritance. He could enjoy his brother's wealth with no risk of ever being accused of murdering him to get it.

While pretending to write his happy news, Jeffries instead copied down the details of the Coopers' new location. After secretly slipping his notes into his pocket, he resealed Matthew's letter and returned it to the manager. "Thank you so much," he said warmly. "You have helped to bring joy to my old parents." He leaned across the front desk and whispered with a wink, "Now, if you happen to see my brother again, you will keep our little secret, won't you?"

As the door closed behind Captain Jeffries, Troussard realized the honorable gentleman did not resemble his brother in the least. *Strange*, he thought, twisting one end of his well-waxed moustache. He shrugged his shoulders and called for the dock messenger. There would be enough time to get the letter to the packet about to sail.

Jeffries left the hotel and returned to his own private room above a dirty tavern at the edge of town. He lay back on his bed and smiled at the ceiling. Raising a finger to stroke the mole on his cheek, he made his plans for Ben's murder.

John kept Prilla loaded, primed, and within easy reach at all times. Except for short trips into the woods to hunt, he stayed near home, guarding his family and the oxen. Ma and Hallie stayed inside the cabin, and he and Ben did all the fetching.

"John, you look as nervous as a bug on the hen-house wall," said Ben as they carried fresh water up from the river. "You've got to get yourself busy on something to take this bear off your mind. Just look out there." He pointed to Jack and Molly grazing peacefully in a patch of prairie grass. "They even *saw and fought* the thing, and they aren't upset any longer. And think of Traveler. She'll let us know in plenty of time if a bear comes into our area."

John knew his friend was right. If he worked hard enough to wear himself out, he was bound to fall asleep instead of lying awake just dreaming up all the horrible ways a bear could lay them all to waste. "Let's get back to work on those shingles, Ben," he said, thinking how strange it felt to be happy about returning to such back-breaking work.

Ben was relieved to see his pal's heart lighten. "John, I have this feeling that your pa is on his way home now," he said.

"Do you think you could ever come to calling him *your* pa, too?" John asked. "I think he'd like that." Ben swallowed back a sudden lump in his throat and held his secret close to his heart. He remained silent.

The boys tore into the cedar logs with a vengeance. They worked steadily through the day, skipping lunch. Then toward evening, as Ben took his turn with the splitter, a knot in the wood caused the dull blade to flip out of the log, end-over-end. Before the splitter landed, Ben's right arm was laid open with a nasty cut.

John dropped the saw and grabbed Ben's arm, pressing the flesh back into place. "Hurry, Ben," he urged. "We've got to get you sewed up right quick." He banged on the door and shouted to identify himself. Rachel read the urgency in John's voice and swung the door open quickly.

"Ben's cut, Ma," John said as he helped his friend to the hearth stool, "and it's my fault, 'cause I wouldn't take the time to sharpen the splitter. Oh, Ben! I'm so *sorry!*"

"It's not your fault, John," said Ben as he watched Ma pluck out one of her long, red-gold hairs. "Well, if hair worked on Old Jack, I guess it'll work on me." He gritted his teeth and looked away from his arm.

"Ben, I'm going to take one stitch here," said Ma, pointing to the corner of the flap of skin. She was looking so carefully at his cut that she failed to see that he didn't care to watch. "I think we can hold the rest together with a bandage."

"Ow!" Ben yelped as the needle pierced his skin. "Ouch! Osha always said you should yell so the dyspepsia won't get stuck in your belly to aggravate you in your old age," he explained sheepishly.

"Then you better yell all you want," Ma said. She reached into the trunk for a scrap of clean cloth and used it to carefully wrap his arm. "Now lie down on my bed for a spell," she ordered Ben as she tied the ends of the bandage. "You've lost some blood." She removed her bloody apron and put it in a pail of water to soak.

Ben opened his eyes to see John's guilty, hang-dog expression, and warned gruffly, "If you apologize to me one more time, I'm going to cast a spell on you!" Then he winked.

John shrugged his shoulders and raised his hands, "Really, Ben," he began …

Ben sat up and pointed a finger at John. "Leave me, wart, and stick to the hinge," he chanted. Both boys exploded with laughter.

For the next hour, John occupied himself by entertaining Hallie. Now that she could walk, she was more fun. Her favorite game was peek-a-boo, and she seemed to believe that no one could see her if she covered her eyes. She could say, "Pa, Ma, and Ben," but she couldn't yet say "John." Instead, she called him "Da." Today, Hallie toddled again and again to the door.

"Da?" she would say, reaching toward the bar.

John could understand her feelings. He enjoyed the safety and coziness of the cabin, but he could never stay inside for long without yearning for the sunshine. He wondered how his ma could stand being inside for so many hours now that Pa was away. John thought of the bear and was grateful that Pa had allowed no windows. He glanced at his sleeping friend. Ben had rolled to his stomach and dangled his injured arm over the edge of the bed. Blood steadily oozed through his bandage and trickled down his arm, dripping from his middle finger to the floor.

"Ma!" he called, "Ben's bleeding!"

Ma hurried down from the loft where she had been working on Hallie's pallet. She lifted his soaked bandage and squinted at the cut. "We've got to stop this bleeding," she said with a frown, "or I'm going to have to do more sewing." Putting her finger to her chin, she thought a minute. "I'll be right back," she announced over her shoulder as she scrambled back up the ladder. The boys listened from below as Ma moved about, apparently searching for something. "Here you are," she said from a back corner of the loft.

She scurried down the ladder with a handful of spider webs. "Thanks to Pa's peepholes," she said breathlessly, "we have just what we need: cobwebs."

John watched his ma proudly. She knew a cure for just about everything, he decided. Some of her cures were not such fun to experience, but it was a comfort that she always knew just what to do.

Ma unwrapped Ben's bandage. "Now, Ben," she warned, these cobwebs have to stop the bleeding, or you know what I'll have to do."

He shuddered, eyeing the needle stuck through her dress. "Yes, Ma'am."

Rachel carefully packed Ben's wound with the silky webs. They quickly worked their magic, and the bleeding stopped. "Now, let's eat," she suggested, for it's getting late, and we must get Hallie to sleep." She dished up a steaming stew brimming with tender bits of a rabbit that Ben had brought down early that morning with his knife. Ma had used the last of her corn meal to create little corn cakes. Ben and John ate like half-starved animals. "That's what happens when growing boys skip a meal," Ma scolded, as she heaped second helpings onto their wooden trenchers.

Finally, the food hit bottom, and the boys' eyes begged for sleep. Hard work, fresh air, excitement, and worry had taken their toll. John carried Hallie up to her pallet and covered her with her quilt. As had happened every night since she began wearing her moccasins, she would not permit him to remove them.

"Suit yourself, you little blond Indian," John laughed, as he returned to the ladder. He helped Ben climb to the loft and tried one final time to apologize for Ben's injury, but his black brother would have none of it. John plumped his pallet and stretched out on the floor in front of the door. Ma banked the fire and sat on the hearth stool, scratching Traveler's ears and searching for ticks. When she found one of the little pests, she pinched it from the big dog's skin and threw it into the fire, pleased with the sizzling sound it made. One dead tick.

"Well, Girl," she said softly, "I think Matthew will be back before long. Then you and Hallie and I can get back outside where we belong." Giving the dog a final pat, she went to bed.

Up in the back corner of the loft, an angry black spider skittered back and forth across the planks, searching for her eggs. She returned again and again to the peep hole where her silken web, filled with her precious eggs, had been until a short time before. The tattered remnants of her web filled her with an urgent need to defend what she had already lost. In the blackness of night, she forged across the floor, looking for revenge. She reached a pallet and crawled across its soft peaks and valleys. Encountering a deerskin moccasin, she climbed to the edge of the soft fur. Turning sharply, she burrowed into the fur and found herself against that hated feel of human skin. Again and again, she buried her fangs into the soft human flesh, releasing her deadly poison until there was none left.

At sunrise, John was awakened by Traveler's insistent pull on his shirt. He scratched her ear and reached for Prilla, understanding that his dog good behavior had earned her some fresh air and exercise. "Come on, Girl," he whispered as he raised the bar and latch.

Ma lifted her head in time to see her son and his dog step into the early morning. A hint of fresh air tugged at her heart as she rose to poke up the fire and stoke it with dried wood. Soon she heard Ben shuffle across the floor of the loft. "How's your arm, Ben?" she called from below.

Ben started down the ladder. "It's stiff and sore, but I think it's healing," he answered. He excused himself and hurried outside to find John and Traveler.

Ma began the endless chore of cooking, and soon the boy's noses led them back to the cabin for breakfast.

"Where's Hallie?" John asked. "Isn't my little Indian awake yet?"

"No," answered Ma. "You'd better go up and fetch her, before she sleeps through breakfast."

John climbed the ladder. "Hallie, Hallie," he said quietly in a sing-song voice. "Ma!" he shouted from the loft. "Come a-running! Hallie's took awful sick!"

Rachel hiked up her skirts and scaled the ladder in record time. Hallie lay moaning in a dream that would not stop. Although she was soaked with perspiration, she seemed quite hot when Ma touched her forehead. Her left leg was swollen and red. Little shivers shook Hallie from head to toe, causing her few little teeth to chatter. John read fear in his ma's eyes.

"Wrap her in Ben's quilt, John. It'll be dry. Then bring her down to my bed," she said.

Rachel struggled over Hallie for hours. She tried every cure she could think of. She brewed boneset tea to make Hallie vomit, but nothing changed. For her fever, she tried dogwood root. She burned juniper wood and held Hallie in the smoke.

John watched the fear in his ma's eyes turn to panic. If only she knew the cure! He stepped outside to fetch more water to bathe Hallie and motioned for Ben to come along. "Ben, what can we do?"

The young black boy shook his head in puzzlement. "We've got to get help, John," he said.

John looked into the depth of Ben's wise, dark eyes and asked, "Do you think the Indians would help us?"

"I've been wondering that myself," Ben answered, "but how can we find them?"

"Well, you know how we have the feeling they're always watching us?" John asked, his mind racing quicker than a bull-snake being stomped by an ox.

"Yes . . ."

"Maybe if we could give them a signal that we need help, well, maybe they'd come a-running. They brought all that clover to Old Jack when he was hurt."

They shuffled their way through dried leaves as they carried the water back to the house, and suddenly, the answer came like a flash into Ben's quick mind. "The spear!" he shouted.

"Wait right here, Ben," John said as he ran to the cave. He returned carrying the long, beautiful war lance, and they picked up their pace, hurrying to the cabin. "We've got to put it where we can be sure the Indians will see it," John planned aloud.

Ben was thinking right along the same track. "Maybe on the roof?"

"Perfect! Don't tell Ma, though; she has enough to worry about."

The boys delivered the water and checked on Hallie's progress. If anything, she was worse. "Ma, I've got to see to Jack and Molly," John said, "and get a couple of important jobs done." He reckoned he wasn't exactly telling a lie if he talked about important jobs.

Ma glanced up at John through eyes glazed by exhaustion. "Go ahead, Son. There is nothing more I know to do. Just don't get too far away, in case we need you."

While Ben kept Rachel talking, John ducked outside with Traveler. As quietly as he could, he climbed the corner logs to the roof and walked as high as he dared. Then he thrust the long, thin point of the spear into the stout ridge pole that formed the peak of the roof.

Hearing the impact of the spear, Ma jumped. "What was that?"

"Oh, John was probably trying to knock that squirrel off the roof again, Ben answered calmly. "He's a fat, tasty-looking one."

Rachel hardly seemed to hear his answer but was instantly calmed by his voice. As she cradled her baby and sang softly to her through the fear-swollen lump in her throat, John raced to the barn and checked on the oxen. When he returned to the cabin, his ma was trying, once again, to cool down her daughter's fever by dabbing hot skin with cool water. "Why don't you rest, Ma, and I'll do that," he suggested. He dipped a clean cloth in the water, wrung it out, and began to gently bathe his little sister.

Ben noticed the breakfast food for the first time. "I think it's well past lunch time. Let's all eat something. This day may turn into a week before we know it." He took Rachel by the hand and led her to the hearth stool. Taking a trencher from the mantle, he filled it with a dipper full of oatmeal from the stew pot. He took the last corn cake from her biscuit tin and added it to the meal. Fetching her spoon from the rack, he handed it to her with the food. Rachel sat silently and ate without thinking.

"This smells good, John," Ben said as he dished up a plate for his best friend. He grabbed a long iron hook and pulled on a swinging iron bar, bringing another pot from the back of the fireplace. It was last night's stew. Using the big wooden dipper which he had carved for Rachel, he scooped up a serving for Traveler and dumped it into her wooden bowl. Soon Ben was bathing Hallie while John, Traveler, and Ma Cooper filled their neglected stomachs.

Licking the last of her stew from her whiskers, John's big brindled dog lifted her head and cocked her ears forward, staring at the door. Padding softly to the only opening into the cabin, she stood listening carefully. Her tail moved in a hesitant wag, as she whined quietly, and then scratched at the door.

"Maybe it's Pa," Ma said hopefully as she crossed to the door. "Matthew? Is that you?" There was no answer. Still Traveler stood alertly with her tail wagging slightly. Ben and John traded hopeful looks, while their fearful hearts drummed out a retreat signal. "Maybe he's too far away from the door yet to hear me," Ma said with a growing smile. She quickly lifted the bar and latch and pulled open the door. In front of her stood two Indian men, who immediately walked into the cabin.

"John!" Ma gasped, as she backed toward the fireplace.

Ben and John stepped toward the Indians, offering them shaky smiles and nodding toward the bed. "Ma," John said in a trembling voice, "don't do anything. I think they came to help us."

With a smile, the shorter Indian pointed to Hallie's moccasins and said something they couldn't understand. The taller man seemed to be examining her left leg. He pulled off her left moccasin and grunted. Gathering Hallie up in Ben's quilt, he carried her across the room and was quickly out the door.

"Where are you going?" Ma shrieked. "What are you doing with my child?"

"Ma, let's go with these men. Look at Traveler. It's almost like they're friends of hers. Come on, Ma, hurry!" John urged, hoping he was right.

The Indians trotted across the clearing quickly, with John, Ben and Ma running to keep up with them. They had stepped into the cold, wind-whipped air without their winter wraps, because they had been too shocked by the Indians' actions to think clearly. When they fell too far behind, the natives waited just long enough for them to catch up, before continuing quickly on their way. They turned on the deer path near the trading tree and followed a smaller path, as it wound through the woods at the edge of the small river.

John no longer recognized his surroundings. They had gone well beyond the territory he hunted for game. Suddenly, the men veered toward a well-worn footpath leading up to the crest of a hill. When the stragglers scrambled to the top, they found themselves at the edge of a clearing similar to their own. In the center of the clearing stood a small Indian village made up of a mixture of buildings. Some were log lodges, which looked as if they had been there for many years, while others were tents made from large animal skins sewn together and stretched over curved poles. Here and there, they saw large huts, which seemed to be covered, top and sides, by huge slabs of tree bark, and from a hole in the roof of nearly every dwelling, smoke curled lazily toward the sky.

A woman ran from one of the tents to meet them as they neared the village. Soon, other Indians had gathered and were talking sympathetically about Hallie. John, Ben and Ma understood none of their strange-sounding words, but they knew from the Indians' voices and actions that they were trying to soothe both Hallie and the nearly frozen trio of settlers. Women and children ran to their homes and hurried back with thick, furry robes, which they put over the shoulders of their visitors, gesturing they were to use them to warm up. The men who had visited the cabin placed Hallie in the arms of a large woman who pulled on Ma's skirts, letting her know she was to follow. When Ben and John tried to join Ma, the two men held them firmly by the shoulders. Rachel and Hallie disappeared into a small hut made of logs, which was set apart from the rest of the tents and lodges. A new group of men led the boys to a leafless shade tree, where each sat on a large smooth stone. There seemed to be several stones arranged in a circle. When John started to sit on one, the nearest Indian stood quickly and moved him away from it. He pointed, instead, to the grass, saying something in his strange language.

Ben was having his own problems. A group of Indians surrounded him. Touching his skin and hair, they smiled brightly and said things that seemed to be compliments. "Thank you," he answered again and again.

Inside the little log hut, Rachel watched as the woman examined Hallie's foot. She pointed to a bright red welt and spoke to her as she did so. "It must be a bite of some kind," Ma said to the woman as if she would be understood. "Why didn't I think to take her moccasins off?"

Saying no more, the woman took Ma's hand and rested it on Hallie's chest, and left the hut. Ma felt better. It was plain to her that the Indians were concerned about Hallie. She liked the way this Indian woman acted. Somehow, she guessed the woman knew what Hallie's problem was and what to do about it.

The woman returned quickly. She opened a pouch which hung from her shoulder and removed handfuls of plantain leaves. Noticing the green stains on her hands, Rachel supposed the woman had just pulled the weeds from somewhere nearby. The woman squeezed the leaves over a wooden bowl, wringing them like Rachel wrung wash water out of clothes. Slowly, beads of bright green juice dropped into the bowl. The woman handed leaves to Ma and prodded her toward the juice bowl. Happy to be doing something to help, Ma squeezed for all she was worth.

The woman lifted Hallie's foot to her mouth several times and sucked on the red spot, spitting loudly onto the ground. She sucked and spit for several minutes, and then she packed the squeezed leaves on Hallie's foot and left the tent again. About the time Ma had finished squeezing all the leaves available, the woman brought in more and dumped them near where Ma squatted.

When about a half cup of green juice had accumulated in the bowl, the woman picked it up. She led Rachel to Hallie's foot and showed her how to rub juice into the bites. Finally, she held the bowl to the toddler's lips. Ma immediately understood and propped up her unconscious daughter, sliding tiny amounts of juice down her throat.

It was done. The juice was all gone. The woman lifted Hallie to her mother's arms and held back the bear skin flap which served as a door. They were to leave. As Rachel walked out with Hallie, the woman stopped her. Shyly, she reached out a work-roughened hand and touched the sleeping baby's soft, golden curls. She smiled into Rachel's eyes and spoke softly in her Indian language.

"Thank you," Ma said. "Oh, thank you!" She fought back grateful tears as she walked to rejoin the boys. The woman followed her and spoke to the two men. They stood, motioned for their visitors to follow, and began the trip back to the cabin. John and Ben removed the fur robes they had worn and tried to give them back, but the people wouldn't take them. They wanted their visitors to keep warm on their trip back home. From the forest, Traveler trotted toward them and dropped into the line of walkers behind John.

Ben studied her carefully. "That dog of yours has known these people for a long time," he said. John nodded in agreement, and in his heart, he wasn't at all surprised.

When they arrived at the cabin, the two Indian men entered and immediately began moving, lifting, poking and searching everything in sight.

"What are you doing?" asked Ma angrily. "If you want payment for ..."

The shorter man spotted the ladder and quickly climbed to the loft, where he continued his search. "Ah!" he shouted, loudly.

There was a sudden thud, and the man came back down the ladder, proudly holding a dead black spider. He lifted it close to Ma's eyes and pointed to a red design shaped like an hour glass on the top of the spider's abdomen. He spoke to her in his language, clearly pointing out that this kind of spider was to be avoided or killed. Carefully, he showed it to the boys, and then he threw it into the glowing embers of the long-abandoned fire. The men gathered the borrowed fur robes and left as quickly as they had come, leaving the door opened behind them. Ben, John, and Ma watched them trot across the open field toward the deer path.

Rachel gently laid her daughter on the rope bed and removed the quilt, handing it to Ben. "Look, boys," she exclaimed happily, "Her rosy color is a-coming back. She's a might cooler, too." Then she sat on the end of the bed and studied Ben and John carefully. "Boys, there's something that's been a-gnawing away at me. How did those Indians know we needed help? Was it a miracle, or did you have something to do with it?" Her eyes narrowed, and she noticed a squirm here and there.

"You tell her, Ben," said John uneasily. "I got to fetch Jack and Molly before dark sets in."

"Jack and Molly have been in the cave-barn all day, John," said Ma. "Now, suppose you both tell me your secret."

The boys began with the mystery of the trading tree and told Ma everything to the last detail. Finally, John climbed onto the roof and got the beautiful lance. It felt good to have it in their home at last.

When John returned from watering Jack and Molly, he found the feathered and beaded spear hanging over the fireplace. "That is where it will stay," Ma announced proudly, "so that our new friends can see how much it means to us." Propped against the stones, stood the black doll, guarding the very center of the mantel.

FIRE EYES!

T WO DAYS LATER, AS DARKNESS settled down, Pa pounded on the thick cabin door. "Name's Matthew Cooper," he shouted, "and I'm hungry for some good cooking!"

Rachel rushed to the door and raised the latch and bar. Pa pushed the door open and stepped inside with a large bag slung over each shoulder. He set them down in the center of the dirt floor and out tumbled ten chubby piglets, squealing their delight at having been set free.

"Actually, I reckon these here little critters are a might hungrier than I am," he said with a wide smile. John and Ben watched as Matthew lifted Hallie to the crook of one arm and pulled his wife into a bear hug. He looked over Ma's head and shot a wink at the boys. "Women," Pa sighed with a smile. "They've always got to have their hugs." A bright blue feather caught Pa's eye, and he stared in amazement at the Indian lance above the fireplace. "John, fetch in the bag of meal for the pigs, while your ma explains this here spear to me."

The pigs were soon happily slurping their way through pans of mash, and the stories began. Pa listened carefully and fired off questions, one after another, until he had a clear picture of what had happened. The men folk paid a late-night visit to the cave-barn so that Pa could examine Jack's injuries. Matthew held the lantern close to the ox's side, as his fingers carefully traced the healing edges of torn hide.

"So, she sewed him up with hair from Molly's tail, did she?" he asked. His huge smile brightened the light of the lantern, and he shook his head. "That woman," he said. "What will she think of next?"

While Traveler licked the piglets clean, Pa gathered his family near and told them of his adventures in St. Louis. He explained that he had left their supplies hidden in the woods near the Mississippi River. Early tomorrow morning, he and Ben would hitch up Jack and Molly and make the day-long trip back to the big, muddy river. They would camp near the Mississippi tomorrow night and would begin the trip home early the next morning. Thanks to Ma's needlework, he said, Jack should be ready for the trip, although Pa promised to keep an eye on his injuries.

"You should look for us along about sundown the day after tomorrow," he said. "Now let's us get some sleep."

John was happy to return his sleeping pallet to the loft. It felt good to turn over his responsibilities to his pa and be a boy again, if only for the night.

From the darkness below, he heard his father's deep, bellowing laughter. "No, I *won't* tell you what it is, or it won't be a surprise!"

As Pa had predicted, the wagon rattled to a halt in front of the cabin two days later, just as darkness began to sift down. Ma danced for joy with each sack of flour, meal, and a cone of precious sugar. Two sides of bacon swung from a corner rafter. Pa had thought of everything. He brought her thread, as well as a bolt of linsey-woolsey fabric to use it on. There was flax seed, so that next year Ma could return to weaving her own fabric. There was enough shoe leather to keep Pa busy all winter making shoes for each of them. Ma was breathless with excitement, as she watched the stack of supplies grow. Finally, Pa carried in a small, wooden box.

"For you, Rachel Cooper, from Captain Jean Baptiste Le Claire," he announced with a flourish.

Ma carried the box to the hearth stool and sat down. "Oh, Matthew! What a beautiful box!" She held it to her ear and gently shook it, smiling at the whisper of a rattle that came from inside. "What could such a beautiful box hold?" she said as she fingered the carving on the lid.

"Open it, Ma, before we all get the dyspepsia just a-waiting!" urged John impatiently.

Rachel lifted the lid and gasped. She held up a necklace made of beautiful, pale purple glass beads. "Matthew," she cried, "why would Captain Le Claire want to give me such a fine necklace?"

"He told me that he wanted the most beautiful woman in the territory to have them, Pa answered proudly. Ma blushed as she clasped the necklace around her neck.

"And now for you, Men," Pa said as he turned to the boys. They traded looks and John gritted his teeth. "*Men,*" he thought. "*That means another job.*"

Matthew carried in a large, wooden crate and set it on the dirt floor. "Will you please open this?" he asked, handing a pry bar to John. The boys worked together to free the lid.

"Save those nails," Pa said, as the iron nails squeaked free of the pine.

With the lid laid back, Ben snatched up the lantern and held it over the open box. He let out a low, surprised whistle. "Traps!" he crowed happily. "Enough traps to go into the fur business!"

Pa removed ten traps and lined them up in the light of the fireplace. "Now Men," he suggested, "this could be the beginning of a business for you. If you want to, you could each take five traps and scratch your name into them. If your trap catches an animal, the pelt is yours."

John and Ben thrilled at the prospect of earning their own money.

"Or, you might want to work together and split your earnings right down the middle," Pa continued. Ben squinted as he sized up his pal.

"Split it right down the middle?" John asked Ben timidly.

Ben sighed with relief. "That suits me," he said, smiling.

With Pa back home, the settlers all drifted back toward more normal days. The bear had not returned, and Pa concluded that it must have been passing through on its way to another area. With good luck, it would not be back. In fact, it was probably already drifting off to sleep for the winter in some den miles away from the Coopers' home. Maybe it would never return. Matthew, John and Ben went to work building a pig pen beside the cave-barn and moved the pigs out of the cabin.

Rachel opened the door wide and swept the hard-packed clay floor. She stood in the sunshine and breathed in the fresh air. For nearly a week, now, the days had been almost as warm as the middle of summer. There wouldn't be many warm days left before the sky started spitting snow. It was settled; she was taking Hallie outside. Ma held out her finger for her daughter.

"Come on, Young Lady," she said as Hallie grabbed her finger, "we are going out for a walk." With Hallie toddling along beside her mother, they stepped through the door. "It's time we got rid of that pig smell," Ma added.

They walked to the corner of the cabin and slowly made their way toward the back. Hallie released her grip on Ma's finger and stooped to inspect a colorful pebble. Ma saw her husband working near the cave and waved. Several minutes later, the two had circled the cabin and neared the front.

"Hallie, we're a-going to the river for a good bath," Ma said with a sudden gleam in her eye. She lifted her daughter and ran into the cabin. "Let's get a chunk of Lady Eleanor's soap."

She raised the lid of the trunk and set aside a new bolt of fabric. Snatching the soap, she turned to leave. "Dear Lord in Heaven!" she gasped.

The large Indian woman who had helped to heal Hallie was seated, cross-legged, on the floor. She gripped a pipe tightly between her teeth and smiled widely.

"Uh, good morning," stammered Ma. She sat on the hearth stool and pulled Hallie to her lap. "How nice of you to come for a visit. Uh . . .thank you for your help. See how well Hallie is?" Ma pulled off Hallie's moccasin and held her tiny foot toward the Indian.

The woman drew in a lung's worth of smoke and blew it toward the mantel. She spoke to ma in her strange language.

"I, I wish I could understand you," Ma said. She moved from the stool and sat on the floor facing the woman. "Rachel," she said, placing her palm on her chest.

The woman tried to imitate Ma.

"Hallie," Ma continued, pointing to her daughter. The woman smiled. She obviously cared a great deal for the little blond toddler whose life she had saved.

"You?" Ma asked, pointing to the woman.

"You?" imitated the woman with a smile, spreading her palm across her chest.

Speaking in her native language, the woman fingered Hallie's blond curls. She took the moccasin from Ma's hand and began a long speech about it. Ma sensed that the woman was telling her that she had made the moccasins for Hallie. She seemed to be instructing Ma about how to make a good moccasin. The needle stuck through Ma's dress suddenly flashed in the firelight and caught the woman's eye. She pointed to it and seemed to be asking something.

"It's a needle," said Ma, pulling it from her dress. She hurried to her trunk and pulled out her precious thread from St. Louis. Soon, she was stitching through her apron, demonstrating the needle's use.

"I just came to tell you . . .'" said Ben as he popped through the doorway.

"Thank you!" shouted the woman with delight. She jumped to her feet and hurried to greet him. Rubbing his hair and smiling with wonder, the Indian spoke to the young man excitedly.

"You," she said, pointing to herself.

"Um-m-m, hello, You," Ben said respectfully. "I'm pleased to meet you."

"Thank you," she said, pointing to Ben.

"You're welcome," he said with a sociable smile. He turned toward Ma and raised his eyebrows in a silent question.

"I think she stopped by for a visit," explained Ma. "Oh, how I wish I could understand her! It would be so nice to have a woman friend again!"

The visitor turned toward the fireplace. She knocked the strong-smelling tobacco from her pipe and tucked it into a pouch that hung from her shoulder. Pointing toward the Indian village, she spoke again in her strange-sounding language and smiled her farewell.

"Good-bye," Ma said. She reached for the woman's hand and shook it respectfully.

The woman looked puzzled and surprised by Ma's action, but she soon overcame her feeling. "Good-bye," she said, shaking Ma's hand energetically.

"Good-bye," Ma said, trying to politely end the handshake.

"Good-bye," imitated the woman.

Ben sensed Ma's problem and stepped in. "Good-bye," he said, waving at Rachel's visitor. "Good-bye."

The woman released Ma's hand. "Good-bye," she said, waving.

When Ben dropped his hand, she stopped waving and stepped through the doorway. Ben and Ma watched her trot quickly across the clearing toward the deer path in the woods.

"I wonder if she could teach me to run that fast," Ma pondered aloud.

A few days later, the woman returned. She brought with her a tall, important-looking Indian man. Pa, who was working on the new pig pen, was the first person they approached. "My name Medicine Stick," the man said to Pa. He pointed to Ma's new friend. "This woman Black Pot."

Pa had been hoping for a chance to meet the Indians. He had worried about how he would talk to them, and here, suddenly, was an Indian who spoke English.

"You," the woman said as she stepped forward to greet Pa.

"Yes," said Pa. "I'm Matthew Cooper. I'm pleased to meet you both." He pointed toward the cabin. "My family would like very much to meet you, Medicine Stick."

"We will come," the man announced simply.

With Medicine Stick's help, the Coopers were able to thank Black Pot for her help with Hallie. As Ma had guessed, the woman had made the moccasins. Soon, the Indians and the Coopers were trading words.

The settlers learned that Medicine Stick had crossed the Mississippi River with a group of four other men from his tribe. They were attacked by a ferocious band of Indians from another tribe, who killed all but him. Just as they were about to take his scalp, a strange white man stepped through the bushes and scared them off with his long rifle.

"I die without this old man," said Medicine Stick. "He take me to his cave. Pull out arrow here, here, here." His audience stared, wide-eyed, at the ugly scars he pointed out on his chest and lower back. "This bad smell man is good. He make me strong. He teach me your word."

John's heart jumped when he heard the Indian say, "bad smell man." Could this man be their dear old long hunter? His common sense kicked in, however, when he realized most of the white men they had met recently smelled bad enough to attract a milk pail full of blue-bottle flies!

"What was the man's name?" asked Pa.

"Name Smelly Jack," answered Medicine Stick. He turned and explained to Black Pot what they had been talking about. She nodded and smiled.

John, Ma, and Pa grinned widely at each other. Shy old Smelly had stepped out of his hiding place before to help someone.

"We know this man. He gave me that rifle," offered John as he pointed to Prilla.

Medicine Stick arose from his squatting place near the fire and walked to the gun to study it carefully. "This Prilla," the man said, stroking the rifle like it was a well-loved dog. "Smelly have two rifle. This one name Prilla."

The Coopers could not talk the Indians into staying to eat with them, and soon their guests were gone as quickly as they had appeared.

During the weeks that followed, the natives paid several visits. Often, Medicine Stick hunted with Matthew, John, and Ben, as they worked to stock up on meat to salt away for the winter. Black Pot showed Ma how to dry meat, then pound it into tiny pieces that she mixed with fat, seeds, and nuts. The Coopers did not like the taste of this mixture, but they knew a time might come when it could keep them from starving. Each time Black Pot finished with a batch of her emergency food, she packed it tightly into a clean deer gut and tied each end of the gut in a knot. This reminded the Coopers of the way the people of Stowe's Fork made sausage from pork scraps and seasonings. John would walk many miles for just a taste of sausage these days, but he wouldn't have stepped across the room for Black Pot's *pemmican*. He thanked her for the armful of stuffed guts she presented to him, just the same.

Ma ranged as far as the river on the other side of the deer path or to the edge of the clearing. She loved her trips out with Hallie. Although the nights were cool, the days continued to be unusually warm. She found as many excuses to get out into the fresh air as she could, because she knew both she and Hallie would be cooped up in the cabin much more during the snowy winter months. The Indians had assured the Coopers that the day would come when the snow would fly, and it would remain cold and snowy for about four or five months.

Black Pot showed her new woman-friend many native plants whose roots would store well through the winter. One day, she brought a small woven basket filled with several of those roots. Somehow the women found a way to communicate with smiles, gestures, and pantomimes, even when Medicine Stick was not available to interpret. Thanks to Black Pot, Rachel Cooper no longer worried quite so much about how she would supplement the meat with vegetables during their first winter in the wilderness.

"Rachel, Medicine Stick is a-taking us up into the hills to hunt for deer," Pa announced early one morning. "There's even a chance we'll bring down a bear. Then you'd have enough grease to last clear through the winter, and you'd get a warm, furry cover besides."

Ma smiled. "You go ahead, Matthew. Hallie and I will keep busy pulling wild onions. We smelled them growing right near our wash hole yesterday. I've been wishing for onions to cook with deer meat, and now I've found them!"

Kissing Rachel, Pa said, "We'll be back before dark so's we can bring in Jack and Molly."

Rachel hurried to finish her morning chores early. She sang as she worked, with Hallie tagging along at her heels. Soon she was ready to go. She gathered up her daughter, a large sack for the onions, and a water bucket. Before stepping through the door, Ma poked the leather latchstring out through the hole above the latch. Now she could lift the latch to open and door from the outside by pulling on the string.

In minutes they had crossed the clearing and were into the woods. She made straight for her washing hole. "There they are again Hallie," she said as she sniffed the air. "Smell them?" Ma followed her nose as she walked along the river's edge. "We're getting closer," she said with a smile. "There must be enough onions growing down here for every man, woman and child back in Stowe's Fork. Maybe I'll just pull a mess of those stinkers for Black Pot, too."

As they neared a large, slow-moving expanse of water, she spotted the onion stalks. They covered the ground at the edge of the deep, dark pool in which Ben and John had caught some of their biggest fish. It seemed to Ma there must be a million onion plants, standing silently in the still air. They had found the onions just in time, she thought. With the first hard frost, their stalks would shrivel up and the big bulbs which bulged up from the dirt would turn to mush.

She sat Hallie down and began pulling up onions, laughing as the toddler tried to imitate her mother's actions. Ma noticed the best bulbs were growing nearest the water, and she concentrated on filling her sack with the large onions from the river's edge. A flock of crows began to squawk their irritating calls, splitting the peaceful silence in two.

"Listen to those crows across the river, Hallie," Ma said. "It sounds to me like they're a-holding court. They do that, you know. They sit around in a circle and scold the crow that has broken their rules. Next thing you know, they chase him away." Rachel straightened up and rubbed the small of her back. She glanced over her shoulder at Hallie, who was taking onions out of the sack one by one and throwing them to the ground. Ma laughed at her daughter and turned back toward the river.

"Hallie, you ..."

Suddenly the huge head of a white grizzly bear seemed to float on the water in front of Ma. She was within five feet of its massive jaws filled with long, yellow teeth, and she could smell the giant's wet fur. It stared at her through blazing, red eyes that seemed to glow like the very fires of hell. Like an approaching ghost in a horrible nightmare, the grizzly rose in the water to its full height and shook the ground under Ma's feet with a thunderous growl. Ma's legs seemed to freeze, but her voice was still just fine.

"Hallie!" she screamed so loudly it hurt her throat. She ignored the pain, bellowing, "Hallie, run!"

Startled, Hallie immediately began to wail, and her cries brought Ma's legs back to life. She turned and snatched up her daughter. Pulling her skirts as high as she could, she ran into the woods as the huge white monster dropped to all fours and pulled itself up onto the riverbank. Roaring with fury, it chased Ma and Hallie.

Ma's bare feet pounded the soft, cool earth of the deer path as she struggled to keep ahead of the grizzly. She remembered Smelly Jack telling them that a grizzly could easily outrun any man, and she thanked her good Lord that she'd gotten a running start in the time it took the bear to climb out of the river. On she ran, her lungs burning as she gulped air to feed her leg muscles.

John was proud of himself. He stood with Prilla cradled over his arm and grinned at Ben. This was the biggest deer he had ever brought down. It had been a good morning. They had saved their shot for large game, passing up chances to easily shoot squirrels and rabbits. At one point, Traveler had picked up the scent of a bear. From her actions and from the size of the tracks, it was an enormous bear that would have filled their bellies for a very long time. They had followed the bear tracks carefully, but the animal had disappeared. Not even Traveler could pick up its trail. Then John had spotted a white tail flicking back and forth from its perch atop the rump of a deer, and thoughts about bear meat disappeared.

The men pulled their knives and began the messy job of skinning and gutting the big buck. For no apparent reason, Traveler suddenly went crazy. She whined and danced, pulling at Matthew and John. She raced down the hill growling fiercely, then returned to whine and pull again.

"Pa, there's something awful wrong," John said. "We've got to follow her."

"We go fast. Leave deer," agreed Medicine Stick.

With John reloading Prilla on the run, the four hunters ran downhill, racing to keep up with Traveler. It seemed to Johnny that he was in the middle of a nightmare, running until his lungs would burst, but getting nowhere. They all feared in their hearts that Ma and Hallie were in trouble.

When they reached the clearing, their senses told them they were right. Jack and Molly huddled near the cave-barn door instead of enjoying the prairie grass. The cabin stood quietly in the center of the clearing, with smoke steadily curling from the chimney. It looked peaceful enough, but the air was too silent. Not a creature made so much as a peep. Something was wrong.

Traveler shot across the clearing and headed straight for the cabin. Smelling the hard-packed clay near the door, she growled fiercely and crisscrossed the ground. The dog's keen nose located the point where the scent led into the field, then she returned to the door where she scratched and whined, begging to be let in. It seemed to the men she had decided whatever had frightened the oxen had left the area. It was safe, at least for now.

Medicine Stick and Matthew reached the front of the cabin first, with John catching up with them quickly. Ben breathlessly arrived to find his three hunting companions staring at the log home in amazement. Something very sharp had slashed deeply into the door and the logs on the front of the cabin. The ugly gouges began a full ten feet or more above the ground. Massive strips of bark had been torn away from the logs and lay scattered on the ground.

"Bear," Medicine Stick announced, looking up at the deep scratches. "Big bear."

Ben panted to a halt as Matthew pounded on the scarred door. "Rachel!" he shouted. "Rachel, answer me. Are you in there? Open the door, Rachel. It's Matthew. It's me, Rachel."

The color drained from Pa's face, and his blue eyes blackened with fear as he slammed his shoulder into the door. His wife wasn't answering. Was she inside? She'd said something about gathering wild onions, but where? The latch string was in and the bar was down. Had the bear mauled her before she could get inside? Was she in there dying? Matthew ran his fingers through his sweat-soaked hair. What could he do?

Ben stepped up and put his ear to the door. "I can hear Hallie. She's crying … sort of," he said.

Pa's face twisted in agony. "We've got to get this door down," he said, banging against it with his shoulder once again.

"But Pa, what if the bear comes back and we need the door up?" John asked as he tugged on his Pa's arm.

Just then they all heard the sound of the wooden bar being lifted from inside. The latch clicked, and the door slowly opened. Ma Cooper stood in the doorway, white from fear and drenched in perspiration. Matthew wrapped her in his big arms.

"Oh, Rachel, Rachel," he cried, "I thought I'd lost you!"

He lifted Ma and carried her to the bed, where Hallie lay whimpering, as Ben, John, Medicine Stick, and Traveler followed. Ma shuddered and pulled herself to the log wall, wedging her back into the corner formed by the headboard and the logs. She drew her legs against her chest, pulling her long skirt down to cover her feet, and sat resting her chin on her knees.

"The bear came back," she whispered hoarsely.

Pa sat on the edge of the bed and lifted Hallie to his shoulder, rocking her quietly. He gently brushed back a stray lock of his wife's red-gold hair and put a big hand on her trembling shoulder. "It's gone now, Rachel, and we're here. Can you tell us what happened?"

Ma spoke of the onion patch and the crows. She told of the huge white bear with the glowing red eyes that suddenly rose up out of calm waters at her feet. She told of the chase and her struggles to get the bar down in time. She had taken Hallie and gone to the loft, and then pulled the ladder up behind her.

"No wonder it took her so long to get to the door," Ben thought to himself.

John stared in horror at his haunted mother and his little sister, who was locked safely in her Pa's arms. Finally, he noticed something which might help everyone take their thoughts off what might have happened.

"Look, Ma," he said cheerfully, "Hallie kept her onion." Hallie's chubby little fingers were curled tightly around the stalk of an onion, and she seemed not to notice she was holding it.

Medicine Stick spoke with sadness. "Spirit Bear. Fire Eyes. He come back. Now no one safe. Fire Eyes come back from hell to take life away."

John and Ben shot frightened glances at each other and crowded closer to Pa.

Matthew settled his daughter beside Rachel on the bed and began to pace. "A bear is a bear, Medicine Stick," he said. "Ghosts and spirits are in our minds."

Medicine Stick slowly shook his head, disagreeing. "Fire Eyes come to our village. He take son of Black Pot. Now Black Pot alone. Every year Fire Eyes come and take our people to hell. Now, Fire Eyes want to take white and black man, too."

"Why do you say he is a spirit?" asked Pa. "Why isn't he just a large, rogue bear that has a taste for people?"

"Spirit is two place one time," Medicine Stick answered. "My people see him on hill and by river at same time. Only spirit in two place one time."

Ben reached for his snakeroot and began to chew it in earnest. When John noticed, he extended a hand, silently asking his pal to share the magic. If there ever was an evil spell hanging round these parts, it was now, he thought.

"Matthew go, take family now. Not safe," warned the Indian.

"No, we will not go," said Pa. "We will stay and kill the bear. We'll hunt him down and kill him."

"Not do," the solemn Indian said sadly. "Every time my people try, bear gone like magic."

Ben locked eyes with his friend. He liked the sound of this bear less and less. Silently, John shot back a look of total agreement.

Matthew Cooper's quick mind took over. "John and Ben, take Prilla and Traveler and go put Jack and Molly and the pigs in the cave. Make sure they have plenty of water and food. Then come back here right quick." He turned to his new Indian friend. "Medicine Stick, can you stay long enough to help us pack that deer meat down to the cabin?"

The Indian nodded yes.

"John, you will have to stay here to guard Ma and Hallie, while Ben and Medicine Stick come with me," Pa continued. "But first, Men, get out to the livestock."

It was easy to get the animals into the cave, because they knew, themselves, it was the safest place to be.

"Look how spooked they are, John," Ben said. "They act like they saw a ghost." He spat out a long stream of snakeroot juice through his front teeth, wiped his mouth on his sleeve and looked at John. "And maybe they did."

When Ben, Pa, and Medicine Stick reached John's deer later that day, they found the huge animal lying just as they had left it. Vultures soared high above the carcass, notifying the flesh-eaters in the area of the free meal lying below.

"With those buzzards a-circling, it wouldn't be much longer until our meat would have disappeared," said Pa, squinting up at the ugly birds.

The three hunters rushed through skinning and dressing the deer, quickly loading the hunks of meat onto the deerskin, which they dragged behind themselves, hurrying back down to the cabin. When they arrived, they were covered with blood, and Pa insisted they go to the river to clean up.

"He just wants to see the spot where the bear came out of the water," thought John, *"and he's liable to get them all killed. What if Medicine Stick is right? What if that bear is the Devil himself?"*

Matthew, Medicine Stick and Ben left the cabin and marched toward the river. By following their noses, they easily found the onion patch. Pa and Medicine Stick examined the huge tracks in the mud and looked for signs that the monster was near, but it was no use. After a quick sniff here and there, Traveler relaxed and moved easily at their sides. The bear was gone. The men washed themselves in the river, and then they refilled the sack with the onions Hallie had thrown. They filled two water buckets and brought them back from the river, along with Ma's precious onions. When Pa opened the bear-scarred door to the cabin, he found his wife and daughter sleeping peacefully, while John roasted fresh venison on the spit.

Medicine Stick ate supper with the Coopers and Ben, and he agreed to spend the night in their cabin. As they sat licking their fingers and chewing hunks of venison, Pa outlined his plan.

"John, either you or I must be with Ma and Hallie at all times. When one of us is a-going out, the other must stay. We have to keep hunting for meat, roots, and nuts," he added, "or we won't make it through the heavy snows." He wiped his greasy mouth on his shirt sleeve and continued.

"Tomorrow, Medicine Stick and I will take Traveler and track Ol' Fire Eyes. We'll take just one day for an all-out bear hunt, and then we must get back to readying for the winter. Ben and John, you will stay here. Except for seeing to the stock, you will stay inside with Ma. You won't have Traveler, so you won't have any warning if Fire Eyes comes back. That means when you're outside, you move like the Devil, himself, is after your hide. Understand?"

"Yes, Sir!" they both eagerly agreed. Neither of the boys wanted to be outside a second longer than was absolutely necessary.

"You just relax and try not to get Ma a-thinking about her big scare," Pa added under his breath. Ben wondered how anyone could relax when a killer bear with red, glowing eyes was lurking out there somewhere, just waiting to attack, but he kept his thoughts to himself.

The following morning, the two bear hunters and their borrowed brindle dog left before sunrise. John and Ben followed Pa's instructions and found themselves with hours of free time in the cabin. Ben finished his carving of Hallie and set it on the mantel. He started a replacement for the carving of Traveler, which the boys had left in the trading tree. John played with Hallie and swept the loft for Ma, and then he sat talking quietly with Ma and Ben, as the young black boy worked magic with his knife.

Well after dark that night, a very weary bear hunter and his equally exhausted borrowed dog returned to the cabin. The bear was gone. Traveler had tracked it through the woods toward the Indian village. The grizzly had doubled back and returned to the hills, then the trail ended. They had searched for the rest of the day with no hint of the huge, white monster. Knowing how bears like to forage for food at night, Medicine Stick and Pa agreed they should each get themselves back to the safety of their homes. They separated at the trading tree.

Pa settled into bed without supper and soon fell into an exhausted sleep. It was over. The bear was gone. Or *was* it?

THE EVIL VISITOR

JOHN MOVED HIS SLEEPING PALLET closer to Ben's, so his whispers wouldn't be heard below. For days, he and Ben had been talking in secret about Old Fire Eyes. As boys have a way of doing, they managed to replace their fear with a good dose of bravery and dreams of heroism. They were convinced that they could kill the giant grizzly if they could track him down. Their biggest problem was finding a way to hunt for the bear without Ma and Pa knowing. It was plain that the bear was considered too dangerous for the boys to even join the adult men on bear-hunting trips. Besides, everyone but the boys seemed to have decided laying in food was more important than killing the devil before he returned to attack them all. After all, what good would food do, if no one was left to eat it?

These days, Pa hunted for meat and left Ben and John at home to do the outside chores and guard the cabin. They were bound by their promise to follow Pa's strict orders. Besides, with Traveler out every day with Pa, the boys were not about to risk being caught off-guard by Fire Eyes. While their bodies toiled away, their minds were hard at work on their secret dream, because they had not mentioned their desire to kill Fire Eyes.

"I'd like to just get a good look at that old grizzly, up real close," John whispered late one night. "If I could get off one good shot, I could bring him down. I *know* I could!"

Ben rolled onto his side and propped his head up with the palm of his hand. "One shot is all you're allowed, you know. It had better be good, or we're both gone suckers."

"We're supposed to be thinking of a way to find Ol' Fire Eyes," John whispered, "not a-worrying about what kind of hunter I am."

The boys listened as Pa's deep, steady breathing turned into snores.

"Ben?" John whispered. "Ben?" he shook his friend awake.

"Wha . . ."

"The traps," John said quietly. "We've got to start our trap lines now. That's the answer!" Ben had fallen back to sleep.

The next morning, John and Ben hung around Pa like a pair of hungry mosquitoes. They had to get their trap lines started, they insisted, or his investment would go to waste.

"I've got to get on with the hunting," Pa said, "or we'll go hungry when the snow's deep. And you've got to protect our ladies."

"Pa, think of the meat we could bring home from the traps each day," Matthew's persistent son dared to say. "There's too much time around here with nothing to do."

To back up John's point, Ben pointed to the finished carvings of Hallie, Traveler, and John that perched on the mantel over the fireplace. "Before long, I'm going to run out of people to carve," he reasoned. "I have so much time on my hands that I feel like my mind's frozen up. Just think of how we could be working on stretching pelts each day."

"Pa, you and Ma hardly even get a chance to talk these days," John added. "Why don't you stay here and visit with your ladies each morning, while Ben and I go work on our trap lines. Then when we get back, you can go out a-hunting." He noticed his mother perk up at his suggestion. "Why don't you at least talk to Ma about it and see what she thinks before you go a-saying no?" He turned quickly to his friend. "Now come on, Ben, let's get out and see to Jack and Molly and the pigs. Heaven knows what trouble those little squealers have gotten into this time!"

John pulled Ben out the door and left Ma and Pa together to talk. He was pretty sure he could count on his lonesome ma to convince her husband that he should let the boys run their trap lines each morning. Traveler loped over to meet the boys, and John rubbed her ears affectionately. "Good morning, Girl," he said. "Do you feel like hunting up some grizzly?"

John's prediction about Ma's powers of persuasion came true, and early the next morning John and Ben hurried out before daylight to set their traps. The full moon was still reigning over the darkness, and the hoarfrost crystals reflected its light nearly as brightly as a fresh layer of snow. There was no need for a torch, for which Ben was grateful. He was overburdened as it was. Because John might need to grab Prilla quickly to defend them from Fire Eyes or some other big predator, they agreed Ben should be in charge of toting the heavy iron traps. As he toiled along with the traps slung over his shoulder, Ben made a mental note to learn how to shoot. They knew likely spots for raccoon, possum, and skunk, but what they really wanted was beaver. Pa had told them that beaver pelts were as good as gold, and gold sounded pretty good to them.

"Let's cut back down the river, away from Medicine Stick's village," Ben suggested. "We don't get down that way much. Maybe we can find some beaver lodges, or maybe some grizzly tracks if we're real lucky."

They hurried to carry out their plan. With a large stone, Ben pounded the stakes into the ground and carefully set the traps to spring shut with the slightest pressure. He uncorked a crock jug filled with putrid-smelling, red-brown liquid and spattered a few stinky drops into the center of the traps. Finally, he carefully laid dried leaves and dead grass over the iron contraptions to hide them. Ben set all ten traps, while John stood watch with Prilla.

"I'm not so sure I'm glad you have that rifle," Ben complained, "'cause now I have to do all the work. We need to think of a different way to do this." He grinned up at his buddy.

When the job was finally finished, the boys hurried off to search a section of forest near their traps. As if she read their minds, Traveler put her nose to the ground and crisscrossed the area, looking for grizzly. They were out of luck, however, and had to give up their search for the day. The time had come to head home. On their way back to the cabin, the boys planned a system. Each morning they would carefully search a different section of land until they found their bear.

Pa was in a happy mood when they returned. Ma had filled him with freshly baked bread and squirrel meat, and she had even found time to trim his shaggy hair.

"Maybe next year we'll have a milk cow," she dreamed aloud, "and I'll churn us up some butter every week. There's nothing like the taste of butter a-dripping off of hot bread to wake a body up. And maybe we can have a batch of laying hens. Wouldn't a fresh egg set well right now?"

John's mouth watered as he listened to his ma's daydreams. His nose led him to the small table they had hauled all the way from Virginia, and he sat across from Ben to wait for his portion of fresh bread and squirrel meat. As he awaited his lunch, he remembered Sunday meals around his grandma's big table back in Virginia. There was usually ham, fresh greens, cool buttermilk from the milk house, sweet butter and biscuits, deep fruit pie . . .

When Ma set a plate of warm slices of bread between the boys, they both reached for the top slice.

"Someone's coming," Ben predicted seriously.

"What do you mean?" John asked. "I don't hear anyone."

"Someone's coming, just the same," said Ben, "because we both reached for that piece of bread at the same time. Now you take it and make a wish for someone nice. Maybe it'll be Medicine Stick."

John rolled his eyes toward the ceiling and sighed. "Ben, that's superstitious." He took the slice, bit off a corner, and began to chew.

"Did you make a wish?" Ben asked.

"Of course not."

"Then we're in big trouble," said Ben as he reached for the second slice. "You just remember what I said."

The boys ate silently, until Ben asked another question. "How is your wart?"

John looked at his trigger finger. The wart was gone. When he looked up, Ben's eyes echoed his warning. *"Remember what I said."*

Early the following morning, while the boys were out tending their trap lines, there was a quiet knock at the door of the cabin. Pa looked at Ma with a silent question. They had heard Ben's warning, and they knew Ben was seldom wrong about anything. Medicine Stick and Black Pot had quickly learned they were to knock and shout their names, and there seemed to be nothing but silence on the other side of the door. It couldn't be their new Indian friends.

"Who is it?" Pa shouted through the door as Ma handed him his rifle.

"It is James Campbell, Sir, from Charleston. I am thinking of settling in the area, and I came to call."

After reassuring himself that his loaded rifle stood within easy reach, Pa lifted the bar and latch and opened the door carefully. Before him stood a middle-aged man in simple, homespun clothing. The man smiled warmly and reached out to shake Pa's hand. Pa obliged the stranger, but his heart warned him that something was not right about this visitor.

"Haven't we met before?" Pa asked, motioning the man inside.

A finger shot quickly to the mole on the man's cheek as his sharp eyes carefully swept the room. Immediately, he spotted the carvings on the mantel over the huge stone fireplace.

"I was wondering the same thing about you," the man responded quickly. "Have you ever been to Charleston?" He raised his eyebrows and smiled earnestly.

"No," answered Pa thoughtfully, "but I'm sure we've seen each other. I wonder where it was."

"I've spent several weeks in St. Louis," the man offered. "Have you been to St. Louis?"

"Yes, I have," Pa said pensively, "but I don't . . ."

"There you have it," the man interrupted through a big smile. "Now tell me. How do you find life out here? How long have you lived in these parts? I hope you will forgive me, but if I am to bring my family to settle, there are things I must know."

"Oh, that's no bother," Ma joined in. "We'd be happy to tell you. We're Rachel and Matthew Cooper. We'd be pleased to have neighbors from the other side of the mountains. Whereabouts are you thinking of settling?"

"Well, I'm looking at several spots in the area," said Campbell. Without giving any information, their visitor asked several questions, eventually getting around to the subject of slavery. "Are you planning to work any blacks on your land?" he asked casually.

Pa blushed as his heart flashed up a warning. "I'm considering it," he said, rubbing his neck, which had suddenly begun to prickle.

"And do you own any now?"

"Yes," Pa answered, almost choking on his lie. "I bought a fine black boy in Richmond before we left."

The man continued to smile as his heart raced. The boy Benjamin was still living with them, then. He pulled one side of the blond mustache he had grown to disguise his looks. "I'll be interested in how it all turns out for you," he said easily as he lifted the latch and prepared to leave. "And now I must be on my way. Perhaps I'll see you next spring. I believe the safest thing to do at this point is to winter in

St. Louis. Thank you for your help." He gave a quick nod and touched the brim of his hat, almost as if he were saluting, and he closed the door behind him.

Pa put his finger to his lips, signaling for Ma to hold her tongue until he could be sure the man was truly gone. A full five minutes later, he opened the door and circled the outside of the cabin. The man had disappeared.

"There was something wicked in that stranger's eyes. They were kind of yellow and kind of green, like a wolf's," Ma said when Pa stepped inside. She stood with her fists on her hips like she was spoiling for a fight. "I pity his wife, and I hope they don't settle here."

"Rachel, I think you're right," said Pa as he returned his rifle to its spot near the door. "Something didn't add up about the man, and I really do think I've seen him before. I felt like the devil himself was a-standing there when I looked into those eyes of his, but I just can't quite remember when or where it was. We should have told him about Old Fire Eyes. *That* would have sent him packing!"

The boys heard about the visitor when they returned, and Ben looked knowingly at John, reminding him silently of his prediction about someone coming. Young Cooper shrugged his shoulders and smiled at his friend. Once more, Ben had been right.

"From now on, Ben, I promise I'll believe what you say," John said, crossing his chest and pointing to the sky as proof. "Now, let's bring in our first catch to show Ma and Pa."

Rachel's eyebrows raised with excitement. "Oh, John! What did you trap? Did you get a beaver? Let's see what you got," she whooped, practically dancing with excitement.

They opened the door. There, lined up neatly, were four animals. There were two raccoons, one opossum and a beaver.

Ma clasped her hands together under her chin. "Boys, you're going to be rich! All the fancy men want to wear top hats made of beaver these days!" she exclaimed. Then she considered the meat under the pelts and wrinkled her nose. "Do you think Black Pot would like to have the meat?"

Pa tilted his head back and roared with laughter. "Rachel, you'd best get used to the idea. Just throw a few onions and some roots into your cookpot, and that meat will taste just fine," he declared. Matthew Cooper wiped a tear from his eyes with his sleeve, and his laughter drifted back down into his chest, leaving him silent for a thoughtful moment. He looked down at the furry critters and shuddered. "After a week or two of getting used to it," he added.

Ma and Pa pitched in. With one animal per person, they quickly skinned, then gutted and cleaned their catch. John carried their leftovers to the pigpen, and the young piglets gobbled up the innards like they were starved. Ma and Pa carried the meat inside, while the boys hurried to the river with their axes. Soon they returned to the cabin with armloads of young willows.

"It's us trappers," John shouted, pounding on the door.

Pa decided to stay home, since there was fresh meat aplenty, and the whole family moved outside for fresh air and sunshine. While Hallie toddled between them, Ma and Pa busied themselves pulling long strips of bark from the young willows, and then stuffing them into a large, wooden pail filled with water. Using shells they had brought back from the river, John and Ben scraped away at the insides of the skins, until there was nothing left but fur-covered hides.

The boys took the willows out of the water and used a short strip of bark to tie each willow into a round hoop. Ben made small slits in the skins near the edges, and John threaded strips of willow bark through the slits. Pulling the bark strip through a slit, then out around the edge of the hoop, then through the next slit, John was able to stretch each hide out tight inside its own, special hoop. They left the rest of the willow whips and bark strips in the water and weighed them down with a large stone. As long as they were kept wet, they could be used later, when more animals had been trapped. As the hides, the bark, and the willow whips dried, the skins would stretch even tighter. When the pelts were completely dried, the boys would remove them from the hoops and stack them neatly in the loft. John and Ben smiled happily at each other while they worked. This was a tough job, but it would pay off for them.

As the Coopers worked away in front of their cabin, a pair of wolf-like eyes watched them from a bluff nearby. Jeffries had found his slave boy. He would wait until he could catch the young man alone, and then he would kill him quickly. The evil captain smiled to himself. It would soon be ended, he thought, collapsing his brass telescope and dropping it into a roomy pocket. In the meantime, he had found himself a comfortable cave to hide in. He must be patient, knowing the right moment would come.

The days slipped by quickly. Each morning the boys left at sunrise to check and reset their traps. Next, they would move on to a new section of land, scouring it for signs of the big, white grizzly. They had sensed, since their first morning out, that Fire Eyes was back in the area, because Traveler had begun to act edgy and nervous. It was as if she knew the beast was out there and something was about to happen.

"Look, Ben," John said one morning as they stepped out the door. "See how Traveler stares up at those bluffs and sniffs the air? I think that's where Ol' Fire Eyes is a-hiding."

Ben watched the dog carefully. "I think you may be right, John," he said. "Lord knows there are enough caves in those bluffs to hide a hundred bears! Let's change our plans and search up there. Maybe we can even bring down a deer, while we're at it. Your ma would sure welcome a change in the meat, and so would I."

"I'm with you," John said as he jogged toward the trap lines. "This morning I checked myself to see if I'm growing a possum tail!"

The boys hurried through emptying and resetting their traps. They caught three large beavers and three raccoons.

"This is our lucky day, Ben," John announced as he reset the last trap and dropped a beaver into his sack. "I can feel it in the air. Luck is all around us."

"Now who's superstitious?" Ben asked with a wink.

They hustled to the long rope they had strung over a limb high-up on the trading tree and tied the bag of beavers and raccoons to one end. Then they pulled the free end of the rope, hoisting the bag about fifteen feet above the ground and carefully tied it to the tree. Now, the animals were safely out of reach of any varmints that hankered for a quick, easy meal. Keeping Traveler between them, they worked their way around the clearing in the shadows of the woods. There would be no way that Pa could see them from the cabin or the cave-barn.

Another pair of watchful eyes had followed their movements for some time, however, and now those same eyes flashed in anticipation. Jeffries smiled and caressed the bone-handled knife that hung sheathed at his side. Ben's time had come. The evil Captain dropped to his belly and slid backward so that his body was well hidden. Then, like a rattlesnake ready to strike, he waited.

"If Fire Eyes is up here, he's a smart old coot," puffed Ben as they hurried upward. "It'd take years to search all these caves and look behind all the boulders."

"But we have Traveler," said John proudly. "Look at her. She's picked up a scent already."

Traveler's back stiffened with interest as she identified two hated smells at once. Her memory flashed back to the evil man who tried to search the wagon in the settlement. He was nearby. The bear that had attacked the cabin was near, too. There was no fear smell on the man's trail. He did not know about the bear. Traveler lifted her head and sniffed the soft breeze floating downhill toward them. Stepping as quietly as possible, she glided up the hill, with the boys hot on her heels.

"This is it, Ben," whispered John. "Stay close behind me."

Ben rested his right hand on his knife handle and fell in step behind John. The determined young hunters watched Traveler closely. Her hair stood up all the way from the back of her head to the top of her rump. Her lip curled in a silent growl that showed her long, white teeth. Silently, she floated forward, sniffing the air.

Traveler reached the mouth of a cave. She stood like a statue and sniffed the cool air drifting out of the cave and dropped to her belly, crawling low to the ground.

"John!" Ben screamed. "Help! He's got me!"

John spun around and raised his rifle. In his sights stood the evil Captain Jeffries, holding a knife against Ben's throat.

"Put than gun down, Boy," the captain growled. His eyes darted quickly between John and his dog as he dragged Ben backward. "You call off that dog," he growled nervously, "or the boy, here, gets his throat sliced right now."

Traveler understood the captain's threat and hurried to John's side.

Jeffries tightened the knife under Ben's chin. "I *told* you to put that rifle down," he growled through yellowed teeth.

John saw a hint bright red blood appear under the business side of Jeffries' knife, and he dropped his rifle, stepping away from it. His dog moved to the side, also. When the murderer backed toward the mouth of the cave, dragging Ben with him, Traveler spotted her chance. Quickly, she jumped on Jeffries from the side, knocking him off balance. Ben rolled onto his side and grabbed his carving knife as the captain swung his own blood-stained blade at the dog. He sliced across her chest, and a bright red stripe immediately appeared on her fur. Ignoring her wound, she dropped to her feet and crouched, ready to spring on Jeffries once more. He raised his knife and moved toward her as John scrambled for Prilla.

"Ben! Roll away!" John shouted, but his voice was buried by the sound of a thunderous growl. Old Fire Eyes lunged out of the shadow of the cave and stood to his full height directly behind Jeffries.

"Run, Ben!" John bellowed, pointing to the giant grizzly standing above his friend.

Ben looked up and a scream froze in his throat. His legs were suddenly too weak to carry him, so he rolled down the hill. Traveler checked her instinct to attack the grizzly. She ran to John and barked frantically, attempting to move him out of the bear's deadly reach.

The boys stared in horror as the grizzly's iron jaws closed over the captain's shoulder. The man screamed in pain and fright. Just getting started, Fire Eyes easily knocked Jeffries to the ground with a giant paw and stood on him, ripping and crushing him with his bloody teeth. It was soon plain to Ben and John that, although the bear continued to toss around the man's body like a puppy playing with a rag doll, the evil caption was already dead.

As John raised Prilla and waited to get a shot off, Traveler lunged at his rifle.

"Traveler, don't!" John screamed above the grizzly's frenzied growls.

But the dog would not stop. She jumped at John's arms and pulled on his pants, growling.

Ben warned John, too. "Come on. We've got to get out of here! Look at Traveler, John. She's bleeding so hard she could *die*," he pleaded. "Come on!"

John snapped to his senses and turned to run with Ben and Traveler. They hurried down the hillside, too afraid and shocked to look back. The big dog was the first to realize they were safe. She slowed to an exhausted walk and, for the first time, she let the seriousness of her wound show.

"She's hurt really badly, John. Look at her," Ben panted. "We've got to get her home."

John remembered the animals strung up on the trading tree. "You start across the clearing for home with Traveler," he said, "and I'll go fetch our catch."

"But what about Fire Eyes?" Ben asked, wide-eyed.

"I'll run," said John. "Look at Traveler. As bad off as she is, she would be angrier than a wet hen if the old grizzly was nearby. Now go to the cabin, and I'll catch up."

John kept his promise. The boys and their dog arrived together to pound on the door, shouting their return. Pa threw open the door and immediately called for Ma, who was up in the loft.

"What's happened to you, Ben? Your throat's bleeding," Pa began as he moved the young black boy into the light of the fireplace. "You look like some fool sliced you with his knife."

Ma spotted the dog's bloody chest. "And look at Traveler," she said. "Is that stripe from a knife?"

While Pa and John lifted Traveler to the wooden table near the fireplace, Ma bathed Ben's neck with cool water and rubbed in a wild alum salve to stop the bleeding. Traveler's wound required needle work. While John held his dog's muzzle, Ma sewed her back together. Soon both patients were resting on the bed and the boys unfolded the story of Jeffries and the bear.

Pa slapped his forehead. "Of course!" he groaned. "That man who came to the cabin the other day! That Campbell. It was Captain Jeffries. I remember those eyes, now. Why didn't I recognize him?"

Ma crossed her arms and stepped in front of John. "What *I* want to know is, what were you doing up on the bluffs? I thought your trap lines were set out along the river," she said firmly, looking John squarely in the eye.

He lowered his head, suddenly fascinated with the packed earth of the cabin floor.

"Son, your mother asked you a question," Pa prompted.

Slowly, John revealed the plan which he and Ben had carried out for the past several days. He watched his Pa work himself into a deep anger, and he knew he deserved whatever punishment his Pa chose to deal out. His best friend had almost been murdered and his dog was badly wounded. Johnny shuddered when he thought of how close they had come to being killed. It was all because he had wanted to be a big hero and shoot Old Fire Eyes. Ben was much braver than he was. All those days, he had walked around hunting for the demon bear with nothing but a knife and a stupid friend for protection. John looked at his parents in agony.

"I'm so sorry," he blurted, looking at his best friend in the whole world. "I almost got you killed, Ben!"

The young black boy smiled weakly at John and his parents. He propped himself up on his elbows and leaned against the log wall. "I've been thinking," he said, "and what I've been thinking is, I don't have to run any more. Captain Jeffries is dead. That devil killed his own brother and tried to kill me, and now he's dead. It's over."

Pa stared into the fire for a long time, deep in thought about the two young men living under his roof. Without realizing it, he had started thinking of *both* of them as his sons. He was one of the luckiest men alive to have such good young men for his sons, provided Ben would agree to the arrangement, he thought. He swung a beefy arm around John's neck and pulled him into a headlock, rubbing John's hair with his rough knuckles. "Ben is right," he said. "It's over."

THE SECRET OF THE CAVE

WITH THE REMAINS OF JEFFRIES buried and prayed over, Ben and the Coopers settled into a truce with Old Fire Eyes. Pa had brought in enough meat to dry or salt down for the winter, and roots and nuts crowded a back corner of the cave-barn. Ben had built two nice bins that stored the food supply out of the reach of the livestock, and soon they were filled to overflowing.

While the boys nailed more shingles onto the roof, Pa built furniture to make their long winter in the cabin more comfortable. He started with a table large enough to seat Ben, all the Coopers, and two guests besides. He made chair frames and sent Ben and John out to strip fresh willow bark to weave backs and seats for them. Finally, he built a small lean-to shelter beside the cabin door so that Traveler would be well protected from the winter's snow and icy winds.

The boys worked over their fresh animal skins each day, scraping them clean and stretching them tight on willow hoops. Medicine Stick and Black Pot dropped in for visits, sometimes bringing other Indians they wanted to introduce. There was always a lesson to be learned from those wise Indians. One day, Black Pot brought a deer hide scraped clean of hair, and she sat, cross-legged, on the floor in front of the crackling fire. With her sharp knife, she cut out a pair of moccasins for Ma. Solemnly, she stuffed small sections of the moccasin pieces into her mouth and chewed them for several minutes, pausing only long enough to spit politely into the fire. Rachel had admired Black Pot's strong, white teeth, and as she watched, she silently wondered if the woman's hide-chewing was the cause. Her thoughts were interrupted when the quiet woman nodded at her hostesses.

"Rachel," she said, handing sections of the second moccasin to her new friend. Ma panicked for a minute, but then she shrugged her shoulders and began to gnaw on the leather. It didn't taste as bad as she had thought it would. As Rachel chewed away, she felt the hide begin to soften, and she smiled, spitting heartily into the fire. The harder she chewed, the softer her moccasins would be. The Indians always had a good reason for anything they did.

Ma spent hours measuring out sections of deer hide for jackets for pa and the boys. Her three men were beginning to look more and more like their Indian friends every day. She learned to make fur-lined moccasins that would keep their feet and legs warm and dry during the cold winter months. With each day that passed, Ben and the Coopers were kept busier than ever.

The boys found time each night to whisper their theories about the where-abouts of the big white bear with glowing red eyes. They were sure Fire Eyes was still in the area. Although he had left the Cooper settlement alone, he had visited Medicine Stick's village twice since that terrible day when Jeffries met his maker at the mouth of the cave. The boys noticed that Traveler's eyes were still drawn to the bluffs overlooking the clearing, and they were willing to bet their entire collection of pelts that the old monster was holed up in one of the hillside caves. He would surely be ready to hunker down for a long winter nap any day, now, so the chance to find him would soon disappear in clouds of blowing snow. As much as they whispered and reckoned, though, they knew better than to risk their lives to hunt the old devil down.

But then one morning, just as the settlers had pulled their chairs up to Pa's new table to enjoy breakfast, their days of safely jawing about the grizzly ended. Fire Eyes was back! Traveler saw him suddenly appear at the pig pen, and she indignantly snorted into warning barks and growls as she streaked toward the hungry raider. Out the door in a flash, the men rushed to back up Traveler's attack, bristling with guns and knives. Fire Eyes swatted at the dog with a huge paw and sent her hurtling through the sturdy pole fence. As the wood splintered from the force of her hit, Traveler yelped with pain, but landed on her feet and scrambled back into the pen to lunge at the giant's muscular haunches.

Pa and John moved in as close to the bear as they dared, but there was no time to get off a good shot. Two young pigs were already dead, and a third was being squeezed to death as the fiery-eyed demon dragged it through the wreckage of the fence. Traveler dove for the grizzly's heels and flanks, but she soon fell behind as the bear sped into the hills with the third pig clamped in its bloody jaws. He was headed for his hideout. Unable to contain his anger any longer, Pa shot at the bear, and a red blossom appeared on its right flank. He had grazed Fire Eyes. No spirit could possibly shed honest-to-goodness blood, as far as Pa could figure.

"Well, at least we know the old boy can bleed," he said, spitting in disgust. "Men, we're a-going after that grizzly and finish him off. Go get whatever we need from the cabin and tell Ma to lock herself in with Hallie. I'll get started with Traveler, and you two catch up right quick."

Strung with shot pouches, possible bags, and carrying Pa's newly made fur-lined coat, the boys caught up with Matthew Cooper five minutes up the trail. John could see that his dog was bruised and badly scraped, but he felt her angry determination to track Fire Eyes. They couldn't have kept her down if they wanted to. She snorted and growled as she nosed out the bear's fresh scent. Spots of blood marked stray leaves and frosted grass. They knew they were on his trail.

The bear had climbed steadily upward, still carrying the pig. The cunning monster had back-tracked twice and even walked several yards in a stream, but Traveler would not be tricked. She led them to the mouth of the cave where Jeffries had died only a few weeks before.

Ben and John were filled with fear at the sight of the cave. Their minds played tricks on them, and again they saw Jeffries meet his terrible end. John reached for his friend and gripped his arm. It was like being in the middle of a nightmare that wouldn't quit.

Pa stood quietly and studied the situation. "Hold your weapons ready, Men," he ordered in a hoarse whisper. "That grizzly is liable to come charging out after us any minute."

They stood their ground while Traveler, sensing that the next move was up to her, crept carefully into the cave. John wanted to call her back, but that would seem cowardly. He watched her pass into the shadows, knowing the Fire Eyes was waiting there to kill her. Tears filled his eyes as he looked at Ben.

It was too quiet. The brindle dog should have been whining, at least. The scent of bear outside the cave was strong enough to curl a hunter's toes. It had to be twice as powerful in the cave. The men waited for the sound of Fire Eyes attacking Traveler, but the cave stayed silent. Then the dog appeared from the deep shadows. She was safe and calm; too calm. The cagey old grizzly had disappeared. Pa looked at the boys with questions written all over his face.

"That cave must go on forever," he said. "Come on, Men. Let's take a look."

With their guns raised to their shoulders, Pa and John advanced toward the cave, while Ben held his knife at the ready and brought up the rear. The trio of hunters edged into the shadows beyond the entrance.

"Wait for your eyes to get used to the dark, and be still," Pa whispered.

As they adjusted to the shadows of the cave, they saw clear signs of Fire Eyes. The bloody remains of the third pig lay in the center of the cave, and spatters of blood dotted the earthen floor here and there. Traveler nosed back and forth, back and forth. The trail had ended, and there was no way out but the way they had come in.

"This doesn't make any sense," Ben observed. "If Old Fire Eyes came out, we would have seen him. At the very least, Traveler would have picked up his escape trail."

Pa paced near the walls, looking for a clue. "That old devil picked himself a good cave," he said. "It's almost hidden from the whole world until you come right up on it." He pointed to a small waterfall pouring through a crack in the ceiling of the cave. It ran onto a ledge about eight feet above the floor of the cavern. "He doesn't even have to leave this place for water," he added.

"But Pa," John interrupted, "where did Fire Eyes go? He disappeared, just like the Indians say."

"I reckon that wily old devil snuck out of the cave right before we got here," reasoned Pa. "I don't care what the Indians claim. He's just a grizzly. He's no spirit, even with those fiery red eyes. I've heard tell that every now and then an animal is born that has white fur and red eyes."

"An albino," Ben offered.

"A what?" Pa and John asked in unison.

"An albino," Ben repeated. "Scientists call mammals that are born with white hair and red eyes 'albinos.' There are even albino men and women, but I've never actually seen any."

"See?" Pa said to John, shaking his head in agreement. "That old grizzly is just one of those albinos. Now, let's get out of here and pick up his trail."

They worked Traveler for more than two hours near the cave, but there was no trail to follow. The bear had disappeared. They had to give up.

When the weary hunters and their dog arrived back at the cabin, they found Medicine Stick waiting for them. "Cooper men come, help us find Fire Eyes," he said excitedly. "Spirit bear come to Proud Face on river. Almost kill her. Black Pot send for Rachel and needle to sew Proud Face."

Ma tucked her needle, thread, and soap into her apron, slung Hallie to her hip, and threw a blanket over herself and her daughter. "I'm ready," she said as she pulled out the latch string and closed the big oak door.

"When did Proud Face see Fire Eyes?" Pa asked as they trotted across the clearing.

"Not long," Medicine Stick answered. "Fire Eyes catch her at river by onions. If Rachel sew her up right quick, she not die."

Pa stared at the Indian in surprise. "But that can't be, Medicine Stick," he panted, struggling to keep up with the Indian's easy strides. "The boys and I just got back from the bluffs. We chased Fire eyes up there. He couldn't be at the river, too. That's impossible. The two places are too far from each other."

When Ben reached into his pocket for a piece of snakeroot, John held out his hand. He wasn't going to be left out when it came to warding off evil. Ben broke off a piece and handed it over to his buddy with a grin. He had known John would eventually decide he was right, after all. Both boys began some serious chewing.

Like a sudden, fierce wind, Fire Eyes had passed through their lives again only to vanish into thin air. While Ma and Black Pot worked over the ragged, bleeding skin on Proud Face's shoulder, arm and side, the menfolk took Traveler out to scout for Fire eyes. Scattered onions, trampled plants, and blood spatters told the story of poor Proud Face's meeting with the grizzly. Traveler scouted up and down the riverbank for the hated scent of the big white bear, but she found nothing fresh enough to justify exhausting her already-tired, injured body.

"Fire Eyes go back to hell," Medicine Stick announced.

"What if he swam down river and then got out somewhere on the other side?" John asked, trying to be helpful. "Shouldn't we cross the river and look over there?"

"That not hell," said Medicine Stick, pointing to the dense forest on the other side.

Pa silenced John with a stern look. Now was not the time to question Medicine Stick's beliefs.

Dragging their exhausted feet, the discouraged hunters trudged back to the village. Proud Face was sitting propped against the huge tree where John and Ben had spent their first day at the village. Indian men and women sat on the flat-topped boulders that circled the tree and listened as her weak voice detailed the attack. Medicine Stick stood beside Pa and explained her story. As with Ma, the huge bear had risen out of the water like a ghost out of its grave. Proud Face had made the mistake of trying to save the onions she had pulled. In the seconds it took to reach for them, the bear caught her.

Pa was startled by the news that the grizzly was bleeding. That meant the bear had been in two places at once. There was no longer a chance that two white grizzlies were living in the area. When John and Ben heard about the bear's wound, they were hit by waves of fear. Could Pa be wrong? Could this animal be the Devil, himself? It was true that Captain Jeffries had been an evil man. Maybe Fire Eyes was the Devil, come back to claim Jeffries' soul for hell!

Ben and the Coopers returned to their cabin in the clearing and tried to pretend that life was back to normal. But it wasn't. Every day that the boys worked their trap lines, they expected Fire Eyes to charge from the forest or rise out of the waters. They began to snap at each other for no good reason. Traveler seemed baffled by Old Fire Eyes. She often disappeared from the cabin for hours at a time, and the boys were sure she was searching the bluffs or riverbanks for some sign of the ghostly grizzly.

Each evening the Coopers pulled their chairs near Ma's cook-fire and puzzled over the strange bear, forming one plan, then another, to kill the creature. They knew he would be back, and they worried about what he would attack the next time. Their talk always ended with no real plan to do anything more than to try to live another day in peace.

Ben sat through their conversations and grew angrier by the minute. It wasn't like Matthew, Rachel, and John to give up. They always fought for what was right. It seemed to Ben that the bear's evil spirit was casting a spell on this family, and he hated what was happening. Besides, Matthew Cooper had planned one last trip to St. Louis before the snows flew, and Ben had hoped to send a letter to his adoptive father's attorney, explaining in detail what had happened, both to his father and to his father's murderer. He wanted to carry out his father's death-bed instructions and free the people of the Jeffries Plantation, so that they could receive their saved-up funds and get on with their lives.

His conscience was gnawing away at his determination to keep secret his true identity and wealth. As soon as he could be assured by Lawyer Calhoun that he could return to tell the law of his father's murder and go on to inherit what was rightfully his without starting a local war, he would tell the Coopers the rest of his story. At the same time, he realized that his determination to return wilted a bit with each day he stayed with this welcoming wilderness family. He was torn between his love of the Coopers and his duty to his father and the people of the Jeffries Plantation. It wasn't helping that the grizzly's threats had brought Matthew's travel plans to a halt. With each day that passed, Ben's frustration grew.

The boys headed out to work their trap lines one cold, ugly morning. As they stepped outside, John whistled for Traveler. The dog was gone.

"Where is that brindle now?" John fussed. "She's never around anymore."

Ben could stand it no longer. "She's out doing what we should be doing," he growled through gritted teeth. He shot an icy glare at John. "She's hunting for Fire Eyes, because she knows we're too cowardly to do it, ourselves."

John walked quietly ahead of Ben, and then turned to face him. "Look, Ben, if it was just up to me, that old devil would have been dead a month ago. You see, I happen to like you. Sometimes I wonder why these days, but I do. I don't want to get you killed. All you've got is your precious knife. What if I can't bring him down with my shot and he takes out after you? What chance would you have with just your knife?"

Ben read the anger in his friend's eyes and understood that John's feelings mirrored his own. The young hunter wanted to get the bear just as badly as Ben and Traveler did. "Look, John," he said, "why don't you let me decide my own life? The worst part of being a slave is not being able to make your own decisions. I feel like I'm still a slave. Do you think I can't make up my own mind about things? I'm not as big as you, John, but I'm at least as smart. I don't have Prilla, but I've got my knife, and I'll match my throwing against your shooting any day. Now, when are we going after Old Fire Eyes?"

John stared at his friend, and his look of surprise slowly transformed into a wide, cocky smile. "How's right now?" he suggested.

They were off. Agreeing immediately to begin at the cave in the bluffs, they headed straight across the clearing. John carefully checked Prilla before they began their climb uphill.

They found Traveler waiting for them near the cave, and her very presence made each of them feel about ten feet tall and strong enough to back a bull off a bridge. Together, the dog and the boys approached the cave's shadowy entrance, where they stopped to whisper their plans.

"Let's send in Traveler first," John suggested, "to smoke the old devil out, if he's in there."

Ben nodded his agreement, keeping his eyes riveted to the mouth of the cave. He drew his knife and held it ready. John motioned to Traveler, and she bravely stepped through the black curtain formed by shadows. Silence. She reappeared and stood, waiting for the boys to join her. Ben wiped his face on his sleeve, surprised that he was sweating on such a cold day, and he eyed John.

"Now where do we go?" he asked.

"Let's work Traveler around this area and see if she picks up anything," John offered.

The sun climbed steadily toward the center of the sky as the dog searched for a fresh trail. Each time she crossed the bear's path, she was drawn back to the cave.

Like two sides of a dog sandwich, John and Ben sat outside the cavern with the big dog between them. The sun had weakened with the oncoming winter, but it still warmed them enough to stop their shivers.

"Well, one thing's plain," said Ben as he pulled a tick out of Traveler's ear. "That old devil sure uses this cave a lot. He's come here from every which way.

Look at all those tracks leading into the cave." He rubbed his cold nose. "But look how few tracks lead back out. You don't suppose the old trickster took to walking out of the cave backwards, do you?"

John propped his elbows on his knees and rested his chin on his crossed arms. "He's probably crafty enough to think up something like that," he sighed. "I've never known Traveler to lose a trail before, but Fire Eyes has her so mixed up, she can't tell which trail is a-coming and which is a-going. We've been in it so many times today that I've just about got this here cave memorized."

Ben stood and headed into the cave, saying, "Boy, my belly's growling so hard it thinks my throat's been cut. If I fill it with a long drink of water, maybe I can fool it into believing I ate breakfast."

John helped Ben climb up onto the ledge that held a pool made by the little waterfall. "Breakfast!" John said with a start. "I plumb forgot about breakfast! Ma must be worried sick about us. We'd better be . . ."

"John," Ben interrupted excitedly, "there's a big black hole in the wall up here. Maybe it leads into another room!"

"What?" John said, hurrying to stand below the ledge. "Can you see in there? How big a room is it? Is the hole big enough for a grizzly to squeeze through?"

Ben forced his fingers into a small crack in the rocky wall and leaned into the hole. "It's as dark as the inside of a cow in there," he shouted over the sound of running water. "I can't make anything out. We need a torch. Can you find a branch and get it fired up?"

"Stay right there, Ben, and I'll fetch one," John shouted over his shoulder as he ran from the cave. His words echoed back and forth off the stone walls and chased him outside.

He raced through the scrubby pines that dotted the bluffs until he found a large, dead branch. He scraped together dried leaves and grass, and then he pulled out his flint and steel from his possibles bag. Traveler ran back to check on Ben while John struck spark after spark until his cold fingers were about to go numb.

Finally, a spark caught, and John knelt low over a smoldering leaf. Cupping his hands around the pile of leaves and grass, he blew gently. The tiny flame grew, and soon a little fire popped and crackled merrily. When he stuck the tip on the branch into the flames, the dead pine needles caught fire immediately. Running back to the cave fanned the flames nicely, and by the time John thrust the branch up to Ben, the pine torch burned brightly.

"Here, Ben," John grunted as he stretched toward the ledge. "Can you reach the unlit end?"

"Hang on," Ben said, slogging through the water toward the burning branch. "I'm coming." Suddenly Ben's feet slipped on the slick floor of the pool, and the rushing waters knocked him onto his stomach. "Help!" He screamed. "John, help!" His voice trailed off as he slid, feet first, through the dark opening and down, down into the darkness below.

John stuck the end of the burning branch between his teeth and clawed his way up to the ledge, carefully crawling toward the huge, black hole. He propped the torch against a stone pillar. "Ben! Ben!" he screamed, until his throat was raw. "Are you there? Ben!"

The sound of falling water was his only answer. John held the pine branch high and squinted into the hole. He saw nothing but darkness. The rushing waters seemed to fall into a black, bottomless pit. "Ben!" John cried again. "Oh God! He's gone! He's gone!"

Frozen by fear and worry for his friend, he held the pine branch in the opening until the flame singed his fingers. Tossing the torch into the water, he sat back on his legs and rubbed his sore hands on his thighs. The blackened branch floated across the pool and fell into the darkness below. He looked down from the ledge and spotted Traveler, watching him from the floor of the cave.

"He's gone, Girl," he announced forlornly. A huge shudder passed through his body and filled his eyes with tears. He climbed stiffly down to his dog. Pulling her into his arms, he buried his face in her furry shoulder and sobbed. Traveler sat quietly with her owner, sharing in his grief.

Young Cooper tortured himself with blame. Why did he listen to Ben? Why didn't he follow Pa's orders not to hunt Fire Eyes? Once again, he had given in to the temptation to be a hero, and he had lost his best friend because of it. He knew he would never forgive himself. After what seemed a lifetime later, when his tears had given way to quiet exhaustion, he struggled to his cold-numbed feet.

"Come on, Girl," he sighed, as he shuffled out of the cave, "we've got to get home and tell Ma and Pa." As John started down the hill, he thought about the deep love that Ma, Pa, and Hallie felt for Ben. Their lives would never be as happy without him. His tears began again, and he sobbed in misery.

Later, he knocked weakly on the door. "It's John."

The latch lifted, the bar scraped, and the door swung open. John stood face-to-face with his father. "Oh, Pa," John cried, burying his face in Matthew's shirt. "Ben's gone. He's dead. He's dead, and it's my fault!" He shook with sobs as his pa held him in his massive arms.

"Ben's not gone, Son," Pa said gently, patting John's back. "He's right here."

"No, he's gone, Pa," the miserable boy sobbed. "He slid down into a black pit, and he's dead."

Matthew Cooper pried John's face away from his shirt and gently placed his big hands on his son's shoulders, turning him around toward the fireplace. "Open your eyes and look," Pa said gently. "Ben is here."

John squinted through his tear-swollen eyes. The young black boy sat on the hearth-stool, wrapped in Hallie's quilt, grinning cockily at his business partner. "I've been swimming, John," he said with a wink. "Where have *you* been?"

John stared at the ghost of his friend. "Ben," he stammered, "I thought you were dead!"

"I thought I was, too," said Ben with a shiver. He pulled the quilt over his shoulders and hunched closer to the fire. "I was sure I was a gone sucker when I slid into that pit." He spat into the fire and stood up, looking eye-to-eye at his best friend.

"John, I know Old Fire Eyes' secret!"

HEROES

L ATE THAT NIGHT, THREE HUNTERS sat near the fire. With Ma
asleep, they were free to plot their plans for Old Fire Eyes.

"It's important that we keep this a secret from Rachel," Pa warned the
boys. "Otherwise, she'll worry and fret until we're all addle-headed.

Ben chuckled quietly. "That's what we used to say about *you*," he admitted.

It was settled. At the first sign of attack, Pa and Traveler would chase the
grizzly into the bluffs, and then hurry back across the clearing and through the
woods to the onion patch. If Ben's predictions were correct, Fire Eyes would make
straight for the cave and ride the underground waterway to the river. He should
pop up from the deep pool right in front of the onion patch. John and Ben would
be waiting for Fire Eyes near the water. If their plan went right, Pa and Traveler
should arrive at the river in plenty of time to help kill the grizzly.

Ben and John agreed to pull in their traps until after they brought down the
bear. They would all stay close to the cabin so they could carry out their plan
smoothly. But Ma sensed that her men were keeping a secret, and there's nothing
a woman hates more than kept secrets, when someone else is doing the keeping.

"Look here," she said, waving her long, wooden spoon. "There is something
a-going on here that I want to know about. You men are strung tighter than Jug
White's fiddle, and I mean to know why." She crossed her arms and looked each

one squarely in the eye. John felt himself blush as his eyes dropped to inspect the floor. Pa cleared his throat, and Ben took a sudden interest in the sharpness of his knife.

"Well?" insisted Ma, glaring at her husband. "Were you a-gonna say something, or were you coughing up a hair ball?"

After trying unsuccessfully to laugh at his wife's sarcastic humor, Matthew developed a sudden interest in the dirt under his fingernails and found a hangnail to gnaw on. But just then, Traveler's angry baying pierced the silence, and all bets were off. The men traded knowing looks and sprang for their coats, rifles and pouches.

"It's Fire Eyes," Pa shouted as they hurried through the door.

"So *that's* it," Ma said. "Hallie, those fool men are a-going after that bear again." She lowered the bar into its brackets and picked up her daughter. "One of these days, someone is a-gonna run out of luck. Let's pray that it's the bear." She hiked up her skirts and apron and, with Hallie perched on her usual place, her hip, she flounced up the ladder to the loft. After settling Hallie on her quilt, she hurried back to pull up the ladder, and she was *still* mumbling to herself.

Hoping to pack on enough lard to last him through the long, cold winter ahead, Fire Eyes had eaten through all the berries in his territory, and so it stood to reason he was hungry for at least one more pig. He had broken through the fence and snatched a young squealer in his powerful jaws. Traveler snarled and snapped at his heels and the angry bear swatted at her like she was a bothersome fly. Pa and the boys raced to the pen in time to see the bear high-tail it toward the bluffs with his breakfast.

Without a word, they separated. John and Ben ran to the woods. As they passed the trading tree, each boy touched it for good luck. They sped down the soft deer path and crossed through the last section of woods. Soon they were positioned behind a fallen Sycamore at the edge of the onion patch. From their hiding place, they could see the river clearly, and it was close enough that John could get off a good, powerful shot, if it happened that Pa wasn't back in time.

He checked the muzzle loader carefully. Prilla was primed and ready. John turned her sideways and gently tapped her on a tree. A tiny bit of black gun powder sifted through the touch hole into the frizzen pan. With the gun powder in the pan, Prilla would be sure to fire when he pulled the trigger.

The tall, black-haired, blue-eyed adventurer propped Prilla across the fallen tree and stretched out on his belly with the gun stock at his shoulder. He was safely hidden from Fire Eyes, as long as the smell of the onions played tricks on the bear's nose. If the grizzly caught a whiff of John or Ben, they were in big trouble.

Lying on his belly beside John, Ben pulled his knife. "My mouth is so dry I'd have to prime myself before I could cry," he said, "so don't let anything happen to you that'll make my eyes puddle up. I'd be likely to cry cotton balls. And you know Old Fire Eyes wouldn't have any trouble finding me if I have big, white cotton balls stuck all over my black face."

He never failed to calm John down with a joke or two, and this time was no exception. Ben could feel John's rigid body relax a bit as laughter gurgled up from his belly.

"Ben, you're a ring-tailed roarer!" John whispered, still wheezing with whispered laughter. "Now shut your mouth, or the air blowing into it will dry it out even more." He shivered with a sudden attack of fear, and the dead Sycamore leaves rattled and rustled, sounding for all the world like a pile of bones.

"S-h-h," John shushed, like it was Ben making the leaves rattle.

Pa and Traveler chased the white grizzly to the edge of the bluffs. To convince the bear that he meant business, Pa shot at Fire eyes and quickly reloaded his gun.

"Come on, Girl," he called to the dog. "This is where we turn around."

As if she instinctively understood, the dog immediately turned. Pa smiled at the brindle streak that passed him, heading across the clearing. She had sensed their plan and was doing her part.

Ben swatted at a hornet buzzing around his ear. "Those danged bees," he whispered. "When the weather gets cool, they'll try to crawl into anything warm."

"S-h-h," warned John, wiping a sweaty hand on his pants.

Suddenly, in a white, foaming blur, Fire eyes rose out of the river.

Great God, Almighty!" John's whisper squeaked. His chest tightened with fear.

The bear still held the pig in its massive jaws. He scrambled to the bank and shook himself like a wet dog. John and Ben were so close to the demon grizzly that droplets of water sprinkled down, drenching them in their hiding place.

Fire Eyes dropped the pig and held it under a huge paw as he tore off a bloody strip of meat.

"Shoot him, John!" Ben whispered.

"I can't!" squeaked John desperately. "His side is toward me. He's got to turn around." He felt sweat trickle down the center of his back. "What's keeping Pa?" Then he was struck with a terrifying thought. Fire Eyes was facing the path that Pa would take to the onion patch. What if the demon bear saw him first? There would be no time for Pa to aim and fire. They had to shoot the bear now.

"He's got to turn around!" John whispered through teeth chattering from pure fright.

Ben looked toward the path and read John's fears. In a flash, he stood up behind the tree. "Hey, you wart!" he shouted, before quickly dropping to his knees.

Fire Eyes wheeled toward the boys and rose to his full height. His nose searched the air and he roared with rage when he smelled the boys.

"*Now!*" thought John. He aimed for the huge bear's throat and slowly squeezed the trigger. Bright red blood immediately stained the bear's neck and chest.

"God! No!" John screamed. "He's still a-coming!" His fingers fumbled as he struggled to open his shot pouch. The huge bear lifted the fallen tree and shoved it aside, standing over the two boys. John grabbed Prilla by the barrel and swung it at the grizzly's head, totally unaware that its hot metal was burning his hands. Fire Eyes knocked the rifle away and lunged for its owner.

John felt himself being lifted high into the air, then dashed to the ground. The giant grizzly pinned John to the ground like a dog preparing to bite into a long, tasty bone. As the weight of the enormous bear's front leg and paw lowered, John's chest burned with pain and he heard popping sounds, as some of his ribs cracked. His face was quickly covered by the blood pouring from the bear's throat, as the animal's massive front leg squeezed the life from him. John's ears buzzed and Ben's screams floated farther and farther away.

"I'm dying," he thought.

In a flash, Ben was on the bear's back. Hooking his legs around as much of the grizzly's back as he could, he grabbed a furry white ear and stabbed wildly at Fire Eye's neck. Again, and again, he thrust his knife into the raging demon, whose deep-throated roars rattled every bone in Ben's body. Thick, warm spurts covered both Ben and John, as the bear's strong heart pumped blood out through the stab wounds in its neck.

With one huge forearm, Fire Eyes held John in place while he focused on his attacker. He lifted his other front paw with its long, sharp claws, and raked furiously, trying to pull the young man off his back. His first swipe at Ben's leg left three long slices in the boy's shin. Still, the brave young man hacked away at the grizzly's neck, screaming all the while.

Traveler streaked into the fight. She, too, sensed that the bear's weakest spot was his throat. She lunged for the bloody fur and bit deeply. Fire Eyes swatted weakly at her and sank to all fours. Pa ran into the onion patch in time to see the bear fall to its chest on top of his son.

"Ben!" Pa screamed. "Get down! Get down! I'll finish him off."

But Ben did not hear Pa. In his frenzy to save his friend, he stabbed away like he was a machine with no off switch. Traveler, too, tore into the grizzly ferociously. Within seconds that passed like hours, Fire Eyes was dead. Finally, Ben looked at Pa through eyes haunted with shock and exhaustion, and he slid off the lifeless bear's back.

"Quick, Ben," said Pa, "John's underneath the bear. We've got to roll Fire Eyes over." The two struggled with the enormous weight of the dead grizzly, but they couldn't seem to move him.

"Wait a minute!" Ben shouted. "We need a lever and a fulcrum."

"A what?" Pa asked.

"I'll be right back," Ben answered. He would explain later. Within seconds, he returned, rolling a large rock up to the bear's side. Immediately, he darted into the woods at the edge of the path, dragging a long oak limb.

"Pull on him with everything you've got," he told Pa, "while I poke this limb in under his chest as far as I can."

Pa understood that Ben intended to use the limb as a prybar, and he jumped to carry out his part of the job. He ran to the other side of Fire Eyes and grabbed huge handfuls of slick, blood-covered fur. Shoving his toes under the grizzly's belly, he leaned back, pulling with every ounce of muscle he had. When the bear began to roll away from the stone, Ben plucked enough strength out of thin air to plunge one end of the limb right up to John's side. He rested the limb on the rock and motioned for Pa to hurry to the far end, which jutted into the air, at least seven feet above the ground.

"Now, grab the very end of the limb," Ben instructed Pa. "Get both your feet off the ground and let all your weight hang."

Already on his way, Pa did as Ben had ordered, and the bear's chest started lifting off the ground.

"Good," Ben said. "I was afraid this limb wouldn't be long enough. Now stay there, and I'll try to drag John out from under Fire Eyes." He fell to his knees and reached under the bear, finding John's deerskin jacket. Carefully, he pulled on the shoulder, swinging John around until he could touch the other shoulder.

Slowly and gently, he pulled John's battered body from under the savage bear. Pa stayed at the end of the limb, still prying the bear up off the ground as much as he could. When Ben gave him a nod, he dropped from the limb and landed on his feet at an all-out sprint.

"How is he?" Pa asked, almost afraid to look, himself.

John was breathing, and Ben could feel that his heart was beating steadily. He looked up at Pa and smiled. "I think he's going to be all right, but it might take a while," he answered.

Leaving Traveler to guard the dead grizzly, Ben and Matthew gently carried John to the cabin and left him with Rachel. Pa hurriedly wrapped Ma's apron around Ben's bleeding leg, and they returned to the river to skin and butcher the huge animal. There would be enough meat to have a celebration feast with their Indian friends, and still have plenty left over to add to their winter stores.

With the help of Jack and Molly, they hauled the huge bear skin and the butchered meat up to the cave barn to keep it safe until they could finish their work. When they reentered the cabin for a well-earned rest, John was awake and lying quietly on Ma and Pa's bed.

"Ma told me what you did, Ben," he said weakly to his friend. "You saved my life."

"Traveler and Pa, too," said Ben with a bright smile. "We all worked together."

"It was you, Ben," John said quietly. "You. My big brother."

"But I'm smaller than you are, and I think I'm probably younger, too." Ben insisted. "I'm not your big brother."

John looked into Ben's deep brown eyes so filled with wisdom. "Yes, you are," he said simply.

Ben reached for John's hand. Exhausted and weak, John fell asleep, comforted by his brave friend. Ben continued to hold John's hand while Ma worked on his own injuries. Until her famous needle pierced a flap of skin on his leg, he'd forgotten that he had been hurt, too. Of course, he made sure to screech his pain every time Ma's needle entered his torn skin. After all he'd just lived through, it would be terrible to die of the dyspepsia.

During the days it took John to recover enough to get out of bed and walk around, Pa, Ben, and Ma scraped the inside of the big white bear skin clean, and Pa used his precious iron nails to stretch it on the side of the cabin to cure in the fresh air. Within hours, Medicine Stick and Black Pot knocked on the door, announcing their names.

Pa swung the door open and smiled warmly at the visitors. "Something told me you might drop by," he said with a twinkle in his eye.

The Indians stayed long enough to learn that John had shot Fire Eyes in the throat and Ben had finished him off, saving John's life in the process. Pa chose not to tell them of the bear's secret underground passageway, but said rather, that they had hunted the bear down. They all stood outside and admired the bear skin, which was already covered with its thick, white winter coat. Cautiously, Medicine Stick reached out to touch it.

"You have big luck, Matthew Cooper," he said to Pa. "Your God strong.

"This God belongs to everyone," Pa answered. "You, Black Pot, John, Ben, Ma, everyone!"

A few days after John's strength had returned and he was back to teasing Ben like old times, a group of Indians came to invite Ben and the Coopers to their village for a celebration. John and Ben were to be honored with singing, dancing, and feasting. The family dressed in their finest clothing and followed the Indians to their village. They were met by men dressed in new leather, feathers, and beadwork. The men presented gifts to John and Ben. There were soft deerskin pouches decorated with beads, feathers, and porcupine quills. There were deerskin leggings and jackets, and finally, there was a brown bear skin with the center scraped clean of fur. In the smooth circle of hide, the Indians had painted the story of the boys and Fire Eyes. In the picture story, there was a trading tree, a cabin, a black widow spider, a war lance, a carving knife, and a muzzle-loading rifle. The boys grinned widely when they saw the pictures of themselves, and they felt proud when they saw the painting of Fire Eyes. They thanked the Indians and joined in the feasting. Their mouths dropped open with surprise when they were offered the seats of honor in the large circle of stones. No longer would they be required to sit in the grass.

Ma admired the beautiful beadwork on the fine clothing the Indians wore for the celebration, and all the Coopers stepped into the circle of chanting villagers, who danced smartly around a huge fire. They listened and watched carefully, as men dressed as a great white bear, a tall white boy and a smaller black boy acted out the drama of Old Fire Eyes departure to other hunting grounds, where it became apparent that he had mended his ways and abstained from eating people. Finally, as the gunmetal gray sky dimmed toward dark, they said their good-byes and headed for the cabin.

"I've been thinking there are lots of things I'm thankful about," Ben commented.

"Like what?" John asked

"Well, like the Indians finally learning to call me Ben instead of Thank You."

For the next few weeks, Ben was very quiet.

"I'm worried about him," Ma whispered to Pa late one night. "He seems troubled about something. Do you reckon he's a-thinking about going back?"

Pa rolled over quietly in their rope bed. "I've been watching him, Rachel, and I think that's what he's puzzling about. Maybe it's time we had a talk with him."

The next morning, Pa leaned back and patted his satisfied belly. "Well, I wonder what the folks back at Stowe's Fork are up to today. Do you reckon Jug White's tuning up his fiddle for a dance tonight?"

"I miss dancing to fiddle music," Ma said with a dreamy half-smile. "Virginia dancing is a mighty sight different from the Indians' dancing."

"Do you know what I miss most of all, Ma?" John chimed in.

Ma squinted into his eyes and laughed.

"Grandma's ginger cookies," they said together.

Ben was silent.

"What do you miss the most, Ben?" Pa asked.

Ben cocked his head and looked somewhere beyond Pa's right shoulder, thinking. "The thing I miss most is actually a person, but he is dead now," he answered. "My old Master Jeffries." As much as he trusted and cared for this Cooper family, he couldn't bring himself to admit he was an adopted ex-slave who stood to inherit two estates. He flashed back to the chance he'd had to tell Osha the good news, and he wondered why he remained tongue-tied. Was it trust, or maybe fear?

The young hero smiled at Ma. "Of course, Osha's cooking was mighty good, and my ma joined me every morning for breakfast in the big kitchen, but Osha had fancy equipment. Your cooking is just as good as hers, and you don't have all the equipment she has."

Rachel moved to the back of Ben's chair and rested her hands on his shoulders. "Ben, stay with us and let me by your ma," she said gently.

"And let me be your pa," Matthew added.

The lump Ben had been carrying around in his throat for weeks finally overflowed, and tears spilled from his eyes.

"You know you're already my brother, Ben, whether you take the name Cooper or not." John said, wiping a shirt sleeve across his own tears.

"Ben, you must be thinking about going back. With Captain Jeffries dead, there's nothing to keep you here any longer," Pa paused, "except maybe our love for you. And besides, you're not a slave here like you would be back there. You're family."

Ben arose from his chair and began to pace. "But truly," he insisted, "I'm *not* a slave! I'm … I'm …" He clamped his jaw together and moved to the hearth stool near the fire. Struck with a case of the shivers, he felt like Atlas, that Greek god he'd read about, who was forced to carry the world on his shoulders. He felt sure Doc Graves, the Reverend Stiles, and Lawyer Calhoun were seeing to the needs of the people living on the Jeffries plantation, but those people could be freed blacks, if only he was there with the key to the hidden box that contained all they needed to begin their new lives. He blamed himself for maybe the hundredth time for running away to save his hide, and yet he knew he had done so out of necessity.

Tom Beadles was probably overseeing the workers, Ben thought, just as he had been doing from the time his father broke his back. Osha would still be keeping the books and making sure the needs of the workers and the household were taken care of, just as she had done before Jeffries' death.

Hoping to give Ben some privacy, the Cooper family headed for the loft of the cabin, intent upon taking care of a made-up project. He was grateful for the time alone to think. He had known from the moment he made those promises to his father, that life would never be the same. To face a group of white people angry over a black inheriting not only a well-respected name, but also two valuable estates and all that went with them, was a fearsome proposition. From where he sat, it seemed to him that facing the wrath of Old Fire Eyes was easier than anything he might encounter back in Virginia.

He wanted to return to the black folk of the Jeffries Plantation and tell them in person of their good fortune. Not only were they all freed blacks, but they could begin their lives with ample money to see them settled in new lives. He recalled again how insistent Charles Jeffries had been about each of his charges learning to read and write and calculate figures to the best of their abilities. Like Benjamin, a few had been exposed to the French language, as well. Now he understood that his adoptive father had done everything he could to prepare the black people of the plantation for their new lives, and he loved the old man even more for his forethought.

It became obvious to Ben that the evil captain had given little time and effort to anything but finding the one witness to his crime. Although he might have sold off or mistreated Ben's people if he'd had the time, he probably did not. He was too obsessed with murdering Ben.

If he left now, Ben might find Le Claire and his men making one last trip along the Mississippi before the waters froze up. After all, there was nothing to keep him here now that the captain was gone.

In his head, he heard Matthew Cooper's voice, saying, "...*there's nothing to keep you here, except maybe our love for you.*"

He had made important promises to his dying father, and he felt honor-bound to keep them. *But I'm so young!* The idea so many responsibilities frightened him. After all, he was still a boy; a very mature boy, maybe, but a boy just the same. And he was black. In all the reading he had done under his father's direction, he had learned a great number of facts. But no one had offered any instruction on how you handle being a black college student or a black owner of valuable property. He dug into his shirt and pulled out a gold ring the evil captain had worn to his death. It had been covered in blood when he pulled it off the dead captain's finger. Later, he had cleaned and shined it and put it on the same leather thong which held the old iron key. Until he was murdered, Master Jeffries had always worn the ring, which displayed the symbol of the plantation. How many times his old master had shown him the ring and promised it would be *his* one day! Ben knew he would give up every valuable he stood to inherit if he could see his adoptive father alive and well. There were so many questions yet to ask. Now, Ben would have to learn many lessons on his own. When he thought about it, he realized the first of those lessons began the day he ran from the plantation.

Ben was half-sick from worrying about what he should do. He recalled the day Matthew Cooper knelt at the edge of the Mississippi River and asked God to send them a sign. If only it were as simple as seeing a black owl, he thought bitterly. He kicked a glowing ember back into the fireplace.

"Maybe it is that simple."

Ben jumped. He could have sworn he had just heard old Charles Jeffries talking to him again. The wind howled down the chimney, and he realized that must have been what he heard.

Just as the Coopers worked their way down from the loft, Traveler scratched on the door and barked. John hurried to the door and lifted the bar and latch. Ben looked up to see Traveler, covered from head to toe with white snow. She padded past John and stood before Ben, shaking off the white, fluffy crystals onto him, as if to say, *"I heard that you wanted a sign. Is this good enough?"* She lay a huge paw across his leg and licked his fire-warmed face.

With the door standing wide open, John was whooping and hollering. "Would you just look at all that snow out there? This is the first snow of the winter, and already it's deep enough to swallow an ox. We're having a regular blizzard, and here's Ben, a-thinking about leaving." He moved to the fireplace and squeezed his friend's bony shoulder. "I'm sorry, Ben, but you're just going to have to wait 'til the spring thaw.

Ben reached for his latest art project. "You're right, John," he said, grinning as he worked to smooth Black Pot's big nose. "Besides, there's so much to be done, anyway. I'm not nearly finished carving all the Indians from the village. Then next spring, you and your pa will need help with the planting."

He stood up and smiled at John and Pa. "And how will the two of you ever raise a barn by yourselves? It takes two of us to run the trap lines, John. Don't forget *that*. And I still haven't learned how to fire a rifle." He pulled on his ear, deep in thought, and then smiled broadly. "If I calculate hard enough," he joked, "I think I can find enough reasons to keep me here at least until it's time to leave for college."

"College?" the three Coopers asked simultaneously.

Feeling suddenly shy, Ben rubbed the melting snow from Traveler's broad, wet back. "Well, I guess there are some things I haven't told you yet, but right now they don't seem so important. I'll take care of that later."

The wind howled once again, and Benjamin Jeffries could have sworn he heard his father's voice saying, *"You bet you will!"*

THE END